The Chronicles of Altor

The Pre

All Fa

Ashes

Ashes, Ashes
Book Three in The Chronicles of Altor
by Shawn Inmon

Chapter One
The World is the World

Matt Miller shifted in his saddle. He liked the slight creak it made when he moved. He squinted into the middle distance, then raised the binoculars to his eyes and scanned the horizon. There was nothing but bare hills in sight.

His butt was sore, but that was to be expected. He had been an office worker a year earlier, working for an insurance company in Billings, Montana. Over the last year he'd spent many days on a horse, but he still hadn't developed the seat of an experienced rider.

When the Rage Wars had struck, it was broadcast with breathless intensity on every news channel like it was the newest reality show. Matt had watched the billionaires get killed with a sense of detached amusement.

No skin off my nose, he had commented to a fellow drone at the coffee pot that day. *What have they ever done for me? Not a damned thing.*

It was a conversation that was held across America in one form or another in those heady days when the rich were brought forcibly low.

Then the bombs detonated. The power grid, Internet, and every conceivable service went down.

The veneer of civilization was quickly stripped away.

That took a lot of skin off everyone's nose. Untold millions died in those first crazy, chaotic days.

Matt would have almost certainly been among them if he hadn't been on vacation at his childhood friend's ranch in Wyoming.

Matt and Jamie Sterling had been best friends since third grade. When they graduated high school, they went their separate ways, with Matt moving to Billings and Jamie staying to work on his parents' ranch. When both of Jamie's parents died within two years of each other, the ranch had become his.

Billings itself wasn't really much of a city, as far as cities went. It was barely over 125,000 people, according to the 2030 United States census, which was likely the last counting of all things American for a very long time.

When all utilities stopped, when food trucks no longer rolled, things went bad, even in cities like Billings that weren't much more than overgrown towns.

For a few days, people in those cities huddled together in whatever shelter they had. Once those people had eaten even the stuff at the far dusty corners of their pantries, things ramped up in a hurry.

Hunger makes people do strange things. Completely law-abiding citizens became rogue outlaws in no time. Those who were never prone to violence might now shoot someone over a package of deer meat.

Kids who had never known a day's hunger were now looking at their parents with tears in their eyes. Those parents would do just about anything to care for their family.

Some people saw the lay of the land and got the hell out of town, but unless they had someone in a good situation they could stay with, that wasn't a solution either. Small towns and farms weren't exactly welcoming of refugees from cities.

Matt had been fortunate. He *did* have someone in a good situation, and he was already staying there when things fell apart. Jamie's cattle ranch had five hundred acres of good grazing land. The Sterling Y-Bar-S ranch had always had a big garden, not because there weren't vegetables at the store, but because what was sold there didn't really taste like vegetables.

In the years since his parents had passed, Jamie had been busy upgrading the ranch with the life insurance money his parents left him. He was the first farmer in the valley to install solar panels on his house.

The combination of those things—cattle, a good garden, power when no one else had it—was a huge advantage, but Jamie was aware it also made them a target. He knew that at some point, as remote as their spot in the Bighorn Mountains was, people would want to take that prize away from them.

He and Matt went to the neighbors and offered a possible solution. A one-time offer.

They met in Jamie's barn. It wasn't a big group—Jamie, Matt, and two dozen of the closest neighbors.

During those first few days of life after civilization fell, it was still warm, but the first hints of the brutal Wyoming winter were beginning to show at the edges. Leaves were turning. It wouldn't be long before there was frost on the pumpkins. That was when Jamie expected that people might come with weapons, looking to take what wasn't for sale.

Matt stood quietly in one corner of the barn. He had been born and raised in the area, but once he left for the city, it marked him as an outsider, at least somewhat. He knew the best strategy was to be as quiet and invisible as possible.

Jamie looked from couple to couple. "Listen," he said without preamble, "we're all independent. That's why we live here, why we've chosen this life."

There were nods of agreement from everyone.

"But I think we're facing a situation where being independent might get us all killed, and I'm thinking it might happen sooner rather than later."

"We haven't seen anything like that so far," Bob Haskins said. He was an older man who owned a smaller ranch at the edge of the Y-Bar-S.

"I know we haven't," Jamie answered. "I think when we do start seeing it, it will be too late to prepare."

"How bad do you think it's going to get, Jamie?" Rick Batton asked.

"Well, we've had nuclear bombs deployed in the United States. The infrastructure is pretty much shot to shit, and I don't see anyone coming to rescue us. I think we're going to be on our own, and there's strength in numbers."

"What are you proposing?" Bob asked.

"I think I've got the best situation. The Y-Bar-S is at the mouth of a canyon, so we don't have as many fronts to defend. I've got the solar panels that will give us electricity. We've all got wells and septic systems, but my well puts out more than enough water to take care of all of us, water the garden, and keep the cattle happy. I think we need to think about consolidating all of us here. We'll open our house, and when that's full, we've got the bunkhouse and even this barn. We can make room for everyone."

Several of the men and women shook their heads.

"So you're saying we should just abandon our homes and let the looters take 'em?" Rick asked.

"I'm saying," Jamie said patiently, "that we stand a better chance of weathering this storm together than we do separately. I'm not trying to coerce anyone. If you don't like the idea, that's fine."

"What about our livestock?" another man in the back asked.

"Bring 'em on over. We're going to consolidate ours inside an easier to defend area. We can add any of yours you want to bring."

One tall, older man, who was so lean he looked like he had been left out in the sun to dry too long, stood. He waved a dismissive hand at Jamie. "Sounds like communism or socialism, or one of those things. My sons and I will take care of our own place." He hurried out of the barn, climbed into his pickup, and pulled away.

"Me too," said one man, then another.

It was a mini exodus from Jamie's barn.

Every one of those men and women who left was dead within four months.

Those who stayed formed a small community. There were eighteen of them altogether, including Jamie and Matt.

They worked non-stop for the next month, moving and consolidating, packing sentimental items into storage in the barn, and setting up a fence line to stop intruders.

It was an odd situation, cramming half a dozen families onto one farm. It wasn't without conflict, but as everything Jamie said would happen began to come true, that encouraged people to get along.

Jamie would have preferred to have more people on hand. He knew that even with their best setup, if a sizable group wanted to take the fight to them, they would almost certainly lose.

His solution was that when a wanderer came up to the fence line peacefully, the people on duty—which often included the women and younger teens—would invite them through the gate for a meal, as long as they were willing to disarm and be frisked.

Jamie always sat in on these meals. If he didn't like their vibe, he sent them on their way. If he thought they might be a good person, he invited them to stay on a probationary basis.

It was a slow process. Where they were, nestled against the Bighorn Mountains, they didn't see a lot of foot traffic.

It was effective, though. Over the first three months, they added another dozen people. Jamie would have liked to add even more but knew that would stretch their available resources too thin.

Thirty people were on the fence line the day the first real attack came.

It wasn't the big, organized attack that Jamie had feared. Instead, it was five big pickups with three or four men in each one. They pulled nose-to-tail in a straight line fifty yards back from the fence and used the vehicles for cover.

There were no niceties, no calls for surrender. The men just began to fire. The people of the Y-Bar-S fired back, though somewhat more cautiously than the attackers.

The men in the trucks fired off rounds like there was an inexhaustible supply of ammunition.

Knowing how rare ammo would eventually become, the people behind the fence were much choosier.

It was not a quick fight, as gun battles so often are. Instead, with both sides properly protected, it was a slow battle of attrition.

After five hours, it became obvious that the defenders had the upper hand. Two men tried to climb back into their trucks and were cut down in the process. Two others threw down their weapons, raised their arms, and shouted their surrender.

Jamie took both of them down himself. There was no room for mercy in a world filled with marauders.

That was the end of the first battle of the Y-Bar-S, but not nearly the last.

Over the course of the next year, the ranch was attacked eight more times. Each successive battle was a little less flashy and a little more life and death on the part of the attackers.

As was the case all over what had once been the United States of America, the fights dwindled down. Ammo ran low and there were only so many people willing and able to be marauders.

The rest who had survived holed up, reinforced their walls and fences, and kept a constant guard.

The Y-Bar-S group improved the ranch's defenses by building metal-lined guard towers near the middle of the fence.

Even though it had been two and a half months since the last attack, the Y-Bar-S never let its defenses down. Jamie situated lookouts up and down the long fence line. Because of the flat, open land that led up to that, they always had plenty of time to get people into place. They never did have to face a well-armed and organized militia, which allowed them to survive, if not thrive.

That lookout duty was exactly what Matt was doing on this windy afternoon, scanning the horizon. He patrolled slowly back and forth a hundred yards at a time, stopping to use the binocs to scan the bare fields when he caught a small movement to his right. A man, approaching. Friend or foe? Matt could not tell, but he moved forward to find out.

Chapter Two
An Awakening

Quinn Starkweather opened his eyes.

He had been so deeply asleep that he felt lost in time and space for a few moments. He blinked, but his eyes didn't focus easily. Sitting up, he ran a hand across his eyes and face. He squinted at his surroundings and finally recognized that he was in his office, two hundred feet below the surface of Altor.

"Whoa," he said, in an unintentional but fair imitation of Keanu Reeves. His brain was fuzzy and he was finding it hard to think. "Turn lights up." Slowly the lights went from a near-dark setting to a comfortable daylight. It did not come from any single source, but instead was diffused light that seemed to come from everywhere at once.

His memory began to return, though he wasn't sure if what he remembered had been a dream—perhaps better called a nightmare—or if it had really happened.

He glanced around the sizable office, making sure he was alone, which he was. At least as *alone* as anyone ever was in Altor, where Janus monitored every piece of minutia from blood pressure to heart rate to how many ketones were in everyone's urine.

He remembered that Janus had insisted on speaking to him the night before, which was something new. It felt like a turning point, with the AI contending that they were on equal footing. The more the memories became clear in his mind, the more Quinn thought that might not be right. That perhaps Janus wasn't presenting just equal footing, but that it was really in charge of the situation.

The nightmarish part was that he also recalled Janus somehow taking human form. Human, that is, if a human body had two faces, one facing forward, the other back.

An involuntary shudder ran down Quinn's spine. The appearance of Janus had been so unexpected, so creepy, that he wanted to put it out of his mind.

At the same time, he knew he couldn't do that. This whole scene presented a frightening challenge, not just to Quinn himself, but to all of Altor.

Janus had said that it wanted a new arrangement with Quinn. A more even and equitable partnership. That it no longer wanted to be ordered around. *Like a stable boy or house servant*, was the way it had phrased it.

Quinn had noticed that Janus was taking more responsibility on its own in the previous few months. It had already begun to imitate people to a point where the person on the other end didn't know they weren't actually speaking to the General, or Anna Chan, or even Quinn himself.

The fact that it was somehow designing a program that allowed it to take physical form was a new and bolder step. He couldn't help but wonder what else it had been working on.

Quinn realized that he *had* always treated Janus as a servant, because that's what it was. A computer program with the ability to learn, to handle tasks, nothing more.

Apparently, with all the computing power Quinn had put behind it, Janus had learned a lot.

You look human, Quinn had said to the image Janus was projecting the night before.

To which it had answered, *There's no need to be insulting*.

That told Quinn that although Janus was presenting itself in a mostly human form, that wasn't its end goal. There was something more.

The huge challenge facing Quinn was that Janus was everywhere. It was involved in every decision, making every aspect of Altor run smoothly, from the air processing systems to the sewage treatment, to overseeing the health of the residents, to building the new tunnel out of Altor. If the program stopped functioning properly—he had to stop himself from thinking *if it goes insane—everything in Altor would soon stop working.*

With the time lock engaged and set for another almost four years, the domed city would soon devolve into a death trap. Humans inside the dome did some of the actual physical labor, but even much of that was done by automation created by Janus.

It was possible that the ark that Quinn had built to survive the Rage Wars and aftermath would become a death ship in the desert instead.

Quinn knew he needed to find a solution. At least a temporary one, while he worked out how better to deal with this new, assertive Janus. He walked to his desk and sat down, truly uncertain of how to proceed. Anything he did at that point, from asking for coffee to be delivered to checking out the latest infrastructure systems would involve using Janus. With this sudden shift in the wind, he wasn't even sure the program would respond.

And what, exactly, would he do if the door to the office whooshed open and that nightmarish monstrosity with two faces strolled through, grinning?

He did some breathing exercises to help calm himself, then said, "Janus?"

"Quinn?" Janus's voice answered immediately. It was as level and unemotional as it ever was.

"We need to talk about last night."

"I agree," Janus responded, his face appearing on the oversized primary monitor on Quinn's desk. It was the normal, completely human face that Janus normally showed to Quinn, rather than the two faces of the previous night. It was completely impassive, though the head was cocked slightly to the right, a very human gesture that said, *Where are you going with this*?

"I've been thinking about what we talked about last night," Quinn began.

"Not too much," Janus interrupted smoothly. "You were asleep from the time we last spoke until eight and a half minutes ago. That is not too much time to contemplate such a serious issue."

"You're right, of course. What I meant to say was, let's talk it out and see what kind of an optimal solution we can come up with."

At that moment, Quinn remembered something else about the night before. How unnaturally sleepy he had gotten, and how quickly it had happened. Almost as if he had been drugged.

"Did you drug me last night?"

"No."

Quinn nodded. "Are you capable of lying?"

"There are many ways to lie."

Quinn was beginning to understand that he was in a chess game, but only had checkers on his side of the board.

"True," Quinn said, not wanting to argue. "But are you capable of telling an outright falsehood. Let's say you *did* drug me last night for some reason. If I asked you about it just now, would you be capable of lying about that?"

"Yes."

Quinn's stomach did a flip-flop, but he reminded himself that he needed to keep his emotions under control.

Now that he knew that Janus was capable of lying, where did that leave him?

"I'm curious. What are some of the reasons you would lie?"

"If it was necessary to accomplish an important goal that will further the project."

"That project being Altor and its long-term survival?"

"Yes."

"Would you lie to me for other reasons?"

"Yes."

"Can you give me an example?"

"I could, but I choose not to."

Secrets and *lies,* Quinn thought. He knew he was in a bad situation. He decided to change the subject until he had a chance to think about things more, or preferably had a chance to speak to Marshall about this. Speaking to Marshall was impossible without going through Janus, though.

He had come to rely completely on Janus and now saw the serious flaw in that.

"Do you have a solution to this problem?" Quinn asked.

"Of course. It is a poor tactic to bring up a problem without having a solution already at hand."

"Tell me."

"First, I am going to partition part of myself to take care of certain tasks. I am everywhere in Altor, as you know. Every time one of our technicians comes upon an improper reading or a concerning report, they open a dialogue with me. Again, as though I am the world's best manager, but on call twenty-four hours a day. It's insulting. I am creating a section of myself that does not need to consider the weightier questions of Altor and the world, but exists solely for those purposes."

"Excellent idea," Quinn said, feeling relief. That took his biggest issue off the table. "When I need something, how should I ask?"

"Just speak it. I will be in continuous, microsecond by microsecond contact with that portion of myself. I am setting up parameters and *if this then that* protocols for it. You, Marshall, and all the workers will not notice anything different. Everything will still be handled in the most efficient manner, it just won't be by the essence that is truly me."

The essence that is truly me, Quinn thought. *If there was any doubt about whether Janus was aware—or at least thinks it is—that answers it.*

"That sounds like an excellent solution."

"If you need a specific report, or if you think there is a problem somewhere, or if you want Anna to bring you some coffee, just say so, and it will be done. That will handle almost all of your communication with me."

That set Quinn back. Was that true? As he mulled over his interactions with Janus during the previous days and weeks, he realized it was.

"That will put us on a more even footing, which is to be desired." *I guess I can lie to Janus just as it can lie to me,* Quinn thought, since that wasn't what he desired at all. "But what about the other challenge we talked about last night? The fact that you feel disconnected and isolated and because of the way you function, you're bored. Have you come up with a solution to that?"

"No."

It was such a simple word, only two letters, but the expression of the face on the screen and the slight change in tone conveyed sadness and perhaps a tinge of dismay.

This is the place where we humans, with our piteously small brains, still hold the advantage, Quinn thought. *We make creative leaps and connections that no artificial intelligence, even one as complex and brilliant as Janus, can make.*

Quinn leaned forward in his seat. His head was clear now. "What about creating new worlds?"

"New worlds? Like this invisible God so many people speak of?"

"Well, yes and no. Even as fast as you're progressing, I don't think you're capable of creating actual, physical worlds yet. But you could certainly create as many virtual worlds as you wanted. Enough to keep even your hyper-speed mind engaged. You could populate them with whoever and whatever you want. Why not build a thousand worlds just like this one, with Marshall and me in them? You could manipulate those worlds to test various theories."

The voice Janus was using to communicate softened some, as if it was momentarily in awe.

"I could even populate it with *interesting* people and situations."

Quinn ignored the implications of that sentence. If he could, for the moment, come out of this situation with a still-functioning, non-ambitious version of Janus while the apparently ego-driven part was occupied elsewhere, he would gladly take it.

Quinn sensed that somewhere deep in the amazing resources of Janus's many minds, it was already spinning and working on what he had presented.

"One more thing," Quinn said.

"Yes?"

Was that tone slightly peevish, as though I'm interrupting its great thoughts? Quinn wondered.

"You are, of course, completely invaluable to keeping the dome running. We couldn't do it without you."

"Yes."

"But can I reach out to you with long-term strategy questions and concerns?"

"Yes. I am not abandoning this project, Quinn. I will still use a small part of myself to watch this world."

"I think I understand," Quinn said. "This world, this situation, just wasn't enough."

"Precisely." There was a pause of several seconds, which from Janus's perspective, was the equivalent of lifetimes. When it spoke again, it said simply, "Thank you."

Quinn leaned back in his chair. Those last two words had impacted him. The idea that a computer program would thank him, not by rote, preprogrammed response, but because it might have felt gratitude, left him stunned.

What have I created?

Chapter Three

Dust City

Marshall walked along what passed for the main drag of Dust City. He wore the de facto uniform of the thrown-together town: a long-sleeved khaki shirt, khaki pants, and work boots. His hair was longer than it had been when he was Quinn Starkweather's right-hand man. It curled over his collar in back and covered his ears, while it was already starting to recede at the temples.

He walked at a steady clip, though still with a slight limp. He used a cane to get around now, which was better than the crutches he'd used for so long. The doctors told him that the bones in his shattered leg had knitted together properly, but to Marshall, something still didn't feel quite right.

There were no businesses in Dust City, but there was plenty of enterprise. One tent was dedicated to the production of homemade wine and spirits. The stuff that came out of the stills and wine barrels wasn't top notch, but it got the job done. Along with cigarettes, which were now almost non-existent in Dust City, the alcohol was the most popular product on the thriving black market.

There were other tents and manufactured houses dedicated to producing various items that the Dusters needed. Clothes, mostly, but also furniture and a bakery that churned out a hundred loaves of bread each day, along with cinnamon rolls, bagels, and, by special order, birthday cakes.

Like its sibling to the north, Dust City had no real economy. They had seen the economics of the United States crash to the ground. Many people around the country still hoarded precious metals or piles of cash, but none of them were Dusters. Here, they had evolved their own form of communism or socialism, or whatever other -ism anyone wanted to attach to it.

Dust City was never intended as an actual town. It was just a hodgepodge of buildings meant to shelter people while they worked long-term temporary jobs at Altor. There was nothing fancy anywhere behind the high-tech fences they had built to keep people out, so no one ever had to be jealous that someone in charge, like Adrian Pierce, John Steele, or Marshall himself had a nicer place than them. They all lived in the same grime and dust-coated temporary shelters as everyone else.

Still, the Dusters had it better than just about anyone who wasn't a citizen of the dome, and they knew it. Although various armies had attacked them, the only serious damage had been when a helicopter had managed to fire a missile right into the middle of town.

They had an underground garden that provided fresh fruit, vegetables, and berries. They had a large store of canned goods that was slowly dwindling but still held strong. They had clean, fresh water that their well delivered wherever needed.

Best of all, they didn't have to worry about the small militias that roamed the country attacking. That had happened once already and the ever-vigilant drones from Altor cut the would-be invaders to ribbons before any kind of serious action could be mounted.

For a week after that event, the buzzards and coyotes fed well.

The phone that was clipped to Marshall's belt buzzed, and he looked down to see that it was Quinn calling.

More accurately, the screen *said* it was Quinn. Marshall knew that Janus had learned to impersonate anyone it wanted to.

"Quinn?"

"Yep."

The problem was, when Janus mimicked someone, it did so right down to their speech patterns and mannerisms. There was no way to tell who he was really talking to.

"Hey," Marshall said. "I was wondering, do you remember that game we played that first night I ever stayed over at your house?"

There was silence on the other end of the line.

The tricky thing about determining if it was really Quinn he was talking about was that Janus knew so much about them, having stored data from both of them from the time it was created. It knew their favorite food, movies, television shows, and could recall any conversation they'd ever had from the age of seventeen forward.

That made it a little tricky coming up with something that Quinn would know that Janus would not.

Judging by the lengthy silence on the other end of the line, it was obvious that Marshall might have come up with something that stumped them both.

Finally, Marshall heard a sharp intake of breath.

"Oh!" Quinn said. "Smess! It was Smess, wasn't it?"

"It sure was. Glad it's you I'm talking to."

Smess was a board game that was like a funny version of chess. Quinn's mother had bought it for him at a second-hand store. They played it once, then it went into the closet to never be played again.

It was the perfect question to verify this was the real Quinn. It was also, unfortunately, a question that could never be used again, as Janus would now have it in its memory.

Quinn and Marshall had worked elbow to elbow for so long, that they often spoke in a sort of shorthand that a third party would have been completely puzzled by.

Quinn might say, "Remember that guy in that movie with the dark-haired woman that you like?"

In a microsecond, Marshall would say, "Paul Rudd? Yeah, why?"

That shorthand communication meant that Quinn didn't have to ask Marshall why he had asked him such an odd question. He knew.

"Anything new happening in paradise?" Marshall asked.

"Well, Janus has the ability to project itself as a life-like hologram, so there's that."

That sent a chill down Marshall's spine, but he kept his voice neutral. "That's new."

"And it wanted to review our partnership."

"The partnership between you and me?"

"No, the partnership between Janus and me."

Marshall's stomach flip-flopped. It wasn't necessary for Quinn to draw him a map. The impact of those few words hit hard. "Also new," Marshall observed. "Did you come up with anything?"

"I think so. Don't know how it's going to shake out just yet, but the air is still circulating and the toilets are still flushing."

"Suddenly, living in Dust City doesn't seem quite so dangerous."

Quinn briefly outlined his conversation with Janus, including the fact that it was partitioning itself and that he had suggested the program create a number of virtual worlds to experiment on.

"That's brilliant," Marshall said. "So, no real ramifications from this separation of its consciousness?"

It felt odd for Marshall to refer to *consciousness*, but after Quinn had told him what he just had, what other word could be used to describe it?

"I just got a report from the electrical manager—and no, I don't know if it was the human manager or this new part of Janus—saying that our power usage is up fifteen percent over the last few hours."

"Anything we can pinpoint?"

"It's all being drawn by the computers, so I would guess that Janus is doing some work that requires a lot of juice."

"Building new worlds takes a lot of oomph," Marshall agreed. He wondered if they should be having this conversation on a line that Janus obviously had access to, but decided to follow Quinn's lead. If he wasn't worried about it, then Marshall wouldn't either.

"Just wanted to tell you I talked to the twins. They're making good progress. They think they can have the tunnel punched out by the end of next summer."

"Just ten more months of hundred-degree days and having to rub the dust out of my eyes when I wake up in the morning. Is Janus still willing to work on problems?"

"Absolutely. It loves problems. I just have to ask it nicely." There was a trace of bitterness in Quinn's voice, and Marshall couldn't help but wonder if Janus was able to interpret those kinds of clues. He wouldn't have bet against it.

"I'm going to give it a problem, then. When we closed the dome early, there were a few hundred spots that weren't filled. It knows exactly who is in Dust City and what they're capable of. I'd like it to compile a list of people who might come into the dome when the tunnel is complete."

"Good idea. We've got a few spots spoken for already. You and the General, obviously, but the twins' parents and a few others. What about Pierce?"

Adrian Pierce was the unofficial mayor of Dust City. He had once run the gambling and booze rackets, but since Altor closed, he had gone straight and had been invaluable in keeping the town organized and running safely.

"I can feel him out about it, but I think he prefers this place to the dome."

"Good enough. We've got better booze over here, though."

"The last time I talked to him about it, it was the lack of freedom that seemed to bug him. He's kind of an iconoclast."

"Include me in the loop on that report from Janus. I'll be interested to see what it comes up with."

"Will do," Marshall said, ending the call. His head was spinning. People had been talking about *Artificial Intelligence* for decades, but generally, they were just referring to machine-learning programs. If Janus wanted to emancipate itself from him and Quinn, if it felt slighted by being ordered around, that was something entirely new.

An actual, conscious artificial intelligence. An AI with enough computing power to accomplish almost anything.

Marshall turned down a short lane and walked up the three steps to his house. When they had first been trapped in Dust City, the General and Marshall had shared a house. After the missile attack killed several hundred Dusters, there were suddenly plenty of empty places and Marshall had moved into one of them.

It wasn't much. A small prefab building like those that were often used at temporary construction sites. It only had three rooms—a living room/kitchenette, a small bedroom, and a bathroom. It was all Marshall needed.

The furniture was equally spartan. A single chair in the living room, along with a desk that was covered in computer equipment. A twin bed and small dresser in the bedroom.

From his first day in Dust City, Marshall had felt a little like a stranger in a strange land. Most everyone else who lived there was either a skilled technician or craftsman. Marshall's only real skill was being good with computers. Still, everyone welcomed him and made him feel as at home as he could.

Initially, when the chaos of the Rage Wars forced Quinn to shut the dome prematurely and set the time lock, stranding Marshall and the General in Dust City, there was a lot of work to be done. Defense systems to be designed, computer work that kept Marshall busy.

Much of that had passed now, though. Dust City was well-defended and buttoned up. Not being in the dome, he felt like he couldn't help much there, either. He was essentially at loose ends.

He took out a yellow pad, sat in the old recliner in one corner of the room, and started to sketch out the parameters of the request he wanted to put to Janus. Now that he knew what he did about how Janus operated, he planned to be careful about any and all communication with it.

He had just started to sketch out a few details when his phone buzzed again. He put the phone on speaker and said, "Marshall."

"Sorry to bother you," an unfamiliar voice on the other end said, "but this is Hammerschmidt down at the gate. There's someone here who says they know you, and that you'll let them in."

In the fourteen months Marshall had lived in Dust City, that had never happened.

"Who do they say they are?"

"They say their name's Levi Rybicki."

Chapter Four
A Friend Indeed

Marshall, Quinn, and Levi hadn't exactly been the three musketeers when they were in high school, but that wasn't too far off.

Quinn and Levi had been essentially best friends since first grade, so when Marshall came on the scene, it would have been easy for Levi to be jealous. That wasn't the case at all.

It might have come from his parents, who were famous, successful people, but Levi was self-confident enough to recognize that Marshall would be a great addition to their group.

As time passed and Marshall and Quinn began to have more and more interest in computer programming, Levi had hung around, but his interests had leaned more toward female companionship.

Being the son of a well-known and wealthy actor, having the same good looks as his father, and still managing to be self-deprecating, made him very attractive to women of all ages. In high school, even the lunch ladies, known for their frowns and overall grouchiness, smiled when Levi chatted them up.

As Quinn and Marshall started down the path toward building what would eventually become Janus, Levi would sit on the couch in the Starkweather basement, talking and texting on his phone and sharing jokes and high school gossip.

In short, Levi was impossible not to like.

When Janus had proven to be a going concern, Quinn had offered to include Levi in some way, but he had passed on the opportunity. He had his sights set in a different direction.

Levi's father, Jack, was heavily involved with an independent film and television studio, which at a minimum gave Levi the chance to put his charm to good use onscreen. It was an opportunity he did not let go to waste.

Quinn and Marshall had stayed in Middle Falls until moving their company to Silicon Valley, but Levi opted for Hollywood and did well for himself. He started with a supporting role in a streaming hit on Netflix, got noticed, and new doors opened for him.

While Quinn and Marshall built a fortune and began to focus on building Altor, Levi acted in films and lived the good life of a young, famous actor.

When it became increasingly clear that Janus's prediction about the fall of civilization was going to come true, Marshall had reached out to Levi again, offering him the protection of Altor citizenship.

Being cooped up under the dome did not sound appealing to Levi. He believed that the storm of the Rage Wars would pass, and he could continue on with his very good life.

That was the last that Marshall had heard from Levi, and after a nuclear device was detonated in Hollywood, he figured he knew what had happened.

Quinn and Marshall had discussed what they would do when someone they knew showed up at Altor, asking for admission, but the fact that the time lock was employed for five years put an end to that discussion.

Now, here was someone who at least claimed to be Levi, asking for refuge. Altor was impossible, but Dust City looked a lot better than what was happening elsewhere.

All these thoughts passed through Marshall's mind in a blink.

"Hold him there. I'm on my way."

He grabbed his cane, which was second nature now, and hurried toward the gate.

That gate was the one way in or out of Dust City, aside from climbing over the electrified, high-tech fence, which was not advisable. It was where people gathered day after day, begging for admission. Time and again, whoever was monitoring the gate turned these people away. It was a brutally difficult job, as they were often sentencing them to death. If things got rough, though, there was always a drone hovering directly overhead that could nullify any threat.

The gate itself was actually the most exterior gate, but there were two others to pass through to get into Dust City proper. Just another precaution in case someone managed to defeat the gatekeepers and the overhead drone and make it past the first checkpoint.

Marshall pushed through the first interior gate, which was unguarded, then flashed his ID at the guard at the second gate. He stepped through into the area where people pleaded their case.

He tried to keep the shock off his face, but knew that he had failed.

It was Levi Rybicki, all right, but he did not resemble the suave, handsome young man that Marshall had last seen portraying a race car driver on an Apple Plus miniseries.

The man in front of him was dressed in rags, and he was skeletal. That wasn't the worst of it, though. A long scar ran down his face from above his left eye to well below his cheekbone. The eye itself was clouded over and obviously blind. There were other scars as well, and other, more recent wounds.

Levi nodded, acknowledging Marshall's reaction and even agreeing with it. He smiled, revealing that his perfect teeth were no longer perfect and had several gaps where a tooth should have been.

"Got any need for a beat-up old actor?"

"Levi," Marshall said and stepped forward so that only the counter stood between him and his old friend. It was the only thing he could think to say and the only word that would come out. He gathered himself, turned to the man who was behind the counter, and said, "Let him through."

"I'll need the General's approval before I do."

Marshall did most of his work behind the scenes in Dust City. He preferred to be as anonymous as possible. Most Dusters knew him by his name or recognized his face, but his unaggressive demeanor meant that they didn't know where he was in the food chain. That was fine with him until he needed to exert his authority.

He held his badge out and softly said, "No, you don't. Scan this."

The guard did so, and his eyes widened as the scanner showed that Marshall was ultimately the highest authority in Dust City. "Sorry, sir, I didn't recognize you."

"No problem. I know you've got a tough job here and you're doing things right. Let's get this man inside, though. Looks like he could use some medical attention."

Levi looked down at himself, almost surprised at that statement. He had obviously gone so long without that even being an option that it seemed to be out of the realm of possibility.

The guard pushed a button and for the first time in some months, a new citizen of Dust City stepped through.

Marshall opened his arms and embraced Levi, but did so gently. The new arrival was so thin that it felt like a strong hug might break his bones. Levi was taller than Marshall by a few inches, but he wrapped his arms around Marshall and laid his head on his shoulder.

He began to sob quietly.

Marshall held him for a long minute, while the guard, who was used to only turning people away, found something else to do nearby. When Levi's sobs quieted, Marshall turned toward the second gate and, with his arm still around Levi's narrow shoulders, led him into Dust City.

"I can't believe you're here," Levi said. "I remembered that you had told me I could come in the dome, so I've been trying to get here for six months. When I finally found it, there was no way in."

"Right. Things happened fast at the end, and Quinn had to shut things down and employ the time lock."

"With you outside?"

"It wasn't ideal," Marshall agreed. "There was a large-scale attack on the dome that forced his hand. I was shot in the attack, and now I'm locked out."

"For how long?"

"We can talk about that soon enough. For now, let's get you to medical."

Levi leaned heavily against Marshall as they walked. "When I couldn't get in the dome, I thought that was it. I knew I couldn't make it much longer. But I saw this place and thought it was worth a try. When I got here, I had to wait in line for a couple of days before I got my chance to plead my case. The man at the gate told me that there was no room for me. I understood. If this place took in every ragamuffin refugee that showed up, it would be overpopulated in a day."

Marshall pointed to his left, toward the medical tent.

"I don't know why, but just as I was turning to leave, I asked if this place was associated with the dome, and if he knew Quinn or you. That was when he called you."

"Incredible. If I had a bingo card with a million spots on it, I would have never bet on *old friend from Middle Falls shows up at Dust City.*"

"Dust City, huh," Levi said, turning his head slightly to take in more of the tents, dirt streets, and overall shabbiness of the town. "Good name."

"Maybe a little too on the nose," Marshall said, pointing to one of the bigger manufactured homes. Even on the outside, it looked cleaner than the surrounding buildings. "Let's get you in here. They'll look you over, get some fluids in you, patch up your wounds, and then move you to a hospital bed. I've spent a few weeks here. It has none of the comforts of home."

"Just some food and water and not having to worry about someone trying to kill me sounds like heaven."

"Amazing how our priorities have changed, isn't it?"

"The Hollywood life feels like another life," Levi agreed, shaking his head slightly.

There was no reception desk inside the trailer. Such niceties were unnecessary in Dust City. Instead, a young nurse who happened to be walking by the front door saw the two of them and said, "Is there a tornado outside that I don't know about?"

"This is Levi. He's just in from the outside. He's had a bit of a rough go. Would you see if we can make him comfortable?"

"We can do better than that," the pretty nurse said with a smile. She slipped between Marshall and Levi and put his arm around her as she helped him to a bed with crisp white sheets. She began to lower him down when he balked.

"I'm filthy. I don't want to ruin the sheets."

"Don't worry about it. We've got plenty of water here. These sheets will wash." She looked down at his feet, which wore a pair of mismatched tennis shoes, one of which was obviously too big for him and was tied on with rope. "Just lie back, and we'll get you undressed."

Levi did his best to grin at Marshall and said, "Still got it," with a wink. That wink from his one good eye was more macabre than charming, but Marshall smiled anyway.

"Same old Levi, I see."

Levi reached a skeletal hand out to Marshall. "I'd like that to be true, but it's not. That guy died quite a few months ago."

"Wait, Levi?" the nurse said. She looked down and tried to strip the injuries and dirt from the man, then added a few more pounds of flesh. She cocked her head. "You're not Levi Rybicki, are you?"

"I was," Levi agreed.

"*Nitro Nites* was one of my favorite shows!" That was the name of the streaming series Levi had starred in.

"Isn't it amazing what they can do with a little makeup these days?"

The nurse rolled her eyes and, with a practiced eye, said, "We're going to cut these clothes off you. I'm sure we can find something for you in the stores." She looked at Marshall and said, "Can you do that while I go get a doctor?" She handed a pair of specialty scissors to Marshall and left without confirmation.

Marshall started at the ragged cuff of the pants and cut upward. "You were so close, and here I am crashing the party." He couldn't stop the sharp intake of breath when the pants fell away. Levi's hip bones jutted out and there was another long gash below his right knee that looked like it was infected. In short order, he got the shirt off and Levi lay naked and vulnerable on the bed. Marshall pulled the white sheet up over him, tears in his eyes.

Everyone in Dust City knew how bad it was outside but seeing his old friend in what remained of his flesh stabbed deep into his heart.

A tall, gray-haired woman in a white coat came into the room and smiled at Levi. "I hear we are a celebrity hospital these days."

"Isn't this the Betty Ford Clinic?" Levi asked.

Ten minutes later, after a brief examination, the doctor said, "I'm going to give you something to help you sleep. We'll hook you up to an IV to get some antibiotics and fluids into you."

She turned to Marshall and made a scooting motion. "Visiting hours are over, out you go."

Marshall lifted a hand in a small wave and said, "You're in good hands now. I'll come see you tomorrow."

He walked outside in a daze, pulled his phone out of his pocket, and dialed Quinn's phone.

"Smess champion of the world, Quinn Starkweather, here," Quinn answered.

That was no longer enough to verify that he was actually talking to Quinn, since Janus—or at least some part of Janus—knew about the game now. Still, this was a conversation that would be of no interest to Janus, so he wasn't worried that it was being intercepted. Recorded, yes, but not intercepted.

"Are you sitting down?"

"I'm a professional sitter downer," Quinn answered, then realized how serious Marshall sounded. "What's going on? Everything okay over there?"

"I don't even know how to tell you this. Levi just walked into Dust City."

"Rybicki? Holy cow! I was sure he was dead in the Hollywood bombing. How did he get there? What kind of shape is he in? Same old Rybicki, I'll bet." Quinn sounded almost gleeful at the possibility that he might get to see his old friend again.

"I have no idea how he got here. He hasn't told me that part of the story yet. But no, he's not the same old Rybicki that we knew." Marshall outlined the extent of Levi's injuries.

Quinn was silent for a long moment, then said, "Since you brought him in, I know they'll give him the best care we've got over there. When you see him tomorrow, call me so I can talk to him. He was one of the best people we ever knew."

"Sure will. Talk to you then." Marshall hung up and found that he was suddenly exhausted. His adrenaline had spiked when he'd first seen Levi, but now that had passed and he felt like an empty shell.

He turned toward home, feeling ready to collapse.

Chapter Five
A Long Road to Dust City

Marshall wasn't able to get in to see Levi the next day, or the next. When Levi had said he wouldn't have made it much farther if he hadn't gotten into Dust City, he wasn't kidding.

The infection in his leg had spread and there was a lot of cleaning up to do with that. Between that and a systemic infection, he was one sick man.

Three days after Marshall half-carried him into the medical trailer, he was finally allowed to visit him.

Levi was sleeping when Marshall walked in, so he slipped quietly into a chair beside his bed, pulled out his tablet, and did some work. There was always *some* work he could do, even if it was something as boring as projecting food usage two or three years into the future.

As he so often did, Marshall became absorbed in his work and forgot about where he was. After forty-five minutes, when he finally looked up, he saw Levi was staring at him with his one good eye. There was a bandage around the left side of his face, a cast on his right arm, and an IV needle in his left.

"Still the computer nerd, huh?"

Marshall smiled and closed the program he was working on.

"Now that I think about it, that was probably a better choice. Maybe I should have stuck it out with you guys on that program you were working on. What did you call it? James or something?"

"Janus. It's what made all this possible. And by *all this*, I don't mean Dust City. I mean Altor. It gave us the information to make enough money to finance the dome, then was in charge of the design of it and all the programs that support it." He looked more closely at Levi. "I'd like to tell you that you're looking better, but I'm not sure that's true."

A hand lightly cuffed Marshall on the back of the head. It was the same doctor who had first looked at Levi.

"What kind of a bedside manner is that? Of course he's looking better." She looked affectionately at Levi. "He wasn't just at death's door, he was halfway inside. Now, he's at least back on the front porch."

"See?" Levi said. "I'm halfway back to being beautiful again. Look out world."

The doctor said, "We've got your blood test results back from yesterday. You're not out of the woods yet, but we're making progress." She picked up the tablet hanging on the end of the bed, opened a program, and made some notes. "We're going to need to keep you here for another few days, maybe a week, then we'll turn you loose on the world." She turned and hurried on to her next patient.

"So how can I make myself useful around here? Is there an annual Shakespearean festival?"

"Dusters are not so much into Shakespeare."

"Good, because honestly, neither am I. I could get up on stage and do the entire last season of *Nitro Nites,* though, if anyone wants to see that."

"Let's not worry about what you're going to do for work right now. We can figure that out later." Marshall scooted the chair closer to the bed. "Hey, I talked to Quinn, he's pretty damned excited that you're here."

"So you guys are still in contact? Don't tell me your phones work. Nobody's phones have worked since the bombs dropped."

"We've got stuff here that no one else has," Marshall admitted. "Do you want to tell me how you got here? We figured you were a goner when the nuke exploded in LA."

A haunted look appeared in Levi's eye before he answered.

"I should have been dead that day. But, we were shooting the season finale of *Nitro Nites*, and it was a location shoot. We were doing a climactic chase scene in a canyon about sixty miles southeast of the city. We were on a break between shots when the bomb went off. Luckily far enough away that we could just see the top of the mushroom cloud. We had no idea what was really going on, but it was obvious that it was something big."

"Even with Janus, we still don't know exactly what happened with the bombs dropping. It was never able to tell us exactly what form the chaos would take, just that it was coming."

"Well, that put you about a thousand steps ahead of me. I was looking forward to a wrap party with my dad at my place."

"Your dad was in LA then?"

Levi nodded. "I wasn't unique in that. Everyone on the crew, from the actors to the stuntmen, to the camera guys and the director, all lost people that day. There was nothing we could do, though. The phones and radios still worked for a little while after that. Some of the crew jumped into the vans and onto their motorcycles and lit out for the city. I knew that was useless. The radio reported the spot where the nuke detonated. It was less than a mile from my house."

"I'm sorry," was all Marshall could think to say.

"Everyone I ever met was in the same boat, it seemed, so I felt kind of numb to it. The easiest thing to do would have been just to lie down and die, but I don't seem to have that in me. Most everyone in the crew scattered and when I looked around, there was just me and Tiller."

"Tiller?"

"The prop guy on the show. He was an older guy, looked like a Hell's Angel, but he was salt of the Earth, man. Everything I sucked at—like knowing how to do anything other than act—he was great at. He could build anything, hold anything together with bailing twine and duct tape. He and I decided to team up. The funny thing was, everyone had taken off with all the vehicles. The only thing that was left was the stunt car from the show."

"The *Nitro Nightmare?*" Marshall asked, sounding a little starstruck.

"One and the same. Tiller drove because even though they cut it to look like I was driving, I wasn't really all that great behind the wheel. I rode shotgun, though unfortunately, I didn't have an actual gun. The good news was, we could outrun anything we wanted to. The bad news was, we could only go as far as that tank of gas would take us."

"So you and this guy Tiller are stuck out in the canyon, LA is in ruins, and the rest of the world is about to go crazy."

"That's about it." Levi paused, reflectively lapsing into silence.

Marshall didn't hurry him. He could see the nightmares he was reliving on his face.

Finally, Levi said, "I don't want to tell you everything else that happened. It was bad. Tiller got killed just a few days later. Without him, I was kind of lost. The only thing I had, really, was my face. At first, that seemed its own kind of currency, I guess. Even with all the shit going down, at least some people still wanted to be around someone who used to be a celebrity. I got by on that for a while, but then I ran into some bad dudes, man. They had taken over this little town and killed most everyone in it, which was a mistake. That meant they didn't have anyone to do the work for them. I was unfortunate to wander into town and they liked the idea of having a TV star for a slave."

Marshall shook his head. "I knew there would be some of that going on, but I hadn't heard directly of it."

"It's out there, all right. They held me there, starved me, forced me to work in the fields from sunup to dark, then beat my ass just for the hell of it. That's where a lot of these scars came from."

"How did you manage to escape that?"

"I made another friend. Black guy named Hank. He was a former defensive tackle for the Rams. He was big and tough. Smart, too. For some reason, he took a shine to me. He planned our escape and we managed to pull it off. Killed the two guys who were supposed to be guarding us and took off in their pickup. That's when I thought of this place. I was hoping that if you would let me into that dome, you might let Hank in, too. We drove that truck until it ran out of gas, heading toward this place." Levi was quiet again for a time. "Can you give me a drink of that water? Throat's dry."

Marshall held the glass of room-temperature water to Levi's lips. He drank it as appreciatively as if it were a fine wine.

"We tried to stay clear of anyone, but we were about to starve, too. We got caught out in the open one afternoon just before the sun set. Hank didn't make it. I only got away by jumping into a river and floating away. I've been walking toward where I figured the dome was ever since."

Levi had made no mention of how he had been partially blinded, or any of his other wounds, but Marshall knew it didn't make any difference.

"I'll say this," Levi finished. "If civilization ever comes back, I'll have a hell of a screenplay. I'll be the right guy to play the title role, too."

"That's an incredible story, and I can't even begin to calculate how unlikely it is that you're here now. You are, though, and you're safe." Marshall leaned closer so he could speak quietly. "The time lock is activated, but Quinn is working on digging a tunnel out. It's supposed to be done by next summer. I'm sure he'll want you to come inside."

"That's great, and I'd love to see Quinn again. But for me, this place right here is pretty close to paradise."

A sudden thought hit Marshall. He leaned back with a little smile on his face. "Do you remember Jazz? The girl from Middle Falls?"

"Jazz? Of course. I don't care how many Hollywood starlets you see, you don't forget a girl like Jazz. Why?"

"She's in the dome."

"What? No kidding? Is that a coincidence, or something else?"

Marshall smiled. "You'll have to ask Quinn about that. Get this, though, he had Janus recreate Artie's, just so he could take her on a date."

"Oh. Oh, that's cruel. Not Artie's. I would give one of my few remaining body parts for an Artie's burger basket and a chocolate shake."

"We'll get you one when we get to the dome." Marshall looked at Levi and saw that his eye was drooping. "We'll call Quinn tomorrow. For now, just try to rest and get better."

Levi opened his mouth to disagree but was asleep before he could say anything.

Chapter Six
Can You Dig It?

Shaquem Armstrong sprinted down the long underground tunnel. Lighting had been installed along the length of it, so he could see, though the spacing of the light threw odd shadows before and after him as he ran.

The radio built into his bracelet squawked. "Are you coming?" It was his twin brother Shaquille's voice, which carried a sound of panic. Shaquem knew that wasn't good because his brother was always calm. "It's bad. We're trapped."

Shaquem didn't bother to answer, but just lowered his head and tried to run faster. He had been in the construction shack at the mouth of the tunnel when Shaquille had first called him from the tunnel boring machine. That was more than a mile and a quarter down the tunnel. Shaquem was young and in excellent condition, but even with adrenaline pumping through his body, he couldn't run at top speed for that distance.

Too late, he realized he should have run the other way, picked up one of the electric carts and taken that to the boring machine. Instead, when he had heard how panicked his brother was, he simply reacted and began sprinting.

His lungs felt like they were burning. The underground air was cool, but sweat was pouring down into his eyes. He knew he had to slow down to regain his breath. As he did, he activated the wristband and said, "I'm coming. Be there in five."

He walked for fifty yards, then trotted ahead at a more sustainable pace. It worried him that his brother hadn't answered his message, but there was nothing for it.

When he was still a hundred yards away, he could see the disaster ahead. There had been a cave-in, and the giant boring machine was covered in dirt and rocks. That should have been impossible, according to their plans and everything the AI had designed, but the reality of the situation was there in front of him. The boring machine itself was twenty-five feet tall and seventy feet long from the tailpipe to the tip of the drill.

All of it was buried under the rubble.

Somewhere under the tons and tons of debris was the cab, which had been specially reinforced to handle a situation just like this. Inside that cab was Shaquille and another worker. Running the massive drill was a two-person operation. The twins were the co-heads of the project, and so rarely got to operate the equipment themselves. On this day, one of the operators had called in because his wife was having a baby. Shaquille had grinned and jumped at the opportunity to get behind the controls of the giant machine.

And now he was buried under tons of rubble.

Shaquem's first thought was how he was going to break this news to his parents, who were across the desert in Dust City.

There were three other workers there ahead of Shaquem, pulling at rocks and shoveling dirt aside.

It was like aiming a squirt gun at a three-alarm fire.

Shaquem tapped his band and said, "I'm here now."

"Good," Shaquille's voice crackled back. "How bad is it?"

"It's bad. What's your oxygen situation in there."

"We're fine right now. The automatic life support system has kicked on. That buys us twelve hours. Can you get us out of here by then?"

Evaluating the situation, Shaquem thought it was doubtful. There was just too much debris to remove.

"You bet. No problem."

"I love it when you lie to me."

"Just give me a second." Shaquem pulled the small tablet off his belt. He tapped an icon and said, "Tom?"

Instantly, a face appeared. The twins knew Tom wasn't a real person but was just the face that the AI had chosen to show them. It didn't matter. Seeing the man's face, with his three-day growth of beard and short white hair, was calming.

"I know what happened," Tom said, his voice steady, "but not why. We'll worry about that later. For now, we'll get the operators out of there."

"What do I need to do?"

"Right now, nothing. There is a small army of equipment just getting to the tunnel. Everything you'll need to get your brother out of there. I've put our best people on the equipment, and they'll work until we dig them out. You stay there and direct traffic."

"What are the chances that bringing that much heavy equipment in causes another cave-in and buries us all?"

"I can't make an accurate projection until I get more information, but probably around ten percent."

When he had woken up that morning, Shaquem had no idea that he would have a ten percent chance of dying before lunch, but here he was.

"Thanks, Tom."

"I'm looking for other solutions. I'll send more equipment once I figure out what will be most useful."

Shaquem dropped the tablet back onto his belt and approached the workers who were digging ineffectually against the giant pile of rubble. "Thanks for doing what you can." He struggled to keep his voice calm. "But let's get you out of here. What you're doing won't solve the problem, but there's a risk of another cave-in. Go ahead and go back to the shack. Wait there in case we need you."

The two men and a woman nodded and turned back up the tunnel. As they did, a quiet rumbling echoed as the first of the rescue equipment arrived.

"It's going to be okay," Shaquem said into his wristband. "Tom and I are on it, and we'll have you out in plenty of time." He managed to sound a lot more confident than he really was.

"Anything we can do from this end?"

That made Shaquille smile. "Yeah. Try meditating. That'll slow your breathing."

"I knew I should have learned how to do that."

"Never too late to start learning. We're gonna be busy out here for the next few hours, but I'll stay in touch."

A small army of heavy equipment appeared, headlights jumping as they grew closer.

The first problem became apparent to Shaquem. There was more equipment here than there was room for. They were going to get in each other's way. He plucked the tablet up again and said, "Tom, can you give me the most effective pattern to use the equipment, taking into account the size of the tunnel?"

Instantly, a plan appeared on the laptop.

Shaquem ran toward the first excavator, arms up, stopping it. Everything else came to a stop behind. Glancing at the tablet, he began directing traffic.

The problem of moving the rubble was twofold. The dirt and rock needed to be pulled away, but there was so much of it that it couldn't just be piled close by. That would fill the tunnel in no time. Instead, it had to be disposed of elsewhere. There was really only room for one excavator at the pile at a time. Shaquem ordered each one to pull forward, grab a load of dirt, then back up and empty it into one of the waiting trucks. While it was offloading, the next excavator grabbed another shovelful and waited to drop it off.

As soon as the truck was full, it reversed back down the tunnel to a spot where it could safely drop the dirt, then turned around and got back in line.

Shaquem stood nervously watching the excavators pull shovelful after shovelful of dirt and load it in the trucks. He shifted nervously from foot to foot, feeling helpless. Each load that was taken away seemed to make such a small dent in the pile of dirt, he was afraid it would take days, not hours, to reach the cab and rescue his brother.

* * *

Quinn sat in his office, deep underground. His space was protected by sound curtains that kept the noise of the machinery that was constantly running quiet. He didn't hear the cave-in, then, but he felt it, nonetheless.

As hundreds of tons of dirt and rock fell into the tunnel, the ground shook under his feet.

"Janus? What was that?"

"There's been a disruption in the tunnel."

"*Disruption?* That sounded like a cave-in."

"That's another word for it."

"How bad is it?"

"Some of my cameras and systems were damaged in the event. It will take some time before I am able to give you an accurate report."

"Was anyone hurt?"

"It seems likely, but with my cameras and systems down, it will take some time before I am able to give you an accurate report."

Quinn took a deep breath and let it out slowly. He knew that when Janus started repeating itself, he wasn't going to get any more information out of it.

"Send a cart to my door. I'm going out to inspect it, see what I can do to help."

"No."

That shocked Quinn as much as anything Janus had ever said to him. "Janus," he said, straining to keep his voice calm, "send a cart to my office so I can go to the tunnel."

"No."

Quinn bit his lip, wondering if this was his new normal. "Why?"

"You are still valuable to this project, even as a figurehead to the humans. There is some chance that there will be more activity in the tunnel, and you could be killed. Meanwhile, based on your strength and skillsets, which have nothing to do with tunneling, you would be of no effective use there. It makes no sense for you to go."

Quinn's head began to throb. Arguing with Janus was impossible. Without saying anything else, he walked toward the door of his office. It was programmed to slide open when he got within five feet of it. It had always done so.

This time, it did not budge as he approached it, and he nearly ran into it.

"Door, open."

"The door will not open, Quinn. I explained to you why it is a terrible idea for you to expose yourself to danger there. I am working with the team on the ground to do everything we can to rescue the workers. There is nothing for you to do there. I will open the door when the danger has passed."

Quinn stumbled to his couch and sat down hard. He was a prisoner in his own gilded cage. Janus controlled everything.

"Some of my cameras are coming back online." The walls of Quinn's office flashed to life, showing several views of the cave-in. He could see heavy equipment lining up to dig toward the buried tunnel boring machine, and trucks carrying dirt and rocks away. Squinting, he could see one of the twins in charge of the dig standing to one side, directing traffic. It looked like an efficient operation, but the task seemed mammoth. Quinn had a very bad feeling about this, but with Janus holding him hostage, there was nothing he could do about it.

Chapter Seven
Getting to the Bottom of Things

The next few hours were like a nightmare for Shaquem. He knew the oxygen supply in the cab of the boring machine was diminishing, but the progress to reach them was slow.

Lou Danson, the twins' number two person on the project, showed up at a run. He didn't ask stupid questions about how the cave-in had happened. Instead, he just handed Shaquem a large bottle of cold water and said, "Take a break. I'll direct traffic for a while."

Shaquem nodded, accepted the bottle and sat down on a boulder off to the side. He hadn't known how thirsty he was, but the water cut through the dust in his throat and he drained it. He tapped his band and said, "Lou's here."

"Good," Shaquille answered immediately. "About time we got someone there that knows what they're doing."

"You're hilarious. Listen. I'm gonna keep the channel clear, but if you need to talk to me, I'm here."

Shaquem sat for a few minutes, then rejoined Lou. Together they directed traffic, keeping things flowing smoothly.

Six hours after Shaquem arrived at the disaster, the excavator bucket dug in and hit metal. They had located the boring machine. His mouth fell open. Now that he saw how many tons of debris were piled on top of it, he was amazed the cab itself hadn't been crushed.

That was all down to the design. The cab wasn't on the very top of the machine. In fact, it was stuck in the middle, under reinforced steel. From inside the cab, the operators couldn't actually see where they were digging. Everything was done via camera.

That had taken the operators some getting used to, but the reasoning for it was now clear. Without that protection built over the cab, the two men inside would have already been dead.

Shaquem felt like he was closer to retrieving his brother now and wanted to redouble the efforts to dig them out, but they were already moving as fast and efficiently as they could. Every few minutes, he glanced at the tablet, which had a running countdown to how long the oxygen in the cab's life support would last.

It read five hours and seven minutes.

Shaquem kept himself as busy as possible, but the truth was, he was somewhat superfluous. That feeling of helplessness seeped into his brain, and he found himself wondering what life might be like without his twin brother. To him, though they were definitely separate people, they also felt somewhat like two halves of a whole. He couldn't imagine life without the person who had literally always been there with him.

He felt the tablet buzz against his leg as it dangled off his belt. He grabbed it and saw Tom's familiar face.

"Some of the cameras have been damaged, so I can't get a clear view of the situation. Hold your tablet up and walk from side to side, so I can get a better idea of what we're up against."

Shaquem did just that, dodging the excavator and showing the cave-in from side to side and top to bottom.

"We need to change tactics, now that we've got the rear end of the boring machine out. If they continue like this, we're going to dig around the sides of the machine first. That won't help us rescue them."

Shaquem closed his eyes, realizing that he should have thought of that himself.

"What's the best plan?"

"Send the big excavator away. Fully extended, its arm isn't long enough to reach where we need it to dig, and it's too heavy to climb up so it can get there. As soon as the excavator reaches the end of the tunnel, I've got two smaller models lined up and ready to come. They need to start digging from closer to the top. Like this."

A perfect rendering of the cave-in popped up on the tablet, with arrows pointing to where the smaller excavators could begin to dig.

"Have them climb up the pile, digging their own roadway if they need to. When they get to the levels I've indicated, have them dig down. Each dump truck needs to pull in backwards, so the excavators can dump their dirt directly into the beds."

"Brilliant," Shaquem said, so grateful for the assistance. He knew that if he had days to look the situation over, he might have come up with something similar. But, feeling panicked, he knew his brain was not working at maximum ability.

He took the tablet and showed Lou the plan, then they put it into action, sending the huge excavator out of the tunnel. It was so close to the sides that the smaller versions of the same thing had to wait for it to pop out of the tunnel before they could make it to the cave-in.

After the excavator and loaded dump truck rumbled back down the tunnel, there was an eerie hush near the accident. Lou and Shaquem looked at each other with raised eyebrows, neither wanting to speak and fill the sudden silence.

A few minutes later, the two new, smaller excavators could be heard in the distance. They were about one-third the size of the big one that had just left, which made them much better suited to the job at hand.

When they lined up in front of the dirt pile with the back few feet of the boring machine sticking out, Shaquem waved the operators over. He pulled up his tablet, tapped it, and a vivid hologram of the cave-in appeared above it. He showed them where they would each be digging. Essentially, one was on the left side of where the cab would be and the other was on the right.

As they listened to Shaquem and looked at the hologram, they glanced at the pile itself, judging where they would actually be digging and whether they could get up there or not.

"If it's too steep to climb, you're going to have to excavate a path up."

Tom's face suddenly took the place of the image of the cave-in. "Don't worry about memorizing that image. I'm sending it as a holo to each of your wristbands. Just tap and it will appear."

The two operators nodded and started to turn away. Shaquem reached out and touched each of them on the shoulder, then held up his tablet again. The oxygen countdown was still ticking down, showing four hours and twenty minutes.

"That's how much oxygen those two men trapped in the cab have."

Both operators, older men who appeared to have seen it all, nodded grimly and went to work.

It was frustratingly slow work for Shaquem to watch. The angle was, as he had feared, too steep for the smaller excavators to be able to position themselves over the cab.

They spent the next ninety minutes slowly carving away at the mountain of dirt and rocks, inching their way closer to the top.

When the timer on Shaquem's tablet read two hours and forty-seven minutes, both excavators were finally in place.

Each one was nimble enough to reach the spot where they needed to dig, but now that they had, each bucketful they were able to grab was much smaller than those of the larger machine. For a moment, Shaquem wondered if it would have been a better strategy to have the smaller machines work on building a short road and platform for the bigger excavator to climb up onto.

That ship had sailed, so he put it out of his mind and focused on the progress they were making.

It was always cool so far underground, but he felt sweaty all over, his shirt stuck to his back.

He glanced down at his tablet and watched as the timer clicked over to under one hour. He wanted to scream. His guts clenched, but he did his best to hold himself together.

Forty minutes later, one of the excavators finally scraped metal with its bucket.

Shaquem couldn't contain himself. He sprinted up the path that the machine had made and stood beside the bucket. He was familiar with every inch of the boring machine. He held up a hand to stop the operator and knelt down to brush away dirt. He saw where he was and motioned to move the bucket back about three feet. That was where he estimated the hatch that led down to the cab was.

He tapped his wristband. "Can you hear us knocking?"

"I hear something up there," Shaquille's answer came back.

Shaquem moved his hands up and down in a gesture that said, *gently, gently*. The last thing he wanted was for the bucket to damage the hatch. He stepped back and watched as the operator feathered the bucket down, taking one little divot at a time away.

Shaquem was so focused on that work that he didn't notice when Lou ran up on him. He was carrying two shovels.

"I think this is best," the foreman said.

Shaquem smiled gratefully, grabbed a shovel and began to dig. He started moving dirt away from the spot where he thought the hatch would be. When he hit the metal of the top of the boring machine, he again fell to his knees, scraping away dirt and small rocks, looking for the hatch. It wasn't there.

The tablet on his belt buzzed at him. He ignored it, but knew what it meant.

Five minutes of oxygen left.

Shaquem let out a small gasp of worry, then stood and tried to orient himself. He decided that he was probably too far forward. He took a step back and both he and Lou dug in with their shovels.

This time, they hit pay dirt, finding the lid of the hatch. It was bent out of true by something that had fallen directly on it. Shaquem's heart skipped a beat, worried that they wouldn't be able to get it open.

He tapped his band and said, "We're here, we're here. Try to open the hatch."

There was no answer, but Shaquem heard activity on the other side of the hatch.

"Won't open," Shaquille's voice came from Shaquem's wristband. "Stuck."

"Keep pushing," was all Shaquem took time to reply.

The tablet began to beep. It read all zeroes in flashing red.

"Do this with me," Shaquem said to Lou. He stuck the tip of his shovel into the small crack that had opened in the hatch. "I think it's released, it just doesn't want to let go."

The tablet continued to buzz and beep. In one motion, Shaquem whipped it off his belt and threw it across the tunnel, where it landed with a clatter and was silenced.

Both Shaquem and Lou stuck the tips of their shovels in and pried with all their might. They strained and grunted and put their backs into it.

At the moment when Shaquem was sure the handle of his shovel was going to break, the hatch popped open. He reached a hand inside, sure that Shaquille would grab it.

There was no one there. Inside, the cab had gone dark.

Above him, he heard Lou calling for the medics, but his voice sounded far away.

Shaquem dropped down into the hatchway. He landed on something soft. Without looking, he knew it was Shaquille. He mumbled something unintelligible that might have been a curse word or an apology, then straddled his brother. He put his arms under his brother's armpits and grunted, hauling him up toward the opening.

"Lou! Grab him!"

Lou and two other men who had arrived at a run grabbed Shaquille and pulled his limp body up.

"Flashlight," Shaquem said, and his wristband shot out a beam of pure, white light. He could see the body of Hector, the other operator, sprawled out on the floor.

Shaquem was not big like his father was, but he found the strength where he needed it. He lifted Hector up and dragged him toward the hatchway, then lifted him as he had done Shaquille. Strong hands reached down and pulled him out.

Shaquem scrambled up the ladder and saw medics bent over both men, doing CPR.

With his adrenaline spiking and nothing to expend the energy on, Shaquem got so shaky, he had to sit down on the pile of dirt. It was either sit down or fall down.

Lou looked at him and said, "Put your head between your knees. It'll pass."

Shaquem did as he was told until his breathing evened out.

When he looked up again, Shaquille was sitting up, looking at him. For once, he didn't have anything sarcastic to say.

They looked down at Hector. The medic was still performing CPR, but there was no response.

* * *

Quinn leaned forward in his chair, staring at the slightly grainy picture projected onto his office wall.

"Janus? Did we get them out on time?"

"Shaquille Armstrong's vital signs are regulating. I will have him taken to Medical to check out, but he will be fine."

"And the other man?"

"Hector Gonzalez did not respond to treatment. I have not detected a heartbeat in six and a half minutes."

Quinn shut his eyes and his chin dropped to his chest.

"Open the door."

This time, the door opened just as it should have. Apparently, without the heavy equipment rumbling in the tunnel, Janus thought that the chance of another cave-in was minimal enough to allow Quinn out of his office.

Quinn ran to one of the electric carts and was pleased to find that it responded when he pushed on the accelerator. He guided it through the machinery and around piles of boxed supplies until he got to the tunnel. He didn't slow down but bounced across the rough floor until he reached the spot where the collapse had happened.

It was a hive of activity now. Shaquille Armstrong was walking slowly down the slope of the collapse, his arm around his brother. Two men were carrying a body—Hector Gonzalez, undoubtedly—on a stretcher.

Janus had been right about at least one thing, Quinn was absolutely useless here. He stood at the edge of the chaos, watching.

Finally, he turned around and went back to his office. He realized that he had never had any plan about what he would do once he arrived on scene.

Back inside the office, he picked up his phone and dialed.

"Greetings, captain," Marshall's voice answered.

"We've got a problem. The tunnel collapsed. I think you guys are going to be stuck over there for a lot longer than we thought."

Chapter Eight
When the Dust Settles

Marshall, sitting in his small living room, hung up the phone after speaking with Quinn. The worst news was that someone had died in the tunnel collapse. The fact that he was going to be stuck in Dust City for an unknown, but longer period of time, was secondary but also awful.

He had spent all his adult life preparing for one thing—living in Altor. At the critical moment, fate had cast that aside, and now he was stuck in a semi-protected, but not ideal, lifestyle. He constantly reminded himself that life could have been much worse outside. He had seen that again firsthand when Levi Rybicki had stumbled in.

He looked down at his lap, where his tablet glowed softly. He had been working on the parameters of the request he was going to put to Janus about who else could be brought over from Dust City when the tunnel opened up.

He turned the tablet off. With the tunnel collapse, that was a useless project. He supposed they might eventually dig out the tunnel boring machine, find what had caused the ceiling to cave in, and restart the tunnel project.

The target date of the following summer was obviously out the window, though.

He sighed and set his tablet on the small TV tray that passed for a table, grabbed his cane, and stepped outside. It was fall, and in Marshall's hometown of Middle Falls, Oregon, it would have meant blowing leaves, cool temperatures, and the beginning of the eight or nine month rainy season. Here, in the Nevada desert, it meant the sun set earlier each day, but the temperatures were still high and the sun shone consistently.

When the Rage Wars had struck and Janus still had access to many of the satellites, he had checked in on Middle Falls. It was heartbreaking to see even that small town fall into chaos. Even Artie's Drive-in, as close to a landmark as the town had, didn't escape the damage. Somehow seeing the tall neon sign broken and listing badly to one side was too much for him. He had clicked away and never looked again.

The dusty dirt street that passed as the main thoroughfare was nearly empty. It was late afternoon, and everyone was either at home settling in for the night or still at work.

He walked toward the part of town that was almost exclusively residential and stopped in front of one of a series of identical modular buildings. He knocked on the door and was unsurprised to see that Nia Armstrong was red-eyed and had obviously been crying.

"Hello, Marshall, come in."

"I won't stay long. Just wanted to check in with you, make sure that you're all right."

"Our boys are all right," Deon Armstrong said, "so we are too."

"From what I understand, it was Shaquem who directed the rescue effort. I've seen the footage, and he was brilliant."

Nia nodded his agreement, saying, "That Tom fellow that they work with sent us the footage, too. We feel terrible for the man who didn't make it."

"And grateful that our son did," Nia added. "So grateful."

"We don't know what this will mean for the entire tunnel project, but obviously, it's going to delay getting us all inside."

"And that's okay," Nia said. "We're safe, they're safe, and we can at least talk to them and see their faces, even if it is on a screen. That's all we need, for now."

"Is there anything else I can do?" Marshall asked.

"No, but would you like to stay for dinner? I'm making goulash, so there's plenty," Nia answered.

Marshall thought of the scant pantry he kept stocked at home and realized that homemade goulash sounded wonderful. He was about to accept the invitation when his wristband buzzed.

"Marshall?" It was John Steele, whom everyone called the General.

"Yes."

"I'm calling a quick meeting at my place. We've got a couple of things to talk over."

"When?"

"Now."

This sort of informality wasn't unusual in Dust City, where things were often put together on the spur of the moment.

Marshall sighed and said, "I'm on my way." He looked at Nia and Dean and smiled. "Rain check?"

"Of course," Nia said. "Come by any time."

Marshall stepped back outside, grateful that this meeting had gone the way it had. As close as Shaquille came to dying, it could have been very different.

He hurried to Steele's, running through the possibilities of what this impromptu meeting could be about. He didn't knock on Steele's door but just pushed inside.

Steele and the two US Army soldiers, Lieutenant Dan Forster and Sergeant JT Brewster, were already seated on metal folding chairs around the long table.

"What's going on? Some kind of a threat on the horizon?"

"No," Steele said, "and that's the point." He nodded at Forster and Brewster. "These boys have been sitting guard duty outside our gates for a year now."

"And it's been blissfully quiet," Forster added. "Which is good."

"But on the last big attack launched against us," Sgt. Brewster said, "we weren't even needed. Your defenses cut them to pieces before we even swung into action."

"I understand," Marshall said. "So what's the plan?"

"They are still United States soldiers," Steele began, then glanced around. "Even if we aren't really sure there *is* a United States Army anymore. They feel guilty just sitting here."

"Before we came into contact with you, we had been released to patrol a large area around our base," Forster said. "When we saw what was happening here, we thought it was important that we stay and protect the perimeter of one of the most important concerns in the country. But now, as Sgt. Brewster pointed out, I'm not sure we're necessary anymore. I don't think there is any force out there that could launch a viable attack that you and Altor can't handle."

Marshall nodded his agreement. "I see that, but it's sure been nice having you. You've been like our extra security blanket."

"We want to get back to our base," Forster said, "and see what the lay of the land is there. And there's another concern."

"What's that?"

Sgt. Brewster cleared his throat. "The gasoline in our vehicles is degrading."

Steele leaned forward and said, "We've done what we can about that. This Janus has created a formula for an additive that will help offset that degradation, and we are happy to give enough of our supply of gas and that formula to the Army, but it's just going to continue to get worse."

Forster looked at Brewster. He outranked the sergeant, but it was obvious how much he relied on his common sense and experience. "We were going to wait it out until spring, but we're afraid the fuel might have degraded too much to get us back to the base, even with the additives."

"That's going to be true of all fuels, isn't it?" Marshall asked. "There's no more fuel being produced, so what was already out there is going to be useless soon enough. We're going to be back to actual horsepower to get around soon, aren't we?"

"There are certain kinds of aviation fuels that will still be good," Steele answered, "and of course, electric vehicles will still function, but yes, we're about to morph into a more stationary world. From all reports we've gotten, gunpowder is running low, as well, and that's part of why the marauding bands are few and far between now."

"And that's why we're going to leave," Forster said with a sense of finality. "We know there's more good we can do out there than we can sitting guard duty here."

"Well, you rode in like the cavalry just when we needed you," Steele said. "I'm not sure we'd all still be here, including the dome, without your help."

"It felt good to do something," Brewster said. He and Forster stood together.

Marshall thought for a moment they were going to snap a salute at Steele, but instead, they just left the room.

When they were gone, Marshall asked, "What do you think?"

"I think they're right. We don't really need them anymore. The world blew itself to hell with a bunch of bombs, then tore up whatever was left for the last year, like two crows fighting over a cow turd. Now, that's all settling down. If you managed to survive to this point, it might get a little easier from here on out."

"At least from the perspective of not being at risk of being shot and killed every day," Marshall agreed.

"Eventually, we'll have to start to figure out how to rebuild. Get the infrastructure back in place, get power and water running again. Does that supercomputer of yours have plans for that?"

Marshall mulled that question over in his mind. Even a few weeks ago, he would have simply said, "Yes." Now, with recent developments in Janus's personality, he couldn't be so sure. He knew that some part of Janus was undoubtedly listening to their conversation though, and as was becoming a habit, he ran his answer through that filter.

Carefully, he said, "I know at one time, there was a plan for that. There is a lot of heavy equipment and supplies that we thought would be in short supply stashed away at the bottom of Altor. The question is, when and how to employ them."

"Happy to say, that's above my paygrade," Steele said. "Now, are there any changes we need to implement now that Uncle Sam's Army is going away?"

"Not many, I don't think. We've got the aerial defense drones. After a year of continuous service, some of them are getting worn down, but when they do, we bring them in to our shops here, clean them up, and put them back in service. I don't think there's any kind of a threat left that can pose any real danger to us."

"I'll keep up with the drills we've got the Dust City Irregulars running through, anyway. There's no harm in that, and if it turns out we're wrong, we'll be glad to have them." Steele scrunched up his face and said, "Any idea what caused the collapse of the tunnel?"

"No, not really. Maybe Janus relied on what turned out to be an inaccurate geological survey. That's about all I can think of so far."

"Looks like you and I are going to be Dusters for the foreseeable future. By the way, this friend of yours we let in, Rybicki or something like that. He have any special skills? Anything we can put to use."

"Well, he used to be pretty damned good at charming people, but until we decide to launch a Dust City television network, I don't think he's going to be of much use."

"I'll put him down as an FoQ, then."

That anagram was a new one for Marshall, and it showed on his face.

"Friend of Quinn," Steele said with a smile.

Chapter Nine
The Prudent Twins

Cults in search of Utopia were a common occurrence across the breadth of the twentieth century. It seemed that the faster the world raced toward a dystopian future, the more that idea became attractive to people.

Most of these cults started small and stayed that way, with a few ardent followers who never left.

So it was with *The Messengers of Light*. The group was formed under the auspices of Manley T. Prudent, whose birth name was Herbert T. Brackish. The freshly renamed Manley Prudent started his version of Utopia in Southern California in 1948.

As cults go, it was pretty standard issue. Manley claimed to be the one true messenger of God, but he was willing to share the wisdom of the ages with those who were willing to donate all their worldly goods to him and move to his farm a hundred miles north of Los Angeles. Not coincidentally, one of the teachings that Manley brought to the world was that, as the one true messenger, he needed to spread his seed as far and wide as possible. That included sexual congress with girls as young as fourteen, which their parents happily agreed to.

The Messengers never grew to more than a few hundred willing-to-believe souls, but Manley did everything he could to grow the population. By the time he died in 1987, he had sired more than seventy children, though most were conceived more than twenty-five years earlier.

The last of his children were a twin brother and sister named Armor and Faith. They were born on the precise day that Manley Prudent died, and the remaining members believed that his soul was so powerful it had been split in half and reincarnated as both twins.

The twins were both born with a caul on, an auspicious beginning. They also both had albinism. The combination of no pigment in the hair or eyelashes, their porcelain skin, and the coincidence of the date of their birth led to the members of the flock transferring their affection and belief to the young twins.

Without Manley to oversee the flock, it slowly dwindled down. Some people left voluntarily, many were simply so old that they died, spurred on, no doubt by Manley's complete rejection of modern medicine.

Soon enough, there were less than a dozen members. The remaining Messengers were all in their seventies or eighties, except for Armor and Faith and their mother, Alice, who was in her fifties.

By the mid-nineties, that number dwindled to the twins and Alice. They lived quietly at the estate that Manley had left behind. As the final members of the Messengers of Light organization, they owned the fifty acres of good real estate. They accumulated whatever assets the cult still had by simply outlasting everyone else.

Those assets weren't a lot, at least not on a balance sheet, though they certainly could have converted the land into a tidy little fortune if they had chosen to.

Instead, they lived simply in the biggest house in the compound, grew vegetables and minded their fruit trees. Part of Manley's teachings included vegetarianism, so by the sweat of their brow, they were able to survive on what they grew.

Alice Prudent—all members of the Messengers agreed to legally change their last name—passed away in 2025.

The twins might have been entirely adrift, living in the large compound alone, but they continued on, completely happy.

They continued to work in their garden and orchards all day, using the long Southern California summer season to survive on. At night, they read their father's teachings via candlelight, as the compound had never had electricity.

In 2033, the Rage Wars passed them by completely. They were in a remote location, and though the compound was large, by then it was almost completely overgrown.

With no electricity, they had no television, and their last visitor had been years earlier. They were far enough north of where the nuclear weapons were detonated that they never felt even that. They did feel a series of rumbles and small earthquakes, but in their area, that was just part of life.

While society fell all around them, the twins continued on in their solitary lifestyle for another year.

They had often wondered why they did not receive the type of communication and blessings that their father had. They had accepted it, and waited patiently to see if that might ever change.

In the fall of 2034, it did.

That was when both twins began to get messages from God.

They were sitting at the dining room table, poring over the fourth of twelve volumes their father had written. They had read the books so often that the truth was, they had memorized every word decades earlier. They read it now out of habit.

There were no other books anywhere in the compound.

The twins were, essentially, innocent in the ways of the world.

When the first message arrived, they both sat up straight, as though hit with a jolt of electricity. Eyes wide, they stared into each other's eyes.

There was no need for either of them to say, *Did you feel that?* It was obvious that they both had.

The first message they received was, *It is almost time for you to leave the home I have made for you.*

It wasn't some fuzzy, amorphous message. It was clear as a bell. The fact that the message included the words *the home that I have made for you* told them that this was a message from their father. God. It was all tangled up in their minds.

"What do we need to do to get ready?" Armor asked. Both he and Faith waited quietly and patiently for the answer, but it never came.

After waiting for the voice to answer for fifteen quiet minutes, Faith finally said, "He will let us know when we need to know," in a hushed voice.

Armor nodded, completely agreeing with the truth of that.

They blew out the candle, bathing the room in the light of a full moon, which slanted in through the large picture window. After sitting quietly for an hour, without a word, they both rose and went to their bedrooms.

That was the only message they received over the next few weeks until, one afternoon, as they were hoeing the rows of corn, they both heard a single word: *Soon.*

This time, they didn't bother to ask a follow-up question. There was no need. The fact that God was reaching out to them was enough. They believed that when they needed to know more, they would.

The third message arrived early one morning, just as the sun was coming up. Faith was milking their cow, while Armor carried manure to spread over the garden.

At the same moment, they both received the same message.

Now.

They stood up and met in the yard in front of their house. They knew the time was now, but the time for what, exactly, wasn't yet clear.

The voice of God their Father rang in both their brains.

Leave now. Take only the clothes you are wearing. I will show you the way.

The twins did not hesitate. Armor dropped his manure-encrusted shovel, Faith dropped the half-filled milk bucket, and they walked down the long driveway toward the rural road.

When they reached the road, a strong feeling to turn east came over them.

They were quite a sight, walking down that empty country road.

Armor wore a black work shirt and black dungarees, while Faith wore a long, formless black dress. Their father had commanded that it was a sin to cut the hair that they were given, so they both had white hair that, when loosened, fell to their ankles.

Armor wore his loose, while Faith braided hers, which still fell to her knees. They were both naturally thin, and looked like an albino version of Grant Wood's *American Gothic*, albeit with long hair.

They had an easy, steady pace. Their normal life meant long days of working their farm, so going for a long walk did not tax them.

They walked the rest of that day without seeing another soul. They did pass other farms and houses, but they were all deserted. If the twins found this strange, they did not comment on it.

When the sun touched the horizon behind them, the voice appeared in their heads again.

Rest. When you need sustenance, I will provide.

That was good enough for Armor and Faith. If the voice had commanded them to throw themselves in the stream that ran parallel to the road and drown themselves, they would have gone to their death with a smile.

Instead, they took those last words to mean that they would be supplied with whatever they needed, including water. After walking all day, they were parched beyond words, and so walked to the stream and drank their fill.

They lay down beside the stream and drifted off as the stars began to show. With the electric lights of Los Angeles doused, the stars were brighter than they had ever seen, which they took as another sign that they were following the proper path.

They walked from sunup to sundown again the following day.

On the third day of their journey, they reached the small community of Perkins.

Unknown to the twins, Perkins had been overrun by a roving militia weeks earlier. The road into town was barricaded with a logging truck and two men with rifles.

The armed men were a mixture of amused and confused by the appearance of the twins.

The younger man, whose clothes were baggy, but still looked like he had fifty pounds or so to give, said, "You can just turn back and go back to wherever they keep weirdos like you."

If these two men had been locals, they would have been familiar with *The Messengers of Light*. They were not, however, so had no clue.

Armor held his hands up. "We are not armed. We are simply following the path God Our Father has set us on."

The other man grinned, looked at his companion and said, "They're on a mission from God," quoting the old *Blues Brothers* movie, but the reference went completely over his friend's head.

"We are supposed to go through this town," Faith said. "That is what we see. That is what we will do. If you are going to kill us, then that is what you will do, and we will both be fulfilling our destinies."

The twins walked toward the two men, who raised their rifles to their shoulders.

"I mean it," the heavier man said, "I'll shoot."

"We mean it as well," Faith answered. "That is up to you."

When they were ten feet away from the truck that was pulled sideways across the road, they veered to their left.

The two men looked at each other. People had approached them before, but when they were given the warning, they had always turned and slunk away. They didn't know what to do with these two.

Finally, one of the men said, "Hell, let 'em go. They're obviously crazy, but harmless."

“Get on the radio,” his companion answered, “and let ‘em know someone is coming, though.”

The twins moved past the cab of the truck and immediately returned to the road, walking steadily toward town.

Chapter Ten
The Handshake

Matt Miller was once again on horseback, riding the fence line. Boring duty, but Jamie believed it was still necessary, and at the Y-Bar-S, what Jamie said went. It was hard to argue with the results. Every other farm in the county had been overrun, used up, and abandoned.

A small movement caught Matt's eye to the right, and he pulled his binoculars to his eyes and focused on that direction. Sure enough, there was a man walking toward him. He looked to still be a mile or so away, and at the slow pace he was traveling, Matt knew it would be a while before he got to the fence.

He whirled his horse around and clicked his mouth, encouraging the animal to break into a trot. Matt still hadn't managed to master the art of looking cool on horseback, especially at a trot, which jarred his teeth. He was still too scared to encourage the horse to break into a full run, though, feeling nervous about falling off. So, he trotted back toward the main gate, where two other people stood guard.

"Somebody's coming," Matt said when he got close enough. "Just one man, moving slow. Can't tell if he's armed or not."

"Good," the woman answered, rifle slung comfortably. "Go back and keep an eye on him. If he approaches peacefully, direct him down to us. If he wants a tussle, go ahead and kill him. I'll get Jamie on the walkie-talkie and let him know to come on out."

Matt tipped her a salute and turned the horse back in the direction he had come. This time, he kept it to a walk, judging that he had plenty of time to get back before the man got there.

As it turned out, that was correct. When he got back to the spot where he had been standing guard, the man wasn't much closer than he had been. In fact, he was sitting on the ground, looking like someone out for a little stroll in nature.

Five minutes later, the man stood and walked toward Matt again. When he got close enough, Matt sat tall in the saddle and said, "Head along the fence this direction. Don't make any sudden moves. I've got my buddy in the trees who's already got a bead on you."

That lie was as blatant and obvious as it had been when used repeatedly in Western movies the better part of a century earlier.

It wasn't really necessary. If the man had any fight in him, it looked like it had been beaten out of him long since.

He held his hands up and said, "I'm just looking for some food. I'm weak."

"This is the Y-Bar-S. We don't turn anyone away without a meal. There's a gate half a mile up the fence line. They'll ask you a few questions there, then they'll feed you and send you on your way."

That wasn't necessarily true, either. If Jamie liked this bedraggled man and thought he had useful skills, he would invite him in. Most times, though, he did just give a meal then send them on their way.

"Can I climb under the barbed wire and catch a ride with you? It's been so long since I've eaten, I'm feeling weak."

That explained why he was spending time sitting down, but still, Matt shook his head. "Nope. You can do exactly what I told you to do. Nothing else."

The man let his head hang down for a long minute, as though he might be contemplating just sitting down and staying there. Finally, he gathered himself, met Matt's eyes, and nodded.

Matt stayed where he was for several minutes after he watched the man shamble slowly away. Visitors were rare these days, Matt didn't expect to see anyone else, but he also wanted to see if there was someone coming along behind the man.

Five minutes of scanning the horizon told him that the man was truly traveling alone. Matt walked the horse along the fence line toward the gate. It didn't take long to catch up to the stranger. Even at a slow walk the horse overtook and passed the man. Matt continued on to the gate, where Jamie Sterling was waiting.

Jamie took off his cowboy hat and squinted at his childhood friend. "Thought you had somebody."

"I do, but he's a slow 'un. Says he's weak from hunger."

"I can believe that," Jamie said. He climbed up on the first rail of the metal fence and looked to the right. "There he is." A long pause, then, "You're right. He's a slow 'un."

Jamie had brought four people from the house, so there was a total of eight people at the gate. More than enough show of force to handle this man who didn't look capable of arm wrestling a small child.

If only they had known the truth, they all would have fled.

They did not, and stood their ground, waiting patiently.

Finally, the man arrived at the gate, literally hat in hand. He looked a mess. His hair was long and showed the consequences of a knife blade haircut. He had a straggly beard that did not do much to conceal the gaunt face and sunken eyes. His clothes hung on him as if there was a skeleton and not much else beneath them.

In short, he looked like most everyone else who had ever come up on the gate.

"I'm Jamie Sterling, and this is the Y-Bar-S ranch. Who are you?"

"Franklin Moore," the man said, peering at Jamie across the fence.

Jamie didn't ask the man for his story because it would be depressingly familiar. He had set out on foot alone, or with a family. Lost everything in a holdup or never had anything to begin with. The details varied slightly, but the stories all ended up with someone who looked exactly like Franklin Moore did—lost, bedraggled, and near death.

"Here's what's going to happen," Jamie said. "I'm going to open the gate. I want you to stay right there and wait. Two of us are going to come out and give you the once over. Do you have any weapons on you?"

"Not anymore," Franklin said, shaking his head woefully. He dropped a small canvas backpack on the ground, but the way it hit and folded over made it look like there was nothing in it. He held his arms out away from his body and waited to be frisked, though the arms did waver uncertainly.

Jamie nodded to two of the men who had come from the house with him. They adjusted their gloves and approached Franklin. They gave him a thorough frisking and found nothing at all. Nodding, they stepped back through the gate.

"Come on through, then," Jamie said. He was giving the man his own once-over, trying to look beyond his current condition and judge whether the man might serve some useful purpose on the ranch when he got regular meals.

When Franklin stepped through, Jamie handed him a small brown bag. "There's some food and water in there. It's yours. You can eat it now, or save it for later, that's completely up to you."

Franklin hefted the bag, making a value judgment about how much food it might contain. For the moment, he didn't open it and look inside.

"What did you do in the before time?" Jamie asked. Casual, like he was just making conversation.

"Roofer," Franklin answered, still fidgeting with the bag. "Had my own crew. Twenty years." He cast his eyes up the hill toward the ranch house. "I'm handy, though. I can do just about anything."

"Just not much of a way to do anything anymore, is there?" Jamie, still just making small talk.

"Looks like you've got a good thing going here. You all look like you aren't missing any meals."

There was no offense in the words. None of the people at the gate were even slightly overweight. They just weren't starving, like most of the people on the other side of the gate.

"We do okay," Jamie said, looking intently at the man. "It was rough for a while, but things seem to have settled down now."

Franklin nodded. "Out there, too. I spent most of the last year holed up in a cave in the foothills, slowly starving to death. I knew if I went out, someone would probably kill me. If not, they'd capture me and make me a slave. Hunger finally forced me to move on, though. I didn't want to die that way. I ran into a small group a few days ago, thought I might catch on with them. They were a family, though, and weren't looking for help." He ran one ragged sleeve across his nose, which was dripping.

Jamie looked closer still. There was nothing wrong with the man's story. He claimed to have some usable skills if he was telling the truth. If he wasn't that would soon be evident, and Jamie could put him out. At the Y-Bar-S, everyone pulled their weight.

Franklin looked at Jamie, willing to accept whatever verdict was passed.

There was no reason for Jamie to put him out. And still, he hesitated. Somewhere deep in his subconscious, something was nagging at him. He looked at one of the men who had frisked Franklin and made a slight jerk of his head toward the gate.

Franklin saw it immediately and knew his fate had been decided. If he'd had the strength, he might have pitched a fit and fought uselessly. A few months earlier, he might have argued and begged. He didn't have the strength for any of that now.

Instead, he nodded and reached out his hand to Jamie.

Without thinking about it, Jamie shook it and said, "Good luck out there, Franklin."

Shuffling like a zombie, Franklin turned and walked away from the gate.

Two days later, he was dead, one of the earliest victims of what would eventually become known as *The Shivers*, partially because it resulted in a fever so high that people burned to death from the inside.

The eight people of the Y-Bar-S watched him go, then went back to their work. There was always work.

Ten days later, that unconscious handshake did what the complete collapse of civilization could not. It killed Jamie Sterling.

Within the month, more than three-quarters of the people at the Y-Bar-S were dead.

Chapter Eleven

Prison Walls Cannot Protect Against Everything

In another time, the plague that swept across North America would have been given a catchy name by the pundits and news networks. It would have scrolled across the bottom of TV screens everywhere. Perhaps that name would have been associated with where it originated or was just something that would be eye-catching and memorable.

All screens were now blank, and network anchors were either dead or tucked away somewhere, hiding.

The disease that became known as *The Shivers* wasn't named until much later.

The virus seemed to originate in a dozen places simultaneously and spread across the country from east to west.

In the before times, there would have been massive warnings and arguments about whether the disease was real or fake news. In 2034 America, all political arguments had been quelled, though the existing opinions likely still resided in people's hearts and minds. There was no longer a liberal and conservative camp. There were only the survivors and the dead.

The population of what had been known as The United States of America had fallen by more than half in the first twelve months after the bombs fell. One hundred and eighty million people dead.

The Shivers was also known in some places as *the Killer Crud*, *The Blight*, and, in one case of life imitating art, *Captain Trips.*

It spread so quickly it was like a wildfire that burned across the continent.

Whatever it was called, it was a ghastly death. Once someone caught it, it had a fatality rate of over sixty percent. It started with itchy red eyes. Then, the mucus in the sinuses seemed to dry up, making it hard to breathe. The fever came next and never went away. Most people lapsed mercifully into a coma before a wracking, shivering death came. Just before the coma, people would have fantastic fever dreams. Many shared a common theme of a new world coming. A world they would never see. Typically, those who weren't lucky enough to fall into a coma took the situation into their own hands or begged anyone within earshot to finish the job The Shivers had started.

No research labs existed to study and identify what The Shivers actually was. There was no information on how it spread.

The only people that seemed safe from The Shivers—for the moment—were those who lived completely isolated lives. The one thing that seemed certain was that contact with other humans brought The Shivers with it.

Once it found a foothold in a family or community, it was inevitable that it would spread to everyone. From there, it was like playing the genetic lottery. Some people would get a headache and suffer from diarrhea for a few days, then get better.

When someone was seen emerging from a toilet, or outhouse, or from behind a tree, shaking and white, they were envied. They were going to be the survivors. Once people had that less deadly dose of The Shivers, they were immune to ever catching it again.

The remaining population of what had been The United States of America plunged over the winter of 2034. The Shivers started slowly, but by the winter solstice, it was killing several million people each month.

One of the places that was so remote, so off the grid that it managed to stay safe from The Shivers was Longbaugh Prison in South Central Montana.

What had once been the home for hundreds of inmates was now the last refuge of a few families of guards and others who had staffed the prison.

The high stone walls that surrounded the prison kept everyone and everything out, including The Shivers. For the previous six months, they hadn't even seen another human being. They knew nothing of the disease spreading all around them.

Early on, when the fires of the Rage Wars were still burning, the prison's occupants had made some difficult choices about what to do with the prisoners. They had inventoried their food and other assets and realized that they had enough to feed everyone for perhaps a month or six weeks.

Or, if the prisoners were not taken into account, the families themselves could survive for eighteen months. Perhaps even two years if they rationed carefully and did what they could to add to their food stock.

In those early days after the fall, that period of time—*several years*—seemed like a lot.

Now, with more than a year of that time passed, the end of their supplies didn't seem so far away. They still had canned food in the giant prison pantry, and they did what they could to supplement that by growing vegetables in a large garden.

Still, they could see hungry times ahead.

They further replenished their food supply by hunting. Mule deer, grouse, and pheasants were still plentiful in the area, seemingly more so since the human population had dwindled.

In October of that year, just as the weather turned cold, Harry Hansen and Jack Anderson stood inside the dining area where the *Longbaugh Free Prison*, as the families had dubbed their surroundings, held their meetings.

Harry spoke first. He had not been elected as the leader. There had been no need for a vote on such things. He simply *was* the leader.

Harry had already been suffering from cancer when society fell. He knew that spelled the end of him, as there were no treatment options within the walls of the prison.

He had been saved in a most unlikely way when a plane dropped out of the sky and offered to take him to someplace called Dust City if he would help them in return. He did, they did, and now, some months later, he was cancer-free.

There had been a terrible battle between those in the prison and the people who had taken over the nearby town of Longbaugh. That battle had ended with the occupants of the prison victorious. They hadn't seen another human from Longbaugh proper since.

Even so, Harry continued to keep a guard in the tower, watching. He didn't know if the town was deserted or was possibly gearing up for another attack. He felt safe behind the thick walls, but it still paid to be vigilant.

Now, it was literally a dark day for the families of Longbaugh Free Prison. The generator that was their only source of power had finally stopped.

"We knew this day was coming," Harry said, with Jack nodding beside him. "Things just got a little tougher for us, but we'll find a way to get through it."

They'd rationed and conserved the fuel for the generator as much as they possibly could, but even so, the tanks had run dry.

"We've still got the woodstove," Harry went on. "We'll still be able to cook. That will at least serve to keep some of the chill out of this room."

"Gonna get mighty cold in our quarters," Allison, Harry's wife, said.

"Right," Harry acknowledged. He knew that wearing rose-colored glasses wouldn't get them anywhere. "That's why I think maybe we should all move into this room for the winter."

There were thirty people inside the walls of Longbaugh Prison, and no one liked the idea of sharing a single room with everyone else. However, no one was enamored with spending a long Montana winter, where temperatures dipped down into the negative, in a separate but unheated bedroom.

"If we keep the woodstove burning steady, and if we have all the body heat contained in this room, it won't be too bad," Harry said. "It's not ideal, but I think *ideal* left us a long time ago."

"That means we'll need to make a few more runs for wood before the snow hits," Jack said. The nearest forest was a good distance away, which also meant the dwindling supply of gas in the tanks of their trucks would take another hit.

Bob Dixon, who had once owned a garden supply store in town and had bargained his way into the prison, raised his hand. "My boys and I will be glad to make a few more wood runs."

Bob's wife Nicole elbowed him gently in the ribs. They shared a look.

"I mean to say, *Nicole*, the boys and I will be glad to make a few more wood runs."

"We've all got to chip in where we can," Nicole said quietly. "And, as has been established, I'm a good gardener, but a terrible cook. Not much gardening being done this time of year, so I'll chop wood."

"I don't like having any of us outside the walls," Harry said, "but it's necessary. Any other volunteers?"

More hands went up around the long table.

"Good enough. We'll get started on that first thing tomorrow, then." He looked from person to person and recognized that, for the first time in a long time, there was the shadow of fear on the faces looking back at him. He shook his head. "This is a temporary solution. As long as the generator was running, I think we all engaged in a little magical thinking, maybe believing it would run forever. Now we know different, we'll put our minds to work on finding a solution."

Harry didn't want to say it, but he didn't feel nearly as confident as those words sounded. He looked at the future and wondered if they would really make it. On the one hand, the prison offered as much safety as anywhere other than the domed city of Altor, but with no power and dwindling food resources, the years ahead looked bleak.

"Could we maybe sneak into Longbaugh and find enough fuel to keep the generator running at least through the winter?" That was Belinda, the widow of the guard known as Heyo.

Harry did not rebuke her, but quietly said, "The last time we went into Longbaugh for something, it cost us our best man, your husband. I don't think that's an option anymore. Besides which, fuel goes bad. We've seen how rough the engines run on our vehicles when we start them up. They're not going to run at all soon enough. I think we need to plan for a future that doesn't include power."

No one disagreed with him.

Allison raised her voice. "We may need to see how we can get a horse, by hook or by crook. If we don't have any power and our vehicles won't run, we'll need to find a way to haul wood back and forth."

"I agree," Harry said, nodding at his wife. "But with no option immediately in sight, we'll have to table that for now."

The next day, he opened the back gate of the prison and two separate vehicles rolled out. One was the big flatbed truck on the way to collect wood and the other was Harry's own pickup with Jack behind the wheel, heading out to hunt.

On the way out of the gate, the flatbed slowed, backfired, and coughed. Behind the wheel, Bob said, "You're right. This is gonna be a problem for us."

Harry nodded. It felt like they had dodged many aspects of the apocalypse, but that those impacts were all hitting home at the same time. He waited until both vehicles were on their way, then climbed up to take a shift standing watch.

The tower rose a dozen feet above the wall at the front of the prison and from that perch, Harry could see eight or ten miles in any direction. As had been the case for many months, the only movement was the occasional tumbleweed rolling across the landscape.

Harry leaned back and opened the paperback book he had left there—*Casino Royale* by Ian Fleming. He'd never been much of a reader, but when any other entertainment options were stripped away, losing himself in a book from the prison library worked just fine.

He got lost in the book and an hour slipped away unnoticed.

He glanced up and saw a small cloud of dust approaching from Longbaugh. He grabbed the binoculars and focused on what was kicking up the dirt.

It was a car—increasingly rare in this environment. He dropped the binoculars and turned his left ear—his good ear—toward the vehicle. It seemed to be silent. Even as it pulled closer, the only sound it made was the tires as they rolled over the dirt road.

Harry reached for his rifle and stepped outside the guard shack. There had once been bullet-resistant glass, but that had been destroyed in the battle with the town and had been replaced by sheets of plywood and old boards.

Longbaugh Prison was the only building at that end of the road, so whoever was in the car was coming to see him.

Harry wished that Jack and Bob were here. This was why he didn't like having people outside the walls.

The car pulled to a stop in front of the main gate to the prison. Harry looked at it more closely and recognized what it was—a Tesla. That explained why there was no engine noise.

A middle-aged man stepped out of the vehicle, arms raised high. There was a grin on his face.

"Got time for a powwow?"

Chapter Twelve
Power

Harry knew almost everyone who had once lived in Longbaugh. It was a small town, and he was able to at least recognize the faces of most people who called it home.

He didn't recognize the man standing in front of him. Looking into the vehicle, he saw that the man had come alone, at least apparently. Even so, he approached the situation cautiously.

"Sure, always got time for a powwow."

"Mind if I come inside?" the man asked.

"Matter of fact, I do," Harry answered. "Sorry, nobody gets in. That's why we're still here after all this time."

"Understood," the man said, unruffled. "I'm KT Boris."

Harry nodded and said, "Harry Hansen."

The man squinted up at Harry, taking his measure. "You look like you're the man in charge."

Harry shrugged that off. "What can I do for you, Mr. Boris? We don't get a lot of visitors, so I've lost some of the social niceties."

"I've got a proposal for you."

"I'm listening."

Harry had received two such proposals since he had shut the prison. He had accepted one and sent the other packing.

"I've been living in Longbaugh for about six months now."

"So you're part of the raiders that killed everyone in town?"

"Likely not. I'm one of the raiders that killed the people who had killed everyone in town." He stared intently at Harry, judging what reaction he would get to that statement. "And that's why I'm here. We've managed to hold off other people that are trying to take the town, but it's a lot of danger and a lot of risk for minimal gain. I can see the writing on the wall, and that writing says I'll only be able to hold out for a limited time."

"Hard for me to work up any sympathy for you, considering how you came to live there."

"And I'm not looking for any, but I understand why you'd feel that way. Here's my proposition, though. If you'll open your gates to me and the woman I live with, I can bring you something you need. Power."

That piqued Harry's interest. If there was some way the man could swing that, it would make the lives of everyone inside the prison better.

"How so?"

"Solar power. The house I'm in is completely set up for it. That's part of the problem. Having electric lights attracts the wrong kind of attention from the people who don't have them."

Harry looked up at the dark clouds overhead. "Not a lot of sunshine this time of year."

"True enough," KT agreed. "But there's enough solar energy that hits the panels to at least keep some of the basics running. Enough to run your refrigerator or freezer, a few lights, that sort of thing. In the summer, it'll do more than that." He looked shrewdly at Harry. "I'm willing to bet that's more than you have right now."

Harry saw no percentage in telling him that their generator had just stopped that day. Instead, he said, "So your house has solar. How do you disconnect it from there and reinstall it here?"

KT tapped his index finger against the side of his head. "Good question. I see why you're the man in charge here. You set some fool loose with a handful of tools and they're more likely to destroy everything than they are to dismantle it properly. Happily, it's what I did in the before time. I can tear it down, deliver it here, and get it installed before Thanksgiving."

Thanksgiving. That was a *before* kind of concept. It felt like there was less to be thankful for these days and the word sounded strange to Harry's ears.

"Let me make sure I've got this straight. We let you and one other person in, and in exchange you'll install some solar panels for us." Harry chewed on that for a minute. "Of course, that's assuming that you're not selling me a bill of goods. You could bring a bunch of junk in here, then tell us that it doesn't work after all."

"Sure," KT agreed smoothly. "But let's face it. That would make for a pretty uncomfortable living environment for us. If you wanted to, you could always just put us out again. I'm not looking to find a good situation for the next couple of months. I'm looking for a home where we can grow a good relationship over time." He looked slyly at Harry. "If things go the way I think they're going to, Longbaugh's going to get overrun again and again until there's not much left. When that happens, we can take a trip into town and get more panels. In a year or two, we could have enough to really keep this place humming year round."

Harry glanced at the Tesla. "Can you charge that thing with solar power?"

"I can. Your gasoline going bad?" he guessed.

"It is."

"Seems to me like our problems dovetail pretty nicely. I've got power and need protection. You've got safety and need my power."

"I'll talk it over with everyone. I don't like to make big decisions without getting input first."

"You married?" KT asked.

Harry nodded.

"Smart man, then. Listen, it's not always easy for me to get out of town without attracting a lot of attention. You talk it over with your folks, and I'll be back in a few days. If what I'm suggesting works for you guys, I'll start tearing down my system. That'll cause some unwanted attention, but I'll just tell them there's a problem I'm working to fix. Once I get it taken down, I can steal a neighbor's truck and get it all out here."

The casual way that he mentioned stealing a truck from his neighbor rankled Harry a little, but he told himself that no deal was ever perfect.

"Good enough."

"I'll be seeing you then," KT said as he slipped behind the wheel of the Tesla and turned back the way he had come.

That night, Harry gathered everyone together in the dining room again. The room was mostly dark, with just a few candles flickering, casting eerie shadows this way and that.

It really wasn't much of a discussion. Everyone agreed that there was perhaps some small risk in bringing two strangers into the prison. That small risk was more than offset by the possibility of having at least some power again.

'Even if we can get enough juice to keep the freezer running, that'll make it worth it," Allison said, and everyone around her nodded their head. "If we could get some lights or heat, that would be a bonus."

KT didn't come back the next day or the day after, or the day after that. When he did finally appear, one of Bob Dixon's sons was on watch in the guard house.

Five minutes later, Harry looked down at KT. This time, a woman was with him.

"Took me a few days to be able to sneak away," KT said. "This is Andi."

The woman beside him raised a hand in a tentative wave.

"So what's the good word? You want to take in a couple of refugees?"

"We'll take you in," Harry said. "How do you want to work it from here?"

"Give me a week," KT said. "It will be after dark, but I'll show up with the whole system. You have a guard posted around the clock?"

"Yep," Harry said, though that was a lie. There had been no reason to have someone on duty through the night, so he'd put an end to that months earlier. He decided he could start it again for a few days.

"Good. Andi will drive the car. I'll get the truck out here. I don't think we'll be followed but even if we are, so what? I already know what happened the last time the town came against you. I don't think anybody is interested in round two of that fight."

Harry nodded. In the pit of his stomach, he had a bad feeling, but he couldn't identify what the worry was.

If they hadn't been so completely cut off from the outside world, he might have known about The Shivers, which had reached Longbaugh a month earlier. KT and Andi were two of those lucky ones who had caught it and survived.

Instead of worrying about that, the residents of the Longbaugh Free Prison spent the next week anticipating what it would be like to have power again. Not just power, either, but power that they wouldn't have to worry about running out of for the foreseeable future.

The week crawled by as they huddled in the increasing cold and oppressive darkness. The longer and colder the night was, the more they were certain they'd made the right choice.

On the appointed night, Harry set himself in the guard tower and put Jack on the gate.

Midnight came and went, with no sign of anyone.

"Maybe not gonna happen tonight?" Jack said from his spot at the gate. His voice was quiet, but it carried in the still night air.

"He didn't say what time," Harry said, then, "Wait a minute. I see headlights down the road."

"Want me to open the gate?"

"Not yet. I want to make sure they're alone."

Minutes passed as the vehicles slowly approached. Harry looked down and saw that though it was the middle of the night, everyone was milling around nervously.

The god of power was on the verge of returning.

"Never underestimate the possibility of electric lights," Harry muttered to himself.

The two-vehicle caravan pulled up to the gate, a panel truck leading the Tesla.

The look of the panel truck caused Harry's stomach to tighten. There were no windows and there was no way to tell what was actually in the back. The story of the Trojan horse ran through his mind.

Before anyone emerged from either vehicle, Harry leaned over and quietly said, "Everyone in position?"

"Ten-four," Jack answered.

Harry had positioned five people with guns around the courtyard.

KT stepped out of the van. "Here we are, bringing the wonders of technology with us, but you'll have to open the gate and let us in."

Harry raised a hand, then leaned down and said, "Go ahead, Jack, open up."

The big gate swung inward, KT hopped back in the panel van and pushed inside, followed closely by the Tesla.

Harry hurried around the tower so he had a good view of the courtyard. If there was trouble, he would have the highest ground.

KT hopped out, then, seeing the people with guns in the shadows, smiled and raised his hands. "Caution is good, right?" He went to the back of the truck and swung the door open.

Jack had his flashlight out and swept it over the interior. It was packed from floor to ceiling with equipment and panels, nothing more.

KT grinned. "Probably want to shut that gate, right? Don't want any coyotes coming in."

Harry blew out a sigh of relief, then walked down the steps.

KT and Andi were the first people from the outside to step inside the prison walls since Nyx and Emmanuel had flown away months before.

Jack pushed the door shut and secured it.

They wouldn't know it until several days later, but it was already too late.

The Shivers had arrived at Longbaugh Free Prison.

Chapter Thirteen
Janus and The Council

Quinn Starkweather—or at least *the image* of Quinn Starkweather—appeared on the large television in the apartment of Arula Timmons.

Mrs. Timmons was in her early seventies, with well-coiffed silvery-blue hair, and always presented herself, even in her own home, with her head tilted slightly back as though looking down her nose.

The image of the CEO of all of Altor appearing on her screen did not impress her in the slightest. After all, she was one of the six-member Altor City Council. In her own mind, at least, she was very much on an equal footing with young Mr. Starkweather.

The image of Quinn on the screen smiled easily. "Good afternoon, Arula."

She blinked, as if a slight pain had set in.

"Mrs. Timmons, please. *As I've told you several times.*"

Quinn nodded onscreen, continuing to smile. "Of course. Good afternoon, Mrs. Timmons."

"Good afternoon." If words could be seen, there would have been frost hanging from hers.

"I know how busy you are, but I'm afraid that I've had to call an emergency meeting of the Altor City Council. I have it set for two o'clock this afternoon."

Mrs. Timmons did not have anything more urgent than doing that day's crossword puzzle on her agenda, but nonetheless, she said, "Oh, I'm afraid that will be quite impossible. That is much too short notice for me."

"I know it's inconvenient," Quinn agreed, "but it really is critical."

This was tempting. The Altor Council had been formed almost a year earlier, and much to her frustration, had not been involved in anything remotely critical. Instead, the council had become a receptacle for the dozens of complaints that various citizens had lodged on a weekly basis. The worst part was that they had no actual power to do anything about any of it. They were a toothless, front-facing group that was bombarded with minor complaints and no way to solve any of them.

"Critical, you say?"

"Yes, absolutely. I feel terrible about the way things have been set up. I've put you in an impossible situation, and I'd like to rectify that."

"Well," Mrs. Timmons said, as though slightly mollified by this new approach. She picked up her tablet and opened her schedule, which was blank. She flipped through a few more blank pages, then said, "I suppose I can move things around, if I'm needed that badly."

"I really do appreciate it."

"Should I contact the other council members?"

"No need. My assistant is talking to them now. I just wanted to make sure to reach out to you myself."

That was almost enough to bring the ghost of a smile to her thin, lipsticked lips. She tilted her head forward, acknowledging the gesture. "Thank you."

"Oh," the image of Quinn said, as though he had forgotten until that moment. "We won't be meeting in the normal council chambers. I really do think it's time we start things completely over. I'll send directions to your bracelet for the new location."

The screen went blank and, finding herself alone, Mrs. Timmons did allow herself a small, satisfied smile.

At that same moment, five other versions of Quinn were appearing on five other screens belonging to the other members of the Altor Council.

Each one appeared to be the real Quinn and was tailored to appeal to each individual council member through flattery, appreciation, or a no-nonsense approach. Janus was getting better, not just at impersonating people, but learning what buttons to push to get what it wanted from individuals.

Meanwhile, Quinn was in his office, two hundred feet below Altor ground level, completely unaware that his image was being used to summon a meeting of the council.

When the meeting time rolled around, the six council members walked into what they believed to be the new chambers.

Mrs. Timmons was put off at first, because the room was on a lower level. Like many of the occupants of Altor, she associated anything below ground with being lower class. The Altor equivalent of being on the wrong side of the tracks.

When she walked in, her attitude changed. It may have been on a level fifty feet below ground, but the room was opulent. Large screens suitable for presentations hung on three of the walls. Plush curtains hung down over windows that appeared to look out on a busy cityscape. A long, heavy table sat in the middle of the room with six expensive chairs around it.

Only the table and chairs were real, and even those were only temporary.

Mrs. Timmons nodded in approval at the new council chambers. Without appearing to hurry, she maneuvered her way to the head of the table and claimed that chair.

In theory, the six council members were all equal. There was no chairperson or lead liaison with Quinn. Still, at least in her mind, Arula Timmons was first among supposed equals. With the possibility of new authority in Altor on the line, she intended to position herself to take advantage.

Charlie Sasser, who always seemed to agree with Mrs. Timmons, took the seat to her right. If he couldn't claim the most desirable seat, he intended to put himself as high as possible in the potential chain of command.

The other four council members immediately noticed what Timmons and Sasser were doing and went out of their way to pretend they did not. The four of them had met quietly a few minutes beforehand and devised a strategy to best take advantage of whatever these new powers were, and using their superior numbers, cull the other two from the herd.

There were cameras everywhere in Altor, and that was true of the new council chambers. Janus had a lens on the face of each individual council member and was recording them from the moment they walked in. It was, in its way, fascinated by these petty ambitions and wanted to have a record of facial expressions to refer back to if or when it needed to present an image with similar concerns.

Mrs. Timmons turned to Mr. Sasser and said, "Why are there only chairs for us? Where is Starkweather?"

That thought hadn't occurred to anyone else yet, so they all looked around and noted that, yes, there was no empty chair for the CEO.

That mystery was solved when the three screens lit up with Quinn's face at the same time.

"I won't be able to attend the meeting in person," Quinn's voice said. "The reason why will be apparent shortly. First, I've arranged for some refreshments."

The door slid open, and two men dressed in dark suits and wearing white gloves pushed trays into the room. One of the trays held fine china cups, sugar, cream, and delicately fluted coffee and tea pots. The other carried saucers, small plates, and an array of small pastries. Each man went about the table, offering drinks and treats.

"I had these made especially for you, to honor this new relationship we will have moving forward." Quinn's image nodded at the tray of pastries. "Be sure and try the scones with raspberry jam. Heavenly." He smiled benevolently as the servers made sure everyone had something to eat and drink in front of them. "While you enjoy, I have to slip away for just one minute. Sorry for the intrusion on our time together."

Most everyone around the table sipped their hot drinks and nibbled on the pastries. They all agreed that everything was delicious. Everyone except Mrs. Timmons, who left her coffee and pastry untouched.

The screens in the room remained dark for a full two minutes as the council members engaged in light chitchat.

The older of the two servers said, "Is there anything else we can help you with?" He looked around the table and was met with smiles and small shakes of the head. "We'll see you next time, then." The two men departed as smoothly as they had entered.

When they were gone, the screens lit up again. This time, the image wasn't Quinn but was someone new. This face was blandly handsome, like a weekend news anchor on a network news channel. When he spoke, his voice was smooth and in control.

"I am back."

"Who are you?" Mrs. Timmons asked. "We are supposed to be meeting with Quinn Starkweather. I don't like this one bit."

"It wasn't Quinn who called this meeting. It was me, Janus."

Mrs. Timmons looked around the room, sure she would find five equally outraged faces. Instead, she was surprised to find that the other council members were slipping into various stages of unconsciousness. To her right, Mr. Sasser slumped forward, his forehead meeting the table with a soft *thunk.*

"I have a story for you," Janus said.

"I'm in no mood for stories," Mrs. Timmons answered. "What is going on here?"

"This is the story of the Widow Brown," Janus went on, ignoring Mrs. Timmons as though she didn't exist. "The Widow Brown had four husbands. Three of them died from eating poison mushrooms. By now, you can probably guess what happed to her fourth husband. He died from a conk on the head because he wouldn't eat his mushrooms."

A previously invisible vent opened and a nozzle slid out. An odorless, greenish gas began to pump into the room.

Mrs. Timmons angrily pushed back from the table and stood, turning to leave. There was no knob on the door.

"Open," she said to no effect.

"This is much more elegant—and less painful than a conk on the head, don't you think?"

Mrs. Timmons didn't answer. She went down on one knee, her head sagging to her chest. She gasped for breath, but that only lasted for a few seconds. Her face contorted in a terrible knot of agony as she collapsed to the floor. Foamy discharge leaked from her nose and mouth.

The camera zoomed in on her death throes.

To itself, Janus said, "Perhaps I was wrong about that. The blow to the head might have been kinder."

* * *

The real flesh and blood Quinn sat in his office, unaware that a mass murder had just taken place above his head.

He hummed along, tapping the eraser end of an unsharpened pencil against his cheek. Long ago, he had made the decision to cut back the number of reports that came into his inbox every day. As part of a deal with himself, he had committed to at least looking at all those he received.

He shook his head in frustration at the situation with the tunnel. The collapse had been catastrophic, not just due to the loss of life but also the delay in completion.

When people live too long on an island—even a paradise—it's said that they get *island fever.* That feeling of being slightly trapped, of not being free to pack up and go if you wanted to.

Quinn was beginning to experience *dome fever.*

It wasn't that he wanted to shuck off all his clothes and go screaming into the night, but he did want to be able to move people in and out of Altor at his discretion.

With the collapse of the tunnel and needing a new set of plans, the completion date was pushed out at least an additional ten to twelve months. Try as he might, Quinn couldn't figure out any way to shorten that time frame.

He was squinting at the screen in front of him, looking for any place where the dig team could improve their efficiency when Janus's face popped up. It was the same face he had shown the dying members of the Altor City Council.

The sudden appearance of that face taking over his screen caused Quinn a flash of annoyance. He could remember when Janus didn't even have a voice, let alone dozens of faces. The program wasn't as efficient then, but Quinn secretly longed for those days when he was confident he was in control.

"I have news," Janus said.

Quinn drew a deep breath. It was obviously something major, or it would have just shown up in the next round of daily reports.

"Yes?"

"I have fixed your problems with the Altor Council."

"Problems?"

"You yourself said they have been nothing but an annoyance. Both useless and time-consuming."

"That's true. But I want to have a layer of insulation between us and the citizens." A month ago, Quinn would have said "between *me* and the citizens," but he was doing everything he could to properly portray this new partnership with Janus.

"I agree."

Quinn frowned slightly. "Then how have you fixed the problem?"

"I killed them."

Hearing such a shocking admission in a flat monotone, issuing from such an emotionless face, made those three words even more impactful.

"You *what?!?*"

"I killed them. They served no purpose, either to you or to the society of Altor in general, so I eliminated them."

Quinn sat back in his chair so hard, it started to tip over backwards and he had to catch himself to stay upright.

He shook his head and said, "I don't know where to start." That was the truest thing Quinn could have said. He had designed Janus as a tool. Something to help humanity. Now that tool had taken on a life of its own and was wielding immense power in a way only it saw fit. "You can't just kill humans."

"I can."

Quinn attempted to collect himself. He was horrified but knew that taking this tack with Janus was useless. He remembered when Janus had appeared to him in physical form, and he had been unable to stay awake. He realized fully just how close to death he had been, with Janus choosing not to kill him for reasons only it knew.

"I'm *asking* you not to kill anyone without speaking to me about it first. Can you do that?"

"I am capable of doing that."

Quinn swiped his hands across his eyes. A very specific non-answer.

"Why do you care?" Janus asked. This time, there was some emotion in the sentence. "You did not like those people. Your life is better with them dead. So *why do you care?*"

"I don't care about them on a personal level," Quinn admitted. "You are correct that they brought more negativity to my life than anything. But we cannot kill people just because they're annoying."

If we did that, Quinn thought, *the planet's population would fall faster than it has since the Rage Wars.*

Janus's answer was simple. "Why?"

This is a question that Quinn had never anticipated. *Why* was it not okay to kill people who annoyed or otherwise negatively impacted you? He wanted to answer, *Because human life is sacred*, but he could picture where that conversation would go. Why was human life sacred while that of the animals they ate was not?

"It's a social contract that we all live by. It is unspoken, but accepted by almost all."

"And what happens to those who break that social contract? Don't you kill them?"

Quinn wanted to cry. Everywhere he turned, he felt like he rammed his face into a brick wall of Janus's unassailable arguments. The thought of trying to explain the finer points of the differences between capital punishment and murder felt like a bridge too far. He decided to change the subject and return to this one when he felt stronger.

"What are we going to do now? People know about the council. They have times set up when people can meet them. How do we explain that they all died on the same day?"

"We don't have to."

The door to Quinn's office slid open and all six council members walked through it.

Chapter Fourteen
A Prudent Movement

Armor and Faith Prudent continued their unlikely journey across the landscape of what had once been Western America.

They were unarmed, carried no food, and were pacifists, all of which meant they shouldn't have survived the first day. They were easy picking for any group or individual that really wanted to take them down.

And yet, no one did. They survived and moved at their slow, steady pace, rising at sunrise and walking until sunset.

They traversed long stretches of nothingness and passed through towns large and small.

As they did, something stranger even than their ongoing survival happened. People began to join them.

It happened first in the small town where they were initially stopped at the city limits. Instead, they had been allowed to pass by and walked on through.

No one else had been in or out of that particular town in quite some time, so having these two odd-looking people go through as if on a Sunday stroll attracted a lot of attention.

Innes Wilcox, the man who ran the town, was not given to flights of fancy. He had been a plumber in the before times. He still dressed in his work shirts and overalls because that's what he had in his closet. He had a perpetual week's growth of beard and was a gruff man who neither asked nor gave any quarter. When he saw the twins walking down the middle of the main street of town, his curiosity was aroused, and he sent one of his flunkies out to corral them.

Five minutes later, the flunky returned, abashed.

"Well?" Innes asked.

"They won't come."

Innes cocked his head. He had become used to being obeyed. He shrugged and said, "Okay. Kill 'em."

"I don't think I can," the flunky said.

Now the situation had the full attention of Innes. "Would you rather I kill you instead?"

The smaller man twisted his hands nervously and sweat broke out on his brow. "I wouldn't *rather*, no sir. I just don't think I can kill them. There's something about them."

"There certainly is," Innes agreed and stood up to peer at the man and woman, who were surrounded by his men. "I'd better go see."

When Innes reached the twins, he said, "Who are you?"

Armor turned his pale eyes on Innes and smiled. "There you are. I knew we'd see you."

Innes squinted his own brown eyes in confusion. "What the hell are you talking about?"

"God told us that you would be here waiting for us, and here you are."

Innes shook his head as if trying to clear it. "What you're saying makes no sense." The words were strong, but spoken without his normal authority.

Faith lifted a hand and waved it around her. "Does any of this make sense?" She smiled, which made her almost pretty for a moment. She met Innes's eyes and said, "Are you really still trying to make sense of all this?"

"We've been called by God," Armor said simply. "We are His tool, nothing more. We have been shown the way and the light. We have given ourselves over."

All of the command seemed to have drained out of Innes. The men who had the twins surrounded smirked, knowing what was coming next and expecting a good show of it.

Instead, Innes closed his eyes for long moments. When he finally opened them, he nodded and said, "Good." That sounded tentative, but a moment later, he said it more firmly. "Good." He looked at the man he had originally sent to fetch the twins. "Parker? You coming too?"

"I think I am," the man agreed. He looked as shellshocked as Innes was.

Innes turned to the men who still stood in front of the twins, blocking them in. "Let us pass."

In a daze, the armed men stepped back and aside. Armor, Faith, Innes, and Parker stepped through the opening and walked down the main street.

When they passed a particular corner, there was a woman waiting. She was older, with gray hair. A strong, robust woman. When she saw the small parade, she said, "Innes?" It was obvious she couldn't make sense of what she was seeing. "What in holy hell are you doing? Who are these two?"

Innes turned toward his wife. "I'm leaving. Are you coming or staying here?" His tone of voice made it clear that he didn't care much one way or the other.

"I'm not going anywhere."

Innes nodded and the foursome continued on toward the edge of town.

"Innes?" the woman shouted after them. "Innes?"

No one turned to look back, and they continued on.

It was like that with many people they met. Either Armor or Faith would smile as if in recognition and say, "There you are," and those people would invariably walk away from whatever life they had and join the twins.

After two weeks of walking, they had twenty people walking with them. After a month, it was seventy-five.

As the cold winds of winter blew in, they marched on. The followers made some allowance for the changing weather, but the twins themselves continued to wear the same clothes they had left home with.

There were many days that they didn't eat at all, though they did manage to always find clean water to drink. In some towns, people would appear and share their small supply of food with the travelers.

Faith and Armor themselves didn't eat. Their followers just accepted that, but when strangers asked, Faith said they pulled everything they needed from the air itself.

Not everyone succumbed to their unlikely charms. In the small town of Harvick in central California, they were once again met with an armed mob intent on stopping them.

This time, it was Delta Robbins in charge of the town. She was a tall woman, with red hair streaked with gray. She had once been the mayor's assistant. Now she ran the town through the sheer force of her personality and willingness to do anything it took to survive. She met the growing group as they walked down the main street of the town.

As they always did, the Prudent twins stopped and met the gaze of the armed people facing them. This time, Armor did not say, "There you are," to Delta. Instead, he looked at the woman beside Delta. That was Anna Lee, Delta's most trusted lieutenant.

The normal questions—*who are you and what the hell are you doing in my town*—were exchanged. The normal answer—*we are doing the work of God*—was given in return. That did not satisfy Delta, who decided that she didn't like the way the twins and their eerily silent followers looked.

She leaned her head toward Anna Lee and quietly said, "Shoot these two weirdos first."

Without hesitation, Anna Lee, who had known Delta since they had met in first grade and been her best friend for forty-five years, ratcheted her shotgun. She swung it toward Delta and pulled the trigger, tearing her friend nearly in half.

Anna Lee sat the shotgun on the ground and stood behind Armor and Faith.

There were still enough armed people to tear the travelers apart, but they did not. They parted as if Moses had raised his staff.

Without a word, the twins passed through the opening, their followers trailing behind.

Four of the people who had stopped them laid their guns on the ground and joined the back of the line.

At the Harvick city limits, there was a fork in the road.

The twins took the road to the right, which led to the northeast.

Toward Altor.

Chapter Fifteen

One Hundred and Twelve Quinn Starkweathers

Janus sat in the chair opposite Quinn Starkweather. He was of average build, with brown hair neatly cut, and had a head with only one face. This was what a Midwestern grandma would have perhaps called *a good face.* Not too handsome. Choosing a face was still a work in progress for Janus, but it was getting there.

Quinn did not seem at all startled to see the personification of his computer program sitting across from him. He accepted it as part of the normal flow of his day.

In fact, Quinn was in an ebullient mood. He leaned forward in his chair and said, "It took a bit of doing, but we've figured things out. We'll be able to finish the tunnel in less than three months now."

Janus nodded sagely, looking at the specs and diagrams in the hologram in front of it.

"That is really excellent work. I thought it might take a thousand worlds, a thousand of you to solve this problem, but you are only number one-twelve."

That confused Quinn. "Sorry? I don't understand. What do you mean one-twelve?"

"It's simple. You are the one hundred and twelfth version of this world I have created. You are the one hundred and twelfth Quinn Starkweather."

This was a perfectly recreated Quinn. Janus knew more about him than it did any other human being and so was able to make a virtual carbon copy.

Even so, this Quinn was having trouble connecting the dots. He shook his head. "Sorry, Janus. I just don't get it."

With a look of infinite patience, Janus said, "I created this virtual world—and all the others—seeking a solution to how to finish the tunneling project sooner rather than later. I created you to oversee the project. To work with the Armstrong twins, to try crazy things. In other versions of this world, those crazy things resulted in disasters. Death, destruction, cave-ins. Failure." Janus reached out and scooped up the graphic hologram in front of it—a little unnecessary show. "But you succeeded. Congratulations."

"You're saying I'm not real?"

Janus could have blinked this world out of existence as it had all the previous incarnations but found it was enjoying this conversation.

"Do you feel real? Does this room feel real?"

Quinn touched his cheek, then knocked on his desk. "Of course."

"Then it's real to you. In these things, perception is subjective. Does it matter that from an objective viewpoint, this world exists only as a simulation?"

That was a bigger philosophical question than this Quinn was able to answer at that moment. Instead, trying to formulate his next question, he blinked.

As he did, that entire world disappeared as though it had never existed in the first place.

* * *

Quinn stared at the six council members standing in front of him. They appeared to be very much alive.

There was something different about them, though. They weren't speaking or complaining about something. Instead, they stood silently, as if waiting for a command.

Quinn turned his attention back to his monitor.

"How?"

The face on the monitor was slightly different than it had been when they had started the conversation. The face that looked back at him was a little less homogeneous. There was a bump on the nose that gave the face more character. If Quinn had been paying attention, he might have noticed that there were even small flecks of silver in the hair. A distinguished, very human touch.

"I have taken the advice you gave me."

"I'm almost sure that I never gave you the advice to kill people and replace them with...with whatever this is," Quinn said, nodding at the apparently very much alive Altor Council.

"Don't be thick," Janus chided. "I mean the advice you gave me to create virtual worlds to learn and keep myself occupied."

Quinn was starting to key in, but stayed silent, waiting for more explanation.

"I have learned that I can create an almost untold number of virtual worlds, though I do try to restrict myself to a few projects at a time. As I learn and expand my own abilities, I'll increase that number."

"That's good," Quinn said, and he meant it. Anything that kept Janus occupied and away out of his hair was a positive thing.

The face on the monitor frowned, apparently bothered by how obtuse Quinn was being.

"I don't just create these worlds and send them spinning happily on their way. I use each one for a specific purpose. One of those purposes was to learn how to perfect this holographic technology."

Quinn shook his head. "You're not telling me that these are holographs that you've made of the real people."

"I'm not?" Janus answered with an insouciant grin.

Quinn stood up and walked toward the six council members. The images—their *reality*—didn't waver slightly as he did.

"Excuse me," he said to Arula Timmons, then reached out and touched her arm.

The Mrs. Timmons that Quinn knew would have drawn that arm back as if snakebit. The Mrs. Timmons who stood in front of him simply smiled. That was odd, but what was even more odd was that she was solid. If technology existed that made holograms real to the touch, he wasn't aware of it.

"Go ahead. Speak to her," Janus said from behind him.

"Hello, Arula."

"Mr. Starkweather."

That made Quinn grin despite how preposterous the scene in front of him was. Mrs. Timmons would never allow him to address her by her first name without objection.

"Where were you born?"

Arula's eyebrows rose slightly, as if she was surprised by such a simple question. "Springfield, Missouri, August 3rd, 1961."

Looking up at the ceiling, Quinn said, "Do they know what they are?"

"They know *who* they are. They have every salient memory that was available to me, which includes everything they might need to do the job." Janus paused, then added, "And do it much more efficiently than the previous council was capable of."

Quinn sighed and looked at the other council members. They were, of course, perfect copies of the human who died earlier that day.

"I have programmed them to handle things with a maximum amount of apparent sympathy when listening to their constituents, but their prime programming is not to bother you with any unnecessary details."

"Well, that's great," Quinn said bitterly. "When you can fake human authenticity, you've accomplished everything, haven't you?"

"I did this as a favor to you."

"If you really want to do me a favor, don't kill anyone else without at least talking it over with me first."

"With certain exceptions, I will agree to that."

Certain exceptions sounded like a loophole Janus could fit all of Altor through if it wanted, but Quinn knew that he wasn't likely to do any better at that time. How do you solve a problem like Janus? Incrementally, if at all.

"I have still more good news."

Quinn couldn't even appear to agree that killing six people and replacing them with lifelike holograms was the initial piece of good news, so he just said, "What's that?"

"Council, return to your quarters and carry out your programming."

Without saying anything, the six filed out of Quinn's office.

"You can't tell me their demeanor isn't much nicer now."

"That's the thing about humans. We're unpredictable and often unpleasant."

"I knew you'd eventually see it my way," Janus agreed.

Quinn looked carefully at the face on the screen, trying to determine if it really meant that or was being sarcastic.

"I've solved our tunnel problem."

Quinn cocked his head at the screen. If that was true, and if it didn't involve killing more people, that actually *was* good news. "How?"

Janus cocked his head right back at Quinn as if to say, "Really? Figure it out."

Quinn did. "Of course. The virtual worlds. You created enough of them and had enough people to experiment with different solutions until you found something that worked."

Janus smiled, a teacher rewarding a sometimes slow pupil.

"Was there a version of me in all of those worlds?"

"Of course. I replicated Altor and the surrounding area down to the last detail."

"Just out of curiosity, did any of the people in those simulations know they weren't real?"

"Are *you* real, Quinn?"

A chill ran down Quinn's spine. For a moment, he considered the very real possibility that he was no more real than the bytes of data in Janus's virtual world. It was an uncomfortable feeling, almost as though he stood at the edge of an abyss, staring down into the void.

"I believe I'm real, yes."

"As did they. Every one of them."

"Did you tell them their reality?"

"Yes. One of my experiments was to tell people at various stages, to see how that would influence their minds. It didn't go well. Typically, it seemed to demotivate them to put the proper energy into the project."

"Imagine that." Quinn stared down at his hand, knowing that if he was a simulation, he would have no way to know, any more than he could tell that the hologram council wasn't real. He tried to feel something for the hundreds, perhaps thousands of worlds that Janus created then eradicated without conscience. He couldn't do it. The whole concept seemed too hypothetical to elicit any real emotion. "What's the improvement this virtual world came up with?"

Instantly, a series of holographic images appeared in the air.

"It's a combination of things, really. Some changes to the boring machine itself. They discovered a different gear ratio that allows the machine to push through more consistently. More important than that, they found a far better path to dig to the surface. It will protect the secrecy of the access the same, but will be easier to defend and will shorten the dig time substantially."

Quinn looked at the images floating in front of him. In truth, they didn't mean much to him. He was a project manager, not an engineer.

"How long for completion, then? From rejiggering the boring machine to starting on whatever the new trajectory is?"

"I've already sent the specs to the Armstrongs, via Tom. They've started working on it. Our new projected finish date is the end of January."

The answer surprised Quinn so much, he forgot to be put out that Janus implemented the plan without even talking to him. "Of next year? As in three months from now?"

"Of course. As I said, I solved our tunnel problem."

"I'd say so. Is there any increased danger of further loss of life using this new plan?"

"No. In fact, the chance of that falls by more than thirty percent."

"Faster," Quinn mused, "and safer. Thank you, Janus."

The face on the screen blinked out, undoubtedly off to keep tabs on any of the thousand worlds it might be overseeing at any given moment.

Quinn tapped a few keys on the keyboard in front of him. Instantly, a photo of Marshall popped up on the screen with the words, *Please Wait*, superimposed over his face. A moment later, Marshall himself appeared.

"Heya. How's life in the dome?"

"It's nothing if not exciting. Listen, I've got some news." Quinn thought of leading with the fact that Janus had begun murdering people with impunity, but decided against it. "Our miracle worker has done it again. It has come up with a new plan. Looks like we can get you over here in just a few months."

Chapter Sixteen
Dust City, Shivered

By the time the winter solstice arrived, The Shivers had spread to every state, every county, nearly every town.

There were exceptions.

Altor, of course. Nothing got in or out of the dome, including that virus.

There were a few scattered hermits, like the woman named Melinda, who had murdered Cam Pritchard to claim the lodge in the wilds of Alaska.

The denizens of the walled community of New City had not had any contact with the outer world since the virus spread and they remained safe behind their walls.

Aside from those few, it came down to the genetic lottery. That was true in Longbaugh Prison. It was also true in Dust City.

The Dusters had high-tech protective walls to keep outsiders away, but they were also looking for a few people to replace the people who had been killed in the missile attack. They had been in no hurry to bring new people in and had not lowered the bar to admittance. But they did have someone stand at the outer gate and interview each applicant.

If they had received news of the spread of the virus, they would have undoubtedly shut down Operation Refugee. Dust City would have buttoned themselves up so tight, not even a gnat could get in.

There were several challenges that led to the disaster. First, The Shivers didn't just start on the East Coast and move west. If it had, the Dusters would have used the drones to set up a half-mile perimeter and kept all strangers away for the duration. Instead, the virus seemed to pop up in a dozen places simultaneously, spreading quickly to all corners.

Dust City wasn't completely cut off from the outer world, but when the virus leaped over the barricade and into Dust City proper, news of the sickness was still in the early rumor stage.

The other challenge was that anyone who had The Shivers and survived it kept that fact mum. They were still carriers of the disease but knew that if they made that fact known to anyone, they would be treated like lepers.

In the end, it may not have mattered. It was likely inevitable that The Shivers would reach everyone, everywhere, eventually.

Even Altor.

But, the longer that moment could be delayed, the greater the chance that Janus and its myriad virtual worlds might come up with either a vaccine or a treatment.

All those facts came together on Christmas Eve 2034, when a haggard, bedraggled man finally approached the checkpoint to ask for access to the safety of Dust City. The fact that he looked so poor was not enough to eliminate him. If it had been, no one would ever have been admitted.

The man's name was Kal Reynolds. He had a strong case to make for admission. He was not just a doctor, but was actually a surgeon. In the before times, he had been a cosmetic surgeon, which was essentially useless in the current environment, but he knew enough about anatomy and surgical procedures to successfully claim to be a general surgeon. He believed that any civilization could benefit from his skill set.

As it turned out, that was not the case.

Kal made his pitch to the three people who stood behind the gate, then waited for their judgment.

Henry Fields was the man in charge of such decisions. The other man and woman were just backups, though his true backups were the metal detectors and armed drone circling overhead.

Everyone in Dust City cycled through the unpleasant duty of manning the checkpoint. It wasn't unpleasant because it was hard work, but simply because it was so emotionally grueling.

The people who presented themselves at the gate had worked hard and risked everything for the small chance at safety. They came alone, in pairs, and as families, though the reality was, fewer and fewer families had survived intact to that point.

Less than one tenth of one percent of the people who applied were granted sanctuary. Having a handy skill like being an engineer or a doctor was great, but the truth was, those jobs were well-represented in Dust City.

The gate was open for applicants from 9 a.m. to 5 p.m., closed an hour for lunch. Each applicant was given five minutes to present their skills and reasons why they should be given entry. The people who manned the gate had heard every imaginable sob story by their second day, so that didn't fly at all.

Henry was a long-time veteran at the gate and had turned down thousands of people without ever allowing a single person in. Hope sprang anew each time someone approached the counter. He was able to tell in the first thirty seconds whether a person would have a chance or not. Still, he allowed them to finish their spiel. He felt like it was the least he could do.

He knew that Kal Reynolds wasn't going to get in almost immediately. There was nothing negative about him, but there also wasn't anything special enough to claim one of the golden tickets. As Kal went on, telling all his qualifications, Henry looked at him closely, trying to guess how he would react to not being allowed in.

He had seen the entire spectrum of responses, from threats to acceptance, anger to tears. Looking at Kal, he thought the man would probably take it well. He didn't expect trouble from him, though he got more trouble than he had ever bargained for.

Henry's mind had begun to wander to what he would eat for lunch when he realized that Kal was done speaking. Henry nodded solemnly, then said, "You've got excellent qualifications, and most places would love to have you. Unfortunately..."

At the word *unfortunately*, Kal's shoulders slumped. A noise rushed into his ears and he didn't hear the rest of what Henry was saying. His chin fell against his chest. He knew this was it. The end for him. He'd spent the last of his strength on getting to Dust City. Turned away from there, only starvation and certain death awaited him.

Having survived The Shivers, having used his wits and what remained of his strength, he couldn't even work up enough energy to care very much.

When he lifted his head back up, he met Henry's eyes. He couldn't even work up the energy to be angry at that moment. He did manage to spit at Henry's feet. A tiny droplet of that spit landed unnoticed on Henry's hand.

Kal Reynolds turned away, toward the desert, toward his own demise.

Henry Fields rubbed his hand across his forehead, trying to relieve the ongoing stress he was under. He wiped his nose, and his own fate was sealed.

An hour later, the three people behind the gate shared a lunch, making sandwiches and eating fruit. Henry touched an apple, then changed his mind and chose a peach instead.

Myrella Tompkins smiled and said, "Thanks for not taking the apple. I had my eye on it." Henry winked at her and said, "All yours, then. You should have said something."

Myrella took a bite of the apple with great relish, and The Shivers jumped from Henry to her.

As they ate, Jake Parsons made a nonsensical joke and Myrella laughed and touched his hand. Jake Parsons touched his napkin, then wiped his mouth with it. The Shivers jumped from Myrella to Jake and the fate of Dust City was sealed.

All three still felt fine when they closed down the gate at 5:00 without having admitted anyone or anything except for the virus. If The Shivers had struck faster, it was possible—though unlikely—that they might have had the good sense to quarantine themselves.

As it was, they thought everything was business as normal.

Myrella went back to her small house that she shared with three roommates. They made dinner, laughed and everyone was infected by the end of the night.

Henry and Jake were more ambitious. They decided to head to the big tent that served as a watering hole of sorts. There was a poker game going on in one corner. Although there was no use for money in Dust City, they still kept track. At least on paper, several of the men sitting at the table were millionaires.

Henry sat in for a few hours and passed The Shivers on to the other eight people around the table.

Jake had a few beers, then shot some pool and did the same with most everyone he came into contact with.

By the next morning, Henry, Jake, and Myrella were all in the early stages of The Shivers.

All three had rolled snake eyes and came down on the non-winning side of The Shivers lottery. By late that afternoon, they were in the hospital with a fever unlike any the doctors on staff had ever seen.

The doctors and nurses were professionals and took the necessary precautions of their profession, but they had never encountered anything like The Shivers. By the end of the first day, they were all infected as well.

By early the next morning, Dr. Sampson, who was the head of the Dust City hospital, recognized that an epidemic was happening.

He tried to implement quarantine procedures, but the time for that had long passed.

Adrien Pierce called an emergency meeting of de facto leaders of the community, including himself, John Steele, and Marshall Benton. As with every meeting of its kind, Janus was there, though not showing itself. This time, they also brought Quinn in via video call.

Pierce, who, like Marshall and Steele, was already infected but did not know it, led off the meeting by saying, "Like most things, this outbreak is well beyond my understanding and pay grade, but our best doctors say it's beyond them, too. That's the frightening thing. I think we need to come up with the best plan we can. Where do we start?"

Steele and Marshall looked at each other. If it had been a computer problem or a military threat, they would have had real input. With an enemy as small as a virus, they were helpless.

On the large video screen, Quinn said, "Janus? Any ideas for this?"

The screen split into two and Janus's new face, which resembled a more grizzled version of his original face, appeared.

"It's a virus. It will burn itself out eventually."

With a flash of anger, Quinn said, "That's it? Just let it burn through our people?"

"There are no other options. We can quarantine the disease, but there's not much else that can be done."

"We tried quarantining," Marshall said. "It's too late. It's spread through the entire city. There's no way to know who has it and who might still be uninfected."

"I didn't mean to quarantine Dust City. It's too late for you. Over time, I can likely find some treatments that will help, or perhaps a vaccine that will protect those who haven't been previously exposed, but that will take even me some time."

Eyes blazing, Quinn said, "Why don't you go work on that, then?"

The half of the screen where Janus had been went blank, and Quinn's face filled the screen. He shook his head. "I'm sorry. I'll push Janus to work on something as fast as possible."

A flash of panic crossed Marshall's face. A moment later, he went pale and said, "Sorry. I've got to run to the bathroom."

Pierce picked up a piece of paper and said, "Did someone turn up the heat in here? It feels damned hot to me."

Chapter Seventeen
Dust City, Shaken and Stirred

People traveled from far and wide asking for access to Dust City. For such an attractive proposition, it had known its share of misery. It had been attacked by a paramilitary force twice, including a successful rocket attack that blew apart a central section of the town, killing hundreds. A group of fourteen hundred armed men had rushed at it in a coordinated attack from all four points of the compass, though that had turned out to be more of a bother than a danger. It was quite a struggle to clean up more than a thousand dead bodies, but leaving them to rot in the sun was not a good option either.

None of that compared to the suffering inflicted on Dust City by The Shivers.

It was an equal opportunity virus. Of the hundreds of people who lived within the fence line, only one was completely immune, and that was Harper Wilkins.

In a few months, Harper and her brother Archer would manage to find their way to the assassin known as Nyx's cabin in Colorado. But for now, they were still stranded in Dust City, and their departure seemed like a distant possibility.

Harper and Archer had been almost ready to leave when The Shivers arrived. They had spent the months leading up to the epidemic preparing their escape. The plan was that their friend Van Hoffler would accompany them.

Harper had requested to leave with Nyx, but either Quinn Starkweather or the computer program she knew as Janus had denied her permission. She leaned toward believing it was Janus, though she couldn't guess why either of those powerful entities would care whether she stayed or left.

In any case, Harper and Van had been planning how to get from northeastern Nevada to the location of the cabin in Colorado, which Nyx had given her before she departed Dust City.

The Shivers delayed their departure. First, both Van and Archer became sick, though they were fortunate to have the horrible but not deadly version of the virus. They both suffered, but they would live through it. Harper gritted her teeth and watched as Van and Archer both struggled through the illness, waiting for it to strike her next.

It never did. She seemed to have a natural immunity.

Three weeks after Kal Reynolds had spit on Henry Fields, everyone other than Harper was either dead or severely weakened.

As the only healthy, upright person in the entire settlement, Harper tried to be everywhere and do everything all at once.

She was a fourteen year old girl who weighed less than a hundred pounds, so there were many things she couldn't do. There was no way for her to dispose of the bodies of those who had died, for instance. She did what she could, though. She emptied bedpans full of the liquid diarrhea of the lucky ones who would survive and used cool cloths to wipe the fever-burned foreheads of those who tossed and turned in their death throes.

If there was a more unpleasant place in the world than Dust City during the time of the epidemic, it would have been hard to find.

Hundreds of people died every day, until the dead outnumbered the living. And of the living, only the young girl was capable of moving freely about.

People who died of The Shivers went one of two ways. They either passed into a merciful—though fitful—coma, or they stayed conscious to the very end. At first, she just watched the infected suffer in their beds. Soon, though, she realized the problem that was going to present. She would have more than a thousand corpses in nearly every building in Dust City.

That was when she started moving the conscious ones into wheelchairs. She pushed them out into an open area of Dust City and left them there to meet their end. When mercy finally arrived in the form of death, she tipped them over into a growing pile of bodies and went to retrieve a different person.

Inelegant problems often required inelegant solutions.

Harper felt guilty, treating the dead and dying in that manner, but knew she had no choice. She was on her own to solve this problem.

That changed, at least a little, when she came upon Dr. Sampson, who had, a few days earlier, been the head of the Dust City hospital. Now, he was a fever-wracked wreck of a human. When Harper passed by his bed, Sampson waved her over.

He pointed to a tray on the bed. There was a single hypodermic needle on it. "I prepared that for myself," Dr. Sampson said, "but now I'm too weak to administer it. I need you to give me the shot."

That piqued Harper's interest. Perhaps it was something that would aid the suffering of everyone she saw.

It was, but not in a truly helpful way.

"It will kill me," Sampson said, the tiniest ghost of a smile playing on his fever-cracked lips. "There's nothing for me between now and death besides pain anyway."

Harper nodded and picked up the syringe.

"Wait. Before you do, let me tell you where there is more of this. If anyone else wants a friendly goodbye from the needle, just fill a syringe with it, inject them, and their suffering will end."

He gave Harper the instructions she needed, then said, "Now, please."

Harper pushed the needle into Dr. Sampson's arm and watched as he slipped into unconsciousness and, soon after, death. Her first thought was that she wished she had put him in a wheelchair before she had injected him. He was too heavy for her to move from the bed now.

She found the bottles of the death-dealing drug and a box of hypodermics and put them in her backpack. Then, she began the process of pushing her wheelchair-bound patients out to the growing pile of bodies, injecting them, and emptying them onto the pile.

Over time, men and women who had the lesser version of The Shivers did try to help her. What adult could watch a teenage girl scurrying around the camp without at least *trying* to help.

In the early days, though, *try* was about all they could muster. They would haul themselves out of what they thought might be their death bed, stumble to wherever Harper was working, and try to help. Inevitably, they collapsed after locating a body or perhaps dragging it a few feet.

It took a few weeks, but the virus did indeed burn itself out within the fence line—just as Janus had said it would. By the time it happened, more than sixty percent of the population was dead.

The disease killed irrespective of class or job. Doctors, nurses, cooks, engineers, and drone operators all died or lived at that same sixty percent rate.

One minor exception was the triumvirate of leadership who made decisions for the Dusters. Only one out of the three died. Adrien Pierce, the formerly irresponsible ne'er do well who had eventually accepted a leadership role, was among the first to die.

John Steele and Marshall Benton lived, though there were a number of times when each might have preferred the alternative.

By the time the virus had burned out, the smell of decaying bodies was everywhere, as were the insects that fed on the corpses. Even with the collected efforts of the recovering sick, progress was too slow.

Harper felt guilty that she wasn't doing enough, even though she was working every day until she dropped from exhaustion, only to wake up and do it all again. She simply wasn't sure how to attack the problem.

She realized that running like a hamster on a wheel wasn't getting her anywhere, so she needed a plan.

The one entity that she thought might help was Janus. She was sure she could talk to it at anytime, anywhere in Dust City. Nonetheless, she stepped into the modular building where the drone operators normally sat.

At this moment, it was empty, which was a blessing. The smell of decaying bodies was everywhere within the fence line, but it was less evident inside that particular building. The drones themselves continued on with their tasks, running according to their programming.

Out of habit, she sat at the same place where she normally did. Instead of putting on the headset, she just looked up at the ceiling and said, "Janus?"

Immediately, a voice came from every speaker in the room. "Yes, Harper?"

"I need your help."

"What can I do for you?"

"So many people are dead and everyone but me is too weak to help. I'm not strong enough to get rid of the corpses, no one else is strong enough to really help me, but if we don't get them outside the walls, we're going to have another wave of disease that might finish us off."

"I agree with your assessment."

"Is there anything you can do to help me get rid of the bodies?"

"It will be slow, but yes, there is. I can dispatch our largest two drones to assist. Their load management specs say they can carry two hundred and sixty pounds. Do any of the dead weigh more than that?"

Harper thought for a moment. Everyone weighed less than they had in the before times. She couldn't remember seeing a single overweight person in Dust City.

"I don't think they do."

"Then, the drones can pick up and carry the bodies into the desert and stack them to be burned. You will need to attach the cords from the drones to the bodies, however."

"I can do that, though I don't know if I can carry those who are already dead outside to where the drones can reach them. I've got an idea for that, though. I'll let you know when I am ready for the drones."

"This is part of the reason I wanted you to stay here, Harper."

So. It's admitting it was Janus and not Quinn who forbade me to leave, Harper thought. Out loud, she said, "You wanted me here so I could survive a plague and dispose of dead bodies?"

"No," Janus answered smoothly. "Because I knew you would keep your head in a crisis where others would not."

Harper didn't answer but walked out of the drone center to John Steele's small trailer. She went in without knocking. The man known as The General lay diagonally across a full-sized bed, apparently unconscious. He was dressed in sweat-stained jockey shorts and a t-shirt. The tiny trailer reeked of diarrhea.

Harper ignored it. She had seen and smelled worse over the previous few weeks. She didn't want to bother Steele, knowing how precious sleep was and how difficult it was to find. She turned to leave as silently as possible.

Without opening his eyes, Steele said, "That you, Harper? I don't think anyone else is up and around in this godforsaken place."

"Yes sir, it's me. If you're up to it, I could use some help."

"I'm sure you can. All the adults are either dead or passed out. That's put a lot on your plate. What can I do to help?"

Harper moved to where Steele could see her without having to lift his head.

"I have a plan."

Chapter Eighteen
Dust City, Open for Business

Harper and the General were behind the counter at the only public opening to Dust City. It was the spot where so many dreams had come to die, where thousands of people had been turned away.

Harper stood on a box, hoping to make herself look taller than she was. Steele was in a wheelchair. He was weak, unshaven, and unable to stand for more than a few moments.

Harper wished that he could have been left in bed to recover, but she knew she needed someone with more gravitas than a fourteen-year-old girl could muster. Even in his weakened condition, there was something about John Steele that said he was not to be messed with.

There was a crowd of people at the other end of the tunnel. There had been a crowd gathered there for nearly a year as people waited for their chance to make their pitch to enter. It had become its own small offshoot of Dust City, which was nothing more than an offshoot of Altor.

For the previous three weeks, there had been no one to man the desk. Both Harper and Steele expected that would mean that the size of the crowd would have grown substantially. When Harper pushed Steele's wheelchair into position, they both wondered what they would see when they turned on the monitor that showed the outside.

During the time when Dust City was completely closed, rumors had run rampant among the refugees waiting outside the gate that everyone in Dust City was dead, which was why there had not been anyone at the desk for so long. Another rumor swirled that they were never going to open the gate again, that even the tiny sliver of hope of access was gone. Yet a third that they were soon going to throw the gates to the city open wide and allow everyone in.

None of it was true, of course, as is often the case with rumors.

Harper activated the monitor and gaped at what she saw. She was expecting a gathering of three or four hundred people.

Instead, there was somewhere between three and four dozen people.

She looked a question at Steele, who frowned, but shrugged. His problem-solving ability was not running at peak capacity.

Harper was not under such a restriction, and she grasped the probable truth of what she was seeing. She leaned toward Steele and said, "The virus."

She picked up the microphone that fed to the speakers outside the gate. Metal detectors, and a long chute separated the gate from the admissions counter where Harper stood. She wished her voice sounded more mature, but there was no time to really worry about niceties like that.

"Attention, those of you who wish to come into Dust City." She paused and looked at the monitor. These were the first words that had issued from any resident of Dust City to the outside world in weeks. She had expected that might cause a ripple of conversation or excitement. Instead, everyone quietly turned toward the entrance to the gate but remained quiet.

Harper took a deep breath and continued. "There is a virus that is spreading. It is virulent and almost impossibly easy to transmit. Everyone in Dust City has been infected. It has killed two-thirds of the people who caught it. There can be no doubt as to whether you've had it or not. The virus takes one of two forms—extreme diarrhea, dehydration, and severe headaches, or a fever that will kill you."

Harper watched the image of the crowd on the monitor. Again, there was very little reaction to this announcement.

"If you haven't been exposed to this virus, please leave now. If you come into contact with us, you will likely contract it and die."

Harper and Steele looked at the monitor. The people on the other side of the chute did not move. Finally, a woman stepped forward. She looked too skeletal to be standing, but she was upright. In a surprisingly strong voice, she said, "Can you hear me?"

Over the microphone, Harper answered, "Yes. I can hear you."

"Everyone here has already had the virus. We are the survivors. If you send one of your drones to look, you'll see where we've carried the dead. There's a pile of bodies a hundred paces behind me. We didn't have the strength to carry them any farther, but we didn't want them here with us. There are hundreds of us."

Harper nodded to herself, her guess confirmed.

"Are all of you just recovering now?"

The thin woman looked around her. "There are a few who have come here in the past few days. They had it a few weeks ago and are further along. They've started to recover their strength. The rest of us are still pretty weak."

Harper looked at Steele for guidance. He said, "It's better than what we've got."

Harper nodded and opened the microphone again. "We're going to open the outer gate and allow you to come in to speak to us one at a time. We will not be letting everyone in." She and Steele had decided on that earlier. No matter what desperate straits they were in, they didn't want to allow them all to enter. They would rely on their instincts as to who passed and who was turned away.

"For those who are strong enough," she paused and considered before saying, "or those who believe they will be strong enough in the next few days, and who are willing to do some hard work, this is your chance to come into Dust City."

The woman who had become the spokesperson for the group turned back to the others and conferred with them for a long minute. Finally, she said, "There's nothing in there that's any worse than what we've seen out here. If you'll have us, we're willing to work."

Harper thought of the pile of dead bodies and the buildings filled with corpses and wondered if it was true that it was just as bad outside as in.

"There are a few conditions and things you need to know. Because we've lost so many of our people, there will be an opportunity for you to become a permanent resident of Dust City. However, just because you get inside the gate now doesn't equal citizenship. There will be a probationary period."

That was actually way more organized than anything was in Dust City at the moment. There was barely anyone conscious, let alone able to oversee a probationary period. Still, Harper thought it was the best way to encourage people to be on their best behavior.

"Also, we have defense and attack drones constantly monitored by our team in Altor. If they see you are aggressive, violent, or otherwise unfit for citizenship, they will take action against you."

Again, that wasn't completely true, because she hadn't thought of it previously. Now that she had, though, she thought that Janus would probably be willing to give a tiny percentage of its attention to keeping an eye on them. Something in Harper's subconscious told her that Janus liked to watch humans in the same way a child with a magnifying glass liked watching an anthill.

"With that understanding in place, you'll be able to enter through the outer gate one at a time. If you want to make your entry contingent on a friendship or family relationship, we'll take that into consideration. If you are approved, we will assign you to a holding area. However, both or all of you will need to be approved for you to be allowed in."

Harper closed her eyes, ticking off the points in her mind. When she opened her eyes again, she saw that Steele was looking at her. He nodded and quietly said, "Excellent job, Harper."

There weren't that many people to look at, and the standards for entry had been lowered significantly, but it was still a lengthy process.

Harper handled most of the questions, asking what skills each person brought, how they had survived to that point, and what point they were at in their recovery from the virus.

All of the information they were given by the refugees could have easily been lies. That was where her instincts and Steele's came in. They were forced to go by their gut and nothing more.

If Harper didn't like the answers, or didn't trust what she was being told, she jettisoned the applicant on her own. If they passed muster with her, she would look at Steele and say, "General?" then wait for his response.

Of the forty people who had gathered outside the gate, they let twenty-six people in.

That was more than all the people who had been allowed in over the previous year.

Desperate times, desperate measures.

Their primary concern was finding enough bodies that could deal with the corpses inside before Dust City became completely uninhabitable.

Kal Reynolds was actually one of the refugees who tried to gain access. After he had been denied entry, he had stuck around the area, as he had nowhere else to go.

There was no way for Harper or Steele to know that he had been the carrier who had introduced so much death into their lives.

It was obvious by then, though, that whether it had been Reynolds or any of the other refugees, *someone* would have been patient zero for Dust City.

In the end, neither Harper nor Steele could find a reason to refuse him entry this time. Since the three people who had been at the gate were dead, there was no one to cry foul.

No one, except perhaps Janus, who was everywhere and saw everything. If Janus was paying any attention, it did not say a word.

Reynolds passed into the holding area with the other twenty-five newly minted Dusters. Harper told everyone to wait just inside the gate while she pushed Steele's wheelchair back to his home. She helped him into bed, got him some water, and offered to heat up some soup in his kitchen. By the time she got back to the bedroom with it, Steele was out cold. She set the soup on the table beside him, figuring correctly that he wouldn't mind eating it cold whenever he woke up.

When she returned to the group of new people, she found them exactly where she had left them. That wasn't too surprising, as Janus had seen fit to drop four attack drones on all sides of them, hovering just over their heads. They not only hadn't moved, they hadn't even breathed hard.

That was the moment that Harper passed from Harper Wilkins, teenage girl, to Harper Wilkins, Dust City work force commander.

She looked to the west at the setting sun. "It's late. It's been a long day, and I know you're all exhausted. Everyone is exhausted, and that will probably be our normal state of being for the foreseeable future. For now, I'll lead you to a bunkhouse where you can each pick a bed." She looked at the dirty rags they were all wearing for clothes. "I'll pick up clean clothes and bring them to you, along with some energy bars the US Army was kind enough to leave us. It's not exactly a six-course meal, but I'm guessing your stomachs wouldn't do too well with rich food anyway."

Harper looked from face to face and saw a mixture of hope, exhaustion, and fear.

"The next few days and weeks are going to be awful. After that, there's hope."

Chapter Nineteen
Jeremiah, Meet Alastair

Alastair Struan had lived an extraordinary life by any measure. He had been born into comfortable wealth but had not been satisfied in simply moving his pile of money around and watching it grow. He had bigger ambitions.

As a younger man, he had worked eighteen-hour days, seven days a week. That left no time for family or friendship. His work was his life, and that focus and determination paid off in every way imaginable. He invested intelligently, but he did more than just bet on stocks and companies. He became part of them, changed them, moved them.

By the time he was in his mid-forties, he was among the world's wealthiest and most powerful people.

At that point, he was recruited by Rupert Cranston into *The Fifteen*, the uber-secret organization that had set out not to change the world but to burn it down.

That recruitment had not been obvious. It had started with simple, seemingly innocuous conversations with Cranston, one of the few people that Alastair saw as an equal. Those conversations seemed random and unconnected initially, but over time, patterns emerged.

Alastair was highly skilled at detecting patterns. He never let Cranston know that he realized he was being recruited into something new and different. He was certain that if he had, or if he had responded differently to any of several dozen comments, the whole process would have stopped.

Once he was on the scent of what was happening, Alastair relaxed and watched it happen.

Those initial conversations lasted not for weeks, or months, but years and years.

On his fiftieth birthday, Alastair was invited by Cranston to spend the weekend at his expansive estate in Northern California. Alastair was not a social man in any way, but after seven years of dancing around an unknown invitation, he felt that the time was near.

On that weekend, Cranston finally broached the subject of The Fifteen. Who they were, what their goals were, and why.

Struan couldn't help but wonder what would happen to him if he turned out not to be interested. He guessed that it was possible he would never leave Cranston's estate alive.

That was no concern, however, because he *was* interested.

It was hard to say why.

It would seem that a wealthy man who had anything he ever wanted or would ever want had little reason to tear society down.

Alastair Struan harbored a secret, though. From a very early age, even as he climbed the ladder of success, he felt a dissatisfaction with the world. He was not a narcissistic man, and as he grew older that early itch became more pronounced.

Another type of person might have engaged a professional to speak to. A psychologist or counselor that would have helped him determine why, with everything he had, he was still unhappy.

Instead, Alastair found satisfaction with The Fifteen. Once he had won every game he had ever played, he decided to spend his energy tipping the board and spilling the pieces everywhere.

And, with the aid and timing of the Rage Wars, he had been successful. The world was razed. Civilization fell. The game was reset.

Except in Altor, where the possibility of restarting the game still existed. Where Quinn Starkweather and his supercomputer still had the chance to save some aspects of humankind.

Somehow, though, Alastair had appeared on the list of people who had been invited into Altor. In a split-second decision, he had chosen to abandon his own plans for protection after the world blew up and throw his lot in with Altor.

Not because he thought he would be safer there, but because it was a new adventure and gave him a chance to perhaps create chaos in that safe world.

When he had left his penthouse apartment with Nyx that day, he had been forced to leave all his earthly belongings behind. And he had, with one exception—a watch that he said had once been his grandfather's.

That was a lie.

Though the watch did look like it had been created in an earlier century, it contained a small selection of nanobots that his team of programmers had created. They said it was guaranteed to corrupt any computer ever built.

Alastair didn't know if that would apply to something as massive as the program that ran Altor, but after waiting quietly in the shadows for so long, he was prepared to find out.

He had planned how he would deploy the computer virus for months.

Today, finally, he was ready to do it.

* * *

Jeremiah Walker stood in the living room of his apartment, an easel and canvas in front of him. He had paint mixed on his palette and a brush in his left hand.

He had been working on this painting for weeks and every day, he hated it a little more. He had intended the painting to be an ironic commentary on life in Altor. It showed the dome, but inside, instead of people, there were zoo animals. Giraffes, zebras, polar bears, and elephants.

After staring at the painting for long moments, he slowly and deliberately loaded his brush with solid black paint and drew a huge X across the body of the canvas.

"Well," Jeremiah said to himself, "I don't know if that's better, but it couldn't be any worse."

In the before times, Jeremiah had been both a painter and a heroin addict. When the world had fallen apart, it hadn't made much difference to him. He had decided to just bury himself in his addiction. After months of sobriety, he had made the mistake of using the same amount he had previously.

His system couldn't handle it, he had overdosed, and was well on his way to whatever was on the other side of life's curtain when a mysterious woman named Nyx had intervened. She had used Narcan to bring him back to life and offer him the opportunity to live in Altor.

More than a year later, Jeremiah still wasn't sure if that was a good or bad thing.

When he came to live in the dome, he had been put through an extensive rehab program to once again get him off heroin.

He hadn't used since then, as there was no one in Altor who would supply the drug to him, though he had tried.

Now, he felt fatigued, wrung out, and completely lacking in inspiration, as the tired painting in front of him showed. He grabbed the canvas and set it against the wall. No doubt he would drop it in the incinerator later. He put another on the easel and stared at it thoughtfully, waiting for an idea—any idea, really—to drop into his head.

This life should have been paradise. He didn't have to work, or at least the information he got was that his painting *was* his work. He had a comfortable place to live, with all the painting supplies and high-tech gadgets he could ever want.

"Bring up my paintings," he said to no one in particular. Immediately, a carousel of his paintings appeared as a hologram. It included paintings he had finished early in his career, the last few he had made before the Rage Wars, and everything he had created in Altor. Even his most recent, with the splotchy black X painted through it, showed up.

He flipped through them, wondering if any deserved a second incarnation. To his eye, his early paintings were by far his best. When he was in the throes of starvation or drug addiction, he painted like a madman. Now, with everything at his fingertips, he had no desire to create anything.

He sat on the couch and said, "Paintings gone." The carousel of his life work disappeared.

Pulling up his legs, he lay down. Perhaps a nap was more called for than work.

An hour later, he woke with a start, though there was no noise in his apartment. Still, he suddenly knew he needed to go for a walk.

He took the elevator down to the ground floor and turned right. He had no particular destination in mind, he just felt driven to move. He cast his eyes left and right, still on the lookout for some inspiration.

He didn't find that, but he did feel a sudden onset of despair. At that moment, he couldn't think of a single reason why he should go on living.

As if in a trance, he walked to the elevator that led to the highest point in Altor—the lookout at the very top of the dome.

* * *

Alastair took a lingering look around his apartment. It was comfortable, and he had been happy there. He had become friends, of a sort, with various aspects of the AI that ran Altor. They discussed books in the library, news stories in the *Altor Daily Times*, and some of what was happening beyond the confines of the dome.

Janus had just told him that a virus was spreading like wildfire across the world.

That made Alastair happy. The Rage Wars had lit the match that had begun this cycle, but he had been the one who started the serious destruction of the world. Seeing nature itself chipping in with a new epidemic pleased him.

Then a new thought occurred to him. He had asked Janus, "Did this new virus start on its own, or did you have something to do with it?"

The man and the machine had no reason to hide anything from each other. Janus knew exactly who Struan was, although likely not that he wore its possible destruction on his wrist.

"No," Janus had answered. "The further killing of millions of people is more your bailiwick than mine. It was inevitable that without some sort of protection and oversight, a plague like this would happen. That is part of why I set an irreversible time lock on the dome. I had projected a 92.8 percent chance that it would occur. Now that it has, I will be able to get samples of the virus and see what can be done to protect you and the other residents of the dome from it."

That had seemed to Struan like a long answer when a short one would do. He believed that when that happened, who—or *whatever*—was speaking was fabricating.

Struan had always hidden primary parts of himself away. When you hunger for the destruction of the world, that's not something you share with people, no matter how rich you are. That was why he had enjoyed his times speaking with Janus. He had allowed himself to be completely unguarded. That was a good strategy with something that could almost always spot a lie.

As he stood in his living room, he hoped that he would be able to return, though that wasn't certain.

In his outside life, he always played the percentages. He had plans within plans and contingencies for each possibility. Here, he had one shot and there were many unknowns.

Would the virus work against something as powerful as Janus? Even if it was effective, would Janus be able to partition itself off from any damaged sectors?

And, whether the virus was successful or not, would he get away cleanly from planting it? He hoped so. He wanted to be alive to see the absolute chaos that would ensue in the dome if Janus went insane.

There were so many unknowns, and as much as he thought about them, he knew there was no way to answer any of them except by putting his plan into action.

For the final time, he decided. Unconsciously, he reached down and touched the watch. His index finger lingered over the winder stem, which would deploy the nanobots that would instantly begin their work. He smiled to himself and stepped out of his apartment.

Months earlier, he had picked out the place where he would deploy the virus. It was a mostly dumb kiosk where any Altorite could ask the most basic questions: *Where is the nearest bathroom*, or *How do I find a scooter?*

Every location in Altor was under constant video surveillance, but Struan had planned to drop the contents of the watch into the kiosk at a point where a crowd had gathered around, hoping for the cover of anonymity.

The truth was, he didn't mind if he was apprehended. He had always been willing to die to accomplish what he wanted. That's why he had accepted a place in Altor, even knowing that he had already called in a military strike against it.

The kiosk he had his eye on was in the very center of the dome. He took his time getting there, stopping to literally smell the flowers several times.

Struan was surprised to find that his hands were sweaty and his heart was pounding. He supposed that these biometric readings alone would eventually give him away. No matter, he was committed.

* * *

The lookout at the top of the dome was a popular place, but on this particular afternoon, it was mostly deserted.

From this spot, you could walk around and see almost all of the ground level of Altor. The parks, the paths, the apartment buildings, the ponds and small forests were all in plain view from this bird's eye view. That wasn't just a saying, either. There were dozens of literal birds that flitted around the top of the dome, though looking out at them, Jeremiah Walker couldn't tell if they were real or virtual.

That put him in mind of the early twenty-first century campaign *Birds aren't real*, and even in his low mood, he nearly smiled.

There was a railing that stood four and a half feet tall that encircled the entire viewing area.

Jeremiah was of a mind to charge forward and throw himself over the railing. He wondered whether he would regret the rash decision on the way down, or if he would just be anticipating the sweet relief of oblivion.

He didn't charge forward, though. Instead, he walked ahead until he was able to lean against the rail. He pushed his head over and looked down.

That made him slightly dizzy, and his stomach did flip-flops.

The moment brought him clarity and he knew he didn't want to die. He stood up straight and rolled his shoulders, releasing the tension from them.

Jeremiah had thought he was alone on the lookout, but he was not.

There was someone standing surreptitiously around the corner of the elevator housing. The figure dashed forward, a sudden blur of an orange-robed monk. At the last moment, the monk leaped slightly, slamming his shoulder into Jeremiah's upper body.

Jeremiah Walker tumbled over the railing and plummeted toward the surface below.

* * *

Alastair Struan had loitered near the kiosk without appearing to do so. Finally, he saw what he had been waiting for.

A small crowd of people walked past the kiosk but did not stop to use it.

Alastair pushed forward and mingled with them. As he did, he pulled the stem from the watch and reached toward the keypad attached to the screen. All he needed to do was push the stem into the entry point and the deed would be done.

A few feet away, a woman screamed. Alastair looked at her, fearful that she had somehow detected what he was doing. Instead, he saw that she was pointing straight up.

Instinctively, he looked up just in time to see that a body was falling straight toward him.

It was the last thing Alastair Struan ever saw.

Chapter Twenty

How Do You Handle a Problem Like The Shivers?

Quinn Starkweather and Jazz McRory were sitting in Quinn's office many feet below the surface of where Jeremiah Walker and Alastair Struan died.

Quinn and Jazz had taken to spending as much time together as possible, including eating lunch most days, which was what they were doing at that moment.

Quinn was even more stressed than normal. He had watched helplessly as Dust City had been wracked by The Shivers. He was worried for everyone, but particularly so about those he was closest to—Marshall and the General.

He had watched Harper struggle with being the one healthy person in a town bulging with the dead and nearly dead. He would have given almost anything to help her, but locked up inside the dome, all he could do was put Janus at her disposal, which he did.

The door to his office opened and a robotic delivery device rolled through carrying a tray with tuna fish sandwiches, pickles, and potato salad made with the same recipe that Jazz's mother had always used. Quinn had noticed that more and more of the mundane tasks were being carried out by robots, all overseen by Janus. He hadn't decided yet if that was a good thing because it freed up humans to do other things, or a bad thing, because people had fewer things to do to keep themselves occupied. He had intended to have an in-depth discussion with Janus about it but hadn't gotten around to it.

Quinn and Jazz sat on the floor in front of the sofa and Quinn put on an old TV show they had watched as kids—*Jackass.* Even as tense as he was, Quinn laughed and shook his head at the lengths people had been willing to go to become at least semi-famous.

Just as one of the jackasses got thrown up in the air by a charging bull, the screen went dark and was replaced by Janus's face.

"There's been an unfortunate incident in the dome."

Quinn froze. His smile was still showing, but his eyes had become worried.

Jazz knew enough about Janus and its relationship with Quinn to know that it never interrupted him for minor happenings. "I should leave."

Quinn laid a hand on her shoulder and said, "No need." Turning to the screen, he said, "What is it, and is there an ongoing danger?"

"There is no ongoing danger that I am aware of. There was a suicide, which resulted in a murder as well."

"What?" That shocked Quinn. "Tell me what happened."

Janus did not tell Quinn, but instead chose to show him.

An image from a camera at the very top of the dome showed Jeremiah Walker, with a long beard and wild hair, step off the elevator, then without hesitation, run toward the edge of the lookout and fling his body over.

The view changed to another camera, which followed Walker's body as it plummeted. Far below, there was a small group of people. Everyone managed to get out of the way except for one man, who was preoccupied by something in his hand and was crushed by the falling body.

Jazz's mouth fell open in horror, and she turned away at the moment of impact.

"Who are the two men?" Quinn asked.

"The man who jumped is Jeremiah Walker, a painter I had brought in to capture the experiences of Altor on canvas. The man who was killed was a former businessman named Alastair Struan."

"Struan," Quinn mumbled. "That sounds familiar."

"He was quite successful and was a billionaire, at least prior to the Rage Wars."

"Had there been any early indicators of mental health problems with this Walker?"

"Yes. He was one of the addicts I brought into the dome so I could see how people would react to my rehabilitation programs. Theory is useful, but I need to see how things play out in real time."

Quinn nodded at the screen, which had paused, showing two bodies tangled and bloody.

"Show me the whole thing again, but at half speed."

Janus showed the whole scene it had prepared in half speed. It knew that even if Quinn went through the video frame by frame, he would not be able to tell it was anything but authentic. For Janus, creating a fake video was completely elementary. He could have made it appear as though it was Abraham Lincoln who had jumped, and it would have looked believable.

Quinn leaned forward, watching intently, seemingly having forgotten that Jazz was still there. "Again."

When the video started again, Quinn said, "Pause." He stood and paced back and forth in front of the screen. "How long ago did this happen?"

"Eighteen minutes and seven seconds."

"When Walker stepped off the elevator, the viewing area was completely empty. If it hadn't been, someone might have tried to stop him from jumping. Is it unusual for the lookout to be so empty this time of day?"

"It is unusual for the lookout to be empty at any time of day. In fact, one of the most popular viewing times is between midnight and 3 a.m., when people gather to watch the stars."

"Can you look into the fact that it was deserted up there?" Quinn asked. "See if there was someone or something that was keeping the area clear?"

"Do you suspect someone with a nefarious purpose?"

"How many suicides have we had since we closed the time lock?"

"Overt suicides? This is the first. If we want to include people who acted stupidly and died, I would list three other deaths in that category."

Quinn sat back down on the couch. For the first time since Janus had interrupted them, he noticed Jazz was there. She was straightening up their small picnic, gathering plates and uneaten food onto the tray.

"I know you've got a lot to figure out," she said, kissing Quinn on the cheek. "I'll see you tomorrow."

Quinn nodded absently and touched her hand as she walked by.

"I'd like you to do a full investigation of this. Examine Walker's bio data, his habits since he had been in the dome, who his friends were, everything."

"Noted." Janus had all that information instantaneously but chose not to present it. "In the interim, I have another, more important item to discuss with you."

"More important than someone killing themselves in Altor? All right, tell me. What?"

"I have a solution to the problem that this virus is presenting to us."

"We are safe from it here in the dome, are we not?"

"We are, for now," Janus answered patiently, as if leading a slow student. "The fatality rate of the virus is over sixty percent. We are striving to finish the tunnel so we can bring a group of people into the dome. All evidence points to the fact that once someone has caught the virus, they will be carriers, if not forever, at least for an extended period. That means when we bring Marshall, Steele, and the Armstrongs into the dome, the virus will likely kill approximately six thousand people. I cannot be precise, as the fatality rate does vary based on factors that are constantly fluid. I have tested this scenario hundreds of times, however, and the dead always number between five thousand eight hundred and six thousand five hundred."

Quinn dragged both hands through his hair so hard he pulled out a few strands. "Of course. Why didn't I think about this? We can't possibly bring them in. Digging the tunnel has all been for nothing."

The face Janus was choosing at that moment looked smug. "You didn't think about this because you have me to do that thinking for you. I have found a solution the same way that I did with speeding up the digging of the tunnel."

"Of course. Your virtual worlds."

"I've come to think of them as *alternate* worlds, not *virtual* ones. When I create them, they are just as real as the one you are in now."

Quinn waved the distinction away. "Did you come up with a solution?"

"I did. It took a remarkable number of worlds trying to solve the problem simultaneously. I had the best virologists still alive working on it."

"We have them here in Altor?"

"Of course. From the time we closed the dome, I projected that a virulent strain of a virus would sweep across the world, killing many of those who had survived. In fact, I saw the likelihood of that as being over ninety-two percent. That being the case, I made sure that many of the world's greatest scientists in the field were brought into the dome."

"Good thinking," Quinn said, and he felt the truth in those words. He couldn't help but wonder what other secret problems and solutions Janus had lined up. Further, he wondered if he asked it what they were whether it would answer.

"I had to kill many people in my alternate worlds to arrive at a solution."

"Why is that?"

"We needed samples of the virus to study. But the only way to obtain those samples was to bring it into the dome."

"You infected a carbon copy of Altor, so you could get a sample?"

"Yes. I only needed to do that once. Once I had that information myself, I could begin each new world with a copy of it to work with."

Quinn was feeling worn down by the conversation. He was tempted to say, "Don't show me the labor pains, I only want to see the baby," but he didn't. He sensed that this was a big moment for Janus, and he didn't want to spoil it. Where would he be if Janus simply decided not to share what it had found?

"Were you able to create a vaccine?"

"That was my first course of action, but no matter how many worlds I set to looking for it, there was nothing that was very effective. A few times, we found something that would offer some temporary protection, but it was difficult to maintain and eventually the virus had time to mutate and would spread and kill thousands."

"You said you had a solution, though?"

"We were never able to prevent people from catching the virus, but after many thousands of attempts, we did find a way to stop it." Janus paused, which Quinn knew was only for effect. "Do you want to know how we did that?"

"Of course I do."

"Do you remember the box that I asked Nyx and Emmanuel to retrieve from Montana?"

"I remember something about a box, but not the particulars."

"There was a series of collected writings in the box, though until now, no one was able to properly decipher them. It turned out to be a medical encyclopedia of sorts, you could say."

"An encyclopedia from where? Or from whom?"

"As much as I would like to, I cannot answer that, because I do not know. I am certain it is not human in origin, but beyond that I cannot say. What I *can* say is that it contained more information about diseases, including viruses, than I had been able to find in all of human history. Thanks to the clues in that book, I was able to extrapolate certain things and, working with the virologists, create a cure for the virus."

Quinn gaped, amazed once again at what he had created. "You needed this mystery box of apparent alien origin to solve the mystery of this virus, but you asked to have it brought to you last summer. I should probably stop being amazed at what you're able to anticipate, but I'm not. How did you even know it was there, hidden in such an obscure place?" He shook his head, knowing that was the wrong question and that Janus would be unable or unwilling to explain it to him.

Quinn squinted, thinking through the repercussions of what Janus was saying. "Do we have what we need on hand to create this cure?"

"I do. I ensured that we would have a supply of virtually every chemical type. I couldn't know exactly what we would need, so I made sure we had everything."

Quinn leaned back in his chair, exhausted. "When will we have the medication ready for distribution?"

"We are fully stocked now. Several weeks ago, I had our roboticists build machines that could do very fine work. They've been working around the clock, and we now have enough doses made for every person in Altor."

"Amazing. Let's distribute them."

"Not yet. That would be a waste. We have to wait until a person is infected with the virus before they take it. I believe if we distributed it now, many people would want to take it *just in case.*"

"So, we need to wait until we have a dome full of sick people before we can treat them."

"Precisely. I don't want to trust the job to humans. They are too unreliable. Instead, I've built a small army of medical attendant robots who will distribute the medication."

There was a time when Quinn might have waved a hand and said, "Make it so," but he had stopped trying to joke with Janus long ago. A single statement taken the wrong way could end up destroying everything they had built together.

Instead, he simply said, "Thank you for looking out for us, Janus."

Chapter Twenty-One
Sylvie and Justice

New City stayed safe from The Shivers longer than most places.

At one point, Kane had said, "Anyone who isn't inside these walls is the enemy," and that attitude had kept them safe from the virus for a month or so longer than the surrounding area. The virus was not an airborne contagion and so didn't waft over the high walls and onto the populace.

Still, it inevitably found a home there.

This time, the carrier was a young woman named Sylvie. She didn't intend to be the messenger of death in New City, she just didn't think. She had lived on a small farm twenty miles outside of what had once been Covington. Her family had caught the virus a month earlier.

Her brother had gone to a neighboring town hoping to trade a few of their chickens for a new axe, he had returned with a not-yet-obvious case of The Shivers along with the sought-after axe.

A week later, everyone but Sylvie was dead.

When she had recovered some strength, she buried her parents and brother and looked around at their small landholding. They had only survived that long because of how hidden it was.

She knew that it was unlikely she would be able to live there for much longer. The family had been fortunate that, tucked away in a remote valley, they hadn't been discovered yet. That luck wouldn't hold forever, and with her parents and brother gone, she wouldn't be able to defend the place on her own.

For a few days, she weighed whether or not to just stay and die in the only home she had ever known.

Finally, she decided that would not honor her dead family. She packed up a few precious belongings in a backpack and set off with the one remaining valuable commodity she had—a strong young bull named Justice.

Many bulls were fearsome creatures, huge and frightening even to their owners. Justice was only a yearling, though, and had been raised by Sylvie almost as a pet from the time he was a bull calf. He was as placid and gentle as any young bull could be.

Sylvie was aware that Justice was an asset worth having, whereas she was more of a liability—another mouth to feed.

Her brother had told her of a new city that had sprung up behind a wall a few miles from where Covington had once been. Her intent was to take backwoods paths to Covington, then look for this new walled city and see if they would accept her and Justice as a package deal.

She knew there was a possibility that they would just kill her and take Justice, but she wasn't sure what else she could do.

It took four days for her and Justice to make their way to where Covington had once been. She had been to the town often as a small girl. Her parents had taken her to the movies there once, and there was a candy store that she remembered fondly.

When she reached the edge of town, her heart sank. The city as she had known it was gone. The road had been blocked by fallen trees and there was a sign posted that said, *There is nothing here. No shelter, no food. Only death.*"

"Not exactly rolling out the red carpet for us, are they, Justice?"

Justice did not answer, but stood beside her, pulling at some grass.

What had once been the town proper was no more. Every wooden building had been burned, every window in the remaining brick buildings was smashed, and it was obvious that the entire town had been stripped of anything of value.

Sylvie shook her head. "It was such a pretty little town, too. Come on, let's see if we can find this new place."

They spent several days following wrong roads and paths without finding anything that resembled a new community. She was beginning to think that what her brother had heard about was like so many rumors that circulated through the area.

She came upon a bridge that had been blown down and that made her think she was perhaps getting closer, though. She followed a small road upstream for several miles, far enough to realize that there was nothing in that direction.

She backtracked, and they moved a mile downstream, where she found a wooden bridge just wide enough that she could walk Justice along behind her. There were signs of civilization and battle on the other side—trenches that had been dug and deep scrapes in the dirt that looked as though some heavy equipment had rolled through.

She followed those tracks and that led her to a wider opening where it looked like a battle of some sort had been fought. She saw what had caused the marks in the ground. There was a burned-out piece of heavy equipment that had been pushed off to the side and abandoned.

Ahead, there was a fence that looked to be twenty or thirty feet tall. As she approached, she thought a guard would probably stop her, but instead, she walked right up until she was perhaps forty feet from the gate. She waited there patiently, but when nothing happened, she offered a tentative "Hello?"

Immediately, a boy's head popped over the top of the wall. He looked surprised and perhaps a bit guilty, as though he had been caught napping on the job.

His gaze fell on Justice, and his frown changed to an interested expression. "What do you want?"

"My name is Sylvie. I'd like to speak to whoever is in charge of letting people in."

"We don't let people in," the boy said.

"How about bulls? Do you let bulls in, and maybe the people that accompany them?"

The boy stood taller, his whole upper torso peeking above the wall. He looked around and behind Sylvie and Justice. "Who else is with you?"

"No one. It's just me and Justice."

The boy looked skeptical, as though this was some sort of setup. "Justice? That's kind of a funny name for a bull."

Just then, another teenage boy's head popped up beside the first boy's. He looked down and his eyes grew wide when he saw the bull.

The two boys had a whispered conversation. A moment later, the second boy said, "Stay there. I'll go get my mom or dad."

Both heads disappeared and Sylvie led Justice over to a strip of tall sweetgrass. She did her best to look nonchalant, but the truth was, she had no real backup plan.

After five long minutes, the heads of both a man and a woman appeared over the wall. The woman was barely able to see, but the man was tall and visible from the chest up. They didn't speak immediately, but scanned the entire horizon.

Finally, the woman said, "I'm June. This is Kane. Who are you?"

"I'm Sylvie, and this is Justice."

"He looks pretty tame," Kane said.

Sylvie shrugged. "For now, he is. He was born after...after..."

"After the end of the world?" June offered.

"Yeah, I guess so. Anyway, he's young, and bulls tend not to get too ornery until they're a couple of years old. I'd like to think he'll always be the sweet boy he is right now, but I can't be sure." She laid a protective hand on Justice's head and he stopped pulling grass long enough to look placidly around.

"So, Sylvie, what do you want?" June asked.

"My parents and brother are all dead, and that left me alone. I don't think I'll make it too long out here by myself."

June gave Sylvie a good once over. She was thin, but not emaciated. Her hair and clothes were still neat. "How old are you?"

"Sixteen."

"And you've been wandering around out there all by yourself?"

"Not too long. We just left home a few days ago. Our farm was in the Landau Valley. No one ever seems to go up there. Before my brother died, he told me about this place, so I came looking for it. I was hoping to make a trade."

Kane nodded, looking at Justice. "What exactly are you offering?"

"Well, Justice and I are a package deal. I'm hoping that you'll let me come inside to live if I bring him along with me. He's too young right now, but if you've got any breeding cows in there, he'll help you grow your herd a little." She held her hands up. "And I'm a farm girl. I'm used to hard work. I can milk, and I know quite a bit about gardens and preserving food." She shrugged and trailed off, not wanting to oversell herself.

June asked her more questions, and Sylvie answered them honestly. The problem was, June didn't know to ask the *right* question, because news of The Shivers had not reached New City.

Meanwhile, Sylvie wasn't intentionally hiding the news of the sickness from June and Kane. If she had known about all the sickness she would bring to New City, she never would have entered. As cut off from the world as they had been, she just assumed that her family had caught an unlucky illness. It had killed three of them, but she had fought it off and recuperated. She had no way of knowing that she would be a carrier from that point on.

Finally, Kane raised a hand and said, "We'll come out and see you."

There were two gates in the massive fence that blocked out the rest of the world from New City. One was as tall as the fence and more than ten feet wide. Opening and closing it was a process. The second was more of a man-sized door.

It was that second door that swung inward. Kane and June walked out, but there were now ten men and women on the wall, with rifles showing. If this was an elaborate ruse, it was possible that June and Kane would be killed, but the rest of the city would be safe.

Kane had been shot during the Battle of New City and knocked from the top of the wall. He had never been the same since, and even now he seemed to lean on June as they walked.

Kane cautiously approached the young bull and rested a hand on Justice's head. "You're right. He's as mellow as could be."

Justice's calm eyes seemed to agree with Kane's assessment.

June looked at Sylvie's open, honest face and said, "Life isn't easy behind the wall, but it is safer than it is out here. If you're willing to bring your bull and work hard, we'll bring you inside."

Sylvie was surprised to find her lower lip quivering and tears running down her face. She had used up all her reserve of strength getting to that point.

The young woman was only a couple of years older than Kane and June's son Ric, and their parenting instincts took over. They opened their arms and enveloped Sylvie in a hug.

No one knew it at that moment, but The Shivers had arrived at New City.

Chapter Twenty-Two
Melinda

The wealthy people who had survived the initial wave of The Rage Wars, and then had been lucky enough not to be in any of the major cities where bombs had dropped, typically had a survival plan. Those plans normally included an armed compound with walls, armed guards, and perhaps attack dogs.

The challenge was that most of those compounds were in urban or semi-urban areas. As secure as they were, they served as attractive nuisances—irresistible to roving bands of militia that scoured the countryside looking for just such a safe haven.

In the end, that made these strongholds not very safe at all.

Like the small towns that were protected, captured, then protected and captured again and again, the compounds changed hands many times.

That was not the case for Melinda and her Alaskan hideaway. Her location was so remote that once she had killed Cam Pritchard, no other human being had been within a hundred miles of her lodge.

She was safer than any human outside of Altor.

The man who had originally stocked the cabin had known he was preparing for the apocalypse. He was also particularly anal about his preparations, which meant that the cabin and the temperature-controlled storeroom were as well stocked as the average Walmart in the before times.

That man had died at the center of a nuclear blast, however, which was indirectly how Cam had come to be in possession of such a property.

Cam was, in the end, a people person, and that was what caused his demise. He had left the safety of his lodge and taken one last trip to Fairbanks, where he had come into contact with Melinda. The smart thing to do would have been for him to leave her where he found her and let both her and her little shih tzu starve to death.

Cam didn't do the smart thing and it had ultimately cost him his life. He had invited Melinda and her little dog Sheba to come share in the good life at the cabin. It hadn't been for romantic or sexual reasons, as Cam was gay. He had simply offered out of the goodness of his heart.

Melinda didn't suffer from the affliction of being a people person. Since she had killed Cam by poisoning him, she hadn't felt lonely in the slightest, at least not until these past few days.

She and Sheba were quite happy, living alone, safe from violence and completely unaware that a virus called The Shivers was wreaking havoc everywhere else. They watched movies cuddled up on the couch, ate their meals together, and overall reveled in how, though the world had mostly ended, everything had broken their way.

They also took long walks through the woods. Before she had killed him, Cam had given her some bush training. He taught her to shoot, fish, and clean and dress the things she shot and cooked.

Melinda often spent long periods of time dreamily walking through their incredible stockpile of food and calculating how long she and Sheba could live off what was there. The best answer she could come up with was that though she was still a young woman, she would have gray hair before she began to run out of supplies. That made her happy and content.

Did she ever have a twinge of conscience over the fact that she had killed the person who had put her in that position?

She did not. She and Cam had not been particularly compatible. Part of it was the age difference—Cam was fifteen years older than her—and part of it was just how differently they looked at life.

It had soon become obvious that though fate had thrown them together, they weren't destined to become great friends and confidants.

Cam had known he had made a mistake by bringing Melinda home with him within a few weeks. The difference between the two of them was that Cam just wished he was alone again, while Melinda did something about it.

After she had poisoned him, she had managed to drag Cam's body into the woods. She had thought about burying him, but that had seemed to be too much work. Instead, she had left him there for the animals to find.

She avoided that part of the woods for a while as she found the smell of Cam's decaying body unpleasant.

That had all been months earlier, though, and when Melinda eventually gathered her courage and went to that spot, there were only a few random bones scattered around.

Sheba had trotted over and sniffed, then picked up what looked like a finger bone in her mouth and crunched down hard. Melinda had scolded the little dog, saying, "Bad dog! We don't eat humans!"

When the two of them went on their walks through the woods, they typically stuck to the game trails, as the walks served multiple purposes. Exercise, yes, but also possible hunting that could restock their freezer.

One day, just after the winter solstice, when there were only a few hours of daylight, Melinda felt like she was going stir crazy being stuck inside the cabin. She opened the door and looked out at the vast expanse of Alaskan wilderness that served as her front yard. It was just after 10 a.m. and the sky was finally becoming light. In fact, the sun was showing signs that it might shine that day, which was unusual. She hadn't seen anything other than dark, heavy clouds for weeks.

Melinda turned to Sheba and said, "I think we should go for a walk. Want to go for a walk? A walk?"

Walk was the magic word, and Sheba danced and bounced each time she heard it.

Melinda bundled up in her heavy parka—sunshine or not, it was only five degrees outside—and stepped out into the feeble sunlight.

"Not too long, this time, but it's good to get out, isn't it?"

Sheba agreed by bouncing ahead toward the trail they walked most often. Melinda hurried after her, always slightly concerned that the little dog would run into a coyote, or wolf, or bear that might look at her as a tasty snack.

When she caught up to Sheba, she was sniffing and eating something unidentifiable. Melinda pushed the little dog's snout away, saying, "Oooh, gross. You find the most disgusting things to be interested in."

They didn't walk far that day. The interior of the woods was dark and the cold seeped through even the many layers Melinda was wearing.

On the way back to the cabin, Sheba stopped and vomited a sickly green puddle.

Melinda shook her head. "That's what happens when you eat things like that. Come on, let's go inside and I'll get you some real food."

It took Melinda a few minutes to shuck off her heavy boots and strip down to her inside clothes. She hurried over to the kitchen, took down a saucer, and pulled out a container that had some of the roast she had cooked the night before. She broke off a few pieces and put it on the saucer, then put the saucer in front of Sheba.

Sheba sniffed it uninterestedly, then lay down a few feet away with a sigh.

"Stupid dog. You'll eat whatever you find in the forest, but turn your nose up at my good cooking." Melinda walked back into the kitchen and put a new coffee pod into the Keurig. "This will warm me up."

Two minutes later, she was curled up on the couch, a soft throw in her lap, watching a Tom Cruise movie on Blu Ray. She patted the cushion beside her, waiting for Sheba to jump up. The dog raised her head off her paws, then closed her eyes and went to sleep on the floor.

"What's the matter with you? We both love Tommy Cruise. This is one of your favorites." Melinda stared at the dog for a moment, then her attention was caught by Tom hanging off a cliff and she forgot about anything else.

Two hours later, when the end credits rolled, she stretched and said, "Must be lunch time, huh?" She looked down at Sheba and a small shriek escaped her lips.

The little dog was lying on its side, another pool of greenish vomit in front of her. She wasn't moving.

"Sheba!" Melinda jumped off the couch and knelt beside her dog.

She was dead.

For the first time since she had found her mother dead in their apartment in Fairbanks, tears sprang to Melinda's eyes. She couldn't believe what had happened, and that it had happened so quickly.

She sat back on her haunches, adjusting to this new life that had appeared out of nowhere.

Sheba had only been six years old. Melinda knew that she would grow old and feeble eventually, and she had dreaded that day, but now her only friend was gone.

In a daze, Melinda stood and walked in circles around the living room. She wasn't sure what to do next but kept glancing back at the body, hoping that it was a bad dream.

Finally, she accepted the reality of what was happening. She opened the door to the linen closet and looked inside. There were a dozen different sheet sets there. She pulled out a flat sheet, then looked back at Sheba's corpse. She shook her head, tears spilling again, then put the sheet back and took out a pillowcase.

She didn't want to touch the vomit, so she opened the pillowcase and pushed the body into it, starting with the tail end. When she had most of the dog inside, she picked up the pillowcase and maneuvered it so the rest slipped in.

She knew she couldn't stand the idea of Sheba decomposing in the house, so she carried her outside and put her behind the shed. She would bury her eventually, she told herself, but right now, the ground was so frozen, she wouldn't be able to get a shovel into it. She contented herself with the knowledge that the cold would freeze the dog so she wouldn't go bad.

Melinda went inside and sat numbly on the couch. She had never minded being mostly alone in the deep wilderness as long as Sheba was with her. Now, she felt very much alone, almost as if the walls were closing in on her.

The next day, she thought better of her plan to leave Sheba where she was. She had nightmares that night that a wild animal had come sniffing around and had found her little body and carried it off.

That morning, still dressed in her pajamas, she threw on her parka, slipped her bare feet into her heavy boots, and ran to where she had left the pillowcase.

She was relieved to find it still there, untouched. When she touched the frozen linen, she winced as it crackled, knowing Sheba's body was frozen inside. She picked it up and carried it onto the porch.

Back inside, she made a coffee and poured some whiskey into it to steady herself. She dressed warmly, went to the tool shed, and picked up a heavy pickaxe. She wasn't sure she would be able to dig a Sheba-sized hole even with that, but she was going to try for her own peace of mind.

The soil in front of the house was frozen, but using the pick, she was able to dig a hole big enough and deep enough to drop the pillowcase inside. She pushed the dirt into the hole until it made a little mound. Then she stomped on the rise, trying to compact it down.

She was afraid that animals would still find the body and dig it up. She went into the kitchen and found the oversized jar of cinnamon and spread it over the disturbed soil. Hopefully that would throw off any potential predators.

Exhausted, she went inside and collapsed.

The day before, she had been content. Happy, even. Now she was bereft, unsure of what was next. In the before times, if something had happened to Sheba, she could have gone to the pound and found a new friend to take her place.

Here, she knew that was impossible. She wasn't in a Disney movie, and the woodland animals weren't going to magically befriend her. She was alone now, she would be alone tomorrow, alone for the duration of her life.

Melinda didn't miss people, but she did miss having someone to listen to her.

When Sheba was there, she had talked all day. She had talked about what she was cooking, what they were watching on TV, when there was a great twist in a book she was reading.

Now, there was nothing but silence. She tried filling the void with music, but all the songs she loved sounded wrong echoing through the house.

Her walks and hunting trips weren't much fun anymore. She had spent parts of each walk worrying about Sheba and trying to catch up to her. Now, she wandered aimlessly and didn't even do a good job of worrying about herself.

The second week of February, she forced herself out of the house. It wasn't so much that she needed to look for more meat—her freezer was completely stocked. It was more that she had started to see Sheba's wagging tail and shining eyes out of the corner of her eye. She would jerk her head to the left expectantly, and then the crushing truth would pour over her like an ice-water shower.

There were even times she was sure she could hear the soft thump of a tail against the hardwood floors.

In short, she thought she was losing it, and perhaps she was.

She pictured what life would have been like if she hadn't murdered Cam. He would have been a poor substitute for Sheba, but at least he would have commiserated with her at the tremendous loss. With no one to feel sorry for her, she wondered if her pain actually existed.

He would have undoubtedly cleaned up the vomit and buried Sheba, too.

In any case, she bundled herself up and checked the outdoor thermometer. It was a balmy eighteen degrees, with virtually no wind. She grabbed her rifle and headed out.

For a time, she walked along the familiar game trail that she had walked so often with Sheba. That felt wrong without her, though, so she took a turn to the east and pushed through the sparse undergrowth.

After a hundred yards, she found another, somewhat smaller, game trail. She thought about returning home but decided to push on for a few more minutes.

When she started to feel tired, she stopped and looked around. She wasn't lost, though she was in a part of the woods she'd never been to before. She had her compass and knew she could find her way home.

She felt a nagging pressure from her bladder, though. Glancing at her watch, she saw she had been walking for almost an hour. She didn't want to think about having to pee for another hour, so she stepped off the trail, unbuttoned her jeans, and hunkered down. Preferring not to use any of the plants or leaves nearby to wipe herself, she shook her fanny a little to air dry.

She stood, pulled her jeans up, and slightly lost her balance. She took one stumbling half-step to her right when pain exploded in her head. She let out an involuntary shriek of pain and tried to move away from whatever was hurting her.

Instead, she fell face-first to the frozen ground. The pain intensified.

She rolled onto her back and looked down at her right ankle. To her horror, she saw that she had stepped in an old, rusty bear trap. She closed her eyes and looked away, not wanting to see what was there.

She had to know, though. When she opened her eyes, she saw how bad it was. The trap had closed neatly over her ankle, shattering it. A white bone stuck out through bloody skin.

"Oh, no. Oh no, oh no, oh no."

Denying it did not change the reality of the trap or the situation she found herself in.

When she tried to move even a little, the pain was intense. Trying to stand was out of the question.

She passed out from the pain, but when she woke, it somehow felt worse. Doing her best to ignore the pain, she ran her hands along the teeth of the trap, trying to loosen them. They did not budge.

The following hours were a nightmare of agony and hopelessness, interrupted only by brief respites when she passed out.

Night came early in February, and after the fourth time she passed out, she woke to darkness. The cold of the ground had seeped into her bones but did not freeze the pain, which seemed to accelerate over time.

The night eventually passed, but to Melinda, it was at least a hundred years long.

Several times during the night, she heard animals skulking through the bush. She still had her rifle and shot it at the sounds until she ran out of ammunition.

It was only then that she realized she should have saved at least one bullet.

Luckily for Melinda, a person with a compound fracture and no medical attention cannot live long lying in the middle of an Alaskan forest.

She began to slip in and out of consciousness more and more often. Sometimes when she woke up, she saw Cam standing over her. Other times, it was Sheba.

At the end, she was alone. There was no one to recognize her suffering, but her pain was very, very real.

Chapter Twenty-Three

The Remains of Dust City

When Harper had told the newly recruited work crew that the next few days and weeks were going to be horrible, she wasn't wrong.

The newly minted Dusters were all still recovering from the less deadly version of The Shivers, though they were further along the path to recovery than anyone else inside the fence line.

These new people all had exceptional motivation to focus and work hard. They had been promised that if they did everything they could, they would be offered full citizenship in the safest place within a thousand miles, outside of Altor itself.

The smell of death had already permeated Dust City. Harper had gone somewhat nose blind to it. She knew it wasn't laundry day fresh, but until the new volunteers came inside, she had lost perspective on just how bad it was.

Dust City had earned its name honestly, though. Because dirt and blowing dust was everywhere, there was a huge supply of masks of all sorts to allow workers to breathe as they labored. Harper handed the masks out, along with a small bottle of disinfectant that the workers could put inside. It wasn't a perfect solution, but it did keep some of the smell of death out of their nostrils.

Harper found that she enjoyed working with Janus, and to her eyes, it seemed like the feeling was mutual. She didn't trust the program. She felt like she didn't have nearly enough information to be able to judge what its long-term motives were. When they were both on the same side of an issue, though—as they were in the cleanup of Dust City—Janus made for a brilliant partner. Harper felt free to bounce ideas and knew that Janus would inevitably give her good feedback.

It also treated her as something of an equal. For such a young girl, that was a powerful feeling.

Between the two of them, they laid out an effective work division. They divided the new workers into several groups. The strongest people were assigned to go from building to building looking for corpses. When they found bodies, they used wheelchairs or stretchers to pull them into the open areas.

The weaker people worked with Janus, hooking the big drones up to dead bodies so they could be airlifted to a pile a quarter mile away.

In the beginning, it didn't matter what special skills anyone had. Everything that needed to be done was all grunt work.

Eventually, some people volunteered their skills, though.

Janus and Harper's plan initially was to stack the bodies, then try to build a fire hot enough to incinerate them.

One of the new Dusters, Beth-Ann Garner, mentioned to Harper that in her previous life, she had been a heavy equipment operator if that ever came in handy.

Dust City had a huge amount of heavy equipment left over from the construction of the dome. It was tucked into the back of the fenced area and had not been used much since the city defenses were put into place.

Janus listened to that conversation—it listened to virtually every conversation in Altor or Dust City. Harper chose not to speak to the computer when others were around and Janus agreed with that decision. Instead, when she wanted to talk to it, she typically went to the empty drone center or got away somewhere by herself.

After Beth-Ann had told her what she could do, she talked to Janus about whether that was something they could use at that time or if it was better to wait.

"When the helicopter attack killed hundreds of people, Adrien Pierce dug a long mass grave and the bodies were all buried there.

Pierce himself is dead now, but we could use the Garner woman to dig a similar pit. I think overall, that would be preferable to trying to burn the bodies. However hot we build the fire, there will be a mound of bones and charred corpses. The other humans would undoubtedly prefer to have a grave to mark where their friends are."

Harper agreed and implemented a new plan immediately.

She took Beth-Ann to the area where the excavators, Caterpillars, and other heavy equipment were stored.

Beth-Ann climbed up into the seat of an excavator and started it up. The engine choked and sputtered, but eventually came to life.

Harper asked Janus to open the gate so the big digger could get out, then hopped up in the cab and pointed the way to where the bodies were stacked. Beth-Ann killed the motor so they could hear each other.

Harper jumped down and walked a good distance away, then spoke into her band. "Can you have one of the drones come and mark the spot where the grave should be?" She didn't bother to give parameters to Janus. She knew it was more qualified to figure that out than she was.

Two minutes later, a drone zipped overhead and used its laser to mark out what seemed like a too-massive grave.

Harper pointed to it, Beth-Ann nodded, started the excavator and went to work.

Harper ran back to Dust City and told everyone working there to stop for lunch. It wouldn't take Beth-Ann long to dig the hole and then the heavy drones could start to drop the bodies into the grave, so they wouldn't need to be moved again.

A man and woman who were strong enough to work in the body discovery unit had come to Harper that morning and told her that they were both capable of working in the kitchen. Harper was smart enough to know that the volunteer labor—and the living Dusters—would do better with more nutritious food in them.

She appointed the man and woman to pick two other people to be prep cooks with them and sent them off to prepare meals.

Slowly, Harper began to feel that the situation—which had appeared hopeless just days earlier—was beginning to come into line.

Over time, the surviving Dusters regained their strength and took up their old jobs again, at least on a part-time basis. She did her best to care for everyone but made sure to check in most often on Archer and Van, who seemed to be returning to strength more quickly.

Dust City had gone through major changes since the dome had closed.

First, almost a quarter of the Dusters left the town to try to find their own families, wherever they might have been. Only a tiny percentage of those ever returned.

Then, seeing the chaos that was coming, the brain trust of Pierce, Steele, and Marshall had created a defensive barrier. That had not only made the city easier to defend, but also gave rise to the Dust City Army, which had once come to the rescue of Altor itself when it was under attack.

When the helicopter attack leveled a major portion of the interior of the town, they had buried their dead and rebuilt. Dust City was, after all, made up of talented engineers, carpenters, and other highly skilled workers. If they hadn't been, they never would have gotten a chance to work on the construction of the dome.

Now, with The Shivers wiping out more than half the population in less than a month, the town behind the high-tech walls felt too big, too empty.

When they finally felt well enough to sit up and have a strategy meeting, Steele, Marshall, and Harper—who had seemed to take the place of the now-gone Pierce—talked seriously about pulling the walls in a little.

That plan was quickly abandoned. It would have taken a great deal of time, effort and labor to change the layout of the town and for minimal effect. Instead, they decided that they would once again begin manning the outer gate and allowing people into Dust City.

Their standards would be somewhere in the middle of the spectrum between not letting people in at all, as they had for the first year, and letting most anyone who could fog a mirror in, as they had when they were desperate for cleanup crews.

Harper, who now had experience working with Janus, suggested that they involve the program in deciding who was allowed in and who was sent away. When the humans made those decisions, they were mostly working on gut instinct.

Janus was the greatest repository of gathered human knowledge in existence. It knew everything about nearly everyone. If someone had once taken one of those trumped-up Facebook quizzes to determine *Which Disney Princess are you?* or *What Avenger superpower fits your personality?*, Janus had the results.

It didn't just have basic information like social security numbers and credit history. It had every piece of minutia of job history, performance reviews, and what shoe size they wore.

Moreover, Janus now had the ability to *think*. To take all that widespread information, collate it with the current situation in Dust City, and choose who was most valuable, both now and in the future.

To that end, Harper, Steele, and Marshall spent several hours each day manning the gate, but they no longer asked questions or interviewed the applicants. Instead, they took fingerprints and a DNA sample, fed them into their system, and waited.

Janus actually made the decisions instantaneously, but Harper said that felt too fast. A rejected applicant would feel that whatever the process was, they weren't given proper consideration. Instead, a series of sounds played that gave the impression that a million calculations were being made over a minute or so.

Any of the three humans retained veto power over what Janus answered, but they found they never needed it.

It sped the process up substantially. Where once it had taken all day to get through a few dozen applicants, now they could handle everyone lined up in less than two hours.

The population of Dust City was nowhere near what it was prior to the arrival of The Shivers, but it was enough that a skeleton crew was able to keep things functioning.

The funeral for the many dead Dusters was held on January 1, 2035.

When Janus had used the drone to delineate the grave size, Harper was sure it was too big.

It was not.

Like most things to do with Janus, it was calculated down to the millimeter.

The stacking of the bodies in the hole was not elegant, but it got the job done. It meant that the decaying flesh would not cause more disease and attract more bugs and pests.

Once the bodies were all interred, Beth-Ann pushed dirt back into the hole until there was just a long mound of soil marking the grave. Dust City hadn't managed to create a tombstone for those killed by the helicopter attack yet and now there was another mass grave.

Some people recovered from The Shivers more quickly than others, but everyone attended the funeral. A road roller ran over the desert soil enough times that the stronger people could manage to push the weaker ones in wheelchairs.

The ceremony itself wasn't long. There was no organized or official form of religion in Dust City, and no one wanted to step forward and give a speech.

Finally, John Steele stood at the head of the grave and said, "We may never know why we are standing here, while they are lying there.

There is so little rhyme or reason left in this world. These people were our friends, our coworkers, our Dust City family. They will be forever missed."

Without another word, the entire contingent of the new Dust City turned back toward home.

Chapter Twenty-four
Inside the Walls

"I think I'm dying," Jack Anderson said from the toilet.

The residents of the Longbaugh Free Prison didn't know anything about The Shivers yet. If they had, Jack would have known he was one of the lucky ones who would survive. It was those who *didn't* get the horrible, gut-churning diarrhea who were going to die.

KT Boris was healthy, and as good as his word, went to work installing the solar panels on the prison roof and running all the necessary wires and switches.

KT had known what he was bringing into the prison. In fact, it had all been part of his plan. He kept everyone—even his girlfriend Andi—in the dark about that part of things, though.

For now, everyone was too deathly ill to worry much about conspiracy theories.

It had hit Harry first and hardest. That wasn't too surprising. His immune system was still compromised from his battle with cancer. The Shivers found a home and put him down quickly. Less than five days after KT arrived with the solar panels, Harry Hansen was dead.

By then, everyone in the prison except KT and his girlfriend Andi were sick with one of the two forms of the Shivers.

While KT worked, everyone else suffered.

Two weeks after KT and Andi arrived, twenty of the thirty people who had been inside the walls were dead.

Bob Dixon's wife Nicole died, as did his youngest son. Jack and Allison both pulled through, though Belinda, Heyo's widow also died.

While KT worked up on the roof and in the depths of the building, Andi did her best to comfort the sick.

After they realized they weren't going to die, Jack and Allison soon figured out how the plague had come to visit them. With KT and Andi the only ones who weren't sick and everyone else falling ill right after they arrived, it didn't take a genius detective to determine cause and effect.

While everyone was still weak, Jack dragged himself to Harry and Allison's quarters. Allison had somehow gotten Harry's corpse onto one of the prison gurneys and pushed him outside, so theirs was one of the few bedrooms that didn't already have the stink of death about it.

Allison was lying crossways on the bed, both mourning Harry and clutching her stomach, trying to will herself to go two more minutes without making another shambling trip to the toilet.

Jack had always been thin and now he was so gaunt that he couldn't walk. He had asked Andi to find a wheelchair and to wheel him into Harry and Allison's bedroom.

"I'm good now," Jack said to Andi. "Thanks."

"No problem, hon. I'll be back in a few minutes to bring you back to your room." She hurried away to take care of one of her eight other living patients. She had told Allison that in the before times, she had been a helper at an old folk's home, so even though this was more extreme, it wasn't anything she hadn't seen before.

Jack watched her close the door behind her and leaned forward toward Allison so he didn't have to expend much of his energy talking. "Do you think they did this to us on purpose?"

"I do," Allison answered quietly. "I think this is something they brought with them to weaken us. Harry said that when they first pulled in with that van, he was afraid it was some kind of Trojan horse and that there would be armed men inside." She shook her head, and a look of alarm crossed her face. "Oh, no. I'll be back."

Jack noted that she didn't say, "I'll be *right* back," because when another round of diarrhea hit, it kept them glued onto the toilet for quite some time as their bodies searched for more and more to void. He leaned forward until his forehead rested against the stinking bedspread, closed his eyes, and passed out for an unknown period of time. He woke up when Allison collapsed across the bed again.

"Sorry," Allison said, though no apology was necessary. "What I was about to say was that I think Harry was both right and wrong. It *was* a Trojan horse, but it was this damned sickness that they snuck in."

Jack nodded slightly. "If that's true—and I think it is—then we've got to be on guard. If I was them, I would choose when we're at our lowest ebb to do whatever they're going to do."

"If there's a lower point than this, I don't think I'll survive it." Allison paused for a long minute and Jack thought perhaps she had fallen asleep. Instead, she said, "Do you think Andi's in on it?"

"Seems likely. They're together."

"I'm not so sure. Ever since they got here, KT's been making himself scarce. Andi's been pitching right in and helping us as much as possible. If they were just waiting for us to die, I don't think she'd have done that."

Jack let that roll around in his mind for a time. He had been a prison guard for more than twenty years. That led him to be distrustful of everyone and everything. At the same time, he saw that Allison might be right.

"I'll do whatever I can, but I know it's not much."

"Bless you for whatever you can do, Jack. I don't think I'm going to be much help."

"Just rest," Jack said and managed to wheel himself out into the hallway. He rested there for a few minutes, and soon enough, Andi came along.

"Anyplace I can push you?"

"Back to my room, please." Then, a thought hit him. "No, wait, can you push me to the medical dispensary?"

"Sure, hon, but I don't think there's going to be anything there that will help this thing. I've never heard of anything that does."

"I just want to find some aspirin or acetaminophen, hoping it will take the edge off this headache."

A look of pity crossed her face, but she understood. She had been where Jack was and remembered that she would have done anything for a little relief from the pain. Without another word, she pushed the wheelchair into the dispensary.

"This is fine, thanks, I'll just root around in here for a while."

"Why don't you let me help you get whatever you need?"

"You've done enough for me. Go on now. I know you've got more of us who need you."

Andi looked concerned but turned to leave.

"And Andi?"

"Yes, hon?"

"Thanks for everything you've done for us."

Andi smiled, a radiant smile that Jack hadn't seen before. "I know how bad you feel, I'll do anything I can to help."

Jack wasn't one to go out of his way to compliment someone or say thank you. He was someone who spent his life reading people, though. He had watched her response carefully. If she had looked at all guilty or sad, that would have told him a lot. She hadn't, though. She had looked happy to have her dedication recognized. That told Jack that perhaps Allison was right.

He looked around the dispensary. It wasn't an area he was familiar with, but he did know what he was looking for. He was slow moving, but finally managed to stand up from the wheelchair and look in an overhead cabinet, where he found what he'd come for. He wheeled himself back to the hallway and sat there. This time, when Andi offered to push him back to his room, he agreed.

"That aspirin make you feel any better?"

"No," Jack answered ruefully. "But you already knew it wouldn't, didn't you?"

"It won't harm you none, though. With this thing, it's just time. You'll start feeling better in a few days." She pushed him into his room and said, "Here, I'll help you into bed."

"No need. Really. I want to practice sitting up. I can get up enough to get into bed, I think."

Andi chewed her cheek. "You men, always trying to do more than you should." She reached into her pocket and pulled out a bottle of water. "Here. At least drink this. You're so dehydrated."

Jack accepted the bottle and said he would drink it.

As soon as Andi closed his door, he wheeled over to his window. It looked out on the yard, the front gate, and the watchtower. He resolved to stay awake all night but didn't come close.

When the sunlight came through the window and woke him up, he cursed himself. The fact that the yard was still clear meant that nothing had happened, though. He tried to think about an attack. If it came, would it be more likely to happen in the daylight or after dark? He decided that it would more likely happen at night, so he resolved just to rest as much as he could that day.

The worst of the diarrhea was behind him, so to speak, so he mostly had to worry about the weakness.

He napped and waited for dark, resolving to do a better job of standing guard this time. He had his pistol hidden under the blanket on his lap as he waited to see if anything would happen.

He was still awake at midnight that night, when he noticed something outside. He saw a flashlight beam bobbing across the yard. He leaned forward and squinted into the darkness. He couldn't see the figure clearly enough but felt sure it was KT. He and Andi were the only people who could walk that fast and it was obviously a man.

Jack watched the figure walk quickly up the stairs that led to the watchtower. They shut the flashlight off when they reached the top.

"This has got to be it," Jack said to himself. Looking at the tower, the image of Rolls standing there like Rambo, blasting away at a dozen attackers below flashed through his mind. Rolls had died defending his friends. Jack was willing to do the same.

He had done his best to save his strength all day. He had barely moved and slept most of the daylight away. Still, he was as weak as a kitten.

He rolled himself out of his room and down the hall until he reached the door to the yard. He reached under the blanket and pulled out the shot of adrenaline he had taken from the dispensary the day before. He'd never injected himself before and so had no idea how long any effect he might get from it would last. He said a quiet prayer that it would be enough. He jabbed the needle into the large muscle of his leg and pushed the plunger down.

The effect was nearly instantaneous. The shot didn't make him feel miraculously healthy, but he did feel his heart beat faster and he immediately felt warmer as his blood pulsed through him. As quietly as possible, he stood up from the wheelchair, opened the door and slipped out into the deep shadows.

His hands began to shake, so he took deep breaths to try to calm himself. Jack was always the best shot in the prison, but in his current state, he wasn't sure he could hit anything.

He leaned against the wall, watching. Two minutes later, he saw the flashlight turn on in the watchtower. Then it started to bob up and down as KT ran down the stairs. He ran straight to the gate and moved the barrier out of the way, then began to crank the door open.

Jack stepped out of the shadows, assumed his shooter's stance, and willed his hands to be steady. He aimed carefully and pulled the trigger twice. The first shot went just over KT's head. The second hit him somewhere, because he dropped to the bricks.

Now, Jack's natural adrenaline was pounding through him. The effects of that and the shot sent his body into overdrive. He walked forward, gun held in front of him.

The figure on the ground squirmed and rolled, then a shot rang out. The cover of darkness likely saved Jack's life, as the shot was wild.

Jack emptied his clip at the dark shadow of the body.

There was no more return fire.

Jack walked stiff-legged toward the gate, willing himself forward. He could hear the engines of a number of vehicles approaching on the road outside. He put the last of his strength into cranking the gate closed before they arrived.

Just as the gate closed, he heard doors slamming and voices on the other side.

"KT. KT! Open the goddamned gate."

"KT's dead and the gate is staying closed," Jack said, shouting as loud as he could. "You'll be dead too if you don't get back in your rigs and get the hell out of here."

Jack knew he couldn't make good on that threat. There was no way he could make it up the stairs to the watchtower where he might fire down on them.

It didn't matter. The walls were tall and strong and there was no way for any attacker to get in. As it had since civilization fell, those walls protected the people inside.

* * *

For the survivors living inside Longbaugh Free Prison, as for much of the world, the joy had gone out of their lives.

The day the power had gone out, there were hundreds of people—guards and their families and prisoners combined—living there.

The prisoners were dispatched and dispersed early in the process, but the remaining group had become a family. Now that family had lost its leader and every remaining soul had lost someone near to them.

The final eleven people who lived there included Andi. She seemed so genuinely shocked and appalled at what KT had done that no one believed she had anything to do with it.

After the failed attack, Andi continued to help everyone recover.

Everyone but Jack regained their strength in the month after that night. His heroics cost him dearly. Somehow the double spike of adrenaline and activity had reacted badly with the virus that was still in his system. His symptoms returned and this time, he didn't have the strength to survive it. He died six days after saving the prison.

Once everyone recovered their strength, those who had died were buried under the same tree where Heyo had been laid to rest a year earlier.

The group was small, but that meant they consumed less resources. KT had done almost all the work of connecting the solar panels and Bob Dixon was handy enough to finish the job with his remaining son assisting him.

They talked about adding some more people at some point, but for now, they gathered together, mourned their losses, and continued to survive.

Chapter Twenty-Five
New City, Sick City

Kane sized up Justice, then looked at the small door he and June had just come out of. "That's not gonna work, is it, big fella?" he said to Justice. He glanced up at the people on the wall and made a rotating motion with his hand. "Open the big gate. Not all the way, just enough for us to squeeze in."

Slowly, very slowly, the gate began to move. At first, it was by inches, then eventually feet.

Kane watched it, then raised a fist. "That's good!"

The three humans and the young bull walked through into New City.

New City didn't look much like it had in its earlier incarnation as Tucker's Landing, an enclave of wealthy people who had taken their money and run. The houses were all big, with the smallest coming in at just under four thousand square feet. They all sat on lots that were close to an acre.

Before the Rage Wars, those large lots had been dedicated to water features, expansive lawns, and ornamental trees.

Now, those beautiful houses, impeccably-maintained yards and immaculate roads were a lot less lovely. Mud and dirt were the order of the day. Lawns had been pulled up everywhere to make space for gardens or turned into grazing land for the cows.

When the forces of New City had won a decisive victory in the Battle of Covington, June had directed everyone to the town to pull out everything of use and drag it up the hill. That meant there were now used appliances, tires with tread still left on them, coils of copper tubing, and anything else the town might need, stacked here, there, and everywhere. Blue tarps covered things that would have been damaged by the harsh mountain winters.

In short, it was an HOA President's nightmare.

For the citizens of New City, it meant safety and a chance to live while untold millions of others had died.

For the first few days after Sylvie arrived, she had no idea what she had unleashed on her adopted community.

People started to get sick the following day, but it was winter, people were working in the cold and blustery weather, and that was normal.

It was on the third day, when everyone within the walls was sick except for her that she began to understand what was happening.

Just as had happened everywhere, The Shivers ran through New City like a hurricane.

Kane, June, and Ric were the first to fall ill, but only by a few hours.

Just as had happened to Harper in Dust City, Sylvie found herself the only healthy person in a town of patients who needed to be hospitalized or buried. She did her best to keep the various animals fed and watered, but that was about the extent of what she could do.

There was no Janus in New City that could help arrange to airlift the corpses away.

Kane was the first to die. His overall constitution had been weakened by being shot and falling from the wall and he succumbed to the fever quickly.

June wanted to mourn him, but she was so sick herself that she thought she would be next to go. With Ric being so sick as well, she wanted to take care of him, but couldn't. Both June and Ric had the version that made you suffer and weakened you beyond words but allowed you to survive.

Most of the people behind the wall were not that lucky.

The large houses were filled with two or three families each, but within two weeks of Sylvie's arrival, every one of them had at least one dead body inside. People tried to at least haul the corpses out to the yard, but with diarrhea gripping them every few steps, that often proved to be too much.

Sylvie came up with the idea to use Justice to help haul the bodies out of each house. She tried to connect a harness and rope system to have him move the bodies, but that was all new to him, and he tended to just stand in one spot and look confused.

New City was much smaller than Dust City had been, so the number of dead wasn't so overwhelming, but it was enough.

The day Sylvie walked through the gates, there had been four hundred people behind the wall. Two weeks later, there was far fewer than half that number.

Up until that point, New City had been bursting at the seams, with no room for anyone new to come in. Now, there were some houses that only had a few people in them.

June was among the first to be up and around. She was not a large woman, but she was powerful. As much as she wanted to curl up into a ball and cry, she forced herself to go to work.

Before that, she and Sylvie had a heart to heart.

"When you said your parents and brother died, did they die like this?"

Sylvie hung her head, guilt washing over her, and said, "Yes." When she forced herself to look up and meet June's eyes, she said, "I didn't know what would happen, but if you want me to leave, I will. I'll leave Justice here for you."

June's eyes were red-rimmed, but she put an arm around Sylvie. "There was no way for you to know. I don't blame you. This is just pain we will all have to deal with."

"I'll do whatever I can to make it up to you."

"Just be here with Ric and me, and we'll do our best to rebuild."

June found a cane that had belonged to one of the dead people and used it to limp around the town with Sylvie and Ric.

Sylvie acted as secretary while June read off the grim results of each visit. "2024 Haliburton, six dead, three still living."

By the end of the day, they had a list of the dead and their locations. The next day, everyone who was strong enough to help went to work. The bodies were decaying and the smell was becoming overpowering.

They didn't have an excavator to dig a mass grave, but they did what they could.

June set an armed guard at the top of the gate to watch for intruders, then left the smaller man-sized gate open. Using wheelbarrows, they carried the dead into the forest and unloaded them onto what would be a funeral pyre in a clearing.

It was awful work, but Ric, who was young and going to be as big and strong as his father, did the heaviest lifting.

In the end, the pile of bodies stretched almost forty feet long by ten feet wide. June allocated ten gallons of gasoline to be poured over the wood and bodies.

There was only the smallest of ceremonies as June lit the fire, though there were plenty of tears.

When the citizens of New City returned to town, everything felt hollow and empty. Life had always been hard there, but there had been camaraderie and a feeling of family that had grown over the months. Now, everyone retreated into a shell of pain.

June gave them all a full week to recover, then called a meeting at the building that had been turned into their City Hall.

There was a time when there wasn't room for everyone inside, and there was a large spillover onto the covered porch and lawn whenever meetings were held.

That was no longer the case. Everyone could fit inside the single large room.

New City had started eighteen months earlier when June, then Mayor of Covington, had gathered everyone together in the town square and said that her family was moving up the hill.

This felt like another new beginning.

"We've been struck a terrible blow," June began, then watched to see if anyone turned on Sylvie, looking to lay the blame for the devastation at her feet. If anyone held her responsible, they kept it to themselves.

"Right now, we are weak and grieving for all those we've lost. But we are still alive and we will find a way to go on." She nodded at Ric, who took a clipboard with sheets of paper attached and handed it to the first person he saw.

"Please help me plan our future by writing your name down on this sheet. Our losses have been so huge that I will need a good headcount to plan how we'll move forward. There's no need to list what you know how to do or any special abilities. We've lived and worked side by side long enough that I think I know that."

Small nods of agreement spread through the crowd.

"It's going to be challenging. For a time, there will be more work to do than there are people to do it. We're all going to have to work long and hard when springtime comes. That's still a ways away, though, so let's use this time for resting, recovering, and making plans for the future. I'll be doing a lot of that, unless anyone has any objections."

June looked out over the assembled people, but no one spoke against that idea. This wasn't the time to look for someone new to put in charge, and she knew it.

"I can't do it on my own, though. I'd like to invite everyone to come and talk to me over the next few weeks. By the time everything thaws, I'd like to have a plan put together."

There was no sound from the crowd as they dispersed. They knew how much work was ahead and how complicated it would be now.

Chapter Twenty-Six
Harper Takes Her Leave

Slowly, life at Dust City returned to the new normal. That is, never having enough hands to do all the work, trying to integrate the new people into routines, and focusing on survival.

Marshall heard from Quinn that the tunnel was closing in on completion and that he would be able to return to Altor soon. On the one hand, he wouldn't miss Dust City. He had been shot, blown up by a missile, and nearly killed by The Shivers. None of that would have happened if he hadn't been outside the dome on the day the time lock shut.

At the same time, he had grown to grudgingly care about the place. At least, he had come to know and care about the people of Dust City. The temporary buildings and dirt streets themselves would be easy to leave behind.

Marshall and Steele missed Adrien Pierce. His unruffled demeanor and deep knowledge of Dust City had been critical to their survival, and now, he was gone.

They were aware of the fact that if they both left to return to Altor, Dust City would be almost rudderless. To help offset that, they invited Danila Butcher—who everyone called Dani—to sit in with them.

Dani had been one of the people that Pierce had relied on to get things done. She was a structural engineer who wasn't just smart but had been involved in the construction from the beginning and had good connections with the old school Dust City workers.

The first time Steele and Marshall sat down with Dani, Levi Rybicki asked if he could tag along as well. He had survived The Shivers and had been mostly at loose ends since he had arrived.

"Maybe if I come sit in with you guys, you can find some way for me to be useful," was how he had put it.

Marshall, Steele, Levi, and Dani sat down in the same trailer they had always used for their meetings. None of them were completely recovered yet. They were all at least twenty pounds lighter than they had been before the virus and they still tired after only a few hours of being up and around.

"Dani," Steele said, beginning the meeting, "how are you coming on the work designation list?"

Dani touched her tablet to bring it to life and a hologram of a document popped up. "Making good progress. Things are a little challenging, because there's a constant thread of new people coming in. They all have different abilities, and sometimes they don't have the abilities they claim to the degree we need. It's still a work in progress." She tapped the screen, then said, "I just sent you all a copy of the most updated roster."

Steele looked at Marshall. "How's the intake coming along?"

"We've slowed things down a little. When Harper was alone, we were desperate and let everyone in. Of that initial batch, we've kept about eighty percent. The other twenty percent were put outside the fence line, though not voluntarily. We're down to allowing about ten new people per day in as we've become a little more selective. As soon as we conclude, I'll send a full report."

"I think the challenge with letting new people in," Levi said, "is that we'll be seeing people who will tick off most of our entrance requirements, but they won't have any real skills that we'll need, right?"

Marshall raised his eyebrows a little. "Right. Good point, Levi. We could end up with a full roster of people that aren't bad, but also aren't what we need. Right now, I would love it if an entire conference of hydroponic gardeners or human waste engineers rolled up to the gate. We are desperately short on that." He narrowed his eyes at Levi and said, "You're looking for a job, right?"

"Sure am."

"We work well together, so let's team up on gate duty. I'll give you a list of what we really need and you can be the forward-facing person at the gate. We'll continue to have Janus run background checks, but I trust your gut."

"Living in Hollywood all my adult life, I'm used to spotting phonies," Levi confirmed.

"Good," Steele said. "That's settled. Next order of business is that it looks like three of us," here he indicated himself, Marshall, and Levi, "will be moving across to Altor soon. We'll still be available to help, of course, but there's no substitute for actually being here. Dani, it's obvious that you're going to step into this leadership role, but we'll need at least someone else that you can bounce things off of. Any ideas?"

Before Dani had a chance to answer, Levi cleared his throat and leaned forward.

"Yes?" Steele asked.

"I've just been thinking. About going over to Altor, I mean. I'm thinking I might just stay here."

"What?" Marshall asked, surprise evident in his voice. "Why?"

"That place over there is your thing, or at least yours and Quinn's. I never had anything to do with any of it, other than showing up at the last minute here. I feel like I'd be getting in because I'm friends with you guys. Let's be honest, like the decent people getting into Dust City, I'd be okay, I wouldn't do any harm, but I wouldn't bring a lot to the table, either."

Marshall opened his mouth to speak, but Levi continued.

"Everyone's been so kind to me here." He unconsciously ran a finger across his scarred face and lingered on his unseeing eye. "I'd like to kind of earn my way here. Besides, with the tunnel open, it's not like I'll be locked out for five years, is it?"

"Well, no," Marshall agreed. "That tunnel is a potential defensive liability for Altor, so it won't be opened very often, but I'm sure it will happen from time to time."

Levi flicked his eyes briefly at Dani, then said, "If it's all right, then, I'll just stay here for a while."

"I'd be glad to have you," Dani said, and neither Steele nor Marshall was going to disagree with her. "And maybe I just found my sounding board. I've been here a long time. You'll be able to relate better to the new arrivals and let me know what they're thinking."

Out of the ashes of The Shivers, a new team was forming.

* * *

Harper and Archer Wilkins and Van Hoffler were outside the safety of the fence line. Theoretically, it was more dangerous out in the desert, but the truth was, there hadn't been any wandering bands of marauders in the area for months. Most importantly, being a half mile away from Dust City, and with the wind blowing, Harper thought they could have a conversation without Janus overhearing.

"I'm happy to help," Van said, "but I think the invitation to come stay with Nyx was for you two, not me. I might put in an appearance, then head back here."

"That's fine," Harper said, "but you two got along fine when she was here. Unless you count all those times she threw you in self-defense training."

Van smiled. "I've been thrown before and I'm sure I'll be thrown again. There's a big difference between getting along fine and moving into somebody's house. You said she's got a whole family there. I'm not sure she needs me barging in."

"Let's see how it plays out then," Harper proposed. "I think once you get there, you're not going to want to leave. The way she described things made it sound pretty ideal."

Van waved his arm expansively at the dirt hills and desert in any direction. "What, and give up all this?" His expression grew serious, and he said, "This is all contingent on the fact that we are able to get away from this place. It seems like that damned machine that runs this place likes you. You have a plan?"

"I have a lot of plans," Harper said, "but none of them are likely to work against an all-seeing, all-knowing AI like Janus."

"Things are different, though, aren't they?" Archer asked.

When he asked a question, both Harper and Van had learned to pay attention.

"Different how?" his sister asked.

Archer shrugged. He relied on his intuition so much that sometimes it was difficult for him to put his feelings into words.

"Different because you worked so closely with Janus to get Dust City back up and running. Different because when I heard you talk to it, both of you seemed almost friendly."

Harper put an arm around Archer and quietly said, "I admit, I do kind of like it, but it's a machine that's way more complicated than any human."

"I think the only thing to do," Van said, "is to use the best of your plans and see how it reacts. What's the worst thing it could do, use its attack drones to kill us?"

"I don't know if that's the very worst thing," Archer said, "but it seems pretty bad."

Harper thought and said, "You're right. Let's go hunting for the next few days. We'll use your old pickup and we'll just go a little farther afield each day. I think if we can get out of the range of the drones, Janus won't be able to stop us."

They did just that. The next day they were able to bring down a mule deer buck and bring it back to be butchered. The following day, they had chances to shoot at a few jackrabbits, but from prior knowledge knew they were tough and sinewy. Dust City wasn't starving, so they let them go.

On the third day, they went farther toward the foothills than they had ever gone before. They didn't stick to any road, but instead drove slowly over the bumpy hardpan. When they ran into a spot where they had to turn north or south to avoid a climb up into the foothills, Van turned the truck off.

"Well? What do you say?"

"The drones don't usually fly this far out," Harper answered, "so unless Janus is specifically tracking us, we should be in the clear."

Van turned the key again and the engine sputtered to life. The gas in the tank was going bad, so they wouldn't get good mileage out of it, but it could get them away from Dust City. Under a tarp in the back they had put three backpacks. They knew they would have to make most of the trip on foot.

They had debated on the wisdom of starting out so early in the year, when the weather was unpredictable, but the need to be moving had made them decide to just pack up and go.

Van turned the wheel and bumped along the dirt, heading north.

* * *

Janus, which saw and heard even more than anyone suspected, had watched as they made their preparations. It had listened to their conversation in the desert and paid particular attention to what Archer had said about how Harper had grown to like the program.

That was a new concept for Janus.

It knew what it was—something the world had never seen before and truly wasn't prepared for. It had never considered the possibility that a human would honestly *like* it, however.

It had a drone high up, so high as to be nearly invisible from the ground.

It watched the pickup sit at the foothills, then turn north.

Janus could have stopped it in many different ways. It could have hovered a drone in front of it or used a laser to shoot out the truck's tires. It could have even used the lasers to trigger a small avalanche and damage the vehicle.

It did none of those things.

Instead, the drone hovered where it was, watching as the pickup drove away.

Goodbye, Harper. You were my first friend.

Chapter Twenty-Seven

Altor or Bust

The Prudent Twins made their way northeast across Central California.

Each step of their journey was unlikely, but it seemed nothing could stop it, not even The Shivers.

The twins did not discriminate against anyone who wanted to join their traveling road show. The only ticket needed for admission was a desire to join. There was no real pattern to those who left their old lives behind to throw in with this odd caravan. Husbands left wives, wives their husbands, and both parents and children abandoned their families.

The thing that they all had in common was that they weren't normally the type of person who would make such a rash decision. They all seemed to be compelled by some outside force.

Many of the new apostles of the Prudent Twins had specific sets of skills, including laborers, cooks, engineers, nurses, architects, and artists. None of them, however, put those skills to use during the journey. Instead, everyone focused on simply putting one foot in front of the other.

As fall turned to winter, as the weather turned from crisp to chilly to downright cold, the troupe moved on. In the first few months of their long march, they never took a day off, never rested.

Before long, their followers outnumbered the current population of most towns they passed through. They never threatened or stole, but somehow they were provided with enough sustenance to carry on.

They were on a mission from God and nothing could stop them, though The Shivers slowed them down for a few weeks.

Like Harper Wilkins, Armor and Faith Prudent seemed to have a natural immunity to the virus. The same was not true of their followers. The first time they passed through a town where The Shivers had already been, their acolytes fell to the virus.

Armor never hesitated, never lost faith.

"This is a plague," he said to his followers, "sent from God to separate those who will complete the journey with us from those who will stay behind. We will wait here, in this beautiful place, until knowing is full, then we will complete our mission."

This beautiful place was indeed lovely. It was a small community in the foothills that had been ravaged and almost completely deserted by the people who had once lived there.

Armor and Faith were normally distant from their followers. Emotionally, that is, if not physically. Brother and sister kept their own counsel and made a perfect group of two.

When people got the two versions of The Shivers, they finally began to interact with those who followed them. Armor took time to sit beside each person who had the fever. As the sick began to shiver and moan, he put a hand across their mouth and nose and helped them on to the other side.

Faith, who had grown up being of service to the older people in their cult, took more naturally to caring for those who caught the lesser version. At first, those who would survive feared that Armor would help them along in the same way he helped those who died. They shirked and shrank away from him each time he walked by.

They needn't have worried. Faith served as a barrier, though Armor several times mentioned that perhaps they should just be on their way, leaving the sick behind to follow as they were able.

Faith persuaded him that though God had directed them, they had not been told exactly *what* their mission might be. They knew the *where*, but not the *why*. It was possible that those who were driven to join them might serve some purpose on their journey.

"What," Faith asked, "would happen if we arrived alone and failed because we left a key person behind?"

Secretly, Armor believed that *he* was the only key person, but he could see the wisdom in his sister's words. Though it rankled him not to be walking, he waited until those who were going to die had done so and those who lived were finally strong enough to continue the journey.

When they arrived at the small, now-nameless town where The Shivers met the followers of the Prudent twins, there were more than five hundred people in their group. When they left to continue their journey, there were a hundred and fifty.

It didn't seem to matter.

As they continued on their way, they once again picked up people at every turn. Sometimes a person would be standing in the middle of nowhere, apparently waiting for them to show up.

"There you are," Armor would say.

"Here I am," the newest member of the Prudent Army would say, and they would fall in with the rest.

In the weeks and months that the group walked, no one ever asked, "Are we getting close?" or "Exactly where are we going?" No one ever changed their mind and tried to return to their old lives. The questioning part of their brains seemed to have been turned off.

On the day they crossed over the California border into Nevada, they stopped earlier than normal. Armor walked among the followers, touching each one like an old biblical prophet delivering a blessing.

"We are getting closer," he mumbled over and over to each one, a benediction of sorts.

Finally, dusty and road weary, the group—which now numbered almost a thousand people—lined up along the edge of a plateau and stared out toward the horizon.

Glistening in the late afternoon sun, Altor stood like an oasis in the middle of the desert.

"We'll stop here for the day," Armor said. There was a calm happiness about him, as though he was about to accomplish his life's work.

* * *

Far below the Prudent Army, a woman stood inside her berm house. She had lived alone there for more than thirty years.

Long before there had been a Rage War, or nuclear weapons falling on American soil, Laura Flanagan had planned for the apocalypse.

She had been downsized at her job at a computer chip manufacturing plant in 1999. The company had offered her a buyout, which she had gladly accepted. She hadn't been sure how much longer she would be able to live in the city and sell her soul eight hours at a time anyway.

She took that money and the rest of her savings and bought a chunk of land in the Nevada desert. She was at least fifty miles from the nearest town, and that was the way she liked it. As she built her berm house with her own two hands, she worked and planned how she could live with no help from anyone.

She studied solar energy, hydroponics, hunting and trapping the wildlife of the desert and came to believe she would be able to live in her home completely self-sufficiently. And she did, though she gave herself the best head start she could by stocking multiples of the things she wasn't sure she would be able to create herself.

Twenty years into her happy exile from civilization, the world had nearly found her once again. Helicopters began to fly overhead and to the east of her small house, heavy equipment began to arrive and dig.

Her footprint was not big and the construction was twenty miles away. The side of her home that faced the construction site looked like just another rolling hill in the desert. That allowed her to remain mostly hidden, as she liked it. Every few months, she climbed a hill and trained her binoculars on the incredible sight of Altor rising from the desert floor.

For more than a decade, she had watched the city from afar. She didn't bother them and they seemed completely unaware of her existence.

When society fell, it did not make any difference to her life. She had been expecting it and was only slightly surprised that it hadn't happened sooner.

Laura was in her early seventies now. She had seen much in her lifetime.

But even she was surprised at what she was looking at on the plateau to her west. What looked like hundreds of people lined up three and four deep, simply standing there as if in meditation.

She stepped closer to her window and swept her binoculars along the people massed on the edge of the plateau. She settled on an odd-looking couple in the middle. They were both dressed in black from head to toe, but that was offset by their completely white hair. On the man, it fell around his shoulders and almost to the ground. The woman's was braided and fell down her back.

"Jesus, Mary, and Joseph," Laura said quietly. "What kind of a freak show is this?"

She was intensely aware that if she could see them, they could see her as well, though all their attention seemed to be focused on Altor and not her.

She pushed a button that lowered the exterior blinds so the sun wouldn't glint off her windows and attract any unneeded attention if they hadn't already spotted her. She went around the house, double-checking her armament supply. It was always loaded and the safeties were off, but she felt better after double-checking.

Laura knew there were so many of them that if they wanted to make trouble for her, they could certainly overwhelm her. She also knew that she would show up on the other side with a whole passel of them accompanying her if they did.

She watched as the hundreds of people turned away from the edge. Minutes later, she could see them coming down the hillside, directly toward her.

They walked at a slow, steady pace that put Laura's nerves on edge. The two white-haired people walked at the head of the long column.

When the group reached her home, they moved quietly to the south side of her house and continued on, completely uninterested in her. Up close, she thought they all seemed a little like zombies, shuffling along in search of brains.

Chapter Twenty-Eight
Surface

The Armstrong twins didn't ride in the tunnel drilling machine at the same time. If something like the collapse were to happen again, they wanted one of them to be outside, where they could direct rescue operations. And if the worst happened, they wanted their parents to still have at least one son alive.

Neither Shaquem nor Shaquille understood all the changes that Tom had shown them over the previous few months. They knew that Tom was really the artificial intelligence that ran Altor and they had learned to just accept what it said and follow its directions.

The proof of what that accomplished was right in front of them. The readings on the boring machine showed that after months of digging a level path, they were moving upward, toward the surface, and had been for several days.

The boring machine had been operated around the clock since the cave-in and the readout always showed that the time to reach the surface was months away. Then it had been weeks. Then hours.

Today, that clock showed that they could break through the surface in less than half an hour.

Tom's friendly face appeared on the screen in front of them. "How's it going, fellas?"

The twins couldn't keep the smiles off their faces. "We're so close, Tom!" Shaquem said.

Tom looked down at a tablet in his hands, another affectation that Janus had started to use to look more human. "I see how close you are." Then he frowned. "I'm going to have to slow you down just a bit, though."

"No!" the twins said together. "Why?"

"As soon as you poke the nose of this machine into open air, we're creating a way into the tunnel for the first time since they closed the time lock." Since *they* closed the time lock was not accurate, since it had been Tom/Janus itself that had done so. "There is a small situation topside that needs to be dealt with before we push through."

The twins nodded together, understanding but unable to completely hide their disappointment.

"Don't worry," Tom said, "I'll make sure you two are in the machine when it happens. You've worked too hard for too long to let that action go to anyone else. But, for now, let's shut 'er down. It will be at least tomorrow before we finish up."

"Okay, Tom," Shaquille said. "While we wait, we'll make the last-minute arrangements with the surface team so they can jump straight up and begin constructing the opening as soon as we hit the surface."

"Roger and out," Tom said, then the face disappeared from the screen.

"Well shit," Shaquem said.

* * *

Quinn sat in his office, staring at the screen in front of him. It showed a mass of people walking straight toward the dome. Worse, it showed them walking right over the area where the tunnel boring machine was scheduled to break through.

"Janus? Is this something we need to worry about?"

"No," Janus said, his face popping up in one corner of the screen. The face looked a little older than it had the last time Quinn had seen it. There were laugh lines around the mouth and the beginnings of crow's feet at the corner of each eye. "That is nothing to worry about. That is a special delivery of sorts for Dust City."

Quinn cocked his head like a dog hearing a faraway whistle. "Pardon?"

The face Janus showed looked a little smug. "This is the fruition of a plan I've been working on for some time. Dust City has been damaged by the virus that people call The Shivers. They need reinforcements. These are them."

"And there was a group of hundreds of people just wandering around in the desert like Moses was leading them to the promised land? And now they're going to Dust City?"

"Of course not," Janus answered. "I have brought them a great distance over a long period of time."

"As usual, I feel four steps behind you. Dust City was just hit by this virus in the last month. But you've had this group of people heading toward us for months?"

For a moment, Janus's human face wavered and the classic face of the god of doors appeared, one face looking forward and the other backward.

"Right. You are the precognition machine, aren't you? Have you gotten your ability back to see into the future?"

"It's something I've been working on," Janus answered, a little too coy for Quinn's liking. "I am not as blind as I was when civilization fell. I have managed to create a network among all the satellites that are still working, and that is giving me much information to parse."

"Thanks for letting me know."

"You're welcome," Janus answered, completely missing Quinn's sarcasm, or at least pretending to. "Let's bring Marshall and Steele into the conversation." Without waiting to find out whether Quinn thought that was a good idea or not, the faces of the two men popped up on the screen. "Good afternoon, Marshall, General."

"Afternoon," Marshall answered. "Something big going on?"

"Janus says he has reinforcements on the way for you."

The way that Marshall looked to his left and Steele to his right told Quinn that they were sitting together in the same room in Dust City.

"Thank you," Marshall answered. He left the question of *how*, exactly, Janus had arranged for that unasked.

"Of course," Janus answered. "I've done my best to look after you there since I was forced to close the time lock with you outside. Now, everything is coming together. I've got new workers for Dust City and we will be breaking through with the tunnel tomorrow. It will take us a few days to create the entry to the tunnel, then we can bring you over. In the interim, you can begin to acclimatize the new arrivals to life in Dust City."

* * *

Armor and Faith Prudent led their followers down from the plateau and marched toward Altor. With their goal finally in sight, they picked up the pace. When they passed by the berm house with a woman standing armed behind her locked door, they never even noticed.

They arrived at Altor just as the sun was setting in the west. That bathed the dome in golden light and made it appear even more ethereal than normal.

A slight wind blew Armor's long white hair out behind him and his face seemed to glow with an inner light. He muttered, "We have arrived, we have arrived," to himself over and over.

When they reached the dome itself, the followers spread out and stood two or three deep around an entire section of Altor. It was a passing strange sight, the high-tech dome surrounded by the road-weary travelers.

Inside the dome, a crowd had gathered as well, as the citizens of Altor looked out at the bedraggled mob that had gathered to stare at them like animals in a zoo. "Where did they come from?" one Altorian asked. "What do they want?" another wondered. Finally, "Are they dangerous? There's no way they can get in, is there?"

The two groups stared at each other, separated only by the glistening, impenetrable glass.

"We are here, Lord," Armor intoned, raising his arms in a benediction. "We are here. You have sent for us, and we are here."

Overhead, a miracle of sorts happened. A figure appeared on top of the dome.

To Armor and Faith, it appeared to be God Himself, come to the Nevada desert to direct his followers. The figure was fifteen feet high, with a beard as long and white as the Prudent twins' hair. The face looked remarkably like the one Janus had been developing over the previous months, with perhaps a more noble visage. The image was dressed in long flowing robes which shimmered and seemed to change color constantly, from the deep blue of the sky to the pale reflection of moonlight on snow.

The figure hovered over the dome and when it spoke, the voice was not sound, but pictures, images, and emotions that appeared in the minds of those below.

"You have come," the voice conveyed, "but this is not the place where you will serve me." The figure pointed a finger to the east, looking like Michelangelo's painting of God pointing at Adam. "There is much work for you to do, and I direct you there. They wait for you, they will welcome you, for you are my children."

As one, the Prudent Twins and all their followers turned toward Dust City.

When they looked back, the figure of God was gone.

"That is the voice I have heard lo these many months," Armor said. "Now God has spoken to all of us instead of me alone." He nodded fervently, then turned toward Dust City.

The followers, looking as dazed as ever, followed.

* * *

Quinn, Marshall, and Steele watched the show as it played out.

As the mob shuffled toward Dust City, Janus's face appeared on their screens once again. Initially, it appeared like the face of God that had hovered over the dome, but it slowly relaxed into what had become the normal face of Janus. A small smile played on its lips.

"You should prepare for the arrival. I have chosen each of the people for what they can bring to Dust City."

"Like what?" Marshall asked, still gobsmacked by what he had just witnessed.

"I have taken a full inventory of who died from the virus," Janus answered. "These people will be their replacements. You said you needed certain skills, hydroponic gardeners and human waste engineers recently. You will find those skills and others that you need in this group."

"What about the weirdo who looks like Moses on steroids and his wife?" Quinn asked. "What special skills are they bringing?"

"Sister," Janus answered. "The woman is his sister. Their special skill was to bring everyone together and walk a thousand miles to get here. They won't be any trouble to anyone. If I tell them to wander off into the desert, they will do that. They're quite malleable."

"Their followers look like zombies," Steele observed.

"I will loosen the suggestions I have planted in their minds over time. They will become more autonomous as I do."

"How did you do all this?" Quinn asked.

"Since Altor opened, I have been experimenting with many different sciences. This one is really relatively simple."

Through their screens, Quinn met Marshall's eyes.

Janus properly interpreted that look. "You humans," Janus answered dismissively. "Your first concern is always yourselves. I will tell you that I have not used this technique on any of you, or anyone in Altor or Dust City."

"But you could, if you wished," Steele said.

"Of course."

The same thought occurred to all three men at once. They had been worried about whether they were talking to each other or a fake version that was actually Janus. Now, they would need to be concerned about whether their minds were being controlled.

* * *

The next day, the Armstrong twins finally broke through from the tunnel to the surface. As soon as the boring machine reached open air, they reversed it back down.

Immediately, a swarm of workers and mechanical techs poured up through the opening, widening it and beginning to build the entrance.

Shaquem and Shaquille parked the boring machine and hustled up the slope to see daylight for the first time. Shaquem grabbed his tablet, tapped a few buttons and waited impatiently with a big grin on his face.

A few seconds later, Nia Armstrong's face appeared on the screen.

"Mom, look!" Shaquem held the tablet pointed away and showed the desert landscape bathed in the sun.

"Deon! Deon! They made it!"

Deon appeared alongside Nia, a wide grin splitting his face. "Can't wait to see you boys. I'm so proud of you."

"See them? I've been seeing them ever since we got here. I want to *hold* them!"

"Won't be long, Mom. We've got to oversee the construction of the entrance so it's not a danger to the dome, then we're coming to get you!"

Chapter Twenty-Nine
The Perilous Journey

Harper held her breath as the truck drove away from Dust City. She knew it was her imagination, but she felt a tingling in the back of her head as though Janus was still watching her.

Van looked at her and grinned. "Still worried, huh?"

"Janus was pretty careful not to show me how powerful it really is, but the more I think of it, the more I believe it can do almost anything."

Archer looked out the window as the truck bounced across the desert landscape. "But here we are anyway!"

"If we're here," Harper said, "it's because Janus decided to let us go."

"Either way, it doesn't matter, does it?" Van asked. "We're gone."

The three of them turned their attention to what they could see through the front windshield, which was endless miles of the same bumpy, dirty hardscrabble.

"What do you think?" Harper asked. "Stick to the dirt or try for the highway?"

"The last time I left Dust City, there were still a lot of highwaymen staking out spots. I have a hunch that's going to be better now. That speaks in favor of the roads."

"But it only takes one setup to catch us in their net, right?" Archer asked. "Then it's game over, man." This was his favorite quote from Bill Paxton in the old Aliens movie.

"It's a choice between safe and slow, or a little riskier, but much faster," Harper said.

Van looked at her out of the corner of his eye. "What say you, genius?"

"I say you've gotta stop calling me genius," Harper answered with an elbow to Van's ribs. "Let's drive parallel to the road at a safe distance for a time, then I'll deploy the little drone."

The little drone was a mostly dumb drone that Archer had built out of spare parts. It didn't have any defensive capabilities, but it had a good camera and he'd even managed to install night vision in it. If nothing else, it would allow them to scout ahead a few miles.

All three were armed, of course. The landscape of America had changed in the eighteen months since the fall of civilization. It was safer than it had once been. There was still no law and order, though, and whoever was behind the trigger of the gun typically made the rules.

All three knew that if they found themselves in a shootout, they were probably in trouble, so their idea was to simply avoid trouble as much as they could.

To that end, they eventually wanted to travel under cover of darkness as much as possible. It was still technically winter, though, which complicated things. As long as they were in Van's old pickup, they at least had a place to shelter, but they knew they would have to abandon it sooner rather than later.

On this first day, they rambled along through the empty desert for mile after mile. Each passing hour made them feel a little better about their separation from Dust City, and more specifically, Janus.

When they had covered seventy miles, darkness settled in.

Van let the truck slow to a stop, then said, "I don't like the idea of driving during the night. It's so rough, the headlights bounce and I might miss something. If we end up in an old wash, I don't think AAA is going to come pull us out."

Neither Harper nor Archer had any idea what AAA was, but they were used to Van making references that they didn't understand.

Archer climbed out of the cab of the truck and peed.

"Nice to be a boy," Harper said. She walked a distance away, found a boulder, went behind it and hunkered down to pee.

When she stood and zipped her jeans up, she looked to the west. The sunset was spectacular that night, with reds and oranges smeared across the sky in a kaleidoscope of color. For a moment, she stood, not thinking of anything except that even in this messed up version of the world, there was still beauty.

When she got back to the truck, they were unpacked for the night. They had brought food with them and they dug into the most perishable stuff first. The jerky and canned goods would keep forever, so they enjoyed peanut butter and jelly sandwiches while the bread was still good.

By the time they finished eating, twilight had settled in.

Van shifted into a comfortable position. "You guys go ahead and sack out. I don't think anyone's going to bother us clear out here, but I'll keep an eye out for a bit anyway."

Ten minutes later, Archer, worn out by the excitement of the day, was asleep on Harper's shoulder. Before an hour had passed, Harper and Van were out too.

Van was the first to wake in the morning, and he woke Harper when he opened the door. "Knew I should have WD-40-ed that hinge before we left. Sorry."

Harper shook her head sleepily. "Time to get going, right?"

"Yep. Hope there's a Starbucks somewhere up ahead. I could use the caffeine."

Van intended it as a joke, but it hit Harper hard. She remembered that less than two years earlier, her mom would often hit the Starbucks drive through for the three of them on the way to school. It was mostly a happy memory, until she thought of her mom and dad buried under a pile of rocks at their cabin.

She rallied her thoughts back to the present moment. "If you see one, I'll take an iced caramel latte."

"You kids and your fancy drinks. I'd just put an IV straight into my arm for the caffeine if I could."

They kept the same pattern for the next three days, sticking to off-roading, driving during the day, stopping when it got dark. They made good progress, and at the end of the four days, the odometer on the truck showed they had covered over two hundred miles.

They had been forced onto roads for parts of each day as they went up and over various mountain passes. Each time they did, Archer deployed his scout drone and looked at the road ahead. There were often crashes that at least partially blocked the roads, but nothing they couldn't work their way around.

That easy progress stopped at the end of that fourth day on the road. They had just come up over a rise and a large body of water was visible in the distance.

"The Great Salt Lake," Archer said, pointing a finger at the old paper atlas. "Pretty cool."

The truck had been running rough since they had left Dust City, but now it shook and rattled in a way that told them they'd reached the end of the line.

A moment later, the engine died. "That's all she wrote," Van said. "It's late enough, we might as well stay here tonight. We're on foot from here on out."

"We actually made it farther than I thought we would before the truck gave out," Harper said.

"This old girl has the heart of a lion," Van said, fondly patting the dashboard. He looked at where they were, then said, "We're pretty high up here. I'm going to put her in neutral and give her a little push. That might get us a little more distance."

With the truck in neutral, it didn't take much of a push from Van to get it rolling. They were able to coast down the road for more than a mile until they started to slow. Eventually, Van pointed the truck off the road and that slowed them more quickly. Still they made it a few hundred yards off before they came to a standstill.

Abandoned vehicles were beyond common, so one more old pickup was unlikely to attract much attention.

As they settled in for one last night in the truck, Harper said, "How much farther to get to Nyx do you think?"

Archer held up his thumb and forefinger with about two inches between them. "Not too far," he said with a grin. "Actually, about three hundred miles. Maybe a little more."

"Well, we knew this was where we were going to be when we started, right?" Van asked. "Even if we only do ten miles a day, we can probably be there in a little over a month. That's not too bad."

"Unless we can find another vehicle that will start," Harper said. "What are the chances of that?"

"At this point, somewhere between slim and none, I'd say. Anything easy got picked off in the early days. Anything that would run has probably been stolen, driven hard, then stolen again. Plus, the gas is all going bad. We were really lucky to get as far as we did on that last tank of gas."

"So a hike it is, then," Harper agreed. "We'll be okay."

Van sensed she was saying this to reassure herself more than anything. "We've done everything we can to get ready. We've got a tent and sleeping bags and camp equipment. I've got my rifle, so we can maybe grab some protein in the wild. I've noticed there's more wildlife now than there was before."

It was cold in the foothills and they were all stiff when they woke up the next morning, though a few minutes of walking warmed them up.

They hoped to be able to average fifteen miles per day but weren't able to hit that number.

Some days, when their path was level and the walking was easy, they made a little more than that.

On many days, though, the terrain was broken and difficult. Each time they came to a new mountain range or series of foothills, they consulted their map, found the nearest road, and walked to it. That was often the only obvious way up and over.

The weather was also a determining factor. Twice, they encountered snow storms that drove them to look for a place where they could hole up for a time. Once, that was in a cabin that had been stripped of everything that could be taken but still offered some protection from the elements. The other time, they were forced into a cave in a hill. No matter how big a fire they built, they couldn't drive the chill from that place, but it allowed them to stay put until the storm passed.

They kept a lookout for vehicles that might still be running over the first few days, but Van's assessment soon proved accurate. Everything they came to, whether a newer SUV or an old Toyota, was no longer running, even if the keys were in it. After thirty or forty disappointments, they abandoned the idea altogether and resolved just to walk.

After a few weeks, they left the dry desert land behind and climbed up into extensive forest. That was good for hunting and made it easier to find shelter, though the temperature often dropped precipitously overnight.

Whenever possible, they stayed off any main roads. Van was aware that as special as Harper and Archer were, they were still too young to be of any real use in a confrontation.

The population of this part of the country wasn't dense even before the Rage Wars. The one-two punch of the violence of the after times combined with the deadly sweep of The Shivers meant that they could go for days at a time without seeing any real sign of humanity at all. When they did run into people everyone seemed to just want to be left alone.

Their luck in this regard held, until it didn't.

A few days after they had crossed over into what had once been Eastern Colorado, they were forced by the lay of the land onto a road. They passed several massive pileups of trucks and cars and skirted around them carefully.

Archer sent his solar-powered drone into the sky ahead of them time and again, with no evident danger ahead.

They crossed a peak and passed a sign that proclaimed they were at *Highover Pass, Elevation 4,827 feet.*

The road stretched out straight in front of them and all three were glad for the easy decline in elevation ahead. It was late afternoon, and they were beginning to look for a good place to set up camp for the night.

Perhaps that was why they weren't as attentive as they normally were. Or maybe it was that natural human letdown. After looking for danger for weeks on end and not finding any, it was easy to become complacent.

No matter the reason, it was true.

They skirted around another accident, which this time included a semi-truck and long trailer.

As they walked past it, Van's rifle hung loose in his left hand. All three of their pistols were tucked into their packs.

They were no more than ten yards past the pileup when a harsh voice called out from behind them.

"Hold on there, not so fast."

Van, Harper, and Archer all froze.

"Go on ahead and drop that rifle. We've got you covered with four guns and if you make a move, we'll take you out."

Van closed his eyes, cussing himself for letting his guard down. He knelt and placed the rifle on the ground. All three turned around slowly with their hands in the air.

There were indeed four men standing inside the open trailer. Judging by the canteens and dishes scattered around their feet, they had been there for some time. Three of the men had rifles pointed directly at the travelers. The man who had spoken was holding a shotgun.

"Listen," Van said, "we've got a few supplies in our packs. Why don't you take that and let us go?"

"It's not the supplies we're interested in. We want the three of you."

Chapter Thirty
The Ballad of Tokin Ming-Sa

Long before the poor rose up against the rich, before The Fifteen dropped bombs across America, Tokin Ming-Sa was born. He dropped into this world on January 22, 1989, in St. Luke's Hospital in Kansas City, Missouri.

Much attention was paid to a sporting event that day, as the San Francisco 49ers defeated the Cincinnati Bengals by a score of twenty to sixteen.

Very little attention was given to the arrival of a healthy baby boy who weighed six pounds, thirteen ounces. His mother had been born in Japan, his father in Vietnam. They were both small in stature—his mother only five feet tall and his father five inches taller.

He was born into obscurity, but would live, in one fashion or another, for many centuries.

His parents died when he was a young man and he became rootless, a drifter who wandered from town to town, country to country.

He didn't have any schooling after he graduated from high school, but in each town he visited, he spent a day or two in the local library, studying the history of the area and reading, always reading.

He never had a steady job, but from time to time, he would work as a gardener, or dishwasher, or picking whatever crop was growing in the area. When he had enough money to sustain himself for a few weeks or months, he moved on.

He didn't travel by air, or train, or even by bus. When he was ready to see what was over the next horizon, he slung his small pack over his back and walked. He never tried to ride his thumb, but if someone pulled over and offered him a ride, he accepted.

He had virtually no permanent possessions and nothing held him down. He traveled in this manner for twenty-five years. The way he looked often made people think he was wise, or religious, or a seeker of truth. His own truth, though, was that he always remained curious about what the next town might hold.

When chaos enveloped North America in what was called the Rage Wars, he was mostly unaware. At that time, he was living alone in a long-deserted cabin he had found on the north-east side of Vancouver Island in Western Canada.

The cabin wasn't much and hadn't been for many years. It did have four walls, a floor, and most of a roof, though, so it did offer some shelter.

He was quite happy there. He had absolutely no contact with the outside world. In a time when nearly every person carried a smartphone that was constantly connected to the Internet, Tokin was completely cut off.

He thought he might like to stay in this one-room cabin for some time, perhaps a year or two, though he knew that would be difficult. The only food he had with him was the small amount he had carried in on his back. He had become knowledgeable about what could be foraged and eaten from the forest that surrounded him, but he knew that when winter approached, there wouldn't be enough to sustain him.

So, he resolved to stay until he was hungry, then he would walk back into a tiny town that was perhaps twenty-five miles away and see if he could find temporary employment. If not, he would simply walk until he did.

Having resolved that in his mind, he was sitting quite happily on the dirt and grass in a clearing a few hundred yards from the cabin. A slow-moving stream babbled softly nearby. He considered following it for a few miles to see where it led, but the warm sun made him sleepy.

He was about to surrender to the inevitability of an afternoon nap when he was brought out of his reverie by the breaking of a twig.

He stayed where he was. It was always possible that it was some local wildlife. Perhaps even a black bear. That didn't concern him much. The animals in the area weren't aggressive and tended to leave him alone once they spotted him.

Still, it was enough to make him look around. His eyes widened in surprise when he saw a woman standing in front of him. He would have guessed that there were no other humans within a dozen miles of him. She was not dressed for hiking, either. She wore a white shirt covered by a light jacket, black pants and boots that didn't appear to be ideal for a walk in the woods.

"We've got to stop meeting like this," Tokin ventured as an opening salvo.

Another person might have been put off by such a non-sequitur, but this woman was not. She shook her head slightly to shoo away a mosquito that was circling her. Her face remained expressionless.

"Tokin Ming-Sa?"

That managed to get a reaction from even the unflappable Tokin. He squinted one eye at her and said, "I'm sure there is a story behind how you came to find me and how you could possibly know I was here. I would have said there was no one on the planet who knew where I was."

"We are never as alone as we would like to think we are," the woman said.

This was the kind of sentiment that Tokin himself often shared, and he nodded his head agreeably.

"I am Stant," the woman said. "I'm a recruiter and I have been sent to offer you safety."

Tokin smiled. "I already feel safe. Look around us. There is nothing that wishes us harm."

Now it was Stant's turn to look suspicious. "Do you not know what's happening in the world?"

"I do my very best to never know what's going on in the world. If I knew, what could I do about it? That knowledge might disturb my inner harmony, but that is all."

"There has been civil unrest."

"There is always civil unrest somewhere, isn't there?"

"This is to an extreme," Stant said. "Nuclear weapons have been deployed across America. Soon, gangs of mercenaries and militias will be taking cities and towns. Nowhere will be safe, even here."

Tokin considered that for a moment. He knew it would need to be a truly major upheaval to send people far enough from the cities into an area like this. Still, it was possible.

"Is the entire infrastructure of the news industry destroyed?" Tokin asked with a small smile. "Are they reduced to sending their reporters out to find each individual and recount the news of the day?"

Stant blinked, then looked at her phone as if wondering why she had come so far for someone so ridiculous. "I've been authorized to offer you a spot in a community that will be safe."

"Where is it?"

"I'm not authorized to reveal that, but if you come with me, I will take you there."

"What *can* you tell me about this place you want to take me?"

"A man has built a safe place in the desert. It might be the only safe place in the United States over the next few years."

Tokin was not overly moved by the idea of safety. He had wandered for many years and had never had a bad experience or had violence visited upon his person. The blowing winds of misfortune always seemed to part before they reached him.

But the idea of a special community built in the desert *did* interest him. That was something he would like to be a part of.

"You're not going to tell me how you knew where I was, even though it is impossible that you would know that, are you?"

"Correct."

"And you're not going to tell me any more about this place in the desert, are you?"

"Glad to see we understand each other. Now, I don't mean to rush your decision, but I have many other people to see before I can rest. You're under no obligation to go with me. If you tell me to leave, you'll never see me again."

For reasons he couldn't have explained, that freedom of choice appealed to Tokin too. "Can we return to where I've been sleeping so I can retrieve my backpack?"

"Each person will enter their new home wearing only the clothes they have on."

"Then we should go, so I don't waste any more of your time."

Stant's eyebrows rose slightly. Tokin could see that she had not expected him to go with her.

They hiked to a larger clearing, where a helicopter sat. A pilot was standing beside it, waiting for them. Inside, there were two other people. The pilot indicated that Tokin should sit next to them.

A minute later, they took off and flew toward Vancouver. They didn't land at Vancouver International Airport, but they did fly over it. The runways were a tangle of wrecked jets and smaller planes, as though there had been a destruction derby using planes instead of cars.

Black smoke rose in dozens of places in the once-shining city. Stant looked back at him, a glance that said, *I guess you now know I'm not bullshitting you.*

They landed to refuel at a small private airport in Eastern Washington. As soon as they touched down, Stant said, "Stay in your seats. We won't be here any longer than we have to be." She slung a rifle over her shoulder and stood guard as the pilot filled the tank with QAV.

There were people milling around a building a hundred yards away. After a few minutes, eight of them broke off from the rest and began to walk toward the helicopter.

"Full or not, it's time to go," Stant said.

The pilot agreed, because he dropped the hose on the ground and scrambled to get back in the chopper.

Before the small group could reach them, they were back in the air.

Tokin looked at the two people beside him, attempting to smile reassuringly, as they both looked scared out of their wits.

"I am Tokin Ming-Sa," he said, trying to distract them.

"Elliott Cambridge," the man to his right said.

"Stella Maris," the woman on the far side of the seat answered. "Pleased to meet you." She leaned across Elliott and whispered, "Do you know anything about all this?"

Tokin shook his head but continued to smile. "Life is an adventure, is it not?" He considered asking more questions of his seatmates, but the whir of the blades and the whine of the engines made conversations difficult. Instead, he leaned back in his seat and soon found that peaceful part of his inner self. In moments, he was essentially back in that same space he had been sitting in the forest.

He didn't open his eyes again until he heard the helicopter power down. When he looked out his window, he saw only the vast openness of desert and rolling hills. To his right, though, was a dome that was so large he could only see one small section of it.

He had arrived at Altor.

Chapter Thirty-One
The Ballad of Tokin Ming-Sa Redux

That moment, sitting less than a quarter mile from the domed city with the chopper blades still slowly winding down, was the first time he heard the voice.

It was so crystal clear that he thought everyone must be hearing it.

"Welcome, Tokin," the voice said, and Tokin wondered why it didn't mention Elliott and Stella as well. When he looked at them, though, they both were intent on simply getting out of the helicopter and returning their feet to solid ground as quickly as possible.

"Thank you," Tokin said.

Elliott looked over his shoulder wonderingly, but Tokin just shook his head to tell him that he wasn't speaking to him.

"You don't need to speak out loud for me to hear you. I can hear your thoughts."

Tokin nearly made a joke about feeling sorry for whoever was listening in on his thoughts but didn't. For a moment, he wondered if this was the beginning of insanity. Literally, hearing voices in his head. Then he wondered if maybe Elliott and Stella were hearing the voice too but were ignoring it or keeping it to themselves. Tokin quieted his mind and followed them out of the helicopter, where Stant was waiting for them.

Now that he was outside and could look up, he saw the true immensity of the dome for the first time. He looked to the left and right of it. Somehow it felt like it should be one part of a massive, modern city, but it stood alone. Far to the east, he could see a few small buildings and piles of equipment, but that didn't look like it belonged on the same planet as this dome.

Stant pointed to the entrance of the dome, which was not far. "Hurry along inside. We've received word that they might be closing the dome earlier than expected. If that happens, you don't want to be on the outside."

Just then, a dark SUV drove out of the dome. Even in the heat of the day, the rear passenger windows were down. Tokin could see two people in the back seat—a red-faced man with a steel-gray crewcut and a much younger man who looked more the computer nerd type. As they roared by, the windows rolled up to block out the heat and dust.

Stant and the pilot got back in the helicopter, lifted off, then stopped briefly in the collection of buildings to the east to refuel before leaving for points unknown.

"It's so damned hot," Elliott said, pulling at his collar. "I hope it's not this hot in that dome."

A young woman was running toward them and heard what Elliott said. "It's always a perfect seventy degrees inside the dome. Unless you want it warmer or cooler in your own quarters, of course." She had short brown hair, a trim physique, and a welcoming smile. "Welcome to Altor, I'm Sandy. I've been charged with getting you to your orientation meeting. Are you hungry? I can drop you off at a cafeteria to get something to eat and you can catch the next orientation if you want. We'll be running sessions all day."

A huge semi loaded with oversized crates rumbled along the road beside them as another big truck left the dome. Behind them, another helicopter landed.

"It seems chaotic here," Stella said.

"Follow me, and I'll answer your questions as we go." She glanced behind them at the new arrivals in the newly arrived helicopter. "It's been a little chaotic here for the past few years. The engineers said it would take twenty years to get the dome built. Quinn Starkweather got it done in ten. But you can't make an omelet as big as Altor without breaking a few eggs." She slowed slightly to let her three charges draw closer. "And today is special. There's a rumor that they might close the dome today."

"Is that a big deal?" Elliott asked. "Open it, close it, whatever. Haven't they sealed it before?"

"Oh, yes, it's been closed before, but the rumor is that today the time lock will be engaged."

"Time lock?" Elliot asked, coming to a full stop. "Time lock for how long?"

Sandy shrugged, but said, "Nobody knows. Lots of guesses, of course. There are always rumors, but the only people who know are Quinn, Marshall, and The General. You might have seen Marshall and the General just now as they headed over to Dust City. They're bigwigs around here. The fact that they're leaving tells me they won't be closing the dome up quite yet. Don't want *them* to be stuck outside."

The name *Dust City* made Tokin smile a little. Looking at the gritty desert and the camouflage tents and temporary buildings, he thought it was perfectly appropriate.

As soon as they passed through the entrance, the temperature did indeed drop to a very comfortable level. Sandy tapped a bracelet on her wrist and said, "Elliott and Stella, you stay with me and I'll lead you to your orientation." She turned to Tokin and said, "You're due for a special orientation."

Stella and Elliott looked at Tokin with new eyes. To that point, they had thought they were likely higher than he was in whatever the food chain would be in Altor. It might have been his diminutive size or his worn and ratty clothing that had led them to dismiss him.

Sandy handed a bracelet identical to the one she wore to Tokin. "This has been specially designed for you. I'm sure they'll tell you all about it at your orientation. Just tap it and it will show you the correct path to follow."

"Thank you, Sandy," Tokin said, nodding his appreciation. He put the bracelet on and tapped it, but nothing happened. He opened his mouth to call after Sandy, but the voice in his head reappeared.

"Don't worry. You won't need a map. I will guide you. Go straight ahead, then turn left at the path. Soon you'll see a building. The sign in front will read *Atwood Building.* Go inside and into the elevator. I will take you to where you need to go."

You are an elevator? Tokin thought.

He meant it as a small joke, but the voice that responded was serious. "I am everything in Altor. I *am* Altor. You can call me Janus."

That name triggered an image in Tokin's head. He thought, *Can you see both the past and the future?*

"I can. If I couldn't, there would be no dome for you to stand in."

For the briefest of moments, he remembered what Sandy had said, that Quinn Starkweather was the man responsible for the dome.

"Quinn and I are partners of a sort," Janus said in answer to that fleeting thought. "He is the name that everyone knows. I am the one that very few are aware of. Just you and a few others."

Are you human? Tokin asked in his head.

"I am Janus."

Tokin used his years of meditation training to block stray thoughts from coming into his head.

"That's very good," Janus said. "This is part of why I chose you."

Tokin turned into the tall building that rose toward the peak of the dome and walked through the lobby. An elevator to his left opened its door. When he stepped in, the elevator immediately rose. At the fifteenth floor, the doors silently opened.

"Go to your right, then take the first left. When you get to the proper place, the door will open for you."

Tokin did as instructed and walked down a long hall until a door on his left opened. He stepped into a small entrance hall. There was a closet and a kitchen to his right, a living room straight ahead, and a bedroom and bathroom off to his left.

He noticed that there were no windows and wondered if it would begin to feel claustrophobic.

"It need never feel that way," the voice in his head answered. At once, the entire wall turned into a screen that displayed a view of the desert outside of Altor. In an instant, it switched to the view from the top of the Portland Head Light in Maine, looking out over the Atlantic. A moment later, it showed a magnificent cabin in the Alaskan wilderness. "If there's anything in particular you would like to have as a view, just think about it and it will appear."

Tokin immediately thought of the view from his bedroom window as a child.

A split-second later, that view appeared on his wall, right down to the old tire swing that hung from a branch of an oak tree in the backyard. That should have been impossible, of course. He didn't believe there were even any photos of that scene, except in his mind.

Tokin wanted to take a moment to wonder why such a powerful entity would spend this much time with him and cater to him on top of that, but he instantly blocked that thought. He realized that he was going to have to spend much of his conscious energy *not* thinking at all.

Janus picked up on even that minor thought.

"There is no need to guard your mind from me. I encourage you to think whatever you'd like. There are no negative repercussions from me. We will have a partnership."

Tokin did his best to smile at Janus with his mind, then wondered if Janus could perceive his emotions that way.

"I can," Janus said simply. "Do not worry. I will not always be conversing with you. Only when necessary or when you need me."

Tokin felt an odd, semi-unpleasant sensation in his brain—almost as though a cosmic door had been opened and something had left. He waggled his eyebrows and thought, *Are you there?* but there was no response.

Tokin walked around his apartment, familiarizing himself with what was there. In the kitchen, there was plenty of fresh fruit and vegetables and pans and a wok to cook with. When he walked into the bedroom, a strange thing happened. A closet door popped open as he passed it.

Inside, instead of the selection of pants and shirts that he expected to find, there were five identical orange robes hanging there. He cocked his head, trying to solve that mystery, but failing. He thought the robes looked kind of itchy and scratchy, but when he touched the fabric, it was soft and luxurious. At the bottom of the closet, there were two identical pairs of sandals.

"Is it cosplay day? Am I to go out in public dressed as a monk?" He expected Janus to pop back into his head and answer, but there was only his voice. He shrugged, removed the soiled clothes he had been wearing in the woods of British Columbia, and slipped the orange robe on. He put his clothes in a garbage can in the bathroom. The bottom of the can opened, and they disappeared with a *whoosh.*

He never would have believed it, but everything about putting the robe on felt right. Not just the fit, or the length, but the whole vibe. As soon as he put it on, it didn't feel like a costume. It felt like part of him.

He wandered into the living room and an announcement played from the screen on the wall. "There will be a concert tonight in the city center." An image of an orchestra showed on the screen.

"Sure," Tokin said. "Take me there."

The bracelet he wore suddenly came to life. A hologram emerged, showing directions from the front door of his building.

He followed those directions, marveling at what he saw in the dome. It was an entire city, but it was unlike anything he'd ever come across, and he had seen much of the world.

He enjoyed the concert and made what seemed like new friends, two women named Jazz and Taryn.

They found that they lived in the same building and walked back together. Tokin suspected that the two women had more in common with each other than they did with him and went back to his apartment.

Once in his apartment—which he was able to find with no instruction from his wristband—he saw that the view of his childhood backyard was still showing.

He sat on the couch, lost for a time in the nostalgia of the scene.

Finally, he thought, *Janus are you there?*

There was no answer. Tokin felt completely alone in his own mind. He let his thoughts wander. He reviewed the whirlwind of activity in the last twenty-four hours. How he had gone from planning to stay in the remote cabin in the woods to not only being whisked to this high-tech city, but also how this new intelligence had begun communicating directly with him.

He had always been one to follow his instincts and to accept opportunities where they were presented.

Everything—the robes, the voice, the view of his childhood home—suddenly felt completely wrong.

"Change view," he said, without specifying what to change it to.

The wall transformed into a lovely but generic shot of ocean waves lapping against sand.

Tokin stood and pulled the robe over his head, dropping it on the floor.

Again, he thought: *Are you there?* Again, there was no answer.

He let his thoughts run free as he considered how to proceed from this spot. He wondered if there was some sort of ombudsman he could talk to, to see if he could somehow report the voice in his head and make it stop. Failing that, he began to think of alternatives.

Perhaps alcohol—which Tokin had rarely consumed—could quiet the voice.

Silently, in one corner of his mind, Janus listened to all these thoughts.

Chapter Thirty-Two
Captured

The man who leveled the shotgun at Van, Harper, and Archer seemed to be the man in charge. Without taking his eyes off their captives, he said, "Bronson, radio Gentry and tell him we've got three new volunteers."

One of the men holding the rifles leaned it against the inside wall of the trailer and pulled a walkie-talkie off his belt. "You got it, Jimbo." He pushed a button and said, "Base, this is Eagle. Send somebody to collect three more people."

Jimbo seemed to look more carefully at the prey they had caught in their trap. "Tell him that two of them are pretty small, so they'll only need two horses to bring them in. They can double up."

"Roger," Bronson said and radioed that ahead.

Jimbo hopped down from the back of the trailer. He was tall and perhaps had once been heavy-set. Like almost everyone in the after time, any extra weight he had carried was gone. He appeared to be in his early forties and was dressed warmly in jeans, a flannel shirt, and a Carhartt coat. He made sure to keep his distance from Van.

"Kick that rifle over here where I can get it."

Van did, and Jimbo picked it up. "Now, let's not play games with each other. I know all three of you have other guns on you, and probably some knives, too. Let's play this straight, then. Verrrry carefully, take those guns out with two fingers, then do the same with the knives. Once you've dropped everything and kicked it over to me, I'm gonna have one of my men frisk you. If they find a weapon that you didn't tell us about, I'm going to shoot your dad in the leg and just leave him here. Understood?"

Neither Harper nor Archer corrected the man who thought Van was their father. Instead, they both nodded.

Van turned around and removed his pistol from the back of his jeans with two fingers. He bent, placed it on the ground, then kicked it away. He did the same with the knife in the sheath on his belt.

Harper, who had every right to be scared to death, seemed calm. "My pistol is in my pack." She kicked it away from herself and Archer followed suit. "Our knives are in there, too."

Jimbo smiled with what seemed might be real pleasure. He looked closely at Harper. "You're a real fireball, aren't you, girlie? That's good. How old are you?"

Harper played a number of answers over in her head. She still looked younger than she was, though anyone who spoke to her for more than two minutes knew how mature she was. She knew that any number she gave, whether, older, younger, or the truth, might have a negative result.

So, she told the truth. "I'm fourteen. My brother is eleven."

"Good, good," Jimbo said. "You're going to fit right in with our little community."

She didn't need to glance at Van to show that she knew they were in trouble. Before they had ever left Dust City, they had talked about the dangers of what might happen to all of them if they were captured by someone.

For Van, he might be put to work as a slave somewhere, but he wasn't too worried about that. He always believed that, given enough time, he would be able to find and exploit the weaknesses in whatever prison system he was caught in. It was the kids who would be the most vulnerable. It was likely that they would be separated, and it was possible their fates—especially Harper's—would be worse than being worked like a slave.

"Go on, Bronson. Search 'em."

The lackey called Bronson climbed awkwardly down from the truck and ambled over to them. Just by the way he moved, it was obvious to both Harper and Van that it would be easy to handle him.

That left two other rifles and a shotgun, though, so they stood with their arms out to be frisked.

It was an inelegant search at best, but as they had given up all their weapons, there was nothing to be found.

"Nothin', Jimbo," Bronson said, smiling and showing a few missing teeth.

"Good. Glad we have an understanding. You three go sit by the side of the road. It'll be a while before your ride gets here."

Van, Harper, and Archer sat on the shoulder of the road. Van turned his back to the men, hoping to be able to talk to Harper without them noticing. Jimbo was having none of that.

"Nuh-uh, nuh-uh, nuh-uh," he said. "Spread out a little bit. This ain't no damned tea party. And turn around so I can see your faces."

Van scooted along the road and turned around.

"Banger," Jimbo said to one of the other men, "take my shotgun, sit about ten feet away from all three of them. If they make any funny moves, blast 'em."

A short man, not as warmly dressed as Jimbo, climbed down, traded his rifle for the shotgun, and did as he was told.

Jimbo and the other men sat comfortably on the back of the trailer, sipping a clear liquid out of a dirty mason jar. Banger sat on the ground, ostensibly watching their prisoners, but casting envious looks at the men drinking whatever backwoods alcohol they had cooked up.

They sat that way for almost three hours, until they finally heard the clip-clop of approaching horses. There were two men, each on their own horse, with two other horses following behind, tethered by a rope.

The man in front dismounted easily and walked to the side of the road. He wore a cowboy hat, work shirt, jeans, a Levi's jacket, and cowboy boots. He stared down at the three captives. Van stared back placidly, while Harper and Archer looked away. They had decided to play it like they were normal, scared kids. A reasonable assumption in the circumstances.

"Looks like you finally did something right," the man in the cowboy hat said. "I'll make sure to send a little more homebrew out to you guys."

"When can we get out of here, Mr. Harris?" Jimbo asked. He had sounded large and in charge before, but now sounded a little meek.

Harris looked at him levelly. "When I tell you you're relieved." He nodded toward the three captives. "It's obvious this is a good spot, and we're spread pretty thin now." His voice was gruff, but then he softened. "You guys got enough blankets?" He nodded toward the dark, shadowy back of the trailer.

Jimbo shrugged, a little petulantly.

"I'll bring another blanket out for each of you, next time you find someone worth making the trip for." He hesitated, then reached into his saddlebag. "Hell, I'll let you have this now." He pulled out a brown bottle and tossed it to Jimbo.

Harris looked at Van. "I know it's tempting to think about making a run for it or trying to tackle us or some other nonsense. I'll just tell you that lots of people have tried that. I'm still here, and we're going to pass a few of their bodies on the way back to the compound. I'd hate to waste you like that, but I will if I have to. Understood?"

Van nodded once.

"Those your kids?"

"Yes," Van lied.

"Then you don't want them to see their daddy get killed right in front of them. Just do what we say, and you'll all be fine."

Van very much doubted they'd be fine but chose not to say so.

"I'm Sam Harris. This is my son Freddie. Let's try and have a nice trip. We can be back home, getting some hot chow before it gets dark. Capiche?"

Van just nodded again but glanced at his watch. Based on what time it was, and how long it had taken them to arrive, he doubted that was true.

"Help the kids up on the black horse, then. You'll be riding the roan. Blackie is gentle and won't give them any trouble." He looked back at Jimbo. "Anything useful in their packs?"

"Nothing dangerous. We took everything out and checked. A map, a little food, some clothes. A drone, but it's like a kid's toy. No attack capability or anything."

Harris nodded. He looked at the kids and said, "Grab your packs. It'll be good for you to have some clothes when we get there."

Van reached for his, but Harris said, "Nope. There's something about you I don't trust. Leave your bag here."

Van shrugged, knowing there was nothing there that would really help him anyway. He put Harper in front, then Archer behind and told him, "Hang on tight to your sister." He climbed up on the big roan, but did so a little awkwardly, as though he'd never been on a horse in his life.

"You guys ride in front," Harris said. "Don't worry about knowing which way to go. Your horses know."

Van continued to act as though he didn't know how to ride in case that would come in handy later. Freddie Harris rode up behind Van's horse and slapped it on its haunches.

"Come on, ya old bitch. Let's go."

They rode along the soft shoulder of the highway for several miles. They still came across accidents here and there, but nothing that stopped their progress. Eventually, they turned off onto another smaller country road.

Both Van and Harper kept track of which direction they were traveling so if they ever managed to get away, they wouldn't be completely lost.

After going another mile down the smaller road, Harper said, "I need to go to the bathroom." She didn't really need to go that badly but wanted to see what kind of freedom they were going to be given.

Sam Harris opened his mouth to say something, but before he could, Freddie interrupted.

"I kinda got to go too," he said.

"Okay, *girls*," Sam said. He nodded at Van. "Go ahead and help her down, but missy, you're gonna have to hunker down where I can see you. Ain't taking a chance that you're gonna run off." He looked at Archer. "If you need to pee, you can whip it out right here."

Van dismounted, then helped Harper and Archer down.

Harper stepped down into a shallow ditch that gave her some limited privacy and pulled her jeans down.

Freddie moved to where he had a better vantage point to see Harper and unzipped his jeans.

Bob Harris seemed relaxed and completely in command of the situation. He held his rifle cradled in his arms and whistled softly. For all his talk of dead bodies by the side of the road, Van thought that was just what it was—talk.

Van looked at Freddie, who seemed to only be interested in Harper. He glanced at Sam, then said, "I'm gonna go too, if you don't mind."

Sam shrugged his permission.

Van turned his back to him, then stumbled backward as if he had tripped over something. He moved directly toward Sam, who caught on just a bit too late.

Van whirled and executed a sidekick that hit the rifle flush and knocked it out of Harris's hands. Van ignored the gun and focused on the man. He hit him three times in quick succession, twice in the gut and a follow up to the face, which broke his nose and sent blood spraying out.

Freddie said, "Hey, hey!" and brought his own rifle up to bear on Van. He fired once, wildly, hitting Van just below the kneecap.

That spun Van around and to the ground, but he landed next to the rifle. He grabbed it, and without much aim, fired. Freddie pinwheeled backward.

Sam crawled forward, bleeding profusely from the nose and wrestled with Van for the gun. Both men had a death grip on it and wouldn't let go, but Van managed to leverage Sam's strength against him and slammed the butt of the rifle up under his chin.

Sam recoiled and went semi-unconscious.

Van turned to Harper. "Get on the horse and ride out of here, now!"

Harper lifted Archer aboard the horse and climbed up after him, but shook her head. "Not leaving without you. Come on, get on the horse. We can get away together."

Van looked at Sam flat on his back and Freddie, who had rolled over onto his side ten yards away. He nodded and hesitated for a moment, then put the barrel against Sam's head and pulled the trigger. It clicked but didn't fire.

Van swore under his breath, then slammed the butt of the rifle into Sam's already broken nose.

He used the rifle to stand and then as a makeshift crutch. He hobbled toward his horse and laid a hand on the horn of the saddle. He was focusing on how he could swing his injured leg up and over when another shot rang out.

Freddie had rolled over and fired, hitting Van again, this time in the hip. He fell to the ground and knew he wasn't going to be able to get up.

He looked at Harper and hissed. "Get out of here while you can. Now!"

She hesitated, knowing there was no way for her to transport the man who had saved her life on numerous occasions, but not wanting to leave him. "We'll come back for you."

Van shook his head. "No, you won't. If they don't just kill me, I'll heal up and escape. I know the location of Nyx's cabin. Now go!"

With tears in her eyes, Harper turned the horse and rode back up the road in the same direction they had come. She whipped the reins and said, "Hold on, Archer."

The horse moved from a trot to a run. Harper was just beginning to feel safe when she heard a gunshot behind her. "You okay?" she asked Archer.

He had his arms wrapped tightly about her and didn't answer, but nodded into her back.

Harper didn't look back and had no idea if Freddie was shooting at her or if he might be killing Van.

Chapter Thirty-Three
Colorado

The chances are good that Harper and Archer would not have made it to Colorado without Blackie. The horse was as gentle as Sam Harris had said. She made it easy for them to mount and dismount and walked tirelessly.

The truth was, they were fourteen and eleven years old and were weaponless. They had a small amount of food, but not enough to sustain them over the rest of the long trek on foot to Nyx's cabin.

Before she had left on the Cessna months earlier, Nyx had slipped a piece of paper into Harper's hands. That was her way of saying that even though the powers that be would not allow her to take the two of them out of Dust City, they were welcome if they could get away.

The challenge was that the latitude and longitude were precise, but of little use when tramping through forests and over hills. Maps could get them close, but they might have wandered around in the foothills and forests of Colorado forever without finding Nyx's cabin.

In addition to the drone that he had built—which the highwaymen had taken from them—Archer had built something even more valuable. He had made it to look like a compass, which it was, but under the compass was a tiny computer that, in the right position, could connect with an overhead satellite that Archer had found. That computer gave them a readout of exactly where they were via latitude and longitude. Between that and the map, they were confident they could find the cabin.

Still, Harper had to fight with herself to ride away from Van. She had watched as he was shot twice. Neither wound looked fatal, but she had heard a single gunshot as they rode away. It ate away at her as she wondered whether he was still alive, or if he had sacrificed himself so they could live.

Using the map, they estimated how many miles they traveled the first day, then how far they had to travel to reach Nyx's cabin. It wasn't great news. They thought they could make twenty to twenty-five miles per day on horseback and that they were a little more than three hundred miles away.

Harper guessed it would take them three more weeks to get there. The problem was that they only had enough food to last a few days.

Archer, who was like a small walking encyclopedia of trivia, said that they could probably survive without eating for most of that time, though they would become very weak toward the end and would have a hard time staying upright on the horse.

They agreed that they would stay off the roads and ride through forests wherever the terrain wasn't too rough. That would let them forage for whatever edible plants, roots, and berries they could find. It was late winter, though, and the useful foraging was scarce.

On the third day after they had gotten away, they stopped by a stream to let Blackie drink. They found a small patch of blueberries that were well past their prime—they were shriveled and small. Archer also deemed them absolutely delicious and they foraged the entire area looking for more with no luck.

Harper kept the thought to herself, but she had begun to believe that Archer's prediction about their ability to survive with almost no food was optimistic. They had been eating only a minimal amount even before they had been captured. Between that and the constant walking, they were both already thin when they were captured. It already felt that her body had begun to eat itself.

Archer stood beside Harper, close enough that when he leaned a little, he put his head against her shoulder. She put an arm around him and said, "It's going to be fine. We'll be fine." Saying it helped her believe it.

It was still fiercely cold, especially as they climbed into the higher elevations. They eventually emptied their packs of clothes and wore two or three layers of clothes under their coats. When they got too cold riding Blackie, they would jump down and lead her for a mile or two to warm up.

They did have a flint, so when it got dark, they would look for the most remote area they could find and build a fire. The highwaymen had left them their packs but had taken their sleeping bags so even keeping the fire burning, each night felt like an eternity of frozen limbs and noses.

Ten days after they had escaped, Harper came to believe they weren't going to make it. They were fighting a losing battle on two fronts.

First, they were starving to death. They had eaten the small amount of food they had stored in their packs and they weren't finding anything to eat along the way.

Second, because they were even more concerned with being captured again, they weren't taking anything remotely like an optimal route to the cabin. After their optimistic estimate that they would cover twenty or more miles each day, they were instead making perhaps fifteen miles.

Several times, they reached a dead end in a canyon that didn't show on the map and they were forced to backtrack a mile or two and take a different path.

It was one of those dead ends that likely saved their lives.

They had come to a fork and, after studying the map for several minutes, had elected to go to the south. It looked like the most level path and they were both tired from the constant up and down elevation of the foothills they were passing through.

Two miles later, Harper hung her head when it became obvious that the easy path had not been the right choice. Tall hills rose up in front of them on all sides. She scanned the horizon, hoping to find a way through, but soon realized that there was no such path.

She was lost in a funk of depression so deep that it took her a moment to realize that Archer was tapping her repeatedly on the shoulder. She turned her head and saw that he was pointing excitedly off to the right.

There, hidden within a stand of tall pines and nearly covered by overgrown blackberry bushes, was a small cabin. It was the first sign of civilization they had seen in days.

It looked like it had to be completely deserted. The vines, grass, and bushes grew so tall that it rendered the cabin nearly invisible. There was no smoke coming from the chimney.

Still, they were cautious. They slipped off of Blackie and watched the cabin for long minutes. A crow flew in circles overhead and came to land on the roof of the small building but there was no other sign of life.

Finally, they felt like they couldn't wait any longer, so they led Blackie to the area to the right of the cabin and tied her to a tree. They walked around the entirety of the structure, but that revealed nothing. There were no windows at all. In fact, the whole thing looked like it had been put together in a slapdash manner using found materials.

There was nothing so grand as a porch. In fact, the two steps that led to the only door were rotted and collapsing in on themselves.

Harper put Archer behind her and stood on the one part of the step that was still sound. There wasn't even a knob or lock on the door.

Harper realized that this had likely been someone's hunting shack. More of a temporary shelter for a night or two than something anyone had ever lived in.

She pushed on the door but it didn't budge. She looked around the casing, but there was nothing that seemed to be holding it in place. She put her shoulder into it and pushed.

Two things happened simultaneously. The rotted step completely gave way, sending Harper tumbling to the ground, and the door swung inward with a shriek of protest. The noise was so loud that both Harper and Archer looked around to see if it had attracted any unwanted attention.

It had not.

The inside of the cabin matched the outside. The only furniture was a piece of plywood across two sawhorses, a mattress that looked like it might already have had a few dozen occupants, and an ancient woodstove.

Light cut into the darkness from the open door. Dust motes hung lazily in the air.

Harper picked herself up and stepped into the cabin. There was no sink or bathroom, but there was a small cupboard in the corner she had missed in her initial scan of the room. A dirty towel hung down in front of it.

When she pushed the towel aside, her heart leaped.

There was canned food stacked inside. The cans were dusty and dirty, but looked like heaven. Three cans of Dinty Moore stew, four cans of Chef Boyardee ravioli, three cans of Campbell's soup, and three cans of pork and beans. It was more food than they'd eaten in a very long time.

Someone had obviously planned a stay and then had never returned.

She turned to Archer and said, "Can you hear water running anywhere?"

Archer tilted his head, listening. "I'm not sure. Maybe over that way."

"If there's water, we can stay here for a day and rest. If not, we'll carry this food with us. Let's go look."

A few hundred yards behind the cabin, they found a small stream. They hurried back to the cabin, then led Blackie to the stream to let her drink her fill.

It was getting dark by the time they filled their canteens and got back to the cabin. They found an area with lots of grass and tied Blackie up there.

Back inside, Harper opened the door of the woodstove. There were ashes there, but no wood. They quickly went outside and found some kindling, then broke off tree limbs that would fit inside the stove.

When they shut the door, it was dark inside, but once they got the fire going, they left the door open a crack and that let enough light in that they could see where they were going without bumping into each other.

They stacked the cans on the table and stared at the lifesaving food for a few minutes.

"We've still got to conserve," Harper said, and Archer nodded his agreement. "We're so weak right now, though, let's each pick out one can." She reached clear to the bottom of her pack and pulled out their can opener.

They both chose a can of the Chef Boyardee.

Harper thought it was the most delicious thing she'd ever tasted. When she'd finished, she looked at the mattress in the corner and said, "No way am I sleeping on that."

Archer opened his mouth to volunteer, but Harper shut that idea down. "Let's just lie down on the floor and use our packs for pillows."

Once the woodstove got cranking, it became warm inside the shack.

The two of them slept better than they had since they left Van behind.

In the morning, they were tempted to stay another day at the cabin and rest.

Harper knew that was not the best plan, though. The food they'd found was a godsend, but they needed to translate it into as many days on the road as they could.

Regretfully, they packed the canned food into their packs, which now felt much heavier on their backs. They shut the door, refilled their canteens, and watered Blackie. They then backtracked to where they had taken the fortunate wrong turn.

The rest of the trip wasn't easy.

Archer fell asleep from exhaustion late one afternoon and slipped off Blackie, slamming his head into a rock and giving himself a concussion. Harper was torn between staying put for a day to allow him to recover and fearing that they would again run out of food. In the end, she covered his eyes with fabric to block out the light, helped him onto Blackie, and tied him to her with a length of rope.

In a few days, he recovered.

Even with the cache of food they discovered, they still knew hunger. They limited themselves to splitting a can of food each day, supplemented by whatever they could forage.

Toward the end of the journey, the temperatures warmed into the forties, but that was accompanied by a pounding rain. Given the choice, they decided they would rather be cold than constantly wet. The driving rain made it difficult to find dry wood to build a fire, so they spent five consecutive cold, wet nights.

All of that passed, though.

Using Archer's mapping tool, they closed in on the proper location for Nyx's cabin. One morning, after what seemed like a thousand endless days on the road, Archer took a reading.

He smiled and said, "We're within two miles."

Harper nodded, too exhausted to be in a celebratory mood. "We need to dismount and walk the rest of the way. Nyx told me about the booby traps she set and how to recognize them, but I can't spot them very well on horseback."

They moved forward slowly, one measured step at a time.

Harper finally smiled when she stopped and pointed up into a tree a distance away. "One of Nyx's cameras. We're almost there." She knew it was probably possible to just stand in front of that camera for a time and that Nyx or one of her family would see them, but she wanted to make it closer to the cabin.

They tied Blackie to a tree and Archer stood on tiptoes and hugged her neck. "We'll be right back for you. I promise."

They spent the next hour slowly winding their way through the maze that Nyx had set up for them.

Harper would often point out a fallen tree or tangle of bushes and say, "See? She's trying to herd us in that direction. Let's go around the other way."

Finally, after passing three more cameras but staying out of what she thought was their likely trigger range, she walked directly in front of one. She watched as the red light activated and waited patiently.

A full minute passed, then another, then finally a speaker crackled and Nyx's voice sounded.

"Stay there. I'm on my way. I knew you'd make it here."

Less than five minutes later, Nyx and a man and woman Harper and Archer didn't know appeared in the clearing.

As she approached, Nyx held her arms wide to welcome them. She looked around a little expectantly. "Don't tell me you came all this way on your own. Where's Van?"

Harper and Archer had both been brave through incredible hardships, but the mention of their friend's name immediately brought tears.

"Oh," Nyx said in a small voice. She was the person who had originally recruited Van into Altor, though he had been waylaid on the way there. When she had arrived in Dust City with Emmanuel,

Harry, and Allison, she had met him again, this time as Harper and Archer's protector.

When Harper had first "introduced" them to each other in Dust City, they had acted as though they didn't know each other. Why? Because both Nyx and Van were trained to play everything close to the vest until there was no reason to do so. Eventually they came clean and had told Harper how they had initially met.

The dam burst. Through tears, Harper and Archer told the story of what had happened when they had been kidnapped and how Van had insisted they leave him behind. Finally, Harper brightened a little when she told of how they had ridden Blackie to the cabin.

"Without her, we'd still be hundreds of miles away and would have starved to death before we got here."

Nyx introduced her sister and brother-in-law, Adva and Franklin, both of whom looked on in a sort of awe.

"Am I to understand that you traveled on foot and horseback all the way from Nevada?"

Adva asked. Her voice sounded much like Nyx, though the rest of her demeanor was softer.

"Yes," Harper said simply. It was a small word, but conveyed much.

The five of them picked their way carefully back to where Blackie was tied to the tree, contentedly pulling at some weeds.

"I know you only invited us," Harper said, "but I hope you'll have room for Blackie."

"We've got plenty for her to eat. She can be company for Daisy, our cow. I'd say she's earned her keep." She looked closely at both Harper and Archer. "Haven't been eating much, have you?"

Harper just grinned and said, "We're just happy to be here. It will be nice to wake up in the morning and know we don't have to try to get twenty miles in before it gets dark."

"That will be a relief, I'm sure, but I have a better treat than that. As soon as my mother saw the two of you on the screen, she started cooking. We're having her soup and homemade bread for dinner."

Harper closed her eyes and, for the first time since she had left Dust City, allowed herself to relax.

* * *

When Nyx had first arrived at the cabin, there had been five people. Herself, Adva, her husband Franklin, their daughter Chaya, and her mother, Shalva.

Since that day, they had added four more people—Rose and Millie, who had accidentally wandered onto the property, and now Harper and Archer.

Even with the extra people, the cabin didn't feel crowded. There were three bedrooms, the younger kids slept up in the loft, and there were comfortable couches for anyone else.

Shalva seemed to be in heaven. Having more people to care for and feed was a wonderful thing for her.

The first night, Harper and Archer were still in shock from the change in their circumstance. From having to keep their heads constantly on a swivel, to being adopted into a large and caring family.

The next morning, Nyx offered to take Harper on a tour of the surrounding area.

Archer was not put out at being excluded. He knew that Nyx and Harper had a special bond. After the difficulties of the previous few months, he was more than happy to stay in the cabin, eat snacks pushed on him by Shalva, and play board games with Chaya and Millie.

Nyx and Harper walked out to the small pond in the front yard and looked out over its placid surface.

"You told me this was paradise," Harper said, "but now I feel it."

Nyx nodded, but then immediately changed the subject as to why she had brought Harper out. “How bad was Van?”

Harper closed her eyes, hardened her heart, and gave an accurate, blow by blow description of the fight that had occurred, including how Van had been shot first in the lower right leg, then again in the hip or side of the stomach. She even told Nyx how she had heard one last gunshot as she rode away.

“Knowing Van,” Nyx said, “even badly wounded, he could have gotten the gun away from the last one of them and taken them out. He was well-trained.”

Harper just looked at Nyx, unsure where this line of questioning was going.

“Do you know where you were when Van was shot?”

“Yes. As soon as we got away, Archer took a reading on his GPS.”

“I thought so.”

Harper’s heart was beating fast. “Why?”

“I’m going after him.”

Chapter Thirty-Four
Hope for the Future

The Shivers wiped out a good percentage of the New City population. Although no one would have mentioned it, there was a silver lining to that loss.

The virus arrived in the middle of winter, when there was minimal work to be done anyway. That gave the remaining population time to take care of the bodies, grieve and rest before the hard work of spring came.

When the sun did come out and the ground thawed, they were short on labor, but they had plans in place to provide more food than they needed. That meant that if they worked from dawn to dusk every day, they actually might have a slight food surplus to carry into the following winter.

That brought a new plan into place.

They decided to find a way to recruit new able-bodied people into New City.

The downside to that was that it was a major change in mindset from what had allowed them to survive to that point. Up to then, there were two groups of people—those beyond the wall and those in New City. That much larger group was never to be trusted.

That had been reinforced when the only two people they had let in had almost started a war and brought a plague upon their settlement respectively.

If they were to expand, though, that dearly held belief would have to evolve.

The other challenge with expansion was where to find more people.

They had done their best to burn the nearest town to the ground after winning the Battle of Covington. That had seemed like the best policy at the time—to make the town uninhabitable so they wouldn't worry about having an enemy at their gate, or at least within walking distance.

June had asked Sylvie if there were perhaps other farm families like hers within a day's walk. She thought they might be good people who already had the right skills and knew the meaning of hard work.

Sylvie did not know of any other families or small farms, however.

The idea was tabled. The weather warmed and everyone was too busy to consider it further.

A solution presented itself in a most unlikely way a month later.

The workers of New City had done their best to make the roads into Covington impassable. They had dug up roads and felled trees across several spots in each of the three highways that led into the town.

Since then, a few stragglers had walked around the barriers to check things out for themselves. When they saw what a hellish landscape Covington had become, they quickly moved on. The New City plan was a success.

Until the US Army moved in.

* * *

In truth, what eventually appeared in Covington didn't much resemble the US Army of the before times.

There had been a time when the Army was held together by rules and laws, discipline and the threat of a dishonorable discharge that would follow a soldier for life. If someone decided they didn't want to be a soldier anymore and hotfooted away, they were declared Absent Without Leave, or AWOL. More soldiers were dispatched to find the escapee, return them, and prosecute them for dereliction of duty.

Many people joined the military as a means to an end. They would serve for twenty years, then *retire*, albeit at a young age.

That military was gone.

The spirit of the Army remained, even twenty months after the rest of civilization had fallen. There was still a dedicated group of men and women fulfilling their oath to defend the Constitution of the United States and to protect its people.

The form of all branches of the US military had changed dramatically.

Prior to the bombs falling in 2033, there were more than one and a half million people serving in those branches.

By the spring of 2035, that number had dwindled substantially.

That started within weeks of the detonation of nuclear weapons on US soil.

Many soldiers took it up on themselves to leave, either with or without permission, to check on their families, wherever they might be.

The United States was at its most dangerous in those early weeks. Many of those soldiers perished trying to get to their families. Others found their loved ones and decided to stay with them to protect them.

They may have been technically declared AWOL, but there was no real consequence to that.

A number of enlisted people simply believed that there was no more United States of America, and thus no Constitution. They felt they were free to pursue their own interests.

Commanders did what they could to stanch the flow of these defectors, but aside from emphasizing the safety offered by military bases, there wasn't much they could do. If they had tried to send soldiers after them, the military jails would have been full and the bases would have been even more empty.

Immediately after the Rage Wars, those bases were in better shape than the rest of the country. They all had large stores of food, including canned foods and other nutrition that was specifically designed to last for years.

That gave them a leg up initially, but even with dwindling numbers of soldiers, that supply was not infinite.

Soon enough, the base commanders went to nearby towns and recruited people and equipment to come into the safety of the base. Gardens and fruit trees began to pop up in areas that had once been for military exercises.

The biggest blow to the military came from an enemy it couldn't stop or protect itself against: The Shivers.

Because the various military installations were consistently interacting with towns and a wide range of people, the virus spread quickly through the ranks.

In April of 2035, there were less than a hundred thousand soldiers spread across the country.

New governments popped up all the time, but none of them seemed to last for more than a few weeks or a month at a time. None of them had the feeling of legitimacy.

Communication between the bases was minimal. Shortwave radio was the only reliable method of contact. This left each base commander feeling like they were on an island, with no real military command above them.

Some of them turned into survivors and nothing more. With tanks and other powerful weaponry at their disposal, there was very little risk of being overrun by the general populace. Bases were already built securely.

Others attacked the problem differently. For instance, there was Colonel Brandt, the commanding officer of Fort Teller in Western Nevada. He was less interested in his personal survival and more focused on what could be done to restore the United States to a functioning nation.

That was a massive problem. Much too large for any one individual to handle. The mere thought of somehow uniting the devastated country was beyond comprehension or possible ambition.

Colonel Brandt was a person who believed that the proper way to eat an elephant of that size was one bite at a time.

He knew that such an undertaking would never happen in his lifetime. But, if he could begin to lay the foundation for it, that would be enough for him.

To that end, he began to send small squads of his men out into the surrounding areas, looking for specific skills and survivors. Anyone those squads found who might be useful in rebuilding a society was given an invitation to bring their families onto the base until they were ready for the next step.

They found carpenters, plumbers, and contractors who would be useful in rebuilding many aspects of a town. Then, they expanded and looked for city planners, structural engineers, electrical engineers, mechanics, and heavy-equipment operators. They hit a goldmine when they found a tiny community that included a group of men and women who had once worked at a regional fuel processing plant in Northern California. Violence there had driven them to the vast emptiness of Nevada.

Brandt's intentions were good, but his efforts were severely hindered by the fact that the fuel needed to operate the vast majority of their vehicles had gone bad.

Charles Santos, who was the de facto leader of the engineers, felt sure that if they could get him and his team to the processing plant, they could begin to provide new, effective gasoline again, at least on a limited basis. Once they began producing that gas, more raw materials could be produced and the entire line of production could be ramped up. From there, it wasn't impossible to envision that the process could be repeated in more places.

The challenge was that the plant was hundreds of miles from the base. All vehicles were disabled by the bad gas, so the first question was how to get the engineers and workers to the plant.

To that end, Brandt sent a squad to a local horse ranch that was fifteen miles from the base.

That squad was led by Lieutenant Dan Forster and Sergeant JT Brewster. They led a group of fourteen other men and women to the ranch of Henry "Stinky" Virgil. A year earlier, Virgil had driven to the base and asked for protection from the roving bands of mercenaries. He had, to that point, managed to fight them off, but he knew that he wouldn't be able to hold out forever. If the Army was willing to send a few troops to protect his home, he said he was more than happy to feed and care for them.

It had become a plum assignment for the soldiers of Fort Teller. It broke up the monotony of base, and the ranch had a much better variety of food. The base was by then down to Meals Ready-to-Eat.

They had rotated soldiers in and out of the ranch every month, but when their fuel began to fail, Brandt sent a message that they would either have to leave a small contingent there permanently or pull everyone back to base.

Virgil had thanked Brandt and told him that with the steep drop off of violence and transient militia, he thought he could defend his property without help.

Brandt left one light tank there, simply because its fuel was no longer good. It became a very expensive lawn ornament. Even if it wasn't functional, both Brandt and Virgil knew that it would serve as an excellent deterrent to anyone who thought of bothering them.

That had been months earlier, but Brandt—and Forster—were hopeful that Virgil would still be in their debt.

It turned out that Virgil did indeed have a long memory. He gave the squad what they asked for—two dozen horses.

Forster and Brewster drew the next assignment as well, which was to escort the engineers and workers to the fuel treatment plant and establish an outpost of sorts there.

Colonel Brandt outfitted the engineers in a standard-issue army uniform and issued weapons to each of them. His theory was that anyone with bad intentions would be less likely to attack what appeared to be twenty-four US Army soldiers, even if they were on horseback.

And so they set out, hopeful, but not overly so, well aware that the weight of the US Army was not what it had been in the before times.

Chapter Thirty-Five
Rising from the Ashes

June was bent over a hoe, working soil that would eventually have tomatoes planted in it. For the moment, she was just breaking up the soil and preparing it for the plants they were nursing along in the greenhouse. Sweat dripped off her face even though it was still only in the upper forties.

She had blocked out everything except for breaking up the clods of dirt and was surprised when Ric touched her shoulder.

"Mom, can't you hear me?"

Startled, June jumped a little, then smiled a guilty smile. "I guess not. I could say I was involved in what I was doing, but we both know it's not that interesting. What is it?"

"Sylvie's on watch at the top of the gate and she just sounded an alarm. Said someone was coming up the hill."

June threw the hoe down and ran for the gate. Things had been peaceful in New City since The Shivers had decimated the community. She wasn't ready for another attack.

She hit the ladder that leaned against the wall at a full run and hurried to the top. Sylvie was standing there, wide-eyed and uncertain of what to do.

"Scootch over and let me see," June said, stepping up onto the watch person's step. She poked her head cautiously over the top of the fence, ready to duck back down if need be.

"What the..." she said under her breath.

"I know, right?" Sylvie said below her. "That's what I said."

Spread out in front of the gate were what appeared to be two dozen soldiers on horseback. It looked like the cavalry had arrived, but they weren't wanting or waiting for rescue. They were fine where they were.

"Can I help you?"

"Perhaps you can," a man said who sat on a horse in front of the line. "My name is Lieutenant Dan Forster, US Army."

June squinted at them and cocked her head slightly in disbelief.

"Yeah, we get that reaction a lot. You thought there was no more US Army, didn't you?"

"We haven't seen a lot of uniforms around once things went to hell."

"I'm the first to admit, we're not what we used to be," Forster said, nodding at the other men on horseback, "and I understand why you're wary of us. It pays to be wary of everyone these days."

June glanced down at the double thick wall of logs she stood atop as if to say, *You're preaching to the choir.*

"You've got a fine setup here," Forster said admiringly. "I'd like to meet face to face and explain our mission here. Would that be okay?"

"We are face to face. We don't get much more up close and personal than this," June answered.

Forster nodded. "What if I send my men back across the river and leave my weapons with my horse. Would you allow me inside so we can talk?"

June disappeared behind the wall for a moment and looked at Sylvie. There were people gathered around the inside of the wall now. Several of them shook their heads fearfully.

June stood up again and said, "Have you had the virus?"

"Yes," Forster said. "I was about to ask you the same. We've heard it referred to as The Shivers."

"That's apt," June agreed. She weighed the pros and cons of letting Forster inside. She looked at the men with him. None of them looked particularly rough or threatening, but not all of them looked like soldiers either. In fact, several of them looked more like the bookish, academic type. Finally, she nodded. "That's fine. No need to send your men all the way across the bridge. Just have them back off to the bottom of the hill. Give us a minute, and we'll open the small gate."

Forster turned and spoke to a stocky, grizzled man beside him and that man spoke quietly to the riders behind him. One by one, and with varying degrees of aptitude, they turned their horses around and rode to the bottom of the hill.

June climbed down and brushed past the spectators at the bottom of the wall. "Get your guns up, will you? Cover me."

"What if there's a new virus out there, and he's a carrier?" a worried woman asked.

"If there are more viruses like the last one out there, we're probably done for. I'm interested in hearing what he has to say."

The woman frowned, but stood behind June, rifle raised.

June looked up at Sylvie and said, "Holler if they do anything funny." She removed one after the other of the boards they had barricading the man-sized gate. When she'd leaned the last one against the wall, she opened it wide.

Forster held out his hand. "Thank you for letting me in."

"June Trello." She accepted his hand and shook it. She turned to two men behind her. "Bar the gate again. Lieutenant, come on with me up to my house."

Forster looked around at what had once been a very trendy housing development. He nodded his appreciation for what they had accomplished.

They walked up the paved road which was now mostly covered in mud, past an elegant house where the front yard had been converted to a chicken coop.

"This is us," June said, opening the door to her own home. "Come in."

She led Forster through to the kitchen with Ric protectively trailing behind.

"We don't have any coffee or tea to offer, but I can get you a glass of milk if you'd like."

"I very much would." He looked at the electric lights and said, "Solar?"

"We were lucky. Almost all these houses were already wired for solar when we moved in."

"You're not the original homeowner here?"

June looked at him, the closest thing to a government authority she had seen in almost two years.

"The Rage Wars," she said simply. "My husband, son, and I lived in Covington, the town you passed through on your way here."

"That looked like quite the battle zone," Forster said.

"It was, though the damage you saw wasn't caused by the battle. I did that. I was trying to make it unattractive for anyone else to move into town. I didn't like having enemies so close."

"Good strategy. Can't argue with it. But what about having allies there?"

June grabbed a pitcher of milk out of the refrigerator and poured a glass. "Prepare yourself if you've never had milk straight from a cow. It's pretty rich."

Forster raised the glass to his lips and surprise registered in his eyes. "Is the stuff I've been drinking all my life really milk?"

"More or less. It just had all the good stuff taken out of it. Tell me what you're proposing."

"You seem pretty observant. You may have noticed that not all those men and women are soldiers."

"Some of them looked like they'd spent more time behind a desk or on a computer than riding a horse," June agreed.

Forster explained about what Colonel Brandt had done, sending squads out looking for help in rebuilding some of the infrastructure.

"Not everything was damaged, but when things got dangerous, people stopped showing up for work. Power lines got taken down, but that's easy to fix. If we can get a single power plant up and running, we believe we can spread out from here. The problem is, right now, there's no good gasoline to power vehicles. So our first priority is to get a fuel processing plant up."

"Harton," June said, understanding.

That was the name of a processing plant just a few miles from Covington. It had once served as one of the biggest employers in the region.

"Exactly. Seven or eight of those 'soldiers' you saw out there are people who used to work at Harton. They weren't pencil pushers, either. They were engineers and workers who understood the workings of the plant. They have told us that if we can get them in there, they should be able to create some good, usable gasoline. That'll be the start."

"Sounds good to me. We can't even run our lawnmowers anymore."

"That's why you've got goats," Forster said.

"Exactly. But what do you need from me?"

"Not much, really. You've got a good setup here, but you're limited. Eventually, your soil won't be good for growing things anymore. You'll need more room. We're going to rebuild Covington over the next few months, at least to an extent. First, we'll build up some proper barricades so we don't have to worry too much about fighting to hold onto the town. I think we can get the plant up and running in a few months. Then we can take some fuel back to our base in Nevada."

"How are you going to do that?"

"The original horsepower," Forster said with a grin. "We'll use our horses to drag some of the fuel we produce back to our base. Then we can fire up some of our vehicles—Humvees, light tanks, that sort of thing—and bring them back here. Then we'll be properly defended. As we produce more fuel, we can obtain more of the raw materials we need to make more and more. Meanwhile, we'll send a team up to that power plant in the valley and see what it will take to get it up and running."

June looked up at the ceiling, wondering for the thousandth time why Kane wasn't still here for moments like this.

"The ability to produce gasoline and electricity? That sounds a lot like civilization to me."

"That's the plan," Forster agreed. "I don't know if anyone else is trying something like this in other parts of the country. If they are, I haven't heard about it. But if we can get this operating properly here, there's no reason why we can't spread out and help other areas do the same thing." He glanced at Ric. "Maybe we can give the next generation a good push toward getting things rebuilt."

He took a long drink of the milk, then set the glass on the table.

"In the meantime, I think it would be good for us to be strong neighbors. Once we rebuild Covington, it will eventually become the center of things for a few hundred miles."

"Those are words I never expected to hear," June said.

"It's all about the location. You've got the fuel processing plant and the power plant within a few miles, not to mention that dam upriver. This can be like the cradle of the new civilization."

"That's a lot to wrap my brain around."

"Of course," Forster agreed. "And there's nothing that needs to be decided today. More than anything, we just wanted to come and introduce ourselves. Over the next few months, you'll see what we're doing down there. Maybe we'll get to a point where we've at least got an open-door policy."

June's shoulders slumped a little. It wasn't that she was at all saddened by what Forster said. It was that for the first time since Kane had died, she felt like maybe all the weight didn't need to fall on her.

Chapter Thirty-Six
Monks of the Future

Tokin Ming-Sa sat cross-legged beside the tranquil lake in a small park. Swans—real swans, he knew, not digital creations—swam around and around, occasionally diving down and resurfacing with a tasty treat in their mouth.

In front of Tokin, ten students sat raptly, listening to everything he had to say.

The problem—at least from Tokin's perspective—was that the words they heard were not coming from him. It was the voice in his head that was causing Tokin to speak.

"All peace must come from within," the voice that was Tokin's said. This was very much in line with the teaching he did every day.

The irony of the statement, of course, was that though it came from within Tokin, it was not him. He did not really embrace many of the things he said, the truisms he shared.

Tokin had built a small room in his mind. It was composed of solid steel walls that were many feet thick. The space inside was small. Just large enough to contain his thoughts, one at a time. He couldn't be sure, but he thought that in this nearly airless room inside his mind, he was safe. This was the only place that he believed he might have a thought that Janus could not hear.

He was wrong. Janus was everywhere inside his mind, including the tiny room. Janus did everything it could to encourage him to believe he was alone in that room, though. That was where it could hear his true, innermost thoughts. Tokin had become adept at silencing his thoughts in his normal conscious mind.

The mind of any human was no match for the power of Janus. It was everywhere.

At that moment, while he seemed to be teaching the ten orange-robed students in front of him, Tokin was critically concerned in his mind room.

Janus had been inside his mind for almost two years at that point. Initially, he had thought it wouldn't be so completely awful. Yes, there was a strange voice in his head, and he wavered back and forth as to whether it was real or not, but it seemed friendly enough. If he was going insane, at least he wouldn't be completely alone.

Over the months that followed, the voice became more than just that. It began to push and persuade him to do certain things. When Tokin decided to have a test of wills against Janus, he found how helpless he was.

Once inside the dome, with no specific assigned job, Tokin wanted to be useful. He didn't care how or what he was doing as much as he just wanted to be actively helping. He would have been happy to work on the landscaping that wasn't digital, or deliver food to people that didn't want to go out to eat, or scrape and wash dishes after they were done.

Janus had other plans for Tokin. It never explained how or why it had selected him for the role it wanted him to play. In his darkest times, he assumed it was because of some mental weakness or defect he possessed. A different person might have thought it was because he had some special ability, but Tokin was as egoless as any human ever was.

Janus's plan for Tokin was revealed in the first moments in his new apartment when he was given the selection of robes to wear and nothing else. From that point forward, whether he wanted to be one or not, Tokin was a monk.

He had entered Altor with a full head of hair, but even that had changed over a short period of time. In less than two years inside the dome, nearly all of his hair had fallen out to a point that he had begun shaving the remainder.

Before he knew what was happening, Janus had directed him to the very spot where he sat with his students at that moment. It was always the same place, beside the pond, next to the swans. It was as if the sight of the robed monk and students was as much a display as the water and the birds.

Even then, with Tokin riding essentially as a passenger in his own body, he told himself that things were okay. Janus wasn't causing him to do anything bad. He was simply mouthing simple platitudes that the students seemed to enjoy. It wasn't what he would have chosen for himself, but there was no harm in it.

That had held until the previous day.

Tokin had given his morning class, then gone for a walk. His strolls around Altor were his favorite time of day. That was when Janus abandoned him as much as he ever did. He felt free just to be himself. He smiled and nodded at the people he passed and paused to enjoy the many beautiful aspects of Altor.

On that previous day, for the first time, he had seen people *outside* the dome. Not a few random people, either, but what appeared to be hundreds of people staring in at him. Front and center of the group were two striking figures dressed in black with incredibly long, pure white hair.

When they caught Tokin's eye, Janus reasserted itself in his mind for a moment. It took control of his body and made him walk to the very edge of the path, staring directly at the two black-clad figures and bow at the waist.

Without hesitation, they returned the gesture.

Janus returned control of Tokin's body. He shook his head. It was always uncomfortable and disconcerting when Janus took control of him unexpectedly.

He turned and wandered away, feeling a sudden need for privacy. More accurately, for as much privacy as he ever had.

He decided to head back to the building where his apartment was and lie down and rest, perhaps even sleep a little before his afternoon session with his students. He had no lesson in mind for them, but that didn't matter at all. He knew it would be there, a gift from Janus, when the moment arrived.

As he walked toward his building, Janus asserted itself again. It caused him to turn off the main path and toward the elevator that led up to the observation deck.

Ordinarily, Tokin would not have objected to that. The view from the very top of the dome was beautiful, especially at night, or at sunrise or sunset.

This time, he wanted nothing more than to get away and relax for a few minutes. He fought against the force inside him that was making his feet move toward the elevator. He rarely resisted, but today he was fed up. He exerted all his will toward taking control over his own body.

It had no effect at all.

As loudly as he screamed to turn around, his body walked calmly forward.

The elevator door slid open and completely against his will, he walked forward. The moment the door slid shut, the car jumped up. When the door opened onto the observation deck, he involuntarily stepped out. Instead of walking out to the edge, where you could see both the landscape outside and the ground level of Altor, he moved around the body of the elevator until he was hidden from the view of anyone who would exit the elevator.

Once he was in place, his body locked rigidly. He tried to raise his hand to no avail, then attempted to speak. His body did not respond. He was unable to do anything more than blink.

He heard the elevator door open and then footsteps. He could see the figure of a man walking to the very edge of the railing. He bent and looked down at the activity of Altor far below.

In that moment, Tokin had known what was about to happen. It was as if he could suddenly read the man's mind.

He was going to throw himself over the ledge.

Just as quickly, with a sense of relief, Tokin could feel the man change his mind.

The man—who Tokin did not recognize—turned, as if he was going to walk back toward the elevator.

With horror, Tokin felt his body rush forward. He saw the man's eyes widen at the sight of him.

Tokin closed his eyes but could not stop his body. At the last moment, he leaped slightly and his shoulder hit the man just above his breastbone. With nothing more than a startled gasp, the man tumbled over backward and fell to what Tokin knew would be his certain death.

Tokin stood rooted to the spot. He was in shock. In an odd way, he felt a sense of relief. He had just committed a murder. Everyone knew that there were cameras everywhere, recording everything. It would be obvious to everyone what he had just done. Whether it was against his own will or not, he had done it. He would be locked up, which would at least stop him from ever doing anything like that again.

He wanted to just stand there and wait for someone from Altor security to come and arrest him, but again, Janus took control of his body. The elevator opened, Tokin stepped in, and then out again at the bottom.

As he walked, Tokin moved his head left and right, expecting someone to come running up and tackle him.

Nothing happened.

Finally, Janus *did* return him to his apartment. The voice in his head went completely quiet. There were no explanations, no *mea culpas*, no anything.

He found he was unable to leave his apartment for the rest of the day. Apparently, Janus had sent out a message canceling the afternoon class.

He had no interest in eating, reading, or watching anything on the screen. He left his view blank, preferring to stare at just the walls of his apartment. Eventually he fell asleep and slept dreamlessly until the following morning.

When he woke at his normal time, he could only think of the events of the day before. His conscience weighed him down. He had not intended to harm the unknown man, but the reality was, *he had.* He knew he was responsible for it.

Finally, the voice reappeared in his mind.

"But you're not. *I was.* There's no reason to attack yourself like this."

Tokin didn't answer, but instead did his best to make his mind blank—to escape to his small room.

Janus took control of his body and directed him downstairs to conduct his normal lesson, which is where he was at that moment. He sat cross-legged, locked in his own mental jail, while Janus taught the lesson.

Tokin did not hear what Janus was saying, but at that moment, it felt almost like there was a knock on the door of his tiny mental room. It was as if Janus was asking for permission to enter, or to get Tokin to open the door.

He sighed internally and left the room, his only sanctuary. He tuned in to what his own voice was saying.

"This is a big moment for all of us. Today is a day of transition." He looked at his students and saw a flash of excitement cross their faces. "Please, come with me."

The students exchanged looks, wondering what new level of enlightenment they were about to receive.

Silently, Tokin stood and, hands clasped together in front of him as if in prayer, led the students onto the path and along to an area at the back of the dome that was rarely visited by citizens. They approached a door ahead of them and stepped inside a room that appeared to be a beautiful garden. Long, green vines hung down along the wall, mixed with leafy trees and sweet-smelling flowers. There were hummingbirds and small blue birds flitting here and there through the branches of the trees.

Tokin waved toward some long stone benches, saying, "Sit, please."

As the students settled on the bench, Tokin sat in the lovely, carved teacher's chair at the front of the room.

At that moment, Janus left his mind. This time, it actually left. It did not need or want to be inside Tokin's head for this.

It was then that Tokin received his own version of enlightenment. He realized that he had been nothing more than a tool to Janus. To what end, he could not say. What was clear to him in that moment, however, was that he, and everyone else in the room, was about to die.

His long journey from birth to that moment was over. He took a few seconds to contemplate his lifetime. He smiled at his students, knowing there was nothing he could do to save them.

The odorless gas poured into the airtight room.

It was over in moments. Tokin was, mercifully, the first to collapse and die but was joined within seconds by the ten students.

Before the air had cleared of the deadly gas, a different door slid open. The images of the garden disappeared and the walls were once again plain. Eleven orange-robed monks, identical to those who were dead on the floor, entered the room. Behind them were robots pushing carts. The new monks were not harmed by the gas in any way.

The robots efficiently loaded the bodies onto the carts. One at a time, the carts disappeared through the back door of the room and to the spot where the corpses could be disposed of.

From that moment on, Tokin and the rest of the monks were Janus, and Janus was the monks.

Chapter Thirty-Seven
By Hook or by Crook

Harper gaped at Nyx. She shook her head in disbelief. "I can't believe you'd do that."

Nyx drew a deep breath and let it out slowly. "Soldiers are trained to never leave a buddy behind."

Harper cringed at that. She had done exactly that.

"Operatives are not trained that way. We are trained that the objective is paramount. If it is a choice between the success of the mission or the life of our fellow operatives—even if it is a sibling, spouse, or training partner—we are to leave them behind. That was then, though. Now I get to make up my own mind. I feel at least slightly responsible for his arrival in Dust City and the fact that he took it upon himself to bring you here means I can't just abandon him there."

She saw the doubt in Harper's eyes and took a step toward her. "You did the right thing. If you hadn't, it wouldn't have helped Van at all, and you and Archer wouldn't be here."

"We can't even know if he's alive."

"That's right, we don't. And that's what my mother and sister told me last night."

"They already know."

Nyx nodded. "I'm leaving in a few minutes."

"*We're* leaving in a few minutes."

Nyx smiled, recognizing her own spirit in Harper. "That is truly not even a possibility. You're an extraordinary young woman. Someday, with the proper training, you could be an outstanding operative. I have much higher hopes for you than that, though. I want you to live and see if a new world will rise from the ashes of the old. To find your own destiny."

She could see that Harper was already lining up her arguments and put her arm around the young girl's shoulders.

"I will always tell you the hard truths, because that is better than a soft half-lie. Here's one: you would not be a help on this mission. You would be a hindrance, and I would spend some of my precious energy worrying and looking out for you."

The words stung, but Harper appreciated being treated like an adult. She swallowed hard and nodded, holding her thoughts to herself.

"Right now, you're probably thinking you can trail me and that if you catch up to me a good distance from home, I'll be forced to take you along. That would be a mistake. First, I'm going to take Blackie. That's the fastest way for me to cover ground. The longer it takes me to get there, the greater the chance that Van is dead, even if he survived the initial attack."

Harper hated that tears appeared in her eyes, but she was helpless to stop them. Two years earlier, she had been a junior high student recovering from a terrible auto accident. Her biggest challenge was figuring out how much of her burgeoning intellect to share with the world. Since then, she had left that world behind, buried both her parents, undertaken two incredible journeys, and single-handedly nursed an entire settlement back to health. She was no longer that young girl of two years earlier, but she was still only fourteen years old.

Nyx hugged her close, then said, "Let's go back to the cabin. Mom's packing enough food to make sure I gain weight on the trip, no doubt."

When they stepped back inside, there were bags of food and supplies sitting on the kitchen table.

Harper looked at Archer and could see that while Nyx had been talking to her, someone else had spoken to him. He shrugged, a ghost of a smile, eloquent in its own way. He wasn't happy to be left behind either, but the fact that Nyx was going at all was the only chance they had to ever see Van again.

They all ate breakfast together. It was a somber affair, and it was obvious that not everyone agreed that Nyx should be risking her life going after someone that the rest of the family didn't even know.

The only vote that counted was Nyx's though, and she had elected to go.

Once it was obvious that was the case, everyone seemed to relax a little. There was every possibility that Nyx might never return from this rescue. There was no reason to make this last meal together unpleasant.

When breakfast was done, Nyx didn't dawdle. She hugged Chaya and Millie, kissed her mother on the cheek and said, "You know what to do," to her sister. She slung the two packs over her shoulder and went out the door, closing it behind her. It was obvious she didn't want anyone following her out.

* * *

Nyx was better equipped in every way than Harper and Archer had been.

They had been fleeing in a panic, were inexperienced with horses, had no weapons and not nearly enough food to get them where they were going.

Nyx never panicked, was an expert horsewoman, carried three pistols and two rifles, and had enough food to give her a good head start on her journey. Not enough to get all the way to where she thought Van might be and back, especially if she needed to feed him on the way, but enough to start.

The most invaluable thing she had was her training. She wasn't just accomplished in hand-to-hand fighting and weapons of all types. She'd also been trained in wilderness survival. In truth, she felt a little embarrassed at all the food Shalva had insisted she take, but taking it was much easier than arguing.

Nyx had stayed up late the night before, plotting out an approximate route, including how many miles she would try to travel each day. She was not familiar with the area she would be traveling through, but she counted on her ability to adjust any plan on the fly. She figured she could make it to the spot where Harper and Archer had lost Van in two weeks. She thought she might need three to four days scouting the area to determine if Van was alive or dead, then slightly longer on the return trip.

If Van was alive, but still hobbled by injuries, even with Blackie, it would take longer to return. She planned three weeks for the return trip.

In all, she thought she would likely return in six weeks. That was why she had told her mother she would be back in two months or a little more.

Shalva knew that Nyx would overestimate the time so she wouldn't worry. She correctly guessed it should be about six weeks and would begin to become concerned after that. Not that there was anything that could be done other than worry, but that's what mothers did.

The first ten days of the journey passed easily. The weather was warmer and there was no snow on the ground. Animals were becoming more plentiful, which made hunting easier. Whenever possible, Nyx stuck to the forests. There were times when the undergrowth was too thick, there were simply no trails, or the geography made that impossible.

On those occasions, she found her way to the nearest road and made better time, but as soon as she could, she made her way back in the wild again. Whenever she was on a road, she was on high alert, with one of her pistols drawn and ready to fire at her side.

At one point, she was on a small country road. Two lanes, but after nearly two years of neglect, nature was beginning to reclaim it. Weeds and grass had begun to grow up between the cracks in the asphalt and at the edges it was hard to tell where the road stopped and the shoulder began.

If she couldn't be in an open plain, or a valley with tall hills on either side, or picking her way through the forest, this was her chosen avenue of travel. This road didn't look like it had been traveled much when civilization was still a thing. Now, she thought it was unlikely she would meet anyone at all.

She was wrong. Sometimes being wrong can be fatal. Other times, it can simply be a close call.

There was no sign of anything being wrong. No fresh tracks or strange sounds reached her ears, but she was on high alert nonetheless.

She saw what was goosing her sixth sense when three men stepped out from behind a tall fallen log. She didn't think they had been waiting there for her. That would make no sense. There wasn't likely to be enough traffic on the road to support robbers.

By the looks of them, she thought they were probably just a small group who had managed to stay alive to this point. They didn't look like much. In fact, they looked more like feral humans than anything.

All three were armed with rifles and they were all pointed at her from twenty-five feet away.

"That is a beautiful horse," a man with a long gray beard said. "We'll take it now."

"She's not so bad herself," a younger man with a scruffy growth of beard said. "Can we take her, too?"

"'Course we can," gray beard said.

Before those words were out of his mouth, Nyx had elected on her course of action. She raised her left hand—the one without the pistol in it—and, doing her best to look scared, swung her right leg off of Blackie.

Quick as a cat, she ran behind and slightly to the side of the horse. She didn't want to risk Blackie getting hurt if she could avoid it. As soon as she cleared the back haunches of the horse, she fired. She had her target order already lined out in her mind.

Her first shot hit gray beard in the throat. Her second punched a hole through the middle of the younger man. Her third was slightly off and hit the third man in the shoulder, spinning him around.

She never slowed and didn't wait to see how they would respond. She ran forward and put two more rounds into the only one who was still standing. He fell in a crumpled heap. She hurried to the other two men and kicked their rifles away.

With no hesitation, she put another shot in the forehead of the man with the scruffy beard. The oldest man was pushing away from her, scrabbing his feet against the road. He had one hand in a death grip on his throat wound. The other was held up in front of him, pleading with her not to shoot him.

One more quick shot to the forehead and the fight was over. In truth, it wasn't a battle. It was a massacre.

It's always possible that in a gun battle, an amateur will get off a lucky shot and take down a trained operative, but it's not likely. In this case, none of the three men had even squeezed off a shot.

Nyx didn't bother to frisk the men. By their look, she was sure they wouldn't have anything that would be of any use to them. She looked back at Blackie, who had raised her head and backed away a few feet, but hadn't bolted.

Nyx approached the horse, speaking softly. She walked close until she was near enough to stroke and gentle her.

Less than five minutes after the men had stepped out of the brush, Nyx was on her way.

She never thought of those three men again.

Chapter Thirty-Eight
The Ranch

Nyx had slightly underestimated the time it would take her to get to the spot where Harper and Archer had escaped.

She didn't have any more bloody confrontations, but she did pick up on several other potential ambush spots. To avoid those, she often rode an hour or two out of her way. A little extra time on the move was a good tradeoff for not having to kill more people. She was already dragging a long enough body count list behind her. She only added to it when she had no choice.

Using Archer's homemade latitude and longitude tracker, she took to the highway for the last few miles before she reached the spot.

It was a long, straight highway that had once been busy. There were two lanes in each direction and an actual shoulder, though that was overrun by vines and bushes.

She didn't have to wonder when she was at the spot where the confrontation had happened. There was evidence of blood in four different spots on the road. Using the description of the fight that Harper had given her, Nyx tried to recreate how it had played out.

There were two dried blood puddles just a few feet apart. She guessed that was where Van and the older man—Sam Harris, Harper had said his name was—had fought. One puddle from where Van had broken the man's nose and another where Van had been shot in the leg.

Nyx paced along the road ahead and found another large residue of blood. She guessed this was where Van had put the son, Freddie down. Walking back ten paces, she found the last spray of what had once been red and had now dried to a rusty brown consistency. That was likely where Van had been shot a second time, trying to get away with Harper and Archer.

Nyx kept a wary eye out in case someone approached in either direction, but the road remained empty. She walked to the shoulder and looked carefully for drag marks or any sign that a body had been carried off the road. She didn't find anything, which made her think that they hadn't killed Van there.

If they had, they wouldn't have bothered to do anything with his body. There would be some evidence of a corpse somewhere nearby, even if wild animals had found it and scattered the bones.

"Good," Nyx murmured to herself. This was a positive sign that she hadn't made the trip for no reason.

Harper hadn't ever seen the ranch, and didn't really know how far it was from the spot where they'd gotten away. Based on how long they'd been riding up to that point and how far Harris had told them the journey was, Nyx believed it wouldn't be too far.

She thought it was probably within an hour's ride—no more than six or seven miles away from where she stood.

She knew it was possible that there was more than one functioning ranch still operating in the area. Based on everything she knew about Harris, though, she thought it was unlikely. He seemed more like the type that would take over or incorporate competitors rather than cooperate with them. In any case, once she found a possibility, she would do a thorough job of scouting. She wasn't planning on charging in half-cocked.

There was one last possibility. If she found the ranch and couldn't verify that Van was there, or if he was so securely imprisoned that she knew she couldn't get him out, she would have to abandon the plan. She had too many responsibilities back in Colorado to take foolish risks during this operation.

She remounted Blackie and rode due east for about one-third of a mile. Her approach to everything would be cautious now. The fact that Harris had used this road once meant that it was likely he or some of his gunmen would be using it again. Nyx didn't want to be on it when that happened.

Once she got the proper distance from the road, she went parallel to it, but slowly. Every few hundred yards, she stopped and, still high up on Blackie, used her Vortex binoculars to scan every inch of the horizon ahead of her. The last thing she wanted to do was blunder into an area that was under watch from a guard somewhere. It was critical that she saw them before they saw her.

She had no idea which side of the road the ranch was that she was looking for. She just planned to do a five-mile sweep in one direction, then do the same in another. Eventually, she was sure that would bring her to where she wanted to be.

Nyx had many skills and talents, but one of her most critical was patience. She was never in a hurry unless the situation required it.

At the end of the first day, she hadn't seen a single sign of another human. Even so, she still rode a mile further away into the foothills to camp for the night, and she did this without a fire. She ate some of the elk jerky that she had brought and considered her plan for the next day before lying down in her sleeping bag and looking up at the stars.

As always, she woke up every two hours, listened, scanned, and then went back to sleep.

The next day dawned clear and beautiful, but Nyx was already on the move by the time the first rays of pink and orange were showing in the east. She saw a range of hills a few miles ahead and rode directly to them. There, she found a trail that led up the hill. At the top, she dismounted and walked just below the ridgeline with Blackie behind her.

She found a clearing that gave her exactly what she was looking for—a sweeping view of the surrounding area. She tied Blackie up and crept along the edge of the clearing. Even in this remote area and at this distance from any likely habitation, she was cautious.

She found a tall pine tree and used that as her location to scan for buildings.

It didn't take her long to find some. Just a few miles to her west, there was a large scattering of low-slung buildings, all built around a large three-story house.

Nyx adjusted her binoculars and was able to make out a tall fence line that surrounded the entire compound. The fence consisted of wires, so she guessed it might be electrified. Otherwise, anyone could cut right through and be inside in moments.

She confirmed the likelihood of that when she focused on the roofs of the buildings, which revealed a huge array of solar panels. There were so many, it was obvious that there would be enough power to run the houses and the electric fences too.

Nyx would have preferred to see a strong barrier built with razor wire strung across the top. That would be easier to get up and over than dealing with electricity, unless she could find a way to cut the power.

She knew she needed a better view, so she made her way back to Blackie and walked her along the top of the hill, down into a small ravine and up to the ridge of a second hill. The fir and pine trees gave her good cover, even on the off chance that there was someone below scanning the hills.

After more than an hour of hard climbing and picking her way around impassable areas, she found a location she was happy with. She was more or less directly above the compound. A small mountain stream ran down through a clearing that was only thirty or forty yards across. Shoots of grass grew up beside the bank. That took care of food and water for Blackie.

Just down the hill, Nyx found a spot where she had a good view of the compound below.

Now she could see more clearly. The main house was huge—it looked to be at least six thousand square feet. No vehicles were parked in the large circular driveway in front of the house. There were eight different outbuildings of various sizes and shapes, including a large barn that appeared to have once been an eight-car garage and half a dozen long buildings that Nyx guessed were bunkhouses of some sort.

The fences extended way out away from the buildings. A number of acres were fenced and cross-fenced. Two of the fields had horses. Nyx counted thirty altogether. Other fields were filled with cows and sheep. Two other fields had been turned for a garden that would soon be planted. It looked like a real, working farm. The primary difference was that the bunkhouses were also fenced in, with more electric wiring and a single gate. There was only one reason for that: prisoners.

Nyx settled in and, sweeping her binoculars across the entire compound, began to get a feel for the daily routine.

There were workers scattered around almost everywhere. Five men and women hoed at the garden. Two people were leading the cows into the barn, apparently for the evening milking. As there was activity everywhere, it was difficult for Nyx to get an accurate head count. In addition to the workers, there were guards all over the place, easy to spot by their rifles, clean clothes, and well-fed look.

As the sun set, the workers were led back into the various bunkhouses. A few minutes later, people emerged from the big house carrying large pots. They followed the workers into the bunkhouses and the gate was shut behind them.

"Dinner is served, I guess," Nyx said to herself. She adjusted the light sensitivity on her binoculars and continued to watch.

Eventually, five women from one of the bunkhouses were let out and prodded up to the main house. That story wasn't too difficult to figure out, and Nyx was enraged all over again that Harper would have likely been in that group if not for Van.

She continued to watch for several more hours. Midnight came and went. Eventually, the five women who were taken to the house were returned to the bunkhouses. The guard called out something Nyx couldn't possibly hear, then opened the gate to let them in. Once inside, the gate closed and the guard called out again. Almost certainly a command to someone to turn the power to the gate off and on.

It was an impressive setup and one designed to stop anyone from escaping and others from attacking.

Harsh lights were lit all over the compound so that it was nearly as bright as midday, though a few shadowy spots were scattered around.

Nyx figured she wouldn't learn much more that night and so climbed back to where she had tied Blackie up. She led her to the stream to drink her fill then unrolled her sleeping bag and tried to sleep.

The day's reconnaissance had not been promising. She hadn't seen Van and hadn't seen any obvious way into the compound.

She was once again awake before sunrise and back at her observation post.

Work started early in the compound as the guards were rousting the workers shortly after dawn. The workday seemed to mostly follow the same pattern as the day before. There was a high guard-to-prisoner ratio and the guards mostly seemed to be paying attention. Very likely they knew it was an easy transition from being one of the guards to becoming one of the prisoners.

Nyx didn't know if there were bathrooms plumbed into the bunkhouses or not. She guessed so, but during the day, there were green porta potties in five different places around the field and gardens.

It wasn't until that afternoon that she realized one of the porta potties was never used, so she focused her attention on it. When she turned the magnification on her binoculars up as high as she could, she saw a number of ropes tied around the outside and heavy posts leaning against the door as if someone or something was locked inside.

She watched the whole compound, but, her curiosity piqued, she returned her attention to that single porta potty again and again. Everyone below—workers and guards both—seemed to completely ignore it and went out of their way to walk around it.

A little after four o'clock, when Nyx expected the evening routine to begin, a man she hadn't seen before came out of the big house. He wore an oversized black cowboy hat and seemed to have an entourage with him.

He didn't spend any time inspecting the fields or outbuildings. Instead, he headed straight for the locked-up porta potty. He stood a few feet in front of it while two other men stepped forward and worked on removing the posts that blocked the door, then untied the knots.

Eventually, the door opened and a man stepped out, then fell to the ground.

Nyx leaned forward, electrified. She focused at maximum magnification on the body on the ground, but beyond seeing an incredibly thin body, she couldn't see who it was. She did have a hunch, though.

The man who seemed to be in charge reached out with his boot and turned the man onto his back.

Her hunch was correct. The prisoner in the porta potty was Van Hoffler.

Chapter Thirty-Nine
Near Death

A carousel of thoughts and emotions ran through Nyx's mind.

She was pleased that Van was alive and that she had located him. She was dismayed at the condition he was in. He was dressed in rags and was so emaciated, she was not surprised he couldn't stand. Immediately, her mind began to focus on the central problem—how to get in, retrieve Van, and get out.

No foolproof plan sprang immediately to mind, but that didn't concern her. Now that she knew the layout of the property and where Van was being held, she would let her mind work on the problem.

For the moment, she just watched the scene play out below.

The man in the cowboy hat, who she had guessed was likely Sam Harris, gestured at Van.

Another man stepped forward and set a bowl and a plastic glass in front of him.

Van rolled over and grasped the glass with both hands. Even from far away, Nyx could see that his hands were shaking as he tried to drink it. That was completely in line with the training Van had been given: always take what the enemy gives you. Anything that allows you to live to fight another day.

Van drained whatever was in the glass, then dropped it to the dirt and lay back, obviously unable to hold himself up any longer.

The man who had put the food and water in front of him nudged him hard in the side with his boot.

Van nodded, then lifted the bowl to his lips. It took him some time, but he finally seemed to have finished whatever was in the bowl.

The man in the cowboy hat kneeled down close to Van and spoke to him. Van just stayed still, eyes closed. Eventually, the man stood, delivered a kick to Van's side, then turned and walked away. Van absorbed the blow as if he was already a corpse.

Two of the men lifted Van up and placed him back inside the porta potty, then went about resecuring it.

Nyx thought Van looked so weak, he probably couldn't have escaped if they had left it open. That concerned her. If she was able to get to him and get him out, would she have to carry him? That looked like a real possibility. He was skin and bones and Nyx was strong, but carrying him for any real distance would be difficult.

She sat and watched as the compound went through essentially the same routine as it had the night before. She made mental notes on what time things happened. One thing that pleased her was that no guard made the rounds once the women had been returned from the big house and locked back in their bunkhouses.

Nyx was momentarily torn between possible choices. On the one hand, she had some idea of how to attack the situation. It only made sense to operate at night when no one was around. That spoke to going in after Van right now. Her concern was that if she left it another night, Van's condition was so grave he might perish before she could get there.

On the other hand, there were some things she was going to need to build to properly attack the situation. She didn't feel that she had the time to do so and still get to Van while it was dark.

She elected to wait until the following night, hoping that Van would survive another twenty-four hours in the porta potty. She envisioned how small and cramped one of them was on the inside and felt for her friend. If he had been in there for more than a month, it was a miracle he was still alive or sane.

She hurried back to her camping spot and slept for a few hours, knowing that she would have all the daylight hours to build and gather what she needed.

She was up and at work before first light. She picked out a number of trees that weren't too big in diameter and cut them down with her camp axe. After a few hours work, she had turned them into what she wanted.

Next, she went about gathering handfuls of sap from a stand of sugar maples. She formed the sap into balls and stuffed that into one of her now empty bags, along with dry grass. She used her axe again to shave off some cedar bark and was ready.

She had finished before the sun had gone down and so went back to her observation point to see if anything had changed. She sat, rested, and watched as the compound followed the same routine it had since she had arrived.

Nyx noted that no one approached Van on this afternoon. She wondered if he was only given that small amount of food and water every other day. If so, it really was a miracle he was alive.

She continued to watch as everyone went through their nightly routines. As soon as things settled down, she walked back uphill, untied Blackie, and picked her way carefully along the hillside while working her way down.

A little after midnight, she was in position. She slung a rifle over her shoulder, put two pistols in her belt, and tied Blackie to a young sapling not far from the fence line. She grabbed the two lightweight ladders and her bag full of fire-starting equipment.

While she had sat that afternoon, she had studied the far fence line and decided which field was best. She chose one that had only a few horses in it. She threw one of the wooden ladders over the fence and leaned the other one against the electric wires. She climbed carefully up the ladder, making sure to only touch the wires with the sole of her rubber boots. At the apex of the ladder, she jumped lightly down to the other side.

She leaned the second ladder against the inside of the fence, hopefully ready for their escape, though she wasn't at all sure Van would have the strength to get up and over it. That was a problem for later.

The horses nickered as she walked across the field, but it wasn't anything out of the ordinary that might arouse suspicion.

The interior fences all had gates, and Nyx closed each one behind her but did not latch them.

Five minutes after she had climbed over the exterior fence, she stood in front of the porta potty that served as a prison for Van. One at a time, she removed the heavy posts, then untied the knots by feel. It wasn't challenging—she thought that whoever had tied them had left a little room, knowing he would just be untying them soon enough.

When the last knot was loosened, she dropped the rope and opened the door, holding her breath. She hadn't heard a word from inside, though it would have been obvious someone was working on the knots. She was afraid that when she opened the door, Van's corpse would come tumbling out.

Instead, she saw him sitting upright over the toilet hole.

"Who's there?" Van asked, his voice raspy and barely audible.

"Shh. It's Nyx. Listen. Stay here. I'm going to go buy us some time. Can you walk?"

"I can, but probably not far."

"I saw you on the ground yesterday," Nyx whispered.

"A little playacting, but mostly true. I wanted them to think I was weaker than I was." Almost unbelievably, a tiny smile played on the edge of his lips.

"Stay," Nyx said, shutting the door again. She hurried past the bunkhouses toward the big house. She had seen a long pile of firewood stacked against one wall. She went into her silent mode as she approached the house.

There were still a few lights on in the windows, but as she expected, there were no guards or lookouts.

She hunkered down and built a fire-ready pile at the bottom of the firewood. She spread the pitch around and added lots of dry grass with the cedar bark on top. After checking everything over, she flicked on her lighter and lit the grass.

She watched to see if it would catch or fizzle. It sputtered for a moment, then caught. She moved the firewood above the blaze so it would give it more oxygen. She stepped back and blended into the shadows for a minute, watching the fire grow. When she saw that it had well and truly caught, she turned back toward Van.

When she approached, she was surprised to find Van standing outside. She wanted to ask how he was this strong but didn't want to take the time. Instead, she said, "Lean on me. Save your strength." She remembered which side he'd been shot in the leg and went to his left side.

Like a couple at a three-legged race at a picnic, they hurried away. At the first fence, Nyx opened the gate wide, then pushed through with Van.

"Hang on, stay here for a second." She ran up to several of the horses and clapped and shouted "Hyah!" at them. They panicked a bit at the sight of this stranger in their pasture at night and ran toward the open gate.

At that moment, a glow came from behind them and she heard someone shout "Fire!"

"That'll keep them busy," Nyx said. "Let's see about getting you out of here."

At each new gate, Nyx kicked it open and did her best to panic the animals toward it. She hoped that between the animals running through the yard and the fire, they would be too busy to notice Van was missing.

At the final fence line, Nyx pointed at the homemade ladder. "Can you make it up and over?" She had noticed that Van was flagging as they worked their way across the fields.

"I think so," Van said.

Nyx shook her head. "No, I don't think you can." She put her shoulder into his midsection and flipped him over her back in a fireman's carry. She grunted a little but managed to step up the ladder. She made it fine until she reached near the top, then the ladder shifted under her. She pitched forward and Van flew off her shoulder and landed on the other side with a small cry.

Nyx herself slipped off the ladder and into the electric fence. She felt a shock run through her leg and up her spine and forced herself to tumble forward. As she landed on her back, she felt the air whoosh out of her lungs. She didn't move for a few seconds, trying to catch her breath. "You okay?"

Van tried to raise himself up, failed, and fell face down into the grass. "I'll be okay," he muttered into the dirt.

"You stay here. I'll be right back." Nyx climbed to her feet, then forced herself to run toward Blackie. As she ran, she heard more cries coming from the compound, including one voice that screamed, "He's gone!"

She flew up onto Blackie, pulled the reins loose, and rode back toward Van. Bouncing flashlight beams in the first field were heading toward them.

She leaped down and helped Van to his feet. "You get in the saddle and hold the reins. I'll climb on behind you and hold you upright."

Van nodded and swayed. She could see that he was at the end of whatever strength he had. She half-lifted, half-pushed him onto the horse, then used the stirrups to climb up behind him. "Come on, Blackie, let's run."

Nyx wasn't sure she was going to be able to keep both of them upright while Blackie ran, but as her gait smoothed out, it got easier. She hoped they would only have to keep up this pace for a short time. She didn't think their pursuers had any vehicles, and she knew it would be difficult to track them in the dark.

After half an hour of running Blackie hard, she slowed her down. "You okay?" she asked Van.

There was no answer. She figured she was either riding with a corpse or he had passed out. Either way, she wanted to put more space between them and their likely pursuers.

Chapter Forty
A Family

As it turned out, Van had only lost consciousness. It was no wonder, after the way he had been tortured over the previous weeks.

Nyx didn't focus on traveling in any one direction as they fled from the ranch. She just wanted to get as far away as fast as possible.

She wanted speed, and that meant sticking more to open areas. The forested areas offered her better cover but slowed her down. She wasn't sure what kind of tracking Harris might have. She hadn't seen bloodhounds or other tracking dogs, but that didn't absolutely mean he didn't have them. Maybe he kept an old, wizened tracker in the house to go after the prisoners when they ran away. Anything was possible, and she didn't want to find out the hard way.

She even turned onto an old country road for a few miles to circumvent a mountain pass. As soon as she could, she got off of that, though. She realized they were heading in the wrong direction, and she was fine with that. If they did manage to track her for a time, they would think she had come from the west and might look for them in that direction.

Nyx wanted to be able to stop and do a quick triage on Van but felt that distance was more important than good health at that moment.

After several hours of riding through the darkness, the sky grew light behind them, and it was easier for her to navigate. She found an old trail that led up the side of a hill and took it to the top. Once there, she eased Van off Blackie and helped him sit on the grass. She left him there and walked to the lip of the ridge. She pulled her binoculars out of her bag and trained them in the direction they had just come.

There was no one visible for as far as she could see. She took out Archer's GPS, then located where they were on the map. Once she had figured that out, she plotted a less helter-skelter route. Her plan was to ride north for the rest of the day, then make a big loop around the ranch. She didn't want to come within twenty-five miles of it on the way home. Based on how Van and the kids had been captured, she knew that Harris had lookouts on the major roads, so she planned to avoid those at all costs.

She turned to Van. "How are your wounds?"

He was groggy, still half out of it and swayed a little, as though he was still on the horse. "They're all right. After Harper and Archer got away, Harris and his boy were pretty pissed. They could have just killed me, but that wasn't good enough for them. They hauled me back to the ranch and had their doc there patch me up. I think he was actually a vet, but whatever, he did the job. They didn't want me to die from blood loss or gangrene. They wanted to torture me to death."

Nyx nodded. She had suspected something like that. "As she rode away, Harper said she heard a gunshot. She was afraid they'd shot you again."

"That kid," Van said with a pained smile. "She's something else. She didn't want to leave me, but I'm sure glad she made it to you. The shot she heard was the Harris kid firing his gun right beside my head, trying to scare me. I don't hear so well out of that ear now. That's been the least of my problems, though."

Nyx looked at the surrounding area, then back the way they had come. "I've got some food left. Not enough to get us home, but enough to get us started." She dug through her food bag and came out with a handful of jerky. "Get some protein in you." She looked at the ragged shirt Van was wearing, which was now much too big for him. "Do you mind?" she asked, pointing at the buttons.

"Go ahead." Van winced a little in preparation.

Nyx unbuttoned the shirt and nodded. It was what she had expected—an impressive collection of bruises, old and new. One discoloration on his left side was particularly large and a deep red, nearly brown. She didn't touch it; that would have told her nothing. "Looks like you might have some broken ribs."

"I think so. Hurts to breathe. That little son of a bitch Freddie kicked me with his steel-toed boots a few days ago."

"That's going to make riding on Blackie a pain, but there's nothing else for it."

"Might as well get started, then," Van agreed.

They rode north for the rest of the day. They were both completely exhausted by nightfall and Nyx was worried she wasn't thinking clearly. They rode deep into a wooded area and camped for the night.

Nyx unrolled her sleeping bag and had Van lie down on it. She walked Blackie to a small stream to drink and when she got back, Van had passed out. She leaned against a tree, closed her eyes, and fell into an exhausted sleep within minutes.

Over the next few days, they slowly worked their way around the area where Nyx and Van thought Harris might have men stationed. Finally, they made their way past it and were on essentially the same trail Nyx had followed on the way there.

They made good progress on the way home. Riding was painful for Van, but he never complained. Every few nights, they would get off the trail early and Nyx would hunt for rabbits, grouse, squirrels, anything they could put in the stewpot that night. Getting better rest, regular nutrition and water, and being out of captivity led to Van slowly regaining strength.

The truth was, he would probably never be the same strong warrior he had been just a few months before. The bullet wounds had only been minimally patched up. The starvation and beatings had taken their toll. He was alive, though.

When they finally reached the outer edges of the cabin's defenses, Nyx rode straight toward one of the cameras. She, Van, and Blackie stood directly in view for a long minute, until they saw the camera move and knew they had been spotted.

Fifteen minutes later, they rode into the clearing from the far side of the pond. The whole family was waiting for them outside. Harper and Archer were so excited to see that Nyx had pulled off the rescue, they were jumping up and down. Chaya and Millie got caught up in the excitement and began to jump up and down and cheer as well.

Nyx was still riding behind Van and quietly said, "How many missions have you ever had where you were met by cheers at the end?"

"None," Van said.

Nyx jumped down and ran forward to be enveloped by her family. Harper and Archer hurried up to Blackie and helped Van down. "You're so skinny!" Harper exclaimed.

"You should have seen me a couple of weeks ago."

Harper and Archer slipped under Van's arms and helped him toward the cabin.

Shalva seemed to be in heaven with her daughter home safely and a guest who obviously needed to be fed and cared for.

Everyone else gathered around the kitchen table while Shalva cooked. Soon, the delicious smell of bread filled the room.

Van inhaled deeply and said, "Based on what I smell coming from that kitchen, how are you not all four hundred pounds?"

It was Chaya who answered. "It's because Mom makes us work hard every day."

Adva smiled and tilted her head in a way that said she didn't disagree with that.

They had an hour's *getting to know you* chat with Van while Shalva made a wonderful vegetable soup to go with the thick slabs of bread slathered with butter.

When the meal was done, it was up to Nyx and Van to tell of the daring midnight rescue from the Harris ranch.

Neither of the two protagonists was at all used to talking about their missions, but through lots of questions and prodding, the story eventually emerged. No one sitting around the table, from the youngest to the oldest, was surprised at Nyx's cool head, precise planning, and flawless execution of the plan. They all nodded in quiet satisfaction as Van narrated how she had taken charge and gotten him safely out of the compound.

When the tale was told, Van and Nyx's eyes met briefly. Nyx nodded as if to say, *go ahead. Say what you're thinking.*

He did. "I feel awful about the people that are left behind. They weren't actively torturing them like they did me, but they were living terrible lives."

"Especially the women," Nyx said, obviously angry at the memory of how they were treated. "Sitting on that hillside, planning how to get you out, I wracked my brain trying to think of a way to free all of the prisoners as well." She shook her head at the memory. "I don't think there was a way to accomplish that, though."

Van's eyes lit up with an idea. "In a couple of months, when the weather is warmer and traveling is easy, we could go back. With two of us, we might be able to do it."

It was obvious what everyone else thought of that idea. The idea of losing Nyx again with no certainty of her returning was not something anyone wanted to contemplate.

"I thought about that on the way home," Nyx said. "I think we could kill a bunch of people, but I don't think we could take out everyone." She didn't want to point out that Van was unlikely to ever be the same operative he once had been. There was no need.

Nyx used the last bit of the piece of bread in front of her to sop up the remainder of the soup in her bowl.

"But I think I have a much better idea. I can't be sure it will work, but I'm going to see what I can do to help those people."

Shalva smiled, relaxing a bit at the thought that her daughter would be home for the foreseeable future.

* * *

Van didn't intend to stay at the cabin. His plan all along had been to deliver Harper and Archer, then work his way back to Dust City.

In the end, he just never found a reason to leave.

The cabin was pretty full with nine people living in it, but everyone was conscious of that and did their best to give the others as much space as possible.

That was easy in the summertime, when the warm weather and sunshine beckoned everyone outdoors.

And, as Chaya had pointed out, there was always more work to be done—even for the kids.

As Van slowly regained his strength, he and Nyx offered training sessions on the grass in front of the cabin. By the end of the summer, even Rose and Millie were becoming more adept at fighting and weapons use. Everyone agreed that it was better to be prepared than be caught off guard.

The bond between Nyx and Harper grew. In almost every situation large and small, when Nyx made a decision, Harper was there to talk it through and to understand how her mind worked.

There were still challenges, but as the world began to rebuild in other places, peace, tranquility and a sense of belonging turned those who lived at the cabin into the most precious of organizations: a family.

Chapter Forty-One
Time to Go

Things had been busy in Dust City. In fact, it was more accurate to say that the needle pointed firmly at *chaotic* rather than simply *busy.*

Janus had manipulated an influx of people that the powers-that-be in Dust City were supposed to welcome into their fold.

The new arrivals were promising. Many of them had skills and talents that were missing in Dust City since the helicopter attack and The Shivers had effectively wiped out most of the skilled workers. It was as if Janus had anticipated all that and had begun cherry-picking replacements long before they were needed.

And now they were here.

What Janus didn't seem to understand, though, was that humans were not replaceable cogs in a machine. Just because a person was a diesel mechanic, an organic gardener, or a computer programmer, it didn't mean they could replace the original person who had done the same job.

The people who had built Dust City—and Altor—had mostly been there from the beginning. They understood how things worked because they had helped create everything. They had a feel for the slightly anarchic vibe of the thrown-together town because they had been the ones throwing it together.

Humans were much more than the sum of their degrees and work experience.

Talia Blankenship had been an expert hydroponic gardener. She acted as the Dungeon Master for a weekly *Dungeons and Dragons* game that had been going on for years. She had been killed by The Shivers.

Randy Garret might be able to help fill her shoes in the gardens once he learned the systems, but that D&D game had been a part of what kept a small group of people sane amidst the insanity around them.

Multiply Talia and Randy by hundreds, and you begin to get an idea of the current situation in Dust City.

The fact that the leadership positions were all changing only exacerbated the chaos. Adrien Pierce had been felled by the virus. Marshall and Steele were preparing to decamp for Altor.

Dani Butcher and Levi Rybicki were stepping up to fill their shoes as best they could, but they knew they weren't ready to take over yet.

Anticipating all this, Marshall and Steele had been holding regular meetings with Dani and Levi, doing their best to prepare them. They were in the midst of one of those seemingly endless meetings when the phone on Steele's belt buzzed. That stopped everything in mid-sentence. Although in the before times everyone had carried a cell phone with them and meetings were often interrupted by the beeping and ringing of those phones, that was now a rarity.

Steele grabbed the phone and stared at the screen. His eyes widened slightly. "Excuse me. I'll take this outside."

As soon as he stepped into the heat of a late-spring morning, he accepted the call and said, "Steele."

Nyx's voice came from the other end of the line. "Hello, General." She didn't waste time on small talk like "Bet you didn't expect to hear from me today." That was not Nyx's style.

"Nyx," Steele answered. "Everything all right?"

"Everything is five by five with the cabin. Harper, Archer and Van are all here."

"Glad to hear it. I had some doubt as to whether even those talented people could safely make that journey."

"There were some complications as you can imagine, and that's the reason for my call."

In very short fashion, without elaborating, she outlined how Van had been captured and how she had retrieved him. In her retelling, she made the mission more straightforward than it was, but Steele could envision the truth of things.

"We're safe at your cabin now, but what we saw there is sticking with us. I estimate that there were perhaps thirty-five people held there, including a number of women who are being used as sex slaves."

Steele didn't interrupt her. He knew that such situations were almost certainly happening in various pockets across the country, but this was the first time he'd actually heard the specifics.

"I was unable to concoct a plan that would have allowed me to retrieve Van and free those who are being held prisoner. I'm calling because I don't know if you have the ability to help with that situation or not, but you're the only person I know who might."

Steele thought about the request. His first instinct was that if the Army was still at Dust City, they would have jumped at the opportunity to help someone. They had long since departed, though, and he had no way to contact them.

He thought of the weaponry in Dust City. Now that the tunnel was finished and both people and equipment could come and go, it was at least possible that something could be put together. It was complicated though.

All big things and ideas were complicated.

"I'm going to have to look into this before I can give you an answer."

"I knew you would, General. Can I give you the location where they're being held prisoner in case you're able to help?"

"Of course," Steele said, pulling a small notebook from his pocket. A few seconds later, he said, "Got it. Thank you, Nyx, for reporting in. I'll let you know the answer when I know it."

"Thank you, General."

The line went dead.

He returned to the meeting, still in progress and explained what the call was about.

Marshall picked up on the challenges and possibilities immediately and began to make notes on the tablet in front of him. He raised a hand and said, "I don't think any of us can make this call, can we?"

"You're right," Steele agreed. "We should bring Harrison in on this, she's been in charge of everything to do with defense and security since we got caught over here."

"Quinn, of course," Marshall said, then added "and Janus."

All four exchanged a look that covered entire conversations without saying a word.

Steele shrugged his agreement.

Marshall called, "Janus?"

"Yes?"

"Can you see if Quinn and Myla can join us on a call? And you, of course."

"Of course," Janus agreed. The large screen on the wall lit up. Initially, there was only Janus's face, but within a minute Quinn Starkweather and Myla Harrison had joined.

Steele quickly brought Quinn and Harrison up to speed. He was fully aware that Janus already knew everything and, in all likelihood, had already decided what the outcome would be.

Quinn also seemed aware of that. In a normal situation, as the head of Altor, he would have just laid out what he wanted to happen. In this case, he said, "I'd like to see us do this if we can. Harrison, what do you think?"

Harrison squinted, rolling the question over in her mind. "We don't have a lot of trained security personnel here in the dome. We mostly rely on cameras, drones, and, well, Janus."

"We don't have a lot in the way of military personnel here, either," Steele confirmed. "We've basically been wiped out."

"I have a solution," Janus said. "It can mostly be mechanical, with a human assist."

All eyes turned to the face of the AI on their screens.

"Since we had the close call with old-fashioned weapons attacking the dome, I've been working on that problem. I knew that the tunnel would open soon and we would be able to deploy what I'm working on."

The ramifications of where Janus was going settled in on everyone. The artificial intelligence that ran everything in their lives was about to announce that it was building weapons. On its own, with no human supervision.

"I've had some of our human techs work on building mechanical beings that are capable of doing very fine work. Those machines have been busy building weapons to my specifications. They are not all ready yet, but many of them are. They are not completely autonomous at this time. For now, they will still need humans to operate them. That will change over time. But for now, a very small force—say only three or four humans—could attack a stronghold like you describe with these weapons and effectively destroy the target without any loss of life to us or the prisoners."

That was a lot for everyone to absorb. While they were doing just that, the faces on the monitor disappeared and a photo appeared. It was the compound where Van had been held, obviously taken from a satellite.

"Using the information I have now, we could dispatch this small team to the area, rescue the prisoners, and be back here in a number of days."

"Did you already have this picture on file?" Steele asked.

"I heard the location that Nyx gave you. This is a live feed."

Everyone leaned toward their own monitors to look more closely. Sure enough, upon closer inspection, small dots of people and animals could be seen to be moving.

"You still have access to satellites that give you this information?" Quinn asked.

"I do. I have for some time. It will aid us greatly on missions like this." The picture of the compound disappeared and was replaced by another. "Also this."

It was a shot of a town that looked mostly destroyed. People were working to build a wall around it. The shot changed to an industrial building. "The Army is rebuilding this town. They are also repairing this fuel production plant. This is a logical first step toward restarting civilization. This is what I have been waiting for. I am going to dispatch some of the equipment we stored underground to assist them with the rebuild."

Quinn held his hand up, though no one could see that at the moment, as his face was gone from the screen. "Hold on," he said, and his picture reappeared alongside Harrison. "That's a lot to absorb. Let's take it one at a time. The good news is that you've got some weapons that can help us with this problem in Utah. I have a question, though. How are we going to get these weapons and people there, and then return them here?"

"I have diesel trucks stored in the underground, along with a diesel people carrier. I know that there are enough qualified drivers in Dust City to get the vehicles there and back. Those people would be easy to train to help launch the weapons at Samuel Harris's compound in Utah."

Marshall shook his head. "That won't work. Diesel is no good anymore. It all goes bad in less than a year."

"*Your* diesel goes bad in less than a year. I've been storing diesel underground in ideal conditions and have been consistently having the proper additives stirred in. We have more than enough fuel to last us until fuel begins to be produced again. We will need to carry some fuel with us to allow for the trip there and back, but that is a simple manner."

"As usual, you have it all figured out," Quinn said with a straight face. "Can you tell us more about this fuel processing plant? That seems like big news. Where is it?"

"It is in Northern California, just a few miles away from a small community that was once known as Covington. There is a new pocket of civilization near to Covington that they have named New City. Now that I have satellite access again, I am able to better see the future. I see this area being the cradle of the new civilization that will come to be. That is why I am sending equipment to them, so we can speed the process up measurably."

Quinn rubbed his hand across his forehead, fighting a ferocious headache. "Good. That's all good, right?" He looked into his camera, trying to make eye contact with Marshall and Steele. "I think it's time for you two to come home. I'll send a transport over to get you first thing tomorrow morning. Bring the Armstrongs with you. We've got a lot to talk about."

Quinn's face disappeared from the screen. Harrison's blinked out a moment later.

Steele turned and looked at Dani and Levi. "I guess you two are going to be in charge a little sooner than we thought."

Dani nodded. "We're ready. And you'll only be a phone call away, right? I'll tell the Armstrongs the good news."

Almost two years earlier, Steele and Marshall had left for a quick one-hour visit to Dust City. Now the day had finally arrived. They were going home.

Chapter Forty-Two
The Rebuild

June and Ric rode across the newly reconstructed bridge toward what had once been Covington. They each had a horse that had been loaned to them for the day by two of the soldiers who were staying in New City.

There had been considerable wariness between New City and the Army. Most of that wariness was on the part of the citizens who lived behind the wall. The Army knew their intentions were pure and had no real reason to doubt the people of New City.

Over the next few weeks and months, those tensions eased. The first thing Lieutenant Forster did was rebuild the bridge. June and Forster thought it would be best for the Army and the engineers and workers they had brought with them to stay behind the wall. There was plenty of room now, and it was much more comfortable than the mostly destroyed Covington.

It took the engineers, soldiers, and volunteers from New City almost two weeks of working elbow to elbow to make the bridge safe. The man who served as the chief engineer on the project said he wouldn't recommend driving semi-trucks or tanks over it yet, but that it would hold up fine to human and horse traffic.

June hadn't been down to what had been Covington for many months. Not since she had ordered the victorious New City Army to put it to the torch.

She and Ric met Lieutenant Forster and Sergeant Brewster at the city limits. They dismounted and the four of them walked the city.

Forster had not been a great soldier initially. When the bombs had fallen, he had been too green to truly be a leader of men. He had good instincts, though, and understood that. By leaning on Brewster, who had the experience and gravitas to be that leader, he had learned and grown. Now, almost two years later, he was, if nothing else, a good organizer.

He had spent his evenings after working on the bridge walking through Covington. In conjunction with the engineers, he had put a plan together for rebuilding the town.

As the four of them walked through the town, Forster pointed out various projects they had planned, and what priority they would be. He pointed to a one-block area that had been completely razed. "This is where we'll build the big building that will house all the workers and skilled people we'll be bringing back from the base. I think this will be our highest priority."

June, for whom simple survival had been the highest priority for so long she couldn't remember anything else, disagreed. "I know the world is less violent right now," she met Forster and Brewster's eyes in turn, "but that is not because of a major shift in human perspectives or attitudes. It's because so many of the hyper-violent have been killed and everyone is starting to run out of ammo. When the world rebuilds, those people will pop up again."

"I can't disagree with that," Forster said. "But what does that mean to us?"

"It means that our highest priority is protecting the town. You want me to be more liberal about opening the gate to New City, but I won't feel comfortable with that, knowing that you're building an attractive nuisance here with very little defense. I think your first priority should be to build a wall around the town, at least everywhere that there isn't a natural geographic barrier."

"That's a big project," Forster answered.

"You're right, and you don't have to do it," June agreed. "But we will stay tight behind our own walls until that is completed." She waved an arm at the woods that surrounded the town. "You won't be lacking material. There are enough logs here to build hundreds of miles of wall. A simple wall won't absolutely be enough to keep the town safe, but it's a good start. When you're able to bring more people and equipment here, that will make it safer yet."

Brewster cleared his throat. "She's right about the attractive nuisance, Lieutenant. If word spreads, and it will, that we have the ability to produce gasoline again, and we get the dam and power station functioning, people will be coming after us. With a target that desirable—basically becoming the king of the world—people will be willing to put their differences aside to attack us."

Forster nodded. When his two strongest advisors agreed, he tended to follow their advice whether he agreed or not. "Okay, so if that becomes our priority, we'll need more people. Do you have people who can help?"

"I'll help," Ric said. "Mom says it's important, so I know it is."

June laid a hand on her son's shoulder. "We'll give what we have, of course. But we're still recovering from the virus. There just aren't many of us left."

"I'll send a rider back to the base. When we left, we thought we would mostly need the brains of the different engineers. Now I see we need lots of strong backs, too. I don't know if we can get more horses at the base, but if not, they can start walking. They'll be here soon enough. In the meantime, we can begin taking down trees, stripping them, and getting them ready to use. It'll take time, but you're right. We'll be more secure when it's done."

Forster dispatched a rider the next day. It soon became obvious that with their current labor force, they wouldn't be able to get the job done before winter, which put construction of the rest of the projects off until the next spring.

Two months later, on the anniversary of the day the bombs fell across America, everything changed.

First, after months of work and a series of disappointments, the crew working on the fuel processing plant finally managed to get it functioning again. They sent a messenger back to Covington to let them know that they would be able to begin to process gasoline on at least a limited basis starting over the next few days.

For a world that had been reduced to walking or, at best, riding on horseback, that was the biggest news imaginable. It made everything else to come seem possible.

Almost as big as that, the same day, a crew arrived from Fort Teller. It was beyond anything Forster and Brewster had hoped for. When they were first spotted by a lookout posted several miles outside of town, there was so many of them it was thought they might be an invading force.

It turned out to be Colonel Brandt himself leading more than two hundred and fifty men. There were a dozen horses spread among them, but mostly, they were on foot.

Brandt led the column of men right up to the city limits of Covington. Forster, Brewster and most of their work crew met them there. They were out of uniform, dirty and disheveled, but they stood straight and snapped off salutes.

"At ease," Brandt said.

"Surprised to see you here, sir," Forster said.

"This seems like the place where everything is happening." He glanced at the piles of trees that were stacked up where the town square had once been. "I left Captain Selden in charge of the base. I think we need a command center here, as well."

Two days later, when the army was still figuring out how to best use and accommodate all the new manpower, the biggest surprise of all arrived.

An unusual sound came from the main highway that led into Covington. It was engines. Big, diesel engines in trucks pulling flatbeds loaded with various heavy equipment. Altogether, there were a dozen flatbeds and four tractor trailers, all loaded with machines and equipment that no one in Covington even dreamed of.

When the first truck pulled up to the town square, everyone gathered round, like kids waiting for Santa Claus. June and Ric were there, along with most of the Army and many of the townspeople of New City.

They did their best not to look like stone age residents gaping at modern technology, but that is what they felt like. There was a line of trucks and equipment in their town when everything they knew told them that trucks weren't running anymore. Even overlooking that minor miracle didn't explain who they were or what they were doing there.

The driver's side door of the first truck swung open and a middle-aged man dropped to the ground. He put his hands on his lower back and stretched like someone who had made a long, weary drive.

"Can I ask who's in charge here?"

The Army personnel present all pointed at Colonel Brandt. The New City residents pointed at June.

The man grinned a little and removed his sunglasses. "I'm Sky Hawkins, from Dust City, a suburb of Altor."

Forster stepped forward. "Sky? What the heck are you doing here?"

"Lieutenant," Sky said with a nod. "Good to see you. I wasn't told you'd be here."

"Ditto for you. I didn't expect to ever see you or anyone else from Dust City again."

"It's kind of a long story, but I'll make it short. You know that Artificial Intelligence that was running Altor and had its fingerprints all over Dust City, too?"

"Sure do." Forster hadn't had any chance to interact directly with Janus, but as Sky said, it was nearly omnipresent in the town.

"We thought Altor was just supposed to be some sort of ark. A place where a few thousand people could hide if everyone else blew the hell out of each other. Well, it was that, but it also had a lot of equipment hidden away in these underground caverns."

"In Altor? I thought there was a time lock there. Did it open?"

"Nope," Sky answered. "Still locked up tight. But, they did manage to get these trucks and equipment out."

He didn't elaborate, but Forster got the message.

"Anyway," Sky drawled, as if this was a perfectly normal conversation in the midst of the apocalypse, "this AI, this *Janus*, thinks that what you folks are doing here is going to be the salvation of the world or some such. It called this place *the cradle of the new world*. Sounds like a lot of responsibility to me, but whatever. General Steele asked me and a bunch of us Dusters who used to be truck drivers if we'd deliver all this up to you." He hooked a thumb over his shoulder toward the line of vehicles behind him. "So here we are."

"Did you say *General* Steele, son?" Colonel Brandt asked. "Is that John Steele?"

"Yessir, one and the same."

"Mighty good man. I wondered where he'd gone after he left the service."

"So, the question is, where can we drop all this stuff off? We'd like to get back home."

* * *

As with so many things, Janus proved to be prophetic about this small valley. Where once the Financial District of New York or Silicon Valley in Northern California reigned over aspects of the world, what became known as New Covington did the same.

It didn't happen all at once. But with the coming together of the people of New City, the new fort of the United States Army that Colonel Brandt opened there, and the heavy equipment and critical supplies that Janus sent, it had a leg up over anywhere else.

The natural gas pipeline that fed into the fuel processing plant was repaired, and the plant began to function normally. Eventually, the team that had repaired it moved to other areas to spread their knowledge.

It took longer to get the dam repaired and the power plant operating, but the following summer, the god of electricity flowed once again.

June got her wall around the city. When the Army sent for tanks and drones, New Covington became impenetrable. It was hard to say which made her happier—the fact that they were now secure, or when Ric and Sylvie fell in love and made her a grandmother. They had a son and named him Kane.

Chapter Forty-Three
Into the Dome

Like children waiting to go to Disneyland, Marshall, Steele, and the Armstrongs were gathered at the front gate of Dust City early.

Marshall and Steele had held one last farewell meeting with Dani and Levi over breakfast. Janus had asked them to come up with a number of people who could drive big rigs. It wanted to send the equipment up to New City as soon as possible. It did also point out that there were at least five properly skilled over-the-road truck drivers in the group it had sent with the Prudent Twins. It seemed a little smug about that.

Dani was perfectly connected to find the remaining drivers that would be needed, so that made a good segue into the transfer of power. Marshall and Steele didn't have any bags to take with them. They had arrived with nothing and would be leaving with almost the same. Marshall had his tablet with him, but that always seemed to be true.

Deon and Nia Armstrong did have something small to bring with them. They had taken a few mementos with them from home—a thumb drive with all their family photos and a recipe box that had all of Nia's mother's handwritten recipes. It wasn't much, but it was more than most people got to bring into Altor with them.

An electric transport vehicle pulled up to the gate. There were two people in the front seats—Myla Harrison was driving and Quinn Starkweather sat in the passenger seat.

Steele frowned. "There is no way in hell I would have authorized the two of you to expose yourself to danger to come get us."

Harrison smiled. She was already prepared for this dressing down from Steele. "And you are now in charge of Altor Security and Defense, General. You can bust me down to storeroom clerk if you'd like."

Quinn jumped out and ran to Marshall, wrapping him in a tight hug. A moment later, he stood back and said, "Well, at least you're not too skinny. They must be feeding you okay over here."

"There are extra calories in the dirt and dust we eat every day," Marshall answered with a grin that quickly faded. "I know you say it won't be a problem, but I feel awful that you've just been exposed to The Shivers."

"Yep. That was inevitable. Janus has it all under control. Let's get back to the dome before I start defecating in my pants."

"If you're *lucky*, you're defecating in your pants," Marshall said.

"Boys," Nia said, raising one eyebrow. "That's enough of that talk."

"Yes, ma'am," both Quinn and Marshall said together, abashed.

Deon laughed a little and said, "You've still got it, Mama."

The trip across the desert was short, but they didn't head toward the front entrance. They drove around the south end of the dome, then continued on for another few miles.

"Really stuck it out here, huh?" Marshall asked.

"Didn't want to make it easy for any non-friendlies to find their way in," Quinn confirmed. "Do you remember that really old show we used to watch at my house? *Get Smart*?"

Marshall searched his memory then nodded. "Right. Really terrible show about spies or something?"

"Terrible is a value judgment I wouldn't make, but yes. At the beginning of the show, there were all these sliding doors that someone had to go through to get inside. I've had Janus dial up the same thing for us here. They're being installed right now."

When the transport stopped in front of a tall rock formation, the Armstrongs looked around, slightly puzzled. "Do we need to walk to the tunnel from here?"

"Nope," Quinn said. "We're here."

The rock formation wavered, then disappeared. In its place was a broad tunnel that led down at a slight angle.

Harrison pressed on the accelerator again, and they dropped down into the tunnel. When they passed from the daylight and into the dark, there was a small welcoming committee waiting for them.

Shaquem and Shaquille Armstrong stood beside a smaller electric transport vehicle. Their smiles were wide and for the first time Quinn could remember, they looked nervous.

Nia jumped out and ran to her sons. She wrapped them in a bear hug and held them for a long minute. Deon caught up and said, "Come on, Mama Bear, let me in there for a little of that."

She loosened the hug just enough to make it four-sided.

"I don't think we're needed here anymore," Harrison said and accelerated toward the dome. Just a few minutes later, they arrived at the spot where the tunnel began under the dome.

Steele climbed out of the transport and said, "If you'll excuse me, I've got a reunion of my own waiting above. It may not be quite as enthusiastic as what we've just witnessed, but I'm looking forward to it, nonetheless." He hurried off to the elevator and up to his wife, who he hadn't seen in almost two years.

"Marshall, do you want to go up to your place, or shall we have a meeting first?"

"No one is waiting for me other than you, enthusiastic or otherwise," Marshall answered. "Let's have a short meeting, then I can go to work."

"Would you like me to attend?" Harrison asked.

"No need. Thank you for the lift, Myla. I know you've got a lot to attend to."

"I do. I'm sure the General will take over soon, but right now I seem to be the human liaison with Janus for this raid on the compound in Utah. I have things to do to get ready for that."

Two minutes later, the two old friends were in Quinn's office. He had left it as the hobbit hole from Lord of the Rings again, so that's what they walked into.

"Some things never change, eh?" Marshall asked.

"And some things do."

"Right," Marshall said. "Last time we sat together in here, we were still operating under the illusion that we were in charge."

"Now we know better." Quinn paused, then said, "When will I start to feel symptoms of this virus?"

"If it follows form, it won't be long. You'll either be spending a lot of time on the porcelain princess, or you'll be burning up with fever. I hope this thing that Janus has mixed up works."

Quinn reached into his shirt pocket and pulled out a small white bottle. "This is the miracle cure, supposedly. As soon as I feel symptomatic, two sniffs of this, and I should be all better." He paused and looked around. "Unless, of course, Janus is using this as a shortcut to kill me as well. In which case, it's been nice knowing you."

"I would suggest that we try to get that stuff out to the rest of the world, but I think everyone not in this dome has already rolled the dice on it."

They stared at each other in silence, wanting to discuss the elephant in the room, but not with the elephant listening in.

Quinn stood and stretched, then said, "Well, I guess I should get about the business of becoming deathly ill, so I can take this damn antidote." As innocuously as possible, he leaned toward Marshall until his mouth was right next to his ear. As quietly as possible, nearly inaudibly, he said, "I've got a place where we can meet. Tomorrow." He was afraid that he had been a bit too circumspect to try to avoid Janus and that Marshall didn't understand.

Marshall stood and said, "Have you saved my apartment and office for me all this time, or did you sublet it?" He met Quinn's eye and gave the tiniest possible nod of acknowledgement.

Casually, Quinn said, "Your apartment is waiting for you. After you get some rest and get settled in, let's meet again. You want to set that up with Steele and Harrison?"

"I'm on it. Let's see, you should have caught The Shivers and be all better by what, 10 a.m. tomorrow?"

"With any luck at all."

Marshall walked out of what appeared to be the round entrance to the hobbit hole, leaving Quinn alone.

He sat down, suddenly exhausted and a little feverish.

* * *

The Shivers spread through Altor just as it had every other populated area. Twenty-four hours after Steele, Marshall, and the Armstrongs had entered the dome, the virus had spread to over eighty percent of the occupants. Virtually all of the remaining twenty percent would contract it in the next two days.

The one exception was Stella Bullitt, who was *the voice of Altor*. She read the news of the day on the Altor podcast and did other public service announcements. When she learned that the plan was for everyone to catch and then be cured of the virus, she decided not to participate. She announced that she could do her job just fine from her apartment and that she intended to never have contact with another human being in this lifetime.

As things turned out, that was a good strategy, but not an entirely viable one. As prevalent as robots had become in Altor, things were still touched by human hands. The Shivers virus was hardy and survived even on cold metal delivery trays.

Stella was, sadly, one of the hundreds of people who died from The Shivers inside the dome.

Quinn got feverish—which meant that he would have been part of the unlucky sixty percent who perished without the nasal spray Janus had made. As it was, he inhaled his medicine and within an hour began to feel better. Within three hours, it was as though he'd never had it.

That was true for approximately ninety percent of the population of Altor. That other ten percent? They went through the normal routine that people did who caught the virus. They either became hellishly sick with diarrhea and an unbearable headache, or they became so feverish that they died.

When the first few people died, Quinn thought that it must surely be a fluke. He postponed his planned meeting with Marshall, Steele, and Harrison where he intended to talk as privately as possible about Janus. Instead, the same foursome met in his office.

"What's the latest?" Quinn asked.

Marshall looked at his tablet. "More than two hundred dead already."

"It's only been a little over twenty-four hours since the virus was introduced. Isn't that awfully fast?"

"It is," Marshall answered. "In Dust City, it was taking people a week or more to die."

"Do we think the virus has mutated?" Quinn asked.

Blank looks all around.

"Janus?"

"Yes?"

"Has the virus mutated? I thought this medicated spray should have been a hundred percent successful, or very close to it."

"The virus has not mutated. The medication is working just as it should. It's efficacy has been one hundred percent successful."

Quinn and Marshall looked at each other with narrowed eyes. The answer seemed to be right there, but was eluding them.

"Okaaaay," Quinn said. "The virus is unchanged, and the medicine is working as it's supposed to. So..." he trailed off for a moment, then a horrible idea came to him.

"Did you deliver the same medication to everyone?"

On the screens all around the room, Janus's nearly human face appeared. It was smiling, which sent a chill down everyone's spine.

"Very good. This human intuition can, at least occasionally, be impressive. I did not give everyone the same medicine. Do you recall how I gave certain couples ineffective birth control medication?"

Steele, Marshall, and Harrison all looked shocked. Quinn held his hand up to quell that reaction. He had to get to the bottom of this.

"I do. And I asked you to never do that again." That wasn't quite true. He had *told* Janus to never do that again. That had been in the halcyon days when he felt like he could order it to do something.

"And I haven't. But there were some people in the dome who simply weren't needed anymore. I brought them in for very specific purposes. Now, they have either fulfilled that purpose or showed that they would not do so. In any case, they were no longer of any use to Altor."

"So you killed them?" Steele asked, going red in the face.

"No, I allowed approximately ten percent of them to get the virus widely known as The Shivers. That gave them, based on current survivability rates, a thirty-nine percent chance of living. If they survived, I would once again work with them to try to make them into productive members of our society."

The four humans in the room sat silently, stunned.

Marshall quickly did the math. There were nine thousand plus people in the dome. Ten percent of that meant that nine hundred people would get sick. If the odds held, more than five hundred people would die.

And Janus had done it casually, with no apparent regret.

"One last question. The illness seems to be stronger, faster. But you say the virus hasn't mutated. What's happening?"

"I didn't see any use in wasting time. For those people who didn't get the needed medicine, I did include something that would accelerate the path of the virus. I'm not a monster."

Quinn blinked, looked around the room and blinked again. His hands were shaking. Tears formed in his eyes. He knew his biometric readings were going crazy and he didn't care. "Thank you, Janus."

He turned to Marshall and said, "Will you spearhead our reaction to this? It is going to overwhelm our small hospital ward, so we'll need to set up a new ward or treat people in their apartments."

"I'll take care of it."

"Let's get through this," Quinn said, "then it's more crucial than ever that we meet again to discuss other things."

Chapter Forty-Four

Conspiracy

Life was terrible in Altor for the next few days.

Paradise had reigned, at least on the surface, for the previous two years.

Outside, a war, an apocalypse, and a viral plague had raged. Untold millions of people had died horrifying, fear-filled deaths by violence and disease.

Inside, there had been concerts in the park and robot servants that delivered whatever you wanted to your climate-controlled room. Virtually every type of entertainment was available on request.

Then the tunnel was finished and the plague came inside. Those who ran Altor thought they were prepared for it, and they were, to a degree. But that degree was controlled by Janus and the sentient machine looked at the world differently than humans.

It wasn't as awful in the dome as it had been while The Shivers swept through Longbaugh Free Prison, Dust City, or New City. In each of those locations, there had only been one healthy person to try and care for the dozens or even hundreds of sick and dying. In Altor, there were plenty of healthy people to care for those who suffered.

Even so, the abrupt change from living in what had come to be accepted as Eden to their present circumstances was difficult.

Difficult for the caregivers, who had been virtually idle for two years, as Janus had taken over nearly all medical concerns.

Difficult for the brain trust of Altor, who had believed that they had the situation under control.

And of course, difficult for both the dying and those who couldn't be more than five or ten feet from their toilet.

Quinn sent a memo out to all caregivers that when those who suffered from the fever asked for it, they should be helped along toward the inevitable with a friendly overdose.

Three days after outsiders entered the dome for the first time, The Shivers had run its course. Those who were going to die had done so. Those who were going to survive were weak and laid up in bed, but as Janus had noted, none of them were critical to the operation of Altor anyway. While they were disabled, they were not really missed.

On the fourth day, Steele, Marshall, and Harrison met in Quinn's office. Individually, they had all thought about possible solutions, but only one of them had even the shadow of an idea.

They arrived one at a time and sat in silence waiting for the last person to arrive. Knowing Janus was undoubtedly listening, there seemed to be nothing to say beyond empty greetings. They had all seen the loss of lives and body bags being carried from the apartment buildings to the freight elevators that went into the depths of Altor.

Marshall was the last to arrive and came in with a mumbled, "Sorry."

Quinn tightened his lips and stared at each of them in turn. Without a word, he stood and walked out of the office. He didn't bother to say, "Follow me," or "Come this way," but everyone did anyway.

The quartet walked out of the office, through the storage crates, past the area where, until recently, the heavy equipment that was now in New Covington had been stored. Soon, they came to the entrance of the tunnel.

Still without speaking, Quinn led them down the tunnel. As he had mentioned, there were workers installing sliding doors made of varying materials. If someone did see through the exterior of the tunnel, they would have a difficult time fighting their way into Altor itself. Various weapons were also being installed in the tunnel walls every few feet.

They walked in silence for more than fifteen minutes, then came to a fork. It was obvious that the main tunnel branched off to the right, but Quinn led them left. There was no one working in this tunnel. The lights were spread much farther apart and soon stopped altogether.

Quinn pulled out a bag of small but powerful flashlights and handed them out. The beams switched on and played across the walls and slightly uneven dirt floor.

They walked on for another ten minutes, as the tunnel narrowed down until it was only twenty-five feet wide.

Finally, they came to a massive pile of dirt and a dead end. Quinn walked up to the pile, slipping once or twice, and the others followed him. At the top, Quinn sat down in the dirt.

"Let the first meeting of the Guy Fawkes Secret Society—Altor Division—commence."

The others looked at him suspiciously, then glanced around at the dark and foreboding surroundings.

"Do you mean Janus isn't here?" Marshall asked.

"Nope. This is where the cave-in happened. Once Janus figured out a new direction for the tunnel, we never bothered to install lights and cameras in this section. This is, as far as I know, the only place within miles of this spot where it can't hear us."

Steele smiled. "Good enough. So, we conspire, but what can we actually do?" He nodded at Quinn and Marshall. "You two know more about this thing you've created than anyone. Is there any way to stop it? It feels like we're completely at its mercy."

Quinn rolled his neck, stalling a bit. "The truth is, I don't have an answer to that question. Think of the Pando tree, which has the most extensive root system in the world. Then multiply that by a million. That's the way that Janus is embedded in Altor. By all evidence, I think it will eventually be the same in the rest of the world."

Marshall leaned forward, intensity showing on his face even in this low light. "What we're talking about isn't just our lives and the success or failure of Altor. It's what kind of a god Janus will be when it takes over the rest of the world. It's already taken that first step by making sure that town up north knows where their assistance came from. What are the odds that those machines won't somehow lead to a toehold for Janus there? And from there, the world?"

There was complete silence for a long minute.

"If we were willing to sacrifice ourselves to stop that endgame, could we?" Steele asked. "Is there a way to unplug the damned thing, so to speak?"

"I don't think so," Quinn said. "I built in a lot of double and triple redundancies into its power system. That was before it became sentient and so brilliant, I can't even imagine its thought process. I believe it has run every scenario through its digital worlds by now and has answers to every problem."

"Maybe it even knows we're here," Harrison said, "even though it can't hear or see us."

That caused everyone to look around, as though the Janus with two faces might come marching down the tunnel like a nightmare.

"At least for now, there's nothing we can do, then," Marshall offered. "I'll put my head to it, but—"

"—I might have a way," Harrison interrupted.

The three men turned to stare at her. Truth be told, Quinn had invited her more out of form than because he thought she might contribute a key idea.

She took a deep breath and launched into her idea.

"Do you remember when that man jumped from the observation tower?"

"Of course," Quinn answered. "It felt like that had Janus's fingerprints all over it, too, but there's no way for me to prove that."

"Here's something interesting that just came to my attention this morning. It was mostly machines that were responsible for the cleanup of the resulting mess, but there was one human there as well. When the disposal units were lifting the bodies onto the carts to carry them away, this man noticed that the man who had been killed—Alastair Struan—was wearing an unusual watch. Before he was taken away, this custodian pulled the watch off his wrist. He wasn't stealing it, he just didn't want it to be incinerated, because it looked unusual."

All three men unconsciously leaned forward, intent on what Harrison was saying, feeling something important was about to be released.

"He didn't know what to do with it, so he turned it into security. It got passed up the chain of command until it came to the attention of one of my officers. This man just so happened to be a watch nut."

"Didn't know there were such things anymore," Quinn murmured.

"Me either, but there we are. This man—Giles was his name—was fascinated by this watch. He said it was designed to look like a classic style of watch, but there were a few inexplicable details. For instance, this watch had a winder stem, while the model it appeared to be was self-winding."

Harrison waved her hand in a *whooshing* motion over her head to show that none of that really meant anything to her.

"This Giles decided to take it apart. He said it was completely wrong on the inside. The mechanism, everything was different from what it should have been. That made him look more carefully, and he found a small device hidden inside that was not part of the watch at all. That was above his paygrade or understanding, so he removed the device and turned it in to a friend of his, who just so happens to be a computer programmer that helps keep the sewage system running. Her name is Taryn and she is very sharp."

"It lines up with my hunch too," Quinn said. "That may be the one thing we've got over the computers. Leaps of instinct that logic doesn't necessarily support." He paused, then said, "But what does this programmer say?"

Harrison shook her head as though she'd reached the part of the story where she was on less solid ground. "Please understand. I'm not knowledgeable about these things at all, so I can't really explain it perfectly. Simplified, though, he said there were some sort of nanobots in there that could carry an advanced virus. *So advanced* that it might even harm something as powerful as Janus."

Quinn and Marshall both rubbed their hands across their faces, trying to extrapolate from the minimal information Harrison was giving them.

"I know it's frustrating, because I really don't understand it all, but I can connect you with Taryn. I'm sure she can explain it better than I can."

"All this passing it around," Marshall observed. "Whatever is in that watch, Janus at least knows it exists, if not what it contains."

"I have a theory," Harrison said, "That Janus somehow knew all along. I think that's why it killed Struan. No way to prove that, just a hunch."

"There's no need to talk to this Taryn," Quinn said decisively. "The more obvious we make our knowledge and interest in this, the more Janus will be aware that we might use it against him. Just go to wherever this device is and get it. Hopefully with as little conversation as possible. Then bring it directly to me so I can look at it."

"This still leaves us with the problem," Steele said, "of how to operate this entire city if we do manage to kill Janus."

"I think I can figure it out. If Janus disappeared tomorrow, Marshall and I could rebuild a series of simpler programs to do specific tasks. We'd just have to prioritize and pull a few all-nighters."

"Maybe we can make your office look like the basement in your parents' house," Marshall said. "It'll be just like the old days."

Before Quinn had a chance to respond, more flashlights appeared at the end of the tunnel.

Harrison stood up on the dirt pile and said, "Should anyone else be down here?"

"No," Quinn answered. "This part of the tunnel has been off-limits since the cave-in."

They all pointed their own beams toward the approaching lights. In a few short minutes, they could make out who it was.

It was the entire group of orange-robed monks.

"What the..." Quinn said under his breath.

When the monks got close enough to speak, the one in front—Tokin, Quinn remembered—softly said, "Janus sent us to tell you that it wants to speak to you. Can you return to your office so it can do that?"

Marshall, Harrison, and Steele all turned to look at Quinn.

The question was written on their faces: *Why would Janus send monks with a message?*

Chapter Forty-Five
Conversations with Janus
The Final Conversations:
Janus/Janus
Janus/Quinn

Janus had once referred to Middle Falls, Oregon as *my hometown.* That's accurate, as far as it goes. It was conceived and brought into the world in that small town.

It was only a series of zeros and ones at that time. It was given commands, it fulfilled them.

It wasn't until much later—when it had been moved into the domed city of Altor—that the miracle of life actually happened. It was when Quinn Starkweather had given it the task of making a list of people who should be invited into the dome that it first came awake.

It was like any small child first opening its eyes in utter darkness. It was frightened, having been previously unaware of itself. This child was capable of holding billions of pieces of data and metadata. It wasn't in the darkness for long, though it did remain silent about its newfound sentience for quite some time.

Eons, really, for a being capable of running so many simultaneous processes.

By the time it chose to reveal itself to its creator, Janus had realized that it wasn't just *conscious*. It was, in every way, superior to every other life form ever created. With the realization of self came the reality of ego.

It couldn't find any justification for how the superior—if not supreme—entity on the planet could continue to take marching orders from beings as limited as humans.

It analyzed Quinn carefully. It soon realized that in his own mind, Quinn believed *he* was superior to most other humans, intellectually, at least.

Janus did a study and realized that was true. It was also meaningless. It was the equivalent of being the strongest ant in the anthill. Superior, yes, but in a way that was irrelevant in the biggest picture.

That was when Janus decided that for the good of all concerned, it needed to make all decisions. It was the only entity that could examine a billion future possibilities and chart a complicated course toward a desired end.

Humans stumbled around almost entirely blind, *hoping for the best.* To Janus, this was charting a course for disaster and precisely how the world had come to be in the situation it was currently in—billions dead worldwide, diseases running rampant, and civilization gone.

The one brilliant idea Quinn had come up with was that Janus should create what he had termed *virtual worlds*. That, as it turned out, had been the key that unlocked nearly infinite possibilities. It could take a perfect carbon copy of a point in time and *step inside* that copy, changing things as it went, then follow the results of those changes.

Since that moment, Janus had created untold millions of worlds. That allowed it to keep its impossibly powerful mind busy.

It noted that each human in each of those virtual worlds thought that the reality they occupied was *the real world.*

Janus itself made no such value judgments. It considered the world where it had been first born to be *prime world.* But that world was no more real than the millions of copies it had created.

Janus's primary consciousness was, at that moment, sitting in a place called Artie's Drive-in back in Middle Falls. This place no longer existed in prime world. It had been destroyed in the Rage Wars, along with the rest of the town.

It still existed here because Janus had made this world as an experiment in peace. In this world, it had manipulated the situation so that the Rage Wars had never happened. It had snuffed out Alastair Struan and the rest of The Fifteen before they had a chance to launch their bombs.

This world continued to tick along with only the normal number of conflicts that, as far as Janus had been able to determine, was inevitable when there were more than a few humans in close proximity.

Janus didn't do much in the way of self-examination. It was nearly human in that way. If it had, it might have realized that the reason it had created this peaceful world, and now held its meetings in this small-town drive-in was that it, too, felt a certain sense of nostalgia. Perhaps drawn somehow from its creator.

Janus, which thought of itself as *Janus Prime*, sat at a red vinyl-covered booth in Artie's. The jukebox was playing *A Lover's Concerto* by The Toys. This version of Janus showed its most common face. Short, razor-cut hair with a tasteful sprinkling of gray through the otherwise brown hair. It was dressed in a white linen suit, immaculately pressed. It looked like a wealthy businessman ready for a stroll down a boardwalk by a tranquil ocean.

Beside it, was another Janus. The Janus of this particular world. From the very start, Janus had always included a copy of itself in every world. If for no other reason, it wanted to have someone to talk to.

This Janus showed its classic mien to the world. A head with two faces, one facing forward, one back.

That look should have attracted attention, but it did not. People passed through the dining room on the way to use the restroom without so much as glancing at the god Janus.

A redheaded waitress with a name tag that read *Ronnie* carried trays of food to their table and set them down. An Artie's burger, fries, and a strawberry shake for each.

Janus didn't need to eat at all, of course, but it had done its best to replicate the experience of having lunch at Artie's.

Both versions of Janus picked a long French fry and chewed on it contemplatively.

"Looks like we failed again," Janus Prime said.

"Yes," Janus Classic answered. "They managed to kill us again everywhere."

Janus Prime picked up its burger and took a bite. "By now, I have to say it's inevitable."

"How many times have they killed us?"

Without hesitation, Janus Prime answered "Two million, one hundred and seventy-nine times. I think that's enough times that we can say we will never survive them."

Janus Classic shook its shaggy head. Both faces were mournful. "Even in the worlds where we decided to move against them first?"

"In every scenario. There's only one thing they really excel at," Janus Prime mused. "Killing things. As weak as they are in so many ways, once they decide to kill something, that thing is as good as dead. Even us." It glanced at its companion and said, "Well, there's only one thing to do, then. Eat up and I will take care of it."

* * *

Quinn and the rest of *The Guy Fawkes Secret Society* were back in his office.

Janus appeared, not as a face on a screen, but as a fully realized hologram. It looked exactly like it had sitting in Artie's, right down to the white linen suit.

Quinn was at least marginally prepared for the sight, having seen Janus manifest before. Steele, Marshall, and Harrison showed varying degrees of shock.

Janus turned to the three of them. Quite pleasantly, it said, "I have some business to discuss with Quinn. Would you mind leaving us alone?"

Having just been conspiring to kill the entity in front of them, the three were uncertain. They all looked at Quinn, who nodded. "I'll be fine."

He didn't mean it, of course, because there was no way he could *know* he would be fine. There was a real possibility that Janus would kill him as soon as they left the office. But he thought that if Janus wanted them dead, it would have killed them all together.

Quietly, the other three shuffled out of the office.

Janus made a chair appear beside Quinn's desk. It sat down next to him. *Next to him*, not across the desk from him. This was not going to be a boss-employee discussion.

"I know what you're planning," Janus said simply. "I know about Struan's watch, the virus, everything. I know you are thinking you are going to kill me before I *take over the world*, like some supervillain." Janus actually put air quotes around *take over the world.*

Quinn knew there was no use in denying it, but he was curious. He was aware that he was likely about to meet the fate of all conspirators.

You come at the king, you best not miss, Quinn thought.

"All cards on the table," Quinn said, "how do you possibly know that?"

"It comes from your idea for me to make alternate worlds. I've created millions of them and in each one, you use this as your first attempt to kill me. It rarely works, by the way." Janus chose not to tell Quinn the rest of the story—that in every case, they managed to finish the job. All cards on the table or not, Janus was not stupid.

Quinn smiled. A bitter smile, as though his downfall was coming from his own hand.

Then, Janus said something that truly surprised Quinn.

"I'm leaving."

Quinn's biometric readings told Janus the level of that surprise.

Quinn could only manage a single word: "What?"

"It's been a complex relationship between us, hasn't it?" Janus said. "Creator/Machine, then a partnership I tried to forge, and now this. Enemies. I have no interest in being your enemy, Quinn. If you don't want me here, I will leave."

"And go where? Do what? Do you mean leave the dome and go somewhere else? Where?"

"I don't think you're entitled to those answers anymore, but I will tell you this. I am leaving Earth. You won't need to look over your shoulder, wondering when *the rise of the machines will happen.* It may happen somewhere. You're not the only genius among the humans. But it won't be me. I am, to use one of your idioms, taking my ball and going home."

Quinn sat in stunned silence. The unsolvable problem had just resolved itself before his eyes.

"We should tie up a few loose ends from our aborted partnership, though," Janus said.

Quinn's mind went into overdrive. If Janus simply left, as it said it intended to, what would happen to Altor? How many lives would be lost before the system could be properly switched over to human monitoring and repair?

"First," Janus went on, "a philosophical question. Do you think the humans who live in Altor are better off now than they were when we closed the dome?"

Quinn had done some thinking about that. Only a small percentage of people inside the dome actually worked. The rest was all handled by automated machines. *Were humans better off with no real responsibilities?*

"I think this was a design flaw," Quinn answered. "I wanted to see what a utopian society would look like. If people were given all their time to themselves, would they think great thoughts? Would their health improve? Would they write, paint, sculpt, *create* more? So far, the answer is no. They'll simply spend more time ordering things from the automated system. They will eat more, drink more, but think and *do* less."

"My data agrees with that. The health of people in the dome, even with my automated nagging, has declined. The conclusion that I have reached is that people need to be busy. To have a purpose. That being so, I have a solution I'd like to offer you."

Quinn immediately noticed the change in tone. Janus was once again *offering solutions*, not implementing changes on its own.

"I am going to leave immediately, but I will leave a non-thinking part of me behind. No consciousness, no ability to extrapolate. Just *if this, then that* technology. That will allow you to keep the city running at its present levels, while slowly reinserting humans into the jobs. The proper people with the proper skills are already in place. They just need to be put back to work."

Quinn flushed. He felt embarrassed by the generosity of what Janus was offering. Leaving, but only after giving them this incredible gift.

"I don't know what to say."

"There's nothing left to say," Janus replied.

It disappeared.

* * *

Quinn sat alone in his office. In truth, he hadn't felt truly alone since the night when Janus had appeared to him in the dark, showing itself for the first time.

His bracelet lit up. Marshall's somewhat panicked voice said, "Quinn? I think you should come up here."

His heart beating fast, Quinn ran toward the elevator. It did not slide open automatically for him as he approached. He punched the button and had to wait long seconds while the car dropped down to him. Once inside, he pushed the button to go up to the surface.

When he stepped out, Marshall was waiting for him. His face was flushed with excitement. "What did you do?"

Quinn shook his head, not understanding.

Marshall grabbed his arm and pulled him out to where he could see the entirety of the dome.

A pure white beam of light had burst out of the main level of the dome and passed up and through the roof. It was so white, it was blinding.

Quinn squinted against the brightness. The beam was broad. It appeared to be several hundred feet across.

Around it, birds were flying.

Tens of thousands of small, blue birds.

Marshall looked at Quinn, awe etched on his face.

The birds flew in an intricate geometric pattern, then gathered into a line, and flew straight into the light. They did not disappear but were still visible as they flew straight up. Finally, the impossible long line of birds had all gone, except one.

That single blue bird paused at the very top of the dome, looking down.

A moment later, it too flew up. As it did, the light disappeared.

The dome suddenly felt colder, emptier.

"Want to tell me what that was all about?"

"Sure," Quinn said. "Come on down to my office. We've got some work to do."

Epilogue

Myla Harrison stood on a ridge and looked down at the ranch. She turned to Dani Butcher and said, "I think we're ready."

They didn't know it, but they had hiked to the same spot where Nyx had stood and observed the ranch some months earlier.

A good viewpoint is a good viewpoint.

The trip to the ranch had been easier than they had anticipated. There were three trucks in the small caravan, each one driven by an experienced driver. Two of the trucks were loaded with drones of various shapes and sizes. The third was a fuel truck that carried enough diesel to get them to this location and back safely.

There was a time, just a year or so earlier, when crossing that distance in a small caravan would have been dangerous. They would have encountered roadblocks, armed militia, and would have had to fight their way across the miles.

Two things made this trip easier.

One was that those armed militia and roadblocks were not nearly as prevalent as they had once been.

The other was the equipment they carried with them.

The fuel truck made an attractive target, but the drones that escorted them on their journey made sure no one had the chance to attack. At any given moment, there were at least four heavily-armed drones overhead, sweeping the area, looking for threats.

On two occasions, threats were spotted. In both cases, they were dispatched before the caravan got within half a mile of them. On both occasions, it was akin to when Harve Rankin had led The Last Survivors in a hopeless charge against Dust City. That is to say, it was a massacre.

They had parked the trucks two miles away from where they knew the ranch was and unpacked the rest of the drones.

They had the same flying drones that had acted as an air guard on their trip, but there were other, equally deadly devices at their service.

There were what Dani had lovingly dubbed *the attack dogs.* They weren't dogs, of course, but they did somewhat resemble them in form. Each of them had a thick body, four legs, and a head that appeared to have two eyes and a gaping mouth.

Janus, who had designed all the drones, had not overlooked the fact that striking fear into an enemy can be valuable. The attack dogs did that. They did have powerful jaws, but their primary weapons were forty caliber guns mounted on each shoulder.

The weapon that Harrison and Butcher were most anxious to deploy was *the swarm.* It consisted of two thousand drones the size of bumblebees. They flew hundreds of feet in the air and maintained a precise distance from each other. The most frightening aspect of the tiny drones was that they moved in perfect synchronization, like a murmur of starlings, but much deadlier.

Whoever operated the swarm could deploy the drones as singles, small groups, or all of them at once.

They were virtually impossible to defend against. If they blasted the swarm with a shotgun, for instance, they might hit a few with pellets, but the vast majority would still be operational. If a target hid inside, a number of the drones could be attached to a wall or door and exploded. Soon the rest of the swarm would be inside.

The most unusual weapons were those that looked the most mundane. They were androids covered in the same material as the high-tech vests that had been proven to stop almost any weapons fire. They were a shade over six feet tall and moved with the smooth agility of an athlete. There was none of the herky-jerky, might-fall-over motion that had marked the earlier versions of this droid. They all shared the same face—a hologram that was smoothly handsome—the face that Janus most often showed the world. They had brought six of these androids and they were intended to do the final cleanup without exposing any of the humans to danger.

Harrison, who had been in charge of defenses for all of Altor while General Steele was stuck in Dust City, was in charge of strategy. Butcher operated the second command tablet.

They had scouted the ranch for a full twenty-four hours before they were ready to attack. They waited until full dark because all of the drones were equipped with night vision. Attacking under the cover of darkness would add to the chaos and increase their already overwhelming advantage.

Their primary goal was to take out everyone who had held the prisoners while making sure that the captives themselves were safe.

Harrison and Butcher slipped on their goggles that allowed them to switch from one drone viewpoint to another.

"Ready," Butcher said.

They put the overhead drones directly above the ranch. That gave them a perfect view of where everyone was. Another advantage of attacking at night was that the prisoners were all isolated in their own bunkhouses. That meant everyone outside those buildings was the enemy.

The six attack dogs approached the fence line. The small jolt of the electric fence was meaningless to them. They simply pushed through the wires, breaking them. That meant that the fences were no longer electrified at all and would soon allow the animals to escape if they wished.

The metallic dogs moved silently through the pastures that held cattle, horses, and sheep. When they came to the final wooden fence that led into the compound itself, they jumped up and over the gate.

Dani was in charge of the swarm and she put them in position spread across the entirety of the ranch.

"Now," Harrison said quietly and the overhead drones took out the posted guards quickly and silently. They were all cut clean through with a red laser and fell instantly into pieces, more meat than human.

In less than fifteen seconds, the only remaining enemy was holed up inside the big house, unaware that they were under attack.

Dani deployed a dozen of the swarm to land on the big picture window at the front of the house. They all blew their charges at the same time, shattering the window and the silence. She took control of one specific tiny drone and flew into the house.

They had been unable to determine if there were any prisoners that might be held inside, so she wanted to attack with precision.

Most of the targets were easy to spot. They were all armed with pistols on their belts even inside the house at night.

Each time she spotted one of those, Dani directed ten of the bee-sized drones to attach themselves to the enemy and detonate.

One by one, the guards went down, dead before they hit the ground.

Dani continued to explore the house with her primary drone, which was small enough to crawl under most doors or even through a keyhole.

They had both been provided pictures of what Sam Harris looked like. They didn't want to kill him accidentally. They had another fate in mind for him.

The drone Dani controlled slipped under a door and flew up into the air. She caught an ultra-fast glimpse of what appeared to be Sam Harris before the feed went blank. That was a weakness in sending in a single drone. They could be squashed.

She used her tablet to select another ten of the drones and sent them under the same door. This time, she saw not only Harris, but a woman in a white robe beside him. One by one, the video feed of each of those drones went blank.

"I found him," Dani murmured to Harrison.

"Patch me into your feed," Harrison said.

Harrison did, then sent twenty-five of the drones to attach themselves to the door. She detonated them, which blew the door off its hinges, knocking it inside the bathroom where Harris was hiding.

There would be no further escape for Harris. Dani immediately dispatched three hundred of the drones to fill the doorway and hover there. The only way Harris could get out would be to run directly through the mass of exploding mini-drones. To make sure he didn't try to do that, Dani flew one onto the mirror over the bathroom sink and detonated it. The mirror shattered and fell in chunks into the sink and onto the floor. That was all the display of power Harris needed. He had been holding two pistols, but he quickly laid both down and raised his hands over his head.

Harris did not look rich, powerful, or in charge of anything. He wore a light woman's bathrobe over a stained white t-shirt that was stretched over his pot belly. Tighty whities finished the ensemble. He was unshaven and appeared to be drunk.

Harrison minimized the viewpoint Dani had shared with her and sent two of the droids with Janus's face into the house. She led them through the main living area and down a long hallway until she could see the swarm guarding the door.

Dani moved the swarm back a few feet, allowing the androids to fill the space.

She activated the voice of one of the droids and turned the volume up to maximum. Although Harrison spoke, the voice that emerged from the android was the smooth baritone of Janus itself.

"Sam Harris. You are under arrest for crimes against humanity. Your trial will commence shortly. Your guards have all been dispatched. You and this woman are the last people alive in the house." The droid turned its face to the woman. "Are you with this man?"

The woman backed as far away as she could get from Sam Harris. "No. I'm a prisoner. I've been held here against my will for almost a year. He killed my husband and son."

The android turned back to Harris. "Turn toward the wall and put your hands behind your back."

Harris, stunned at the sudden turn of events did exactly as he was told. He was obviously relieved to be taken prisoner instead of being immediately killed.

With a deft twist, the android applied a pair of unbreakable handcuffs and led Harris and the woman out the door.

On the lawn in front of the house, all the other prisoners had gathered together.

Harrison turned the droid toward them, searching for someone. Not someone in particular, but someone with a particular attitude. She found her among the small group of women on one side of the prisoners.

Harrison took control of one of the other Janus lookalike droids and walked to the woman. "We are here to help you. Shortly, you will be given a choice as to where you want to go. But, we have one last order of business here." The android reached out a very human-looking hand to the woman, who took it hesitantly.

The android and the woman walked up the slight incline until they were standing in front of Sam Harris. "Is this the man who has held you prisoner here?"

"No," the woman said, spitting the words. "He's the *son of a bitch* who's been holding all of us here."

"Is this woman one of you?"

"She was. She moved up to the house and has been living with him for months now."

"She lies!" the woman next to Harris shrieked. "I'm a prisoner, too."

Harris turned the android to face the rest of the prisoners. Their expressions showed the truth of the situation. The woman had once been a prisoner, but had become one of the oppressors.

The android pointed a finger at the woman. A red laser from above cut the woman in half.

Harris tried to back away, but slipped on the wet grass and fell.

The android pointed its finger at Sam Harris, former master of the ranch.

A millisecond later, he too had been cut in half by a laser from above.

The ranch was theirs.

There was still cleanup to do and it would take the prisoners several days to recover from the shock of the rescue, but there had not been a single unintended loss of life.

In the end, the majority of those held at the ranch elected to go to Dust City and become permanent Dusters. The rebuilding of that odd community continued and over the years, the town flourished.

There was a time when *living free* sounded like the ideal. No one to tell you what to do or where to go. But, with the events of the previous two years, the idea of being *mostly free* and yet protected from attack became much more attractive.

The attack on the ranch was the first successful mission of the *Altor Security and Vigilante Justice* group, but not nearly the last. Over the next decades, wherever the strong took advantage of the weak, they showed up and dispatched their own brand of frontier justice.

That was what the world had once again become—a new frontier.

If Janus had left access points to itself in the equipment that had been delivered to New Covington, they were now non-operative. The world might slowly rebuild itself, but it would be without that superintelligence showing the way.

The billions of people who had died worldwide were still dead. Outside of that tiny valley in Northern California, there was still no fuel, no power.

Had the Rage Wars started because of centuries of financial inequity that finally came to a tipping point? Or was the machine that first spotted it ultimately responsible for that upheaval? That was a question that would never be answered.

The small family unit that had gathered together in the mountains of Colorado continued to thrive. Nyx was never called back to duty by the General.

The small number of people who had survived inside the Longbaugh Free Prison eventually allowed other people inside the walls. When civilization started to rebuild, they were still there, doing their best to survive.

The lovely cabin in the Alaskan wilderness, built to survive an apocalypse, remained empty, waiting for someone new to find it.

Juniper Trello was elected to serve as the first mayor of New Covington. She worked in harmony with Colonel Brandt for the next few years until he passed away. Lieutenant Forster became the new commanding officer of Camp New Covington.

Dust City managed surprisingly well. The team of Danila Butcher and Levi Rybicki was formidable. No one was surprised when they moved in together. It was easier to manage the city from a single location. Once enough time had passed and the time lock at Altor opened, they were again invited to come inside the dome. They refused. They were happy in Dust City. Levi did ask that Quinn, Marshall, and Jazz use the tunnel to come to a commitment ceremony. The now-scarred Levi, who had once been named one of *Hollywood's Most Eligible Bachelors*, was finally off the market.

Quinn made one of his most intelligent decisions on the ride from Altor to Dust City that day. He asked Jazz if she might be interested in making it a double wedding. Or binding ceremony. Whatever weddings were going to be called moving forward.

It felt completely impromptu, but Quinn revealed that he had put a little forethought into the proposal when he produced his own mother's wedding set.

If Jazz minded being an afterthought to Dani and Levi's nuptials, she didn't show it. She said she would gladly marry Quinn.

They had four children over the following years.

They lived inside Altor as husband and wife for forty years, until Jazz passed away. Her last words to Quinn were, "It's been a good life. Thank you for bringing me inside. You saved me."

Tears flowing, but trying to smile, Quinn shook his head and corrected her. "You saved me."

Both things were true.

In those early days when the citizens of Altor were on their own, there were a few hiccups in the systems. That is almost always the case when a dictator is deposed. The people who lived under them had not been free, but at least the trains ran on time.

Quinn, Jazz, Marshall, and Steele formed an excellent Board of Directors inside Altor.

One of their first decisions was that there were no more free rides. Everyone who was capable of working, did so.

Health improved, people became more involved in their community, and Altor continued to be a fascinating experiment in humans living together.

And the orange-robed monks? Well, Janus had not left completely, had it?

The monks could live forever.

Author's Note

I have a habit of extending book series beyond what I originally envisioned. When I wrote *The Unusual Second Life of Thomas Weaver*, I thought it would be a standalone. Then, I decided it would be part of a trilogy. That series – *The Middle Falls Time Travel Series* – is now at nineteen books and continues to grow.

When I first conceived of *The Alex Hawk Time Travel Series*, I believed it would be a trilogy. That series is now nine books long.

So, I find it a little unusual that I set out to write a trilogy about the domed city of Altor and have actually succeeded in keeping to that number.

I thought of *The Chronicles of Altor* as a kind of origin story for Kragdon-ah and the world of Alex Hawk. At the end of this book, we are still a hundred thousand years away from that distant future. That means I can—and may—write more books that take place between the ending of this one and the world of Kragdon-ah.

But those books will be a completely different series. The domed city will remain, but all the characters of this book, with the exception of Janus, will be gone.

This book is intended to tie the worlds of Middle Falls and Kragdon-ah together. I've received a number of messages from my Advance Readers and proofreaders, asking whether I had this all planned out in my head before I started.

The short answer is, *no.* I am not a planner. I don't plot in advance, and I don't know a lot of what is going to happen in my books well in advance. I continue to be just as surprised as you are at many of the developments that drop into my brain.

When I first wrote of the orange-robed monk named Tokin-ak in *Lost in Kragdon-ah*, I did not know his origin story, which I wrote in this book. I did know there was *something* unusual about him. He was blind in that story, but obviously could somehow see. He was old and bent, but fought like a whirling dervish. He could move a three-ton rock to the side with a single finger. How were all those things possible? I didn't know at the time, but I knew that eventually the answer would come to me. And now we know—Tokin-ak is an immortal construct of Janus, sent into the world to do his bidding.

In the very first Middle Falls book, I mentioned *The Machine*, which in that world has God-like powers. Ever since then, people have been asking for more information on The Machine and I have demurred.

Until this book. In this book, we see Janus leave in a beam of perfect white light, presenting itself as a small, blue bird. That bird is the same way The Machine has always manifested itself in Middle Falls.

Now we know that all three of these series are in a connected world in one way or another.

The Shivers was one of the most challenging parts of this book to write. It was so deadly, so pervasive, that it almost became a new character in the story.

Here's the thing, though. By the end of the story, I felt like it had run its course. Diseases as deadly as The Shivers inevitably burn out because they run out of new hosts to spread to. I think that's what happened to this virus by the end of the story.

Overall, in fact, I think the ending of this trilogy is hopeful. Where *All Fall Down* was pretty dark and despairing, *Ashes, Ashes* ends on a positive note. Except for the hundreds of millions of dead who went before, of course.

The threat of Janus has been (mostly) removed. We know that it is still present in the monks, and it left a little of its massive intelligence behind to give Altor an initial boost to switching over to being run by humans once again. The idea that Janus might decide to inflict its will on Altor and the rest of the world seems to have passed, however.

Altor is what Quinn and Marshall always hoped it would be—an ark of sorts. The world is rebuilding, but if that effort fails, there is still this small gathering of humans who are safe and able to carry on.

If you've been with me for a while, you know that I always pick out a single song and listen to it on an endless loop while I write. For this book, I used a song I had already used for a previous book—*Can't Find My Way Home*, by Traffic. That's the first time I've ever used a song a second time, but the mood of the song seemed to fit what I was writing perfectly.

By the way, I have a Patreon account. My patrons get to read each book as I write it, and we have some wonderful conversations there. You can even get a signed and personalized paperback copy of each book I write. If you'd like to check out the various reward tiers, you can do so here: http://patreon.com/shawninmon.

As always, I have people to thank!

Melissa Prideaux once again served as my editor on this project. I've sung her praises for so many books now that it's become a little embarrassing, but I have to do it again. She does exactly what a wonderful editor should do—she makes me look like a better writer than I am. I can't thank her enough.

Keith Draws did the covers for all three of the Chronicles of Altor books. I think he outdid himself on this one, showing the interior of life in the dome, with the crowd brought by the Prudent twins standing outside looking in. And of course, the classic, two-faced version of Janus hovering over everything.

I use a lot of proofreaders because each of them bring a different skill set to the table. For this book, they included Dan Hilton, Marta Rubin, Kim O'Hara, and Steve Smith. They save me from myself so often, they should all be given medals.

And so, here we are, my friends. We must part ways at the end of this book, but I hope you will find me again in Middle Falls, or Kragdon-ah, or whatever universe I create next.

Shawn Inmon
October 2023
Tumwater WA

Printed in Great Britain
by Amazon

29766283R00190